Sullivan Road

Pierce Lehmbeck

AuthorHouse™
1663 Liberty Drive, Suite 200
Bloomington, IN 47403
www.authorhouse.com
Phone: 1-800-839-8640

© 2009 Pierce Lehmbeck. All rights reserved.

No part of this book may be reproduced, stored in a retrieval system, or transmitted by any means without the written permission of the author.

First published by AuthorHouse 1/5/2009

ISBN: 978-1-4343-3553-1 (sc)

Library of Congress Control Number: 2007906845

Printed in the United States of America
Bloomington, Indiana

This book is printed on acid-free paper.

DEDICATION

TO DOUG AND JACK Milne, Bucky Clarkson, James F. Bailey Jr., and my beloved Karen Armel, I express gratitude for patience and understanding. The 20-year journey from concept to completion involved talking to those who lived much of it and have survived, a reconnection with feeling, and a long, long journey of rediscovering the soul.

Pierce Lehmbeck
September 1, 2008
Jacksonville FL

PROLOGUE

April 12, 1942

'...*when the roll is called up yonder, some of y'all Sullivans is apt to be missin'.*'

– Preacher Prentiss Pemberton

IT WAS A PROUD little church, nestled at the intersection of two coral-colored sandy roads emerging from piney woods, magnolias, and moss-draped oaks. A newly applied coat of whitewash covered its aged clapboard siding and the tin roof reflected back to the heavens the brilliance of early morning sunshine. Not even the robins, mockingbirds, wrens, thrushes, or crows seemed willing to break the hypnotic silence.

Then, through open windows and a double-wide canopied door, a chorus of two-score voices arose…

> *I come to the garden alone, while the dew is still on the roses,*
> *And the voice I hear, falling on my ear, the Son of God discloses.*
> *And He walks with me, and He talks with me,*
> *And He tells me I am His own;*
> *And the Joy we share as we tarry there,*
> *None other has ever known…*

He speaks, and the sound of His voice
Is so sweet the birds hush their singing.
And the Melody He gave to me
Within my heart is ringing.
And He walks with me, and He talks with me...

Without a prompt, the congregation swung into what it knew was Preacher Prentiss Pemberton's favorite hymn:

When the trumpet of the Lord shall sound,
And time shall be no more,
And the morning breaks, eternal and fair;
When the saved of earth shall gather
Over on the other shore,
And the roll is called up yonder,
I'll be there...

When the roll is called up yonder,
When the roll is called up yonder,
When the roll is called up yon-deeer,
When the roll is called up yonder
I'll be there...

Preacher Pemberton, a tall, slender, black-haired young man with a back as straight as a store-bought hoe handle, stood rigidly erect behind the podium of the small Methodist church, one arm moving up, down and sideways with the old hymn's pulsations. Sung by an overflowing congregation, it reverberated off bare pinewood walls and rose and fell between tin roof and worn oaken floor. The wooden shudders were open, and the sun's slanting rays lit one side of the dim interior.

Putting the hymnal to one side and opening a Bible, the preacher motioned for the congregants to sit down. He cleared his throat, and for a long moment said nothing while his eyes roamed from front to back of the dozen rows of the benches serving as pews. They'd had backrests until his arrival a year earlier; he'd had them removed, believing alert congregants listened better than comfortable ones.

In a deep, practiced voice, he began…

"Oh, what a wonderful hymn and y'all do such a fine job of singin' it. And such a 'propriate hymn, 'cause we all know that Momma Susan, that fine, that wonderful woman, will be there when that heavenly roll is called up yonder, with the Lord's trumpet soundin' and time won't be no more. Just like that fine old hymn says…"

Momentarily, he paused; store-bought shoes and boots grated on the hardwood floor, and coughs and the clearing of throats broke the silence. No one would sit easy while Pemberton was standing up there in his pulpit.

"…Oh, I know how much y'all are sufferin' today, and I'm sufferin' with y'all. But we all got to thank our Savior that our beloved Susan is not sufferin' no more. Never ag'in will she have to feel the winter's cold, cold wind comin' down across them open fields and creeping into the very bones of her old body, which was her frail home on this here frail earth for nigh on to 74 years. Never ag'in will she have to recollect the pain and the hunger she felt as a child, up there in MacCrainey County, up near where the mountains start risin' toward our Savior's Heaven. Oh, she talked lots 'bout that crumblin' shack with a dirt roof that was mostly open to the wind and rain and cold comin' over them open, rocky fields her momma and daddy had to work like a mule to keep them and her alive.

"For that was Susan Virginia Summerford Sullivan, who could see and feel the good in all things, and see the hope, even in the earthly pains God let her feel so she'd know she was goin' to a better place, and that it was in Heaven with Him.

"Oh my friends, I beseech y'all never to forget that all of us are hopeful of goin' to Heaven, and bein' right there with her, and most important of all with the Good God Almighty and our Savior Jesus Christ. None of us wants to wind up in that other place, Satan's place, full of damnation and ever-burnin' sulphur fire, and there ain't nothin' worse'n that kinda fire.

"So it behooves us, all of us, to pray for Susan on her journey to God's land, and to take to heart and mind once more the remembrance of what is goin' to be required of us if we're ever goin' to get to Heaven, to God, and to all our loved ones that already made that divine journey.

"We all know'd that Susan was the stick'um that held the Sullivan family together, and I know'd better'n most that it warn't no easy chore. 'Specially after her beloved husband Niall Barnabas passed on nigh on to six years ago."

With his voice rising like a storm-driven wind that had found opening among the hills, Preacher Pemberton picked up the pace and increased the volume.

"But we who know the will of God know'd that Niall Barnabas Sullivan was a drinkin' man. He was killin' hisself day by day, and that for sure warn't the will of God then and it ain't today. Oh, Niall Barnabas mostly was a good man, and God willin', that goodness got him through them Pearly Gates and Susan's gonna be with him, right after we've prayed one last prayer for her soul and laid her in the holy ground so's them angels will know where to find her.

"And Niall Barnabas didn't beat his wife, like some we know, and he didn't take the peachtree switch to his young'uns less they had it comin'."

The minister paused again, thumbed a few pages of the Bible. Then he looked up, scanned the front two rows of benches, and began again.

"What I'm goin' to do now," he said, "is ask y'all Sullivan men and Liza Jane, y'all's sister, to let me give you some fatherly talk. Oh, I know y'all are all growed up and older'n me. But y'all and the other folk here about made me your minister, y'all's linkup with God."

The Sullivan men, the five wives still living, Eliza Jane, and the four grandchildren old enough to attend the service, filled the front benches on both sides of the aisle in front of Grandma Susan's coffin. Her sons, all but Liam and Dru, had carefully pieced it together from slabs of a cedar tree elder brother Jim had selected and cut down weeks earlier, after

They had sensed their frail mother was nearing the end of her life. She hadn't smoked or used snuff and rarely had she been sick. She had, Doctor Frank Arlis said, simply run down and used up her allotted time in this world.

Dru and Liam hadn't had the stomach to help make her final bed, as they chose to describe the sweet-smelling, flower-covered casket laid out before them. As one, all the Sullivans now looked up from it, set their chins and fixed their eyes on Preacher Pemberton. He was a tough-talking young man, who'd once sent a deceased man on his way, saying: "Now we all know where old Malcolm is goin', so we ain't gonna waste no time talkin' 'bout him. Better that we talk 'bout the livin'!"

Looking down at the grieving and apprehensive Sullivans, and with a final swing of his eyes across those seated behind them, Preacher Pemberton cleared his throat and began.

"There's a bunch of y'all; ain't no other family 'round these parts to compare. And let's not forget the brother and his wife who God called to Himself before what y'all claimed was their time – George Dewey Sullivan and Lora Murphy Sullivan, God rest their souls. Sometimes it seems hard for us common folk down here to see how the Good Lord up there can help us make things that kill us, like that there train what run over that automobile they was in. But we know it ain't ours to question Him or His reasonin', and let's be proud that we had George and Lora with us, for however long it was.

"Let's sing to their mem'ry. Turn to page 102 and let 'em hear y'all up there in Heaven, where they're listenin' in with their Good Lord. Sing it sweet and sing it from your hearts."

All creatures of our God and King,
Lift up your voices and with us sing,
Al-le-lu-ia! Al-le-lu-ia!
Thou burning sun with golden beam,
Thou silver moon with softer gleam!
O praise Him, O praise Him,
Al-le-lu-ia! Al-le-lu-ia…

The preacher cleared his throat again, and took a sip from the glass of water that always was on the podium, placed there by his shy, retiring wife, Missus Lavonia. Some believed she was afraid of folks, and maybe even of Preacher Pemberton himself. Most times she said nary a word when the preacher was around, and she wasn't around much when he wasn't.

"Now, I know ya'll Sullivans are a stickin'-together family. But I ask: Are y'all your brother's keeper? Your sister's keeper? Oh, y'all get together once in a while, mostly to blaspheme and tell stories that are mostly lies…"

A spattering of chuckles rose from the rear benches, and Pemberton's dark eyes flashed from beneath his slicked-back black hair; the laughing stopped almost as quickly as it had begun.

"C'mon now, y'all calls it jokin' 'round and say it's only funnin'. But y'all know the truth, and the Good Lord for certain knows.

"And John, you come up here on a Sunday when you get the chance and you talk about the scriptures real good. But, John, you know the Lord knows you go off and suck the pi'son of likker right through them same lips. And you get drunk, and in times like this, with that big old war goin' on, lots'a men do. But that don't make it right.

"And, John, most men don't get drunk and go home and beat their wives, who they say they love and care for."

Preacher Pemberton didn't say anything more right off; he seemed to be selecting his words carefully before letting them go. Then he started up again, talking directly to John's wife, Jewell Ellen Powell Sullivan.

"Mornin', Jewell. You're lookin' right fine on this fine mornin'. Lookin' right brave, too, and I just know your momma-in-law is smilin' that you are. I hope you ain't smilin' 'bout what I just said 'bout John. One of these days he might hurt you real bad.

"And Jewell -- and I reckon you, too, John – you got a fine boy in that there Bo. I hear-tell he went off to school at five and did two grades in the first year. That'd mean he's done worked his way to the third grade and he ain't seven yet. That right?"

Jewell smiled nervously and elbowed John. They were unstintingly proud of their oldest son, Beaujames. Bo was the six-year-old's nickname; proud that his firstborn was a son, John had been drinking at the time and had said he wanted a special name. He seldom used it himself.

"Well y'all got a right to be proud and you keep on pushin' him. He'll make all of us proud.

"And, Jim, good God-fearin', God-lovin' Jim, 56 years young and a deacon in this here church. The load now falls on your shoulders, if it was not already. I know you been a lonesome man since Abigail left this old world lo so many years ago, and I know you done your part and more. But, Jim, I know and you know that a family that pulls together is gonna do good down here and for sure is gonna be welcome up there in the House of the Lord.

"But lookee down that row of your brothers, their wives, your sister and them young'uns, and re-commit yourself to keepin' 'em together, to havin' 'em stand together like a family oughta. There's John and Liam and Jessie. And Rufus and Dru Winnifred and Liza Jane, too. You love 'em all, I know you do. God knows you do. But God wants you to love 'em even more now your beloved Momma Susan is gone. And you gotta show it every day.

"Liam, you're kinda shiftless lots of times, ain't you? Don't know how you keep up that big old house you built. If I was you, I'd thank the Good Lord every day for givin' me such a good woman as Mollie.

"And you, Jessie, you see yourself as the funny man in this here family. Always tellin' a joke, always got some funny comeback when somebody else's trying his best to be serious-like. Why don't you hush sometimes and listen to some of that serious talkin' and maybe, jus' maybe, you'll learn a thing or two that's worth learnin'."

Preacher Prentiss paused, placed both elbows on the podium, closed one eye, and stared with the other straight at Dru. He started to speak, stopped, took a deep breath, and began again.

"Now comes Dru Winnifred Sullivan. Taller'n the rest, muscles tryin' to bust the seams of that there store-bought suit. Prime of life at 36, you are. It's took your momma's dyin' to get you into this here House of the Lord. Your own momma!

"Jim, she was a momma that wanted Dru to get a good schoolin', but she didn't get no help from the rest of y'all to get him to go get it. Don't y'all feel loads of hurt down deep, hurt that's burnin' there 'cause you didn't help her with Dru? Help Dru see what's right? Do what's right? The Lord above knows he won't listen to me.

"And Dru Winnifred, if'n you ever do come to God and His church, you are gonna learn that havin' a good woman, a *good* woman, Dru, is one of His greatest gifts. And sin ain't to be mistook for love. You oughta know that, and if'n you don't you are gonna learn it the hard way, I promise at the altar of God!"

He paused once more; then, as though the sounds of shuffling shoes and the clearing of throats had given him renewed energy, he looked straight at John.

"And John, there really ain't much more I can say to you or 'bout you. You are the youngest brother, just 35, though I hear-tell you been tellin' folk it's more like 30. Is that because Jewell is 24? John, you don't have to lie 'bout your age. You are a lucky man, and what's more the Good Lord has graced you more than most men in Shannon County, with good schoolin', with a chance to serve your country, even if it was before the devil got this big old world war to goin'.

"All of us know He let you get good learnin' up there at that Em'ry Academy, and that He helped you get in the Army Air Corps and fly up there in them clouds close to Him. All of us here is sorry that you got hurt so bad when you crashed that aeroplane, stayed so long in that hospital, and came back home a drinkin' man.

"But the Lord also gave you a good, lovin' family and you oughta take care of it and not go beatin' up on it, or lyin' 'bout it. There hain't no more I can say to you, 'cept maybe to ask you to help Jim pull your family together. You got the smarts; use 'em! You got the grit; use it to fight the devil that keeps leadin' you back to that jug! And let us bury that jug right here today, with Momma Susan. She'll know where to pour it out, and that's right on Satan's hellfaire, where it and ever' jug full of that vile pi'son oughta be poured."

Though it appeared that Preacher Pemberton was about to wear down, he wasn't quite through. He paused, deliberately, picked up the Bible and held it to his chest. For the first time, he smiled – John later would describe it as a wicked leer – and concluded: "Y'all oughta know that, while we was singin', I got to thinkin' that when the roll *is* called up yonder, some of y'all Sullivans is apt to be missin'. I sure hope I'm wrong, but I ain't so sure."

He waited til the feet-shuffling and throat-clearing subsided, and then he was talking to the women.

"Jewell, Annie Mae, Mary Ruth, Alma, Mollie. Y'all are good wives and mothers, and I know y'all are standin' by your men and always will.

"But for the sake of Momma Susan, for the sake of y'all's Good Lord, make a vow today to help these men to do the right thing and take care of one another so all y'all, all y'all's young'uns and their young'uns, can count on livin' in the House of the Lord forever.

"And now, let us sing one more fine hymn and then we'll say a final prayer for Momma Susan, before we take her to that holy ground and give her to her Savior. Y'all please turn to page 62 and sing it loud for our dearly departed."

I've wandered far away from God,
Now I'm coming home;
The paths of sin too long I've trod.
Now I'm coming home.
Coming home, coming home,
Never more to roam…

With the congregants standing and singing, Preacher Pemberton walked slowly to the front door and to his accustomed handshaking position. Looking into the woods across the sandy road, he frowned. Sitting in or standing by a wagon partially hidden under oaks, pines and waist-high shrubs were Marybelle and Buttonbottom Higginbotham and their six children – Delphi, Lonny, Sonny, Cricket, Mary Sue, and baby May.

In so many ways, they had become a practical and spiritual extension of the Sullivan family; but they were Negroes and Negroes did not go into white churches, no matter what the circumstances. They had their own, a mile or so behind Tip Evers' store back in the woods close by the Big Springs Swamp.

The Sullivans, their friends and Preacher Pemberton buried the Sullivan matriarch and beloved conscience in red clay behind the Deep Springs Church, right next to her husband. The fact that Niall Barnabas Sullivan had been born in 1860 and had died in 1928 already was written in the family Bible. On the line below, his wife's name, birthplace and date of birth had been written in her own delicate script: Susan Virginia

Sullivan, b. 1868. Had she lived til September, she would have been 74.

As her eldest son, Jim was to write the place and date of her passing. Many weeks would pass before he managed to do it, and no one ever asked him why.

BOOK I

THE PIGSTY MURDERS

"I been a good nigger, Mistuh Sheriff Nobles. None'a dis here family has ever caused no trouble an' it ain't goin' to. What I'm a'gonna do now is put my trust in you an' pray fo' the Lord to he'p you find out what went on here, an' who kilt my boy Lonny.

"Havin' said that, suh, I'm gonna go sit by my boy an' hol' Marybelle's hand. It's likely I'm a'gonna cry some, even if she doan. I'd be mos' grateful if'n you'd leave us be fo' a while…"

CHAPTER 1

'We've got a problem, Buddy-ro…'

—Bo's braver self

BEAUJAMES (BO) SULLIVAN RACED bare-footed down Arrowhead Hill and slid to a stop at the edge of what to him was the most fearsome place in Shannon County, Georgia, and maybe the whole world…

…Banshee Swamp, a terrible-awful, monster-infested green wall that stood between him and the one man he trusted more than anyone else he knew. Trouble was he didn't know whether his Uncle Dru's trust included helping a boy keep the sinful secret the devil and Magalene Boru had heaped upon him.

Bo had to know; he had to muster the gumption to get through Banshee Swamp one more time. His soul, and especially his switch-sensitive bare legs, depended upon it.

Gumption already had gotten him through an hour hiding in the barn loft, fearful that his uncle might have betrayed him to his momma and that she'd be coming with a peachtree switch. It had helped him stare down rats, deal with worries about snakes, and with how he'd get by that cantankerous old rooster and its blood-letting spurs waiting at the foot of the ladder.

Gumption also had helped him through the nightmarish remembrance of the time he had killed a momma bird and her babies with a thrown rock; and, thank the Good Lord, it had provided the teeth-gnashing strength to survive visions of the long-beaked, long-clawed, red-eyed, vengeful poppa bird that wouldn't let him alone when he was trying to sleep, nighttime or daytime. And if that weren't enough, he'd been replaying happy-sad visions of his daddy making slingshots for him and his brother one day and beating up on his mother the next.

Bo had snuck by the rooster and Momma Jewell; he'd cleared the hill and had closed his eyes and raced toward the swamp determined to sprint right on through it. It wasn't large, extending about 150 yards east and west and no more than 50 yards deep where the rut road cut through. He could see the other end, like he was looking through a tunnel he'd seen in a picture show in Mayo.

It had been three years since he'd gone through the tunnel alone for the first time, and he kept telling himself there's no reason to be scared. He was seven years old now, and what he oughta be is ashamed that he was still scared of it.

The first time, he had dropped down on his belly and looked all the way through and out the other side. And remembering that he'd seen train robbers do it in a picture show, he'd placed an ear on the ground and listened hard to find out if a herd of buffalo or a rip-snortin' locomotive might be coming up on the other side.

There hadn't been and that had been peachy-good; he hadn't needed other worries while trying to escape the terrors lying in wait on either side of the narrow road, which was filled with mud holes, stumps, fallen limbs, and other gosh-awful toe-stubbers.

His daddy, John Sullivan, and his Uncle Dru claimed they'd heard the most fearsome wails on God's green earth coming out of the place; and, they said, those horrible wails got ear-busting loud when anything smelling of humankind, farm animals, dogs, or cats ventured near it at certain unholy times. And when the wailing wore out the wailers' voices, they'd pound on Injun drums, hollow logs, turned-over pig-boiling vats, milk pails, and anything else that'd make a noise.

Uncle Dru had said – more'n he needed to, Bo felt – that the swamp was the home of Shannon County's banshees, the ugliest, meanest hags there ever was or ever would be.

Looking honest-to-goodness fearful himself, Uncle Dru had gone on to say that banshees were ugly old women who had come from the old country after they had been given a choice: spend their worthless, troublemaking lives in stinking Irish jails or get on a boat and spend them in the New World, which was America, which was where Georgia and Shannon County were located…

Which was where this gosh-awful, God-forsaken, fearsome Banshee Swamp was located…

And that wasn't the worst of it. Saying they wanted him to live a full life, John and Dru had told Bo the swamp was haunted by the ghosts of people, mules, cows, pigs, dogs, and cats who'd gone in one side but never came out the other. Never seen again, Uncle Dru had said, pushing his sweat-stained, shaped-by-hand felt hat back on his head and looking as concerned as a loving uncle could look.

Daddy John told Bo how he could keep from being scared nigh on to death: "First, stay home. And if you can't do that and want to risk a whippin', use you noggin. Don't cross that Satan-made swamp unless you've got a grownup with you, and the best kind of a grownup to have with you is me or your momma."

Well, it hadn't taken Bo long to see through his daddy's reason for giving that advice; so he'd kept on sneaking over whenever he felt the reason was important enough and he might be able to get over and back without being missed at home or captured by some God-awful nether-world critter. "Nether" was another word he'd had to ask his daddy to cipher; he'd been told it had something to do with being secret or hidden, and that was enough to make Bo latch onto the word and store it in his mind-bank of places to avoid.

Once, and only once, he had tried to avoid the swamp by circling through a cornfield. Pushing through stalks that reached three feet or more above his head, with nothing to see but the sky above … that had been scary enough. But halfway around he'd come upon a snake and he'd skedaddled back to the road, where he decided it looked like rain and he'd better go on back home. Now he wouldn't chance that field even in the middle of the winter, when it was as bare as a front yard swept clean with broom straw and all the snakes not living in Banshee Swamp were wintering in the barn.

Bo figured he'd made another error in judgment – as his daddy sometimes said he'd done when he'd riled his momma or another grownup – by asking his Uncle Dru whether everybody and everything that had gone into the swamp hadn't come out; the Good Lord must have taken mercy on some of them, he reasoned. Dru had said he didn't personally know for sure, but as for himself he was too mean and ugly for a ghost to bother; and those terrible, awful banshees knew he wasn't the marrying kind and they let him be.

"You, howsumever," he'd added, "maybe you hain't growed enough to get mean enough to scare 'em off, and you for certain ain't of marryin' age."

Bo half believed him and half didn't, but up to now he'd managed most of the time to get through the swamp. What he'd do is get right to the place where the road ran under the trees, grit his teeth, close his eyes, and tear out running.

Maybe, he was thinking on this already terrible day, it would be smarter to go on back home and keep praying Uncle Dru hadn't told what he'd seen: Bo sitting up in a chinaberry tree, trying to strip back the skin over the tip of his penis, as Magalene Boru had told him to do. The reason, she said, was that it'd work better when they played Doctor Pete. Magalene was 10 and bigger, and when she wanted to play, Bo didn't have much choice.

Today, Bo didn't think too long about going back home. His braver and equally concerned inner self popped up and told him they had a problem and they'd best do what it took to find out what Uncle Dru saw or didn't see.

Telling his braver self "Okay, Buddy-Ro...," Bo gritted his teeth, closed his eyes and took off running. He knew he was inside the woods when he felt the cool air and smelled water. He ran harder and harder, until he hit some infernal snag and hurt his bare toe something awful and fell all sprawled out in a mud hole. Before you could count to one, he was up and running again, leaving a trail of mud whenever his bare feet hit the ground, which wasn't often.

He didn't open his eyes until he ran smack-dab into a blast of hot air; like a furnace, it was, but nothing akin to the Hades he had just escaped. Stopping to catch his breath, he looked back in triumph and shouted, "Beat you again, by jiminy!"

He shouted it right out loud, and told himself he didn't give a hoot if a banshee, ghost or any other nether-world critter had heard him and was thinking about coming up the road after him. Looking down at his muddy cut-off overalls and throbbing toe, however, he wondered whether one of them hadn't tripped him and stomped him in the mud before he could get up and get away.

Anyway, he decided, that's what he'd tell Uncle Dru…

Dru was short for Druid, the name given by his passed-away father, Niall Barnabas. Most folks, kin and otherwise, felt Druid was a mite presumptuous and rarely used it; a simple man oughta have a simple name, they said…

Today, Dru was in his usual place, sitting beneath the huge old water oak that provided his midday shade. Two huge sycamores grew nearby, and when the afternoon sun moved westward the shade from the sycamores would slip in and relieve the oak, whose shade had retreated toward the barn. Dru's wired-together old rocking chair was tipped backwards; his boot-covered feet were propped on rocks piled around the base of the tree, and a toothpick extended from his teeth. The rocks atop the pile were stained from years of being splashed by Dru's long-distance brown tobacco spittle.

His eyes were trained on Bo, as they had been ever since the boy had come running out of the swamp. He smiled, chuckled and, with a quick movement of his tongue, switched the toothpick to the other side of his mouth.

The northern edge of the swamp was only 200 yards from where Dru sat. He watched his nephew, wondering why he didn't seem to be in a hurry; occasionally, the boy stopped and appeared to be rocking back on his heels, perhaps to give his bare feet some relief from the sand's heat. He also appeared to be doing his best to act as though he didn't have a worry in the world; like he had just happened along, and his uncle had just happened to be there.

Bo dropped onto the sand beside Dru's chair and began stirring it with a small stick. Dru took a plug of tobacco from a pocket on the bib of his overalls and bit off a chaw. The toothpick remained.

"What've you been in, boy," he asked from beneath a wrinkled brow.

Bo told him about how a banshee or a ghost had thrown him in a mud hole, but he got away.

"Uh-huh."

Both sat quietly. It was hot, so hot Bo could smell his uncle's man-smell – a mixture of sweat, tobacco and, as often as not, barn manure. Bo didn't mind the odors; he figured he'd smell the same way some day, and they certainly were better than the terrible-awful smell of the honey pot he had to pull from the beneath and bed and dump in the fields each morning.

Bo glanced up several times. He was fascinated by his uncle's eyes, which were a deep blue and a vivid contrast to his darkly tanned skin and the ever-present, blue-black stubble of his seldom-shaved chin.

But, truth be known, Dru's silence was scaring the devil out of him; he took it to mean there was no question but that he'd been seen committing a sin. Gathering up his gumption, he spoke up, a mite louder than he'd intended.

"Real hot, ain't it?"

"Yup."

The boy wondered what to say next, and guessed the best thing was to ask the nagging question. He stirred the sand some more, then leaned on an elbow. His stomach felt like it had dropped beneath his hiney and he was sitting on it.

"Uncle Dru, did you see me sittin' up in that there chinaberry tree?"

"Yup."

The abrupt, matter-of-fact response startled Bo. Unable to speak for some time, he finally blurted, "Well, you didn't say nothin'."

"You were busy."

That also hit hard and Bo gulped. His uncle must have seen it, all of it, he reckoned.

"You seen?"

"Yup."

Bo sat up.

"But you didn't say nothin'."

"No cause to."

"But you seen what I was doin'?"

"Yup. Just told you so."

Way down the road somewhere a crow cawed, and out in the barn the mules, Jennie and Fran, began kicking the wall and one another; Dru heard and mumbled, "Danged fools oughta know it's too hot to get too close to one 'nother."

Bo didn't hear; a storm of confusion was whipping around in his head, shutting out everything else. He turned toward his uncle, tucked his knees beneath his chin and wrapped his arms around them. Even in the shade the sand was hot.

"I was scared you was gonna tell Momma. And maybe Daddy."

"Why'd I go do a thing like that?"

"I just thought you'd a'done it."

Dru didn't reply and Bo added, "I was scared."

Dru pulled the 'pick from his mouth, smiled and gently ran a work-toughened hand across Bo's cowlick, which covered most of the back of his head.

"Now why'd I tell? You was just findin' out about yourself and that's about as natural as it gets."

When Dru said it, "natural" sounded like "gnat-er-al."

But Bo knew what he meant.

He blushed and knew his face was red; he could feel it burning, like when he'd been in the sun too long. He opened his mouth a couple of times, but didn't say anything, and neither did Dru. The crow had gotten closer and was cawing up a racket. The barn was quiet.

When one did speak, it was Bo. "Is it a bad thing? Somethin' inside tells me I ought not be doin' it."

"It'd be bad if'n you're still doin' it when you get to be my age."

"You ain't a bad man, Uncle Dru. You ain't still doin' it?"

Dru didn't answer, and the crow could be heard again. He was far off, 'way down over Bo's fearsome swamp.

"You reckon I oughta tell Momma and Daddy?"

Dru shrugged. "I wouldn't bother, boy. Likely they knows anyways. Your daddy for sure."

Bo looked up, his mouth agape and his eyes wide open.

"How'd they know?"

"They'd remember and they'd know. That's all."

After a moment's cause, Dru asked, "How long you been doin' that?"

Bo pushed the sand with his bare feet, trying to decide how to respond; finally, he figured it would be best to tell the truth. Sometimes, he felt, Uncle Dru was his best friend in the whole world, even better than Lassie and his gone-to-Heaven dog, Spot.

"Well, ever since Magalene said I oughta do it."

Dru dropped his feet from the rocks and sat up, so quickly it gave Bo a start. "Magalene? What'd she tell you?"

His sudden interest scared Bo and he didn't know how to reply.

"C'mon, boy, what'd she say?"

"Well, she told me that if'n I… if'n I'd skin it back all the way, it'd work better."

Bo paused, stirred the sand some more and figured he'd better start telling the story another way. He knew he was blushing again, because his cheeks were burning again. And he feared he was about to start stuttering, which his daddy said was the surest way to let somebody know he was telling a fib, or was about to.

He decided to remain truthful. "Uncle Dru, you ever play Doctor Pete?"

Dru looked down at him, smiled from ear to ear and let go a mild but prolonged laugh.

"Doctor Pete! Doctor Pete! Good Lord, boy, you mean Magalene's been playin' Doctor Pete with you? Why, you ain't nothin' but a tadpole and she must be ten by now. At least that!"

Not knowing how to take Dru's laughter, Bo looked at him real hard for a real long minute.

"I'm goin' on to seven come Thanksgivin' and I'm already goin' to the third grade and Magalene hasn't hardly even been to school. Besides, she says I'm plenty big enough."

Bo's head drooped and he stirred the sand with both feet, vigorously and with evident agitation. "Ceptin' down there," he added, so quietly Dru almost missed it.

Dru leaned close to the boy. "It'll grow, Bo, it'll grow. But when'd this start? How long's this been goin' on?"

Made braver by his uncle's soft words and clear interest, Bo told him.

"Since 'bout Christmas time. Every time I go to Tip Evers' store she comes outa her house and takes me into that shed by the pig pen and says we gotta play Doctor Pete. I tell her I hain't got the time, and that Momma'll be mad if'n I tarry; but she always makes me do it anyways."

Bo said "it" the same way he'd say snake or peachtree switch.

Dru stared at him, eyes flashing and toothpick dancing. Suddenly, he began to laugh, got up and walked around the tree, shaking his head from side to side. Occasionally he stopped and smiled, and sometimes it was a nervous smile. Bo wondered why.

Finally, Dru squatted next to him and roughed up his hair, like he was giving him an Injun haircut, but not so hard that it hurt like a real Injun haircut.

"Tell me, Bo, do you know where Magalene got that name? Her whole name is Mary Magalene, if you didn't already know that."

"Magalene? Mary Magalene? From her momma, I reckon. She hain't got no daddy I know 'bout."

"Well, her momma got it from the Bible and church folk say it Mag-da-lene, not Mag-a-lene. Some say the woman that had that name in the Bible wasn't the kind a good man oughta be around. Preacher Pemberton, he says so. Your daddy, he says don't pay no mind to what the preacher says; the Good Lord knew she was a good woman."

"You think Magalene's a good…" Bo didn't get a chance to finish the question.

"Now that there name you got," Dru added, like he'd just thought of it. "Beaujames! What was your Momma thinkin' when she hung that one on you?"

Now Bo shrugged. "She didn't. Daddy did. Momma said he'd been so happy and he said a first boy was special and he wanted me to have a special name. She said she let him pick. Didn't want to hurt his feelin's, she said.

"It could have been worse," Bo mumbled. "She said he'd been thinkin' 'bout calling me Fauntleroy…"

"Faunt what? Migosh, be musta been drinking. What kind of a name is that?"

"It's Donald Duck's middle name, Uncle Dru. Didn't you know that?"

"Well, 'scuse me, boy' I sure didn't know that."

Bo ignored Dru's mild sarcasm, and added, "I don't mind the name. Not much, anyways, if it don't get 'round too much, like at school."

Bo thought about what he'd just said and about what his uncle had said, and figured maybe he'd ask his momma about Mary Mag-da-lene, and whether his own name was in the Good Book. Dru was nudging Bo's arm and asking something again.

"Tell me, boy, was there any fuzz on it yet? Gawd, she's got to be 10 if she's a day."

"Fuzz? Where?"

Dru grinned and nudged him again. "You know where. C'mon, now, tell me."

Bo said there was, but there wasn't much.

"Could you do it okay? Did she like it?"

Bo thought some, then decided he'd best keep telling the truth.

"Well, she said if I got it skinned back it'd stand up better and we could do it better."

"Did she show you how?"

"She was tryin' to t'other day, but Aunt Sara came and chased us outa the shed. Oh Lordy, she was mad! Aunt Sara, I mean. Magalene, she just cried. And I figured if Aunt Sara was mad, Momma would be mad, too."

After stopping a moment to pick up a small stone and throw it away, Bo went on, very quietly…

"I just took off runnin', like I should'a done when I saw Magalene waitin' for me…"

Sara was Magalene's momma, but Bo always called her Aunt Sara. She wasn't really his aunt; she was a Boru and no kin whatsoever. But his momma had said it was polite to call folks like her "aunt." Showed respect, even if it weren't deserved, she'd said. Bo wasn't sure what she meant by it not being deserved; but he recollected Aunt Sara didn't have a husband and figured maybe that had something to do with it.

At the boy's last answer, Dru had stood, raised his arms straight up and let out a belly whoop that Bo figured must have scared the daylights out of Aunt Liza, who was in the house and always took a nap this time of day. The whoop gave him a start, anyway; prickled the skin on the back of his neck, too.

Dru kept on laughing, bending double and holding his knees tightly.

"Sara mad? Sara mad? Hoo-hah! Sara mad! Ho boy, you don't know the half uf it. Sara get mad? Whooo-eeee!"

Bo figured he knew one thing, maybe two. His Uncle Dru sure didn't make sense some time; and the other was that he hadn't told on him and he could go home, which was through those woods and past the banshees, ghosts and other nether-world critters…

Bo told his uncle he'd better get back home and hurried away. He stopped down the road, just before the turn that'd take him down to the swamp, which now was maybe three chunks of a rock away, when the rock was the right size.

Looking back, he could see his uncle standing in the shade of the oak tree, rolling a cigarette. He could make them with one hand and said he'd teach Bo how some day. Bo wondered whether Dru was going to keep the chaw and the toothpick in his mouth while he smoked the cigarette. He did some time and folks said that was real special.

Dru was sweet on Sara. Folks said so, and Bo had no reason to think it wasn't so. He'd also overhead the same folks saying Dru may have been Magalene's pa. That didn't make no sense at all, he reasoned.

Bo recalled what his momma had said: that Dru just hung around their place so much because it was close to Sara's, which was off to the east a piece and around a bend. The house was a weather-beaten old shack that had a dirt yard with a falling-down shed, an outhouse, a pigsty, a pecan tree and two big old chinaberry trees that Magalene said angels lived in. She claimed you could see them shining through the leaves; but Bo knew it was the sun doing the shining and the wind-tickled leaves caused the sunbeams to dance around and send down silvery and golden shafts, which sparkled brightly and sometimes blinded a boy's eyes if he looked straight at them.

His momma had said so, after Aunt Liza – she was a real aunt – had told the same tale to keep him and Arlis out of her fig tree. It hadn't worked; when she was napping or on the other side of the house, they'd raid the tree anyway.

Maybe Uncle Dru was sweet on Aunt Sara, Bo was thinking; but he sure had a funny way of showing it, laughing crazy and acting the fool Bo knew he wasn't.

Bo wiped the sweat from his forehead, looked down the deeply rutted sand road, and shouted real loud so he'd feel brave: "One, two, three, four, I ain't scared no more! And ready or not, here I come!"

This time he avoided the mud hole and didn't stop until he was on top of Arrowhead Hill.

CHAPTER 2

'Lordy, Dru, don't you come 'round tonight...'

–Sara to herself

TWO MILES SOUTH OF where Dru now sat, Magalene Boru danced in circles around the base of a chinaberry tree in her dusty front yard. The sun was directly above the tree and its rays, filtering through the wee, shimmering leaves, filled it with the sparkling "angels" she loved so dearly.

She was singing to them...

Angels in the treetop,
Angels in the treetop,
Come visit with me,
I'm as lonely as can be.

Angels in the treetop,
Angels in the treetop,
It ain't gonna rain today
And you can stay and play...

Watching from the porch, her frowning grandpappy shook his balding head; his scruffy, grey beard swung back and forth across a matted, bearlike chest visible through the gap in a buttonless shirt.

"Sara, you gotta do somethin' with that there Magalene," he growled. "I keep tellin' her there ain't no angels in that tree, but she won't stop singin' to 'em. Drives me crazy, like she already is…"

Sitting in the porch swing, and without looking up from her knitting, Sara responded, "Oh, Daddy, she's gotta believe in somethin'. Leave her be."

To herself, she added, "Ever'body's gotta believe in somethin'…"

"What'd you say, girl?"

"I said you oughta let her be. She's not botherin' nobody and at least we know where she's at."

"Well, I know where her butt is and I'm gonna put a switch on it if she don't start actin' like she's got some sense."

Stepping down on the flat rock serving as a porch step, he looked toward the southwest.

"The hell with it. It's gonna rain and I'm goin' to take myself a nap. Goin' to Tip's to play cards tonight."

"You mean poker, don't you? Hope you got some money. I hain't seen any in awhile…"

"And you ain't gonna if I… Whoa, was that thunder I heard? Damn weather. You can set your watch by the storms we get ever' day."

"You hain't got no watch."

"Shush, gal! Don't need no lip from you…"

He stomped into the shack, shaking the floorboards and slamming the screen door behind him. Sara flinched, and looked to see whether the door was still on its handmade cowhide hinges.

"Good riddance," she whispered. "Sleep your life away for all I care…"

Everybody called the elder Boru "Old Man Boru"; nobody on this side of Big Springs Swamp knew his first name, and didn't bother to ask. He'd just shown up one day a few years back, with

Sara, six-year-old Magalene and eight-year-old Bertha sitting atop a wagonload of household furnishings. To those brave enough to ask, he said he'd known James Kincaid from a long time ago and, since the sickly, white-haired loner had passed away, he didn't need the place no more. James also had come over from the other side of the swamp, back in '32, after the colored folks who lived in the shack had picked up and moved. They'd built a better one back in the woods to be closer, they said, to kinfolk.

Except for concern about the quality of folks who came over from across the swamp, no one had objected then and no one did now – not so Old Man Boru could hear, anyway. When "T'other Side" was mentioned in this part of Shannon County, it generally was done the same way folks talked about the devil, fallen women, drinking hard liquor, fighting, or gambling. All of those activities were commonplace over there, and had been since before anyone living today could recollect.

John, Jewell, Bo, and Arlis, who now was going on three years old, lived the closest to the Boru's – across a muddy, snake-infested three-acre woodlot that shielded both abodes until winter's cold stripped the leaves from all but the pines and cedars.

Being a devout Methodist and having a kindly heart, Jewell went out of her way to make the Borus feel welcome. Being an educated man, John felt, he said, that being uppity around folks who had less than you was not right. He didn't say so, but he liked the fact that Boru always kept a rope-attached jug cooling in the well. He also enjoyed looking at Sara, who seldom wore more than the weather and propriety required.

Mostly by instinct, and the tell-tale signs one man sees hanging on another, John knew Dru's "secret"; truth be told, so did everyone else up, down and close by Sullivan Road.

The affair was now two years old and Sara wasn't so naïve as to believe that no one knew. That concerned her greatly; if her poppa found out, it'd likely be the death of Dru. He didn't like Dru one bit; he didn't like any man who dared look at her, especially like a dog in heat. He was a most possessive man.

Sara cringed at the thought; like a cat shaking a mouse to break its spine and hasten its demise, she shook hers and looked toward Magalene. The girl was sitting at the base of her chinaberry tree, playing with a strand of her long blonde hair. The clouds had sent her angels into hiding.

"Where's Bertha," Sara called.

"Over there."

"Over where?"

"Over there sittin' against the shed. Readin'."

"You could use some readin' yourself, girl. You want to wind up like your momma?"

Magalene said something Sara couldn't hear.

"What'd you say?"

"I said," the girl said more loudly, "I like my momma the way she is…"

Without responding, Sara went back to her knitting – and her thinking. It had been three weeks since Dru had come over on a Saturday afternoon, when everyone else was in Mayo shopping and exchanging news or what passed as news. She'd missed his visits, but hadn't been able to tell him so.

Sometimes Dru surprised her at night, calling like a bird from the woodlot when he figured her poppa was off playing poker or carousing, as he sometimes did, on T'other Side. She'd respond by appearing on the porch and hurrying to the barn, where they'd rustle the hay til one or the other had had enough.

Visualizing that, Sara smiled. He was a big, strong man, all right; but she was eight years younger than his 36, and she generally wore him down til he feigned a plea for mercy.

Then another vision suddenly flashed across her mind and a frown replaced the smile. She was expecting another visitor tonight.

"Lordy, Dru, don't you come 'round tonight. Please don't…."

But Dru already had made up his mind, and on that rainy, omen-filled evening he headed her way. After he and Jim had mounted the wagon and checked the westernmost cotton field for weeds and Bo

Weevils, he hurried through Liza's dinner of pork chops, greens and boiled potatoes and excused himself.

"Somethin' I gotta tend to," he said.

"Why, it's rainin' out there, Dru," his sister declared. "Can't it wait? I got no time to spend nursin' you back from pneumonia or worse…"

"Won't wait," Dru said over his shoulder. He took his felt hat and slicker from a hook by the door and disappeared into the gloomy night.

Without looking up, Jim said, "Reckon he thinks…"

"Hush now, Jim. Bad enough he's goin' over there to see that there Sara woman. We talk about it and first thing everybody'll know."

Though the rain had settled into a drizzle, Dru didn't care one way the other. His determination helped the first quarter-mile go quickly, though his hat became waterlogged and his boots heavy with mud. Pausing, he stomped the boots to shake off the muck; then he gave his slicker a thorough hand-brushing and shook his soggy felt hat til it was shapeless.

Looking back, he could barely make out Bo's fearsome swamp, which loomed between him and Jim's place. Sodden, low-hanging clouds hid the tops of the tallest pines, oaks and cypress, while the shorter oaks and the ground-hugging evergreens, honeysuckle, plum thickets, and briars appeared to be cringing from fear of the grey monster of which they were parts.

From where Dru stood, the monster appeared as a prehistoric dinosaur, rising from the descending darkness on the east, pushing its midsection bulk into the clouds and dropping to the ground again to the west.

"Ho," Dru said aloud. "if that thing was belchin' lightnin' and them thunder rolls was a'comin' outa that place, it'd be like Hell itself."

Dru looked the other way, down Arrowhead Hill toward John's place, and wondered whether the boy in his soul – the boy who wouldn't let go – caused him to keep Banshee Swamp alive and real; Lordy, he wanted to be a boy again, to feel the tingle run up and down his spine when he approached that swamp. Wouldn't it be great if he could be a boy with Bo, to feel and share all the wild and wonderful feelings a boy experienced? He'd never had such a buddy. Never!

A lamp glowed from John's front porch, and he sensed Bo was out there reading by its flickering light. Likely it was casting shadows about the small porch, and maybe even flickering on the bushes Jewell had planted close by. He imagined the cricket sounds and the frog croaks reaching Bo's ears, and the smells of summertime flowers in the breeze that must be fanning the boy's hair…

Likely Bo was reading one of his Tarzan books; and if he were, all he'd need to complete the setting would be an imagined lion's roar and a terrified monkey's screech. That, Dru reasoned, was why a boy needed a Banshee Swamp in his life; it fired his imagination and he'd go looking for more between the covers of a book.

Smiling a gentle smile and shaking his head with equal gentleness, he thought of how much he loved Bo, and of how grateful he was that Bo surely felt he was very special, too.

"Likely you don't know it boy, but you're awful good for me," Dru said in the barely audible voice of a man talking to himself. "I don't know my numbers too well, can't hardly write and ain't much good at readin'. But sittin' with you while you're a'studyin' is helpin' me likely as much as the studyin's helpin' you.

"And just knowin' you're listenin' when I'm talkin' helps me make out things that are hard to figure. And I don't have to worry that somebody's gonna snort high-'n-mighty-like and tell me I'm as slow in the head as a mule at sunset. So long's a boy like you is 'round, I'd druther be a boy…"

Another pause, another thought… "Well, mebbe not all the time. A man's gotta be a man when it comes to lovin' his woman."

He stepped out again, his feet feeling the way along the slippery, grass- and weed-covered ridge dividing the wagon ruts. The rain had picked up again and rushing water was cutting the ruts deeper still, and in some places they were too deep for safe footing. The wet

Georgia clay was as slippery as an eel flopping around on a creek bank; he'd given up marching to a cadence.

Dru focused his thoughts on Sara, and a sober, straight-ahead stare replaced his smile while he plumbed his inner feelings. "She's a good woman, no matter what anybody says, dagnabbit," he said firmly and out loud. More softly, he added, "I kin talk to her and she sees where I'm comin' from and maybe where I'm goin'. That's 'specially good, 'cause I for sure ain't sure most times."

He thought of the way she took him into her shuck-filled bed, sometimes even when Bertha and Magalene were home and no further away than the yard. And when the girls already were in the bedroom shared with Sara, she'd sit him on a straight-backed chair, hoist her skirt, and crawl up on his lap with legs spread. He loved it when she did that; she was doing it her way and he reveled in the pleasure he saw in her eyes.

He figured she was maybe 28 years old, and knowing Magalene was 10 helped his figuring. He didn't like to think about Bertha's age – she was 12 – and told himself it didn't matter anyway. Sometimes he worried about being eight years older than Sara. And he didn't think he was a pleasing-looking man; manly maybe, being tall and lanky with arms that could wrap all the way around a bale of hay and legs that could reach out and eat up the ground.

But his looks didn't appear to bother her and, by golly, she sure liked the manly part. The top of her head barely reached his chin; her blonde hair cascaded nearly to her waist, and some extended in teasing little loops around her ears and forehead. "Spit curls," she called them. She was full-breasted and, Dru thought, "good as that is, it ain't her best part."

Her best part? Dru splashed on and worked the question around in his head. A man who hadn't had much loving from a woman, any woman, really gets to loving breasts, "honey-muffs," "hev'nly tunnels," and, of course, love-making. But Sara had become so much more and, when the good feelings were cresting and his self-doubts ebbing, he managed to tell her what she meant to him down deep…

"Down there where the Godspot lives, and ain't nobody gonna fool a Godspot."

Sara said she didn't know whether she had a Godspot. He'd helped her find it, or at least where it oughta be located, and said it could be her best friend when he wasn't around. His God talked to him from down there, he said. She had asked why he said "his God" when he didn't even go to church, but he had dismissed the question with a shrug of one shoulder.

They were a great deal alike. She couldn't read, write nor figure much, either. And she understood why he stayed by himself so much. In a very real sense, he thought, it's like a pair of Canada geese who'd mated. If one died, the other wouldn't take another mate. He'd told her that was the way he felt. She'd cried, softly, and he almost had. He'd never had a mate, and he didn't like to think of the mates she'd had, even though he didn't know who they were or how many there'd been.

Dru slowed as he neared a turn in the road, at the northeast corner of the woods separating John's farm from the Boru place. He knew that Sara knew, and didn't mind, that he fantasized that she'd always been with him, though the real intimacy hadn't begun until some two years ago.

And he was aware that she wished he wasn't so self-conscious and sensitive about what he was not. They'd spent hours talking about it. He offended easily, and she'd told him several times that talking to him was sometimes like feeling the stove to see if the fire's going.

Being next to last on the string of Sullivan offspring, he had felt during his early years as though he'd been the real runt of the litter and the momma hog always was shoving him off her teats. But in his case, the shoving had been done by the poppa hog, who didn't have any usable teats but had something else a baby needed: love, attention, and gentle touches.

As the years passed the poppa hog seemed to feel Dru was always where he shouldn't be: underfoot. Jim, Liam, Jessie, and Rufus felt they were too old to have any truck with him, and younger brother

John had been too young to sustain his interest. Sister Liza had been more interested in growing up and getting out.

There had been one special time, down at the swimming hole – everybody called it "the Ford" – when Dru had opened up his soul for Sara. He'd told her nobody had seemed to care whether he spent more time away from the school than in it. Despite Momma Susan's pleas, Daddy Niall Barnabas Sullivan had worried so much about the crops, livestock and things the family didn't have that he hadn't paid much attention to what they did have.

"Hell's faire," Dru had said in agitation, "the only time our old man ever wanted us 'round was when he was suckin' the jug and runnin' off at the mouth 'bout that there Ire-a-land. He'd get to rantin' 'bout the high-falootin', slave-drivin' English; said they'd had a boot on the I-rish neck so long nobody could remember when it got put there."

With head-shaking firmness, Dru had told her it'd never been clear why Momma Susan had married so mean a man. What was clear, he said, was that Niall Barnabas had dearly loved her; she'd had blue-green eyes, red hair and ways that put the lie to stories about red hair and terrible tempers. She also had a loyalty that had never faded. It would have been nice, Dru'd told Sara, if her big heart and loving gentleness had been big enough for both of them.

"But it warn't, dagnabbit. Good as she was, a boy needs a man in his life and that man oughta be his daddy! There warn't no way to please that man. I mean, she'd pile his dinner plate full and he'd still ask for more; let one of us do that and you'd think the garden had dried up..."

Their father, Niall Barnabas, had selected Dru's name and Momma Susan had reluctantly accepted it. Dru was short for Druid, and Druids were priests in long-ago Celtic society, of which Ireland was a part. To get a hold on all that hard-to-imagine stuff, his oldest brother, Jim, had put aside his Bible long enough to do some reading about the Celts; he'd learned Druids were the smart folks among their people – doctors, folks who told kings and queens what to do, and settled arguments that kept families under the same roof and held clans together.

They'd also practiced human sacrifice; and while Jim couldn't bring himself to think of his brother as filling any of those big shoes, he sure couldn't imagine Dru hurting a living thing. He'd seen him step around a roach and grinned at the memory of their sister Liza raising cain because he hadn't killed it.

Niall had defended his choice of names. "Druids believed," he'd said, "everything started and ended in nature, and that everything was hitched to everything else. That's why a circle was their symbol. We're farmers, by God, and we gotta believe in nature. And we sure as the devil gotta understand it.

"I'm hopin' Dru will be the one to do that."

One thing Momma Susan had done in trying to please his daddy, Dru had related, was sing the old Irish songs; she said those touched the heart more than any she'd heard at social gatherings or, God forgive her, even in church. While she sang, he and his brothers sat close by, listening and wondering how songs so sad could make a body feel so glad.

Dru had put it just like that, and Sara had told him those were feelings she could understand and had felt herself; and hearing him express them the way he had, with all that passion, had made her believe they were indeed made for each other.

"Maybe this is what love is like. Maybe it's comin' onto our time, Dru…"

Oh, how that had warmed him. And it had made him talk more on that day down there by the ford, to really get it all out. He'd said the Sullivan "at-hair" – he'd been told that was Irish for daddy – had gotten more and more bitter and Momma Susan had stopped singing when he was around. And that was terrible-awful bad, Dru said. Nobody had blamed her; but for certain he, at least, had blamed their daddy.

Little by little, like the leaves, branches, and the spinning bugs being carried away by the water coursing through the fording place, he'd shared his feelings and beliefs with Sara. And she'd told him it wasn't surprising that he'd become what he was: "A real, honest-to-goodness lonesome man, like the really honest-to-goodness lonesome woman I am."

And she'd gone on to say there was nothing wrong with being as they were and, besides, being alone and lonely gave him more time to think about her and to come visit more often.

But so far Sara never had said much about herself; she'd never said much of anything that would leave the door ajar to the questions she knew he wanted to ask. And when he'd managed to raise some gumption and slip one in, she'd lean against him and say something sweet but sad.

"Oh Dru, you know how much I care about you, and that oughta be enough. You don't want to know if'n I've been hurt and who might have done it. Ain't it enough to know that it hurts me to think about it. And specially to know how I'd feel if'n I talked about it. Besides, this is today and there's just me and you and we don't need nothin' else."

Rounding a corner, Dru saw a pinpoint of light coming from the only window looking onto the Boru front porch. To his left lay a field of soggy cotton, to his right the woods. He had prowled those woods as a boy and, more recently, as a man keeping an eye on his beloved while hiding from the eyes of her father. Pine trees, shrub oaks, several persimmon trees, briar patches, and honeysuckle vines grew right up to the edge of the Boru yard; deep inside, moss-draped water oaks hung over a cypress-studded half-acre pond that couldn't be seen from the road, even in daylight.

Energized now by the light from the shack, he stepped out briskly, grinning at the sucking sounds made by his boots as they freed themselves from the mud. He was still grinning as he stepped onto the porch, shook himself and removed the slicker. Sara was visible through the window, and right away he saw she was talking to somebody and enjoying it.

But he was surprised when she stopped abruptly and looked with wide, wondering eyes toward the front door. Dru sensed his stomping had alerted her; his next thought was that maybe Old Man Boru hadn't gone off to play poker after all, though he'd never seen Sara smile or heard her laugh when her pa was around.

No question about it: he had interrupted something important and that the interruption had set her to acting strangely. He watched as she placed a hand over her mouth, started shaking the other in the direction of the back door, obviously telling someone to go out that way and do it quickly.

Dru walked to the west side of the porch and jumped to the muddy ground. The rainwater running off the tin roof doused his bare head and his back, and for a brief moment he had trouble seeing in the dark. Then the back door opened and a man emerged, raising an arm against the rain. He was tall, broad-shouldered and didn't have a slicker…

And the light coming from the door illuminated his bare back and his smooth, black skin.

Sick to the stomach, knees trembling, Dru sat down on the edge of the porch, almost missing it. He heard the door close and, despite the rain drumming on the tin roof, he could hear the man sloshing around the far side of the shack. Dru didn't even move when, a moment later, Sara opened the front door and called out softly…

"Who's out there? Anybody out there?"

And he was still sitting on the edge of the porch when the door closed, clutching his water-logged felt hat while his tears mixed with the drizzle. Dru sat paralyzed, unable to move even if he had wanted to; and he remained there until the light no longer shone through the window, and he sensed Sara had gone to that shuck-filled bed, and he imagined with his ears the crumpling sound as it accepted her body…

Then his eyes revealed the vision his mind had conjured – of a man in the bed with Sara, a black man…

Only the worst kind of a white woman would be alone with a black man, in her own home and at night. And to take him into her bed! He could be lynched and she…

He didn't want to imagine the consequences for her. His runaway mind screamed for him: "Sara, Sara, what have you done? Why, why, why…?"

After another long and painful moment of gnashing his teeth and fighting back tears, he stood and walked back the way he'd come, dragging his slicker with one hand and carrying his sodden felt hat in the other. The tears mingled with the rain and blinded him – blinded him to everything but his own self-doubt and a stomach-cramping feeling of betrayal.

"Damn you, Sara!" he suddenly shouted into the dark, wet night. "Damn you to tarnation! Ain't there nobody in this whole world for a man like me? Ain't there nobody I can believe in, nobody I can trust?

"Dear Lord, what's the matter with me? I wish I was dead…"

CHAPTER 3

Death in a pigsty

WHILE DRU TRUDGED FORLORNLY home, the night's nastiness already had reached several miles further south, into the thick, water-logged stand of woods known Smoky Hollow. There, Marybelle Higginbotham and her 16-year-old son, Lonny, were sharing the glow from a single lamp in a wee shack alongside Big Springs Swamp. With only the pine-log rafters between them and the tin roof, the pounding rain often made conversation impossible.

Buttonbottom and the girls already were asleep, the man on a straw-stuffed mattress and the children snuggled against one another on pallets spread close by the small fireplace. A bunk-bed, built against the south wall, was empty; it belonged to the oldest Higginbotham son, Delphi, who was out on an errand. Frail, 18-month-old May slept in a fruit crate at Marybelle's feet.

Lonny gave up trying to read the picture book Jewell Sullivan had given him; the light was too dim and he had something else gnawing at his mind. He got off the floor and walked to a rear window, pulled aside a blanket covering the hole where a pane had been, and stared into the darkness.

Marybelle knew why and smiled. His prize pig was out there in the sty and Lonny was concerned that it might drown or catch its death of colic. He'd told himself several times that he should have put a better roof on the pig's hut, and that maybe he should have spread more weeds and tree branches and palm fronds on its bed.

When the pounding rain ebbed to a gentle patter, she said, "That pig's gonna be jus' fine. Pigs know how to take care of themselves." Without looking up from her sewing, she added, "Better'n most folks know how…"

"Aw, Momma, the rain's quittin'. Can't I go out there now an' see to him?"

"No, not now, Lonny-boy, we been over this afore. You ain't goin' out there on a night like this'un. The Good Lord's havin' His say an' He's sayin' you gotta stay in here where it's warm an' safe. You get back over here an' you read that book Miss Jewell give you."

Lonny muttered something inaudible, but returned to his place on the floor and picked up the book. Soft-spoken Marybelle expected to be obeyed; he'd learned that as a toddler and seldom tried to test her will.

"That Miss Jewell's is one'a God's treasures," she said in a voice so low Lonny barely heard.

"What you say, Momma?"

"I was talkin' to my own self, son, but I was sayin' Miss Jewell is a fine lady."

"Yessum, she is."

With a furrowed brow, and an occasional glance toward the covered window, he ran his fingers across a page of the book. He couldn't read many of the words, and Marybelle couldn't help him. But Miss Jewell did, on those days she'd drop by to see whether the Higginbotham's needed anything – old clothes she'd picked up at the church, medicine for May, and especially vegetables from her garden.

Jewell always had a good garden, carefully cultivated on a plot that was larger than her own 800-square-foot house; a five-foot wire fence kept most animals out. The Higginbotham's garden, dug out of root-tangled soil in a small clearing, seldom produced well. The sun reached it for only three or four hours a day and it was open to the deer, raccoons, possums, rabbits, squirrels, and other creatures living in the woods.

Ironically, the Higginbothams survived in great part because of the animals that ate their vegetables. Buttonbottom didn't own a gun, but need had made him a respected trapper. He also was an expert with a slingshot, which had become a more lethal weapon since red rubber had become available for inner tubes in automobile tires.

The rain had begun to subside again when a bolt of lightning slammed into a tree not far from the shack; the resounding "ka-bammmm!" woke May, and Marybelle reached down to shush her and adjust her blanket, another gift from Jewell. Lonny had gotten up and stood at her side, looking down on the child. Marybelle looked at him and he looked back, his eyes pleading.

Placing a hand on one of his shoulders, she shook her head from side to side and smiled. "Oh, Lonny, if'n you just gotta go see to that pig, you wait a few minutes to see there ain't no mo' lightnin' an' then you go look. But you wait til I say so…"

Gradually, the rumbles moved farther and farther away from the little shack in the woods; the rain went with it and Marybelle told Lonny he could go outside. She lifted the crate containing the child, placed it by her bedside and lay down next to her husband.

She loved her man, and she seldom looked at him without smiling and shaking her head about how a man named Erasmus had come to be known as Buttonbottom.

Several years earlier, during hog-killing time at Jim Sullivan's place, he'd gone into the outhouse, dropped his pants and sat down. Looking up, he'd seen a snake staring back at him. Not bothering to see what kind, he'd bolted out the door, tripped over his overalls and landed face-down with his bare butt exposed.

Horrified, Marybelle had shouted, "Button yo' bottom, you crazy man!"

And someone else, someone laughing uncontrollably, had shouted, too.

"Buttonbottom! Hey, 'Rasmus, you got a new name!"

The story had spread throughout Shannon County and, in time, Buttonbottom Higginbotham was proud of his nickname.

Before falling asleep, Marybelle thanked her Good Lord for all His blessings, and especially for her husband.

Sometime later Marybelle awakened. The lamp still burned; the fire in the fireplace was dying, but still had the strength to reach with flickering fingers into the room's recesses. Lonny was not on his pallet. Looking about the shadow-filled room, she called softly, "Lonny-boy, you best git on that floor an' git some sleep. You in here, boy?"

Del answered from the bunk bed. "I been home awhile, Momma, but I hain't seen him. Maybe I should'a woke you up."

"Shhh, Delphi, he's gotta be in here someplace…"

He wasn't. Knowing she must have been asleep for at least an hour, Marybelle got up and went to the door and opened it. The rain had become a mist and a bright moon was trying to break through clouds that appeared be racing off toward the northeast. She could barely make out the pigsty.

She stood there for several minutes, shivering in the nighttime dampness. Nothing moved, in the pigsty or the yard. "Lordamercy, where's that boy?" she said as she lit a coal-oil lantern and took wrap from a nail next to the door.

"I'll go, Momma," Del called from his bed.

"No, no, you stay where you is…"

Stepping around the puddles she could make out, Marybelle made her way toward the sty, ignoring the questioning "cluck, cluck" of chickens sleeping under the house. The stile Lonny had made for stepping over the board fence emerged from the darkness and she mounted the first step.

"Lonny?" There was no answer, and the sty seemed empty. Nothing moved.

"Lonny, where are you, Lonny? You're scarin' me half to death, boy."

Then she saw a form, face down and spread-eagled in the mud. "Lonny!" she screamed and clambered over the stile.

The boy was dead; blood oozed from a large wound on one side of his head and disappeared in the black, clammy mire in which he lay. As she knelt in the mire by the body, her knee hit something that felt like a length of iron pipe. It was a small shotgun, a .410.

The pig was gone.

Sheriff Carl Nobles didn't arrive until morning, after Del had raced through the darkness to Tip Evers' store and pounded on the door. Seeing Del, Tip was angry and was about to slam the door in his face until the young Negro pleaded with him

"Please, Mistuh Tip, somebody done kilt Lonny and we needs the sheriff. I can't run all the way to Mayo, suh. I jus' can't…"

"Killed Lonny? Who'd kill Lonny?"

"Lordy, I don't know. But somebody did, wit' a shotgun. Please, suh, can you…?"

Evers dressed quickly. Getting into his pickup to go for the sheriff, he told Delphi to come with him.

"I can't, Mistuh Evers. Momma and Daddy, they 'bout outa their heads. I gotta get back home."

Buttonbottom had pulled the body from the mud and had taken it into the shack, where he placed it on the bed. Marybelle sat next to Lonny throughout the remainder of the night, wiping the mud and the caked blood from his black skin and trying not to look at the gaping hole from which it no longer oozed.

Rocking her body back and forth, she didn't stop crying or praying until the sheriff arrived. Then she wiped her eyes, put on the stoniest face she could muster, and went to let him in. No one outside her own family, not even Jewell Sullivan, had ever seen her cry.

Sheriff Nobles appeared sympathetic, entering the shack with hat in hand and concern on his swarthy, bearded face. Taking

Buttonbottom onto the porch so they could talk privately, he said, "I shore am sorry 'bout this, 'Rasmus." He'd called the grieving father by his given name, thinking it was proper under the circumstances. He added, "Who'd have cause to kill Lonny?"

"Dat's what we been askin', Mistuh Nobles, suh. Ever'body love dat boy."

"You think mebbe he walked up on whoever took that pig?"

"Could'a been, suh. We thought o' that."

"Hmmm. I don't know of any white man 'round these parts who hain't got 'nough pigs of his own…"

"'Scuse me. Mistuh Nobles, suh, you ain't thinkin' no nigger kilt Lonny fo' that pig? Niggers hereabouts kno'd that was Lonny's prize pig an' that he was gonna show it in the 4-H show come next month. Mistuh John, he fixed it so a colored boy could show his, an' you know he had Lonny in mind when he did it."

"I ain't sayin' a nigger might'a done it, 'Rasmus. All I'm saying is…"

"An' 'sides, they know when it's come time to kill that pig they gonna get part of it anyways. All us niggers share what little we got."

The sheriff frowned and turned away momentarily. "Well, alright, 'Rasmus, but how come you moved the body, er, Lonny from where he was kilt? You know we got to investigate this killin'."

Buttonbottom looked the sheriff in his blue eyes and set his face real hard. Through gritted teeth, he said, "Hain't no man on this here earth gonna leave his boy stretched out dead in the mud of a pigsty, Mistuh Nobles. Not this here man, anyways…"

The sheriff didn't respond; he looked away and wiped his hands on his trousers. Buttonbottom wasn't finished…

"Seems to me, suh, my boy is dead wit' a hole in his head an' we agrees that hole was made by a .410 shotgun, a little thing folks use for varmints an' such. An' the pig's gone. What do it look like to you, suh?"

Nobles backed off and turned away. Walking toward the empty sty, he said just loud enough for Buttombottom to hear, "You know,

'Rasmus, it's jus' possible Lonny'd taken a gun out there to be safe an' shot hisself by accident…"

"No way, Mistuh Nobles…"

"…Or maybe he was so upset at losin' his pig he shot hisself in his misery."

"Lonny never had no shotgun, Mistuh Sheriff. He never had no kind'a gun. There ain't no gun on this place."

"Maybe he went off somewheres an' got hisself one…"

'Rasmus took a deep breath. Twice, he opened his mouth as if to say something, then chosed it. After a long silence during which the sheriff continued to peer into the sty, the Negro said softly, "Ain't no way, suh. Ain't no way…"

Nobles didn't say anything for several minutes. He walked about the wet yard, as though hoping to find a footprint or some other clue. He had a problem, a big one: he knew that many farm families had .410 shotguns, but had no way of knowing which ones. How could he possibly go round white folks' houses asking if they had owned a .410 shotgun like the one that killed Lonny Higginbotham? And if so, where was it?

Buttonbottom, meanwhile, was wishing he had a shotgun – a .12 gauge or bigger. He also was praying that he'd have the wisdom to seek his brethren's counsel before he set out to do something he would regret.

For fear the sheriff might read his mind, Buttombottom couldn't bring himself to look him in the eyes. He didn't have Marybelle's inner strength and he'd never pretended that he did. Meekness, acquiescence, compromised feelings – they had dominated his life; he knew it, hated it, and had promised himself that someday he'd throw off their painful yoke; he saw nothing Godly in them.

When he finally did look at the sheriff, however, he'd forced himself to put aside his hatred and examine each word before he spoke it.

"I been a good nigger, Mistuh Sheriff Nobles. None'a dis here family has ever caused no trouble an' it ain't goin' to. What I'm a'gonna do now is put my trust in you an' pray fo' the Lord to he'p you find out what went on here, an' who kilt my boy Lonny.

"Havin' said that, suh, I'm gonna go sit by my boy an' hol' Marybelle's hand. It's likely I'm a'gonna cry some, even if she doan. I'd be mos' grateful if'n you'd leave us be fo' a while..."

CHAPTER 4

Bereavement for the Higginbothams, a mysterious letter for John, and a man-sized worry for Bo

WORD OF LONNY'S DEATH spread quickly, jumping up Sullivan Road from Tip Evers' store to the Dunaway farm, skipping the Boru's and landing on the porch where Jewell was shelling peas. Horrified, she called John from the kitchen.

"Somebody's killed Marybelle's Lonny," she shouted. "Tip just come by to tell us. I gotta go…"

"Hush, Jewell. You want the boys to hear you?"

"Let 'em hear, John! I hain't got no time to worry 'bout that. Marybelle needs me!"

"She's going to get plenty of help from her own kind. You know that. Best thing to do is let her be til…"

"Get outa my way, John. If you don't want hitch up Junebug, I will. Just stand back and take care of the boys, wherever they got off to."

"Where's Tip?"

"Can't you see him? He's already goin' over that hill to tell Jim and Dru…"

John helped Jewell pull the wagon from the barn and harness the mule, then watched until the rig disappeared behind the woods to the east. Sadly, and with a knot in his stomach, he turned to thinking about his own relationship with Marybelle. They shared several secrets and he never doubted that they would remain secrets.

Twice when Jewell had gone off to visit her sister in Sligo, John had gotten falling-down drunk. Both times Marybelle had sensed it, had picked up the boys, and had taken them home with her. He'd learned early-on to wait til he was sober before attempting to retrieve them; she'd check his eyes, his breath, and the steadiness of his hands before she'd let them go.

Once he'd begged her to clean up the mess he and his drunken fish-fry pals had made, and she had done so. He'd tried to pay her, but she had refused to accept the money. "Not for somethin' like this, Mistuh John. This here's the devil's work and I ain't gonna take no pay fo' cleanin' up the devil's work. I jus' pray the Good Lord don't see me doin' it."

He had found other ways to pay her back and ease his guilt. Like Jewell, he sometimes took vegetables to the Higginbothams, as well as an occasional slab of cured ham. Always Marybelle hesitated to accept the gifts; she'd hem and haw, but finally bow when John reminded her that they were for her family and not just her.

With a shrug, John turned away from the road and the memory. He fixed a noontime dinner, joined the boys at the table and then sent the boys to the bedroom for their naps: Arlis on the bed and Bo on a pallet, a blanket spread on the hard floor. Pallets were uncomfortable and when Bo noticed that his daddy wasn't in his usual place – on the make-do settee – he got up and took over the awkward but more comfortable piece of furniture. Jewell had said it was make-do because it had to serve until $10 had been saved to buy a real settee, if more important needs didn't pop up first.

What it was the frames of three old rocking chairs tied together and the rockers removed; all but the two outside arms had been sawed off at seat level. Three feather pillows covered by an old quilt completed the make-do, and a full-sized man could rest on it reasonably well if he didn't mind his legs hanging over one end.

Bo hadn't been happy with his daddy's response about the absence of his momma: "She's gone to help a friend. That's all I need to say."

So he feigned sleep and did what he often did: he stared at the pine ceiling and imagined that the various knots were animals or something else just as interesting. He stared hardest at a large, oval-shaped knot that John had said was the face of God, who kept watch over them while they slept. Bo had replied it looked like a pine knot to him, a response that had gotten him a firm but friendly glance and an admonition.

"God – or I should say, any man's God – is in everything, and if you look hard enough you'll find him." Bo had wondered why he'd said "any man's God"; maybe, he reasoned, Uncle Dru had told him about Godspots.

Getting off the settee, Bo crept by his sleeping brother and headed for the front porch. Being "not more'n a baby just out of diapers," as Bo liked to put it, Arlis was not subject to the rule banning daytime use of a bed.

Reaching the front porch, he took the dipper and scooped water from the tin pail hanging from a joust. Most folks had wooden buckets, which kept the water cooler and tasting better. Their wooden bucket had sprung a leak when the water froze last January and hadn't been replaced.

He looked up and down the road, and saw his daddy down by the mailbox, so intent upon reading something that Bo figured it must be extra-special important. The Sullivans rarely got mail, and sometimes the postman came around just to let them know he hadn't died or broken a leg or anything like that. And sometimes he stopped off just to sit a spell and talk about crops, the war and what others were doing. He genuinely liked to gossip and sometimes he'd lead folks into asking a question that gave him the opportunity – such as, "Passed the Shaughnessy house this morning…"

He'd leave it at that, knowing the unfinished sentence was apt to prompt a question about what he had seen or heard. Even a simple "Oh?" opened the door.

His name was Fred McCann and, being a mailman and working for the government, he was expected to have the latest inside information about the war. John and Jewell generally listened with appropriate attentiveness, nodding often and saying, "Uh-huh … Well, how 'bout that? … You don't say? … Damn them slant eyes to hell…" John cussed; Jewell didn't.

After Fred left, however, John nearly always shook his head and averred there was no way Fred had an inside track on anything; he just listened to the radio more than most folks who had them, and a lot more than those who didn't have them. And, by golly, he listened to his radio so much because he had more time to listen than real, honest-to-goodness working folks.

Secretly, Jewell liked Fred's gossip, and if Fred said something to indicate Mrs. Shaughnessy hadn't looked well, she'd likely pack a basket of food and be out the door before the day was done.

Bo liked to see Mr. McCann come around because he'd let him sit in the passenger seat of his Model A Ford, and sometimes he'd let him play with the steering wheel. If no one was around, Fred joined in the fun. While Bo pretended to be driving, the mailman sat in the passenger seat calling out warnings: "Watch out for that mud hole on the right… Attaboy, you missed it… Start brakin' now; that corner's closer'n it looks and Mollie (his pet name for the Model A) ain't the lady she used to be… That's a rattlesnake up ahead. Go ahead and run over it if you can."

Mister McCann was – to Bo, anyway – a lot like his Uncle Dru. Several times he'd come close to telling him so, but didn't; he knew some folks didn't see his ill-educated, poor speaking, church-avoiding uncle as he did and wasn't sure the mailman would appreciate the comparison.

The mailbox was about two good chunks of a rock to the east of the house, at the foot of the road coming south over Arrowhead Hill. John didn't look up as Bo approached. Extending a hand, he placed it on the boy's head and roughed up his hair. He continued to read, sometimes frowning, sometimes grinning, and sometimes scratching the side of his head as though, Bo figured, he needed some help making sense out of something he'd read.

"I can read, daddy. Why don't you let me see that letter?"

"I know you can read, boy, but this one's too hard and it's personal."

"But why…"

"Hush, Bo!"

Bo took a step backward, out of reach of his daddy's hair-tousling hand. He didn't have to worry about being hit; John lost patience from time to time, as he had done now, but he'd never hit either him or Arlis. Not that Bo could remember, leastways.

Like his daddy, Bo's momma was always saying how important it was to be able to read and write, and that her boys were going to be good at both. She'd taught Bo his ABCs, how to spell all the days of the week, and how to count to fifty before he was five years old. She'd started him on spelling the months of the year by the time she'd taken him to the school; impressed, the teacher had given him credit for kindergarten, started him in the first grade, and soon moved him to the second. Now Jewell was hard at work on Arlis, and Arlis was just coming up on three years old.

John continued to read. The minutes passed slowly, so slowly that Bo felt time wasn't moving much faster than the buzzard circling above the cotton field. Concentrating on the buzzard and thinking of its God-assigned chore of eating dead things, he was reminded of Preacher Pemberton; and he got to thinking maybe that man could read as good as his daddy. He seemed awfully good at reading from the Good Book at church but, truth be known, Bo often wondered whether the preacher was reading or making it up as he went along. The preacher seldom looked at the Book, and mostly just waved his arms and said things that sounded real smart and uplifting – Jewell had told him the meaning of that word – and sometimes scary. Bo already knew the meaning of that word.

The preacher's raving and ranting was especially vigorous and scary when he got to talking about Satan and his netherworld, where sinners were burning up in fire and brimstone, right now and forevermore.

Bo had tried to picture sinners burning up and figured they probably raved and ranted like the preacher. But he had never come across any brimstone when looking for arrowheads, none that he would have recognized, anyway. Some tom-fool visitor had set him atop a hot stove when he was three, however, and even hearing the word "fire" rekindled the memory. He'd never forgotten the pain and still had a scarred hiney.

So deeply was Bo thinking about the reverend that he didn't notice when John finished reading, folded the letter, and placed it in a shirt pocket.

"What're you thinking now, Bo? That I'm bein' mean? I don't mean to be, but, boy, sometimes you tug at a man's patience til it's about to break."

"No, no, Daddy, I got to thinkin' about Preacher Pemberton and I was wonderin' where he came from and how he got to be so mean."

"Well now, I'll overlook your disrespect for the man…"

John grimaced, then grinned, frowned, and started again. "Ah heck, he is mean, ain't he? Pemberton's just the latest Methodist minister to come here and likely he'll move on once he thinks he's got folks thinkin' the way he wants them to think, which is to think like he thinks.

"Started out a long time ago, maybe a hundred years ago. The big shots in the Methodist Church – they were somewhere up north or maybe over by the Georgia or Carolina coasts – sent circuit riders to bring the word of God to the heathens out here in these backwoods. I'm told some stayed where they lit, but others wanted to keep on moving. Reckon they figured it was better to find more heathens and leave the saved souls to the care of the next minister."

Bo listened with eyes spread the width of his wrinkled forehead. He asked a flock of questions: "Where's up north, how far's the coast, what's a circuit, and did the rider come on a mule or a horse? What's a hea-'thun, and you didn't say if them that come first was as mean as Pemberton, ah, Mister Preacher Pemberton…"

John ignored all but the last of Bo's run-on questions. He grabbed ahold of that one and launched into another tight-lipped, firm response.

"Probably they were, son, but if you think the Reverend Pemberton is mean you haven't been told about the Catholic priests back there in Ireland. When I was a boy like you, Poppa Niall Barnabas'd rear up on his heels and bray like a mad mule about what his own poppa had to say about those priests.

"'Stricter'n a mad schoolmarm canin' a malcontent,' your grandpa'd say, and he'd look angrier'n a wet cat while sayin' it. Never satisfied, never with a nice word to say to nobody! Miss a mass and the door was barred and the poor soul was left out in the cold to wander 'round as free game for the devil!'

"Why son, Poppa Niall said – and I've done enough reading to believe it's so – that if a woman slipped up and admitted she liked makin' love, ho-man, was she in trouble!

"'Makin' love,' Poppa Niall told us, '"was for makin' babies and had nothin' to do with likin' it…'"

John stopped cold right there, sensing that his strong feelings had taken his explanation beyond the bounds of what a boy should know. He frowned, genuinely regretting his slips of the tongue, and grinned at Bo, whose gaping mouth reflected genuine shock at what he'd just heard.

For sure Bo had been knocked back on his heels; but his reaction had been prompted by the recollection that Magalene had said those words – "makin' love" – and, by jiminy, he was too doggone young to be making babies.

Seeing that Bo's face was radiating various shades of crimson and that he appeared to be having trouble breathing, John squatted, placed his hands on the boy's shoulders, and looked him square in the eyes.

"You alright, boy? You ain't about to pass out, are you? Lordamercy, what I said couldn't have been that bad. Think of it as talk between men…"

Bo met his daddy's stare, got hold of himself, and did some quick thinking, the kind of fancy on-the-spot cogitating that had gotten him out of tight spots in the past and would in the future.

"Uh-uh, naw, Daddy, those priests must have been some kinda mean. But the more you talked the more things I thought 'bout and wanted to ask…"

"That's enough, Bo. Maybe some other time. And don't go askin' your momma about what I said. It's likely I've told you more'n she knows herself."

Bo managed a grin, and told himself that, by golly, he'd heard all he wanted to hear, said all he wanted to say, and certainly had no more questions to ask. Not of his daddy, anyway. But for sure he'd have words and questions for Magalene, if and when he ever saw her again.

John stood and looked toward the house. "Make a deal with you, son," he said. "You don't tell your momma we got a letter and we'll go swimmin'."

Nearly forgetting his fears and the give-and-take of the "deal," Bo reacted excitedly. "Down to the creek ford, Daddy? Right now?"

"Not today. Your momma's gone off to help somebody through a bad time and I ain't certain when she'll get back. We may have to fix our own supper."

Briefly, John thought of telling him about Lonny; but he decided that was something Jewell should do, if it became necessary. She was good at such things; he wasn't.

John lifted Bo off his shoulders, swung him around once, slapped his behind and gave him a running shove toward the house. Then he went on across the yard to the barn, climbed to the hay mow, shoved the hay to one side, and carefully deposited the letter alongside the two stone whiskey jugs and a coffee tin containing a few dollars in bills, some change, and a silver dollar Momma Susan had given him for learning a bedtime prayer when he had been about Arlis' age.

She'd taught it to her children and grandchildren: "Now I lay me down to sleep, I pray the Lord my soul to keep. If I should die before I wake, I pray the Lord my soul to take."

Since he'd returned from the Army, John had added his own concluding words: "And as I go through other days, I pray the Lord to guide my ways."

Today, he was thinking his "ways" had better be right, and that he'd need all the direction he could get.

CHAPTER 5

Jewell and Sara melt the ice at the ole swimmin' hole; Bo fears he's in hot water

THE SUN WAS ABED when Jewell got back from the Higginbotham's, and John heard Junebug's tinkling tack and sand-softened "clip-clop, clip-clop" before the wagon emerged from the darkness. The mule's gait was slow and Jewell's shoulders sagged; clearly, she was worn out and, he suspected, heartbroken and painfully frustrated.

He knew the Higginbothams: always willing to help, but incapable of accepting help when it might tarnish their image of themselves. Independence and strength, it was; pride was sinful and the word was not spoken in their household.

Though she saw the glow of John's cigarette, Jewell had given the mule its head and let it pass on by the porch and go to the barn. There she dismounted and, without benefit or need of being able to see, began to unhitch Junebug.

She heard John walk up behind her, but didn't react until he said, "You gonna tell me what's going on?"

Then she turned and pressed her face into his chest. "John, that sheriff is sayin' Lonny likely killed hisself – killed his own self, and with a shotgun! Oh, how could he be so crazy as to think anything like that?"

Unable to contain herself any longer, Jewell broke down and cried; her whole body trembled and John increased his hold, pulling her closer and kissing her matted hair.

"Where was he shot, Jewell?" It was a whispered question, said after she had begun to regain some control of her emotions.

"In the side of the head. Oh, it was awful to see!"

For a long moment both were silent. John remembered Lonny as a smiling, attentive boy who doted on animals, especially farm animals; once he'd had a nanny goat, and the life seemed to have been taken out of him when the goat had to be slaughtered and eaten.

But suicide? "No way that boy killed himself, Jewell. Nobles is trying to protect his own self. It's doubtful any Negro would've killed him, but you can be sure Nobles ain't gonna try to go about this county saying a white man could have done it."

"I know that, John. That's what's so sad. But to say Lonny killed hisself, and in that filthy old pig pen. Lord help Marybelle and her family. They're actin' so brave…"

"That's what it is, Jewell – acting. They're all hurting. We know that…"

"Yes we do, John. I jus' wish they'd treat us like family, like we try to be."

"I know, honey. But we gotta try to see it their way. Maybe we can't – maybe we never will – understand how they really feel about white folks. We pretty well know the 'why', all of us…"

Momentarily silent, he added, "Maybe better than they do."

John's shirt was wet with Jewell's tears now, and he hoped she had cried herself out. Gently, he took her by one hand and led her to the house. Then he returned to the barn, finished unhitching the mule and put it away.

Bo was up early, hurrying around the house and doing little chores he sometimes had to be reminded to do. John knew why. Bo had not forgotten his promise to take the family swimming. He nudged the boy to the front porch and said, "Your momma's not feeling too good, Bo, and we may have to put off swimming for another day or two."

Jewell overheard and stepped onto the porch. "I truly ain't feelin' good, Bo-boy, but maybe a trip to the swimmin' hole will make me feel better. You know how much I love goin'."

Surprised, John stared at her, letting his eyes ask the question.

"No reason we can't go, John."

Bo didn't wait to hear more; he bolted through the front door to get his swimming suit, a pair of cut-off jeans.

"Couldn't this wait til after they've had the funeral, honey?" John said.

"Ain't gonna be no funeral, John. Not one we can go to, anyways. You oughta know that by now."

Negroes in Shannon County had their own funeral services, at their own church. Afterwards, they took the deceased into the woods, to their own secret places, and buried the bodies.

Looking into Jewell's eyes, John said, "Okay, honey. If you're really up to it."

"I am, John. I've prayed 'bout it and the Good Lord says to get on with our lives..." Pausing momentarily, she added, "And He says there ain't no reason to tell the boys 'bout Lonny. Not now, anyways."

The swimming hole was a fording place on a creek a mile east of Tip Evers' store, and Jewell loved swimming almost as much as hoedowns, church socials, and going to town on Saturdays. And at all of them she did her best to project her "Julie" image; folks called her by that name when she let her hair down, laughed a lot, sang country songs, and often became the life of the party.

Much, much earlier, the ford had been part of an Indian trail, which led southeast across the narrow, spring-fed creek and skirted massive Big Springs Swamp. Time and heavy use, especially back when the route was the only one cutting through the region, had packed the ford's clay, rocks and gravel so tightly they resisted even the heaviest of rain-swollen gulley-washers.

On good days, the cold, crystal-clear water cascaded from beneath the foliage to the north and ran into a high-banked outlet thirty yards to the south. Because the narrow outlet couldn't accept all the water at once, it backed up to form a deep, sandy-bottomed pool shaded by a moss-draped oaks, magnolias, cypress, and sun-hunting vines. Smaller trees hugged the bank; bushes, briars, honeysuckle, and a tangle of other vines provided a wall of privacy around its edges.

Some described it as an Eden without the apple; others said the apple was there, but beware the consequences.

Bo truly loved the ford, but his elation about the three-mile journey from home cooled considerably when Junebug hauled the wagon around the corner and the Boru shack came into view. What his daddy had told him about Irish priests raced around and around in his head, so fast he felt dizzy and had to take a steadying grip on the side of the wagon. His head felt as though that angry daddy bird was pecking at it, from the inside out, and he wondered how that wee, harmless-appearing thing between his legs could cause so much trouble.

"'Makin' love was for makin' babies and had nothin' to do with likin' it...'"

Lordy, he thought, what if Magalene is home and wants to go with us? It'd be a long time before he'd get up the gumption to ask her if she was wanting to make a baby when she made him play her game. Already he was thinking he oughta ask Uncle Dru what to do; he kept secrets and was truthful with him. Hadn't he said the banshees in Banshee Swamp had let him alone because he was too young to be the marrying kind? And didn't marrying have a lot to do with making babies?

Despite his best efforts, Bo's cheeks were as a red as a male cardinal; Jewell noticed and reached back to feel his forehead. "Somethin' botherin' you, Bo? Are you feelin' up to this, honey?"

"Oh, yes ma'm! For sure I am." And he quickly added what he hoped would be a suitably evasive reason for his long face and radiant cheeks: "I was just hopin' all that rain didn't dirty up the water…"

He was still holding his breath as they neared the shack, and his thoughts were coming lickety-split; they were telling him that somebody would tell on him and Magalene sooner or later, and he was praying for later.

Magalene wasn't home and neither was anyone else, but John "whoaed" Junebug anyway. The whole family knew why: the Borus had a privy and they didn't.

"Anybody need to go? Don't want anybody messing up the swimming hole."

Jewell smiled, then frowned. "That ain't funny, John. You don't like the Borus, but you don't mind using their outhouse. When are we gonna have one? It's been years since you built our place and we still hain't got a privy!"

The Borus' outhouse had been there when they'd moved over from the other side of the swamp. Standing several feet from their back door, it was a deep, two-holer with a door that latched from the inside.

John told folks he hadn't put up an outhouse because they smelled so bad and the fields did just fine; few believed the excuse, especially in light of the fact that he was an educated man. Even drinking men had outhouses, and may have needed them more than regular folks, the reasoning went.

Nearly every day, Jewell and Bo complained about not having a roofed-over, closed-door, outside place where they could relieve themselves; Bo even said he'd dig the hole if someone would help. He was the "fortunate soul," as Jewell wryly put it when John could hear, whose first morning chore was to take the "honey bucket" from beneath the bed and dump it out of smelling range of the house.

Jewell told the occasional visitor to whom she had to shamefully apologize that John was a lazy man; and if he was out of hearing range, she'd sometimes add, "That's what lots of schoolin' can do to a man. Too smart to dig a hole; too smart to chop down a tree and split it into planks; too important to go askin' for the old lumber on another man's fallin'-down buildin'! Says an outhouse smells awful and we ain't even got the money for all the lime it'd take to kill the smell.

"Ha! You don't see him takin' them pots out ever' mornin'…"

All the Sullivans, those under her roof and the kin scattered around the county, knew that when Jewell peppered angry words with "ha!" it was best to find a hiding place. "Ha!" was as close as she ever came to cussing.

For sure, John knew it and he hadn't responded to Jewell's "That ain't funny…" He'd just snapped the reins and told the mule to move along. She did and, perhaps sensing the moods of those she was pulling, covered the miles quickly. And it wasn't long before she'd pulled them down a rut road that was little more than a gully and halted before the massive canopy of trees hiding the swimming hole.

"Uh-oh," Jewell whispered. "You hear what I hear?"

The sounds were soft, muted and pleasant, and it was clear womenfolk were making them; the voices were familiar and Bo was gripped again by tummy-knotting fear. Magalene? Bertha? Their momma? He wouldn't know for sure until his momma went down to see if it was all right for men and boys to come down.

Jewell returned quickly and confirmed Bo's fears. "It's just Sara and her young'uns. Said come on down. They got dresses on, so it won't matter none if you don't look too close."

She looked straight at John when she said the last part; he raised a shoulder as if to protect himself, laughed, and dropped to the ground, while Arlis slipped over the wagon's side and disappeared under the trees. Bo held back, trying unsuccessfully to shoulder the watermelon. He was in no hurry, looked and felt somewhat ill, and again his momma noticed his strange behavior.

"Lordy, boy, wasn't it you who was a'wantin' to go swimmin' so bad?" She smiled one of her I-know-what-you're-thinkin' smiles and, with Bo wishing she'd just go away, put her arms around his shoulders and told him exactly what he did not want to hear.

"Oh, Bo, you don't have to be shy 'round girls. They ain't gonna be messin' with you, and there'll come a time when you'll be beggin' Bertha and Magalene to go swimmin' with you."

Bo frowned, swallowed hard, and decided he'd better make the best of the situation. Maybe Magalene would be smart like him and pay him no attention, so no one would suspect they'd been playing Doctor Pete for some time, and that it had been Magalene doing the begging.

"Okay," he responded grudgingly. "I just wish Uncle Dru was here."

Sara stood waist-deep in swirling brown water, the top of her cotton dress glued to her breasts and the bottom stretched and wagging from side to side in the current. Spinning leaves, water bugs and an occasional small tree branch danced around her.

"Where's Dru," she called. "I was hopin' he'd be with ya'll."

Mesmerized by Sara's partially exposed body and deeply disappointed by the water conditions, John responded, "Don't know," so quietly she asked a second time.

"Damned if I know," John shouted. "We haven't seen him today."

"Probably sleepin' under his tree," Sara mumbled, her disappointment showing.

Bo's also was, though muddy water had little to do with it. There she was, Magalene, sitting like she didn't have a care in the world. He'd become convinced that her intentions from the beginning had been to get him into trouble, too. What a numbskull he'd been…

Bo remembered how his uncle had reacted when he'd told what Magalene had been teaching him, especially when he'd mentioned how Sara had gotten so angry when she'd found them alone in the shed. Bo wasn't sure she actually had seen them doing anything; perhaps she simply had not wanted them to get the chance.

Bo recollected how his uncle had just about busted his britches laughing about Sara's anger; and while he still wondered why, he decided that what Uncle Dru knew about her was his own business and, Aunt Sara, being a woman and not really his aunt, wasn't worth thinking about anyway.

"I got bigger troubles," Bo muttered to himself, looking for a place to hide.

Bo's momma stepped into the water, revealing her own slim attractiveness. Bo remembered how she'd looked just before Arlis had been born; despite himself, he almost smiled when he recollected that even she had said she looked like a watermelon ready for picking.

Magalene was slim, too, but she wasn't much to look at; Bo was telling himself that when, suddenly, a notion slapped him from inside his head. He stooped, picked up a pebble and chunked it close by where Magalene sat. Scrambling to her feet, she looked around, smiled at Bo, and waded into deeper water.

For sure she wasn't swollen up. Bo felt relieved, really relieved; but he also was a bit riled that she'd have the gumption to smile at him.

He thought about his Uncle Dru and wondered where he was. Then he joined Arlis, who already was splashing around in the creek some distance from where Magalene now sat. Not much of a choice, Bo figured. Just the better of two bad ones…

Sara was looking downstream, clearly lost in her own thoughts. She remained haunted by the feeling that perhaps the noise she'd heard on her porch the previous night – the one that had caused her to send Del out the back door – might have been caused by Dru.

Jewell, meanwhile, was figuring she might have a chance to turn a bad day into a good one. Casting a sideways glance at John, she rolled her ankle-length calico dress up to her knees, tied it in a knot and waded out to stand next to Sara. Perhaps, she reasoned, this was the opportunity she had been looking for.

Sara spoke first. "Hey, Julie. Warn't it awful 'bout Lonny? Near to broke my heart."

"It was. Did break mine, I can tell you. Specially since I went to offer help and they didn't want it."

Jewell wrapped a red bandana around her honey-blonde hair and tied it up in the back. After a moment, she said, "Sara, you sure set me to wonderin' sometimes 'bout your interest in Dru. If you like havin' him 'round so much, why don't you tell 'im so he won't be so gosh-awful shy."

Jewell figured she knew Sara better than most folks on this side of the Big Springs Swamp. Reminding herself that they were standing in Big Springs water, she felt bolder and her eyes hinted of mischief. She looked skyward, asked the Lord's forgiveness for having said "gosh-awful," and decided the moment was right for pressing on and getting some answers.

"Was that question too personal-like, Sara?"

"Well now, Julie," Sara said, calling Jewell by the name she knew she preferred, "Dru knows I like him, an' I do try to let him know. I can't figure if'n he's just too shy to b'lieve it or if'n he's just too thick to let it sink in real good."

Sara matched Jewell's mischievous look. "But just 'cause a gal likes a man don't mean she's pinin' for 'im. I mean, Dru's not the biggest fish in the pond by no means, an' he ain't the best lookin'. A woman with two young'uns an' no man may be needful, but it don't mean she needn't be p'ticular."

She's being coy, Jewell told herself. But having decided to make the most of the moment, she asked a question she'd wanted to ask for a long, long time.

"I'll bet the girls' daddy musta been somethin' special," she said, doing her best to appear a touch envious. "I'll bet he was a..."

Sara knew Jewell was fishing, but she had been in such water before. She had an answer that always shocked and generally sent the curious on their way with an empty croaker sack.

"I wouldn't say they was special," she replied, somewhat sadly. "One wasn't special at all, not at all. I thought the other'n might'a been, but he's gone an' that says 'bout all there is to say." Momentarily silent, she picked a leaf from the water, and added, "Each girl had her own daddy..."

Sara turned away, but not before Jewell had seen the sadness in her eyes, and in her voice. "An' it really is my own business why I didn't make him own up an' marry. Maybe I warn't of a mind to marry back then, knowin', like most folks don't seem to, that a man an' a woman are gonna change an' maybe won't always be fit for one 'nother."

Looking downstream, where the water pushed into a twisting, turning tunnel of low-hanging vines and heavily leafed tree limbs, Sara smiled serenely and, Jewell thought, purred like a cat that had just been fed newly churned cream.

"But, I can tell you this," Sara said so softly Jewell could barely hear, "that Dru can swim like a fish an' just keep on an' on, like there ain't no end. Once I asked him to swim as far as he could down thataway an' come back an' tell me what he found…"

She was pointing to where the stream turned a corner and disappeared. Turning back to Jewell, she raised her voice and, with a finger wagging and one eye closed, spoke firmly and right at Jewell.

"Why, he was gone nigh on to half an hour, an' when he came back he was swimmin' strong an' comin' right back through that openin'. Ohhh, that made me feel good, just like a woman gets to feelin' when a manly man has excited her right down to her core."

Jewell didn't respond right away. She'd had such feelings, too, and they no longer embarrassed her. But she also had felt Sara's obvious excitement that Dru had "…just kept on an' on, like there ain't no end" – and the feeling did bring a slight redness to her cheeks.

Though she realized that she had put the conversation on the course it had taken, she found herself thinking that Sara hadn't been in church in a long time, if ever, and certainly didn't know the way of the Lord.

She also was thinking that Sara wasn't telling the truth about a lot of what she was talking about, and that maybe she was living in a pretend world. Jewell knew about pretend worlds. For the most part, she'd put her own aside when she was the only one of five sisters and a brother still living at home, and her momma had told her she'd better go get John before somebody else did.

And her momma had said it knowing that her daddy, Liam Powell, probably wasn't going to outlive that awful consumption that was eating up his lungs. Having been born a Napier and having French blood, Julie's momma also knew what it took to get a man.

Thinking things weren't going the way she had hoped, Jewell cleared her head and looked straight at Sara; annoyance had replaced frustration, and her voice showed it.

"Well, now, I ain't suggestin' that you oughta think about marryin' Dru. Seems to me there's more women 'round who don't have a man than there's men who don't have a woman. Seems to me he'd do for keepin' a body from gettin' lonely an' for keepin' a body from..."

She was going to say "from getting cold," but didn't.

"Ahem," Sara responded, "are you suggestin'..."

"Oh, I ain't suggestin' nothin'," Jewell said, cutting her off, laughing nervously, and splashing water with both hands. "Besides, there's that Beatrice over on the other side of Munsterville and she sure seems to like Dru."

She told herself she hadn't meant to say that. But she wasn't really sure.

"Oh, I know about Bea, or Be-a-tress," Sara replied. "Dru, he won't talk 'bout her, but other folks do. They say she's hurtin' bad for a man an', livin' with her widow ma like she does, she hain't got much to look fo'ward to..."

Sara turned away again, so Jewell couldn't see that her bottom lip was trembling.

"Maybe Dru knows all that, too," Sara finally said. "It don't take no halfwit to put two an' two t'gether an' figure out why Dru don't go to town on Saturdays much no more. He ain't goin' near a woman who makes up in designin' ways for what she ain't got'n looks..."

After a considered pause, she added, "An' I ain't 'bout to tell you where Dru spends his Saturdays when he don't go to town. Likely you know anyways."

Suddenly, she reared back and swung an arm through the water, sending waves rolling toward the opposite bank. Then she stood, shook the clinging dress away from her body and smiled sympathetically.

"Julie, don't look so concerned. I know what folks say 'bout me, an' I ain't deaf to what they're saying 'bout me'n Dru. He's a good man, gooder'n most give him credit for bein'."

Wringing out her dress at the knees, she tried to put her thoughts into words which wouldn't offend, or that might leave herself open to more questions; and in a soft and almost inaudible voice, she went on, without looking up.

"I'd like a woman friend, I really would. It's just that there's some things I ain't ready to talk 'bout, an' maybe I can't talk 'bout 'em. Maybe I never will be able to talk 'bout 'em.

"Seems to me all of us got some hurts, some worse'n others. But that don't make us bad folk, an' it ought'na make folks feel they got a right to talk 'bout 'em an' think all kinds of bad things, which maybe ain't so. Not down deep where it counts, leastways."

With a rising and firm voice, Sara added, "An' 'specially when they got no say-so or control over 'em..."

She finished wringing the dress, swung it to and fro and released it to the current once more.

"I hain't got the book-larnin' you got, an' for sure I hain't got what John's got. My larnin' has come the hard way; you know what they say: Try it an' if'n it don't work, try somethin' else.

"Well, I tried thinkin' with my head – you might say brains – an' that didn't make things no better. Doin' that got me into lots of trouble, an' I figured the reason was that I was actin' on what I'd seen an' heard goin' on 'round me. Didn't have no momma to tell me right from wrong. An', lordamercy, it didn't do no good to ask daddy.

"Then I tried to shut down that no-good head an' listen with my heart. That was fine for a while, but ever' time my heart'd pick out what looked like a good man for me he'd turn out to be a bad man, out to git what he could git an' then git…"

Fingering a twig and twisting her lips into a bitter, secretive smile, she went on. "An' it didn't take this woman long to see that if'n you ain't willin' to play the game the way it's played, you might as well curl up an' die. An' I ain't dead by a long shot!"

Looking at Jewell, she smiled weakly and nodded toward John. "Folks talk 'bout him, too, an' they say he's a bad man who sometimes beats up on you. I think he's more'n likely a good man who is maybe a little bit sick an' don't know what to do 'bout it."

Turning away again and looking downstream, she concluded, "Lots'a men are like that, an' I've know'd some. They got secrets an' try not to talk 'bout 'em 'cause they don't know for real what's grippin' 'em, an' wouldn't know how to explain it nohow. I 'spect you got a good man, who keeps tryin' to be better. Some don't try."

After a brief, introspective pause, she spoke so softly that Jewell almost missed hearing her. "An' some don't even know their place. Some are gonna sin, even if they knows in their hearts it's the worst kind of sinnin'."

Jewell didn't know what to say, so she didn't say anything. She looked hard at Sara in a soft way, and decided that perhaps there was more to her than met the eye, especially if the eye didn't know what to look for. At any rate, she reasoned, this young woman deserved better than she was getting.

And after a long and awkward moment, after she'd also smiled sympathetically, she got up and called to John. "I'm gettin' hungry, an' if you haven't got anything better to do than sit there and smoke yourself blind, why don't you cut that watermelon?"

John was dying to know what Jewell and Sara had been talking about, but decided there wouldn't be any point in asking. "Fine," he said, dowsing the cigarette butt and getting up off the sandy embankment. "But first I'm gonna get these girls movin'."

Startled, Bertha looked fearfully over her shoulder, rose quickly and hurried into deeper water.

Magalene laughed and sat where she was, until John scooped her up, carried her to where the boys watched with wide, surprised eyes, and plopped her down between them. Rubbing the splashed water from his eyes, Arlis laughed and tried to climb onto Magalene's back.

Bo turned away and went into deeper water, trying to swim hard and fast like his Uncle Dru. He wanted very badly to be able to swim into that outlet, around its bend and, unlike his Uncle Dru, never come back.

CHAPTER 6

Bo's worry ends, John's begins, and Dru is saddled with another

WHILE BO-BOY WAS DEALING with his misery and thinking of his Uncle Dru, the man and his misery were sitting on the boy's front porch whittling and watching the sun dip toward the western woods. Sara was on his mind and he had no way of knowing that his absent kin had been with her at the swimming ford, or that Bo needed him.

When John looked over Junebug's bobbing head and saw his brother, he nudged Jewell; then they agreed in a whispered exchange that they wouldn't mention they'd seen Sara unless Dru flat-out asked. Dru had never owned up to having a relationship with her anyway…

When Bo spotted his uncle, he whispered a prayer of gratitude and tried to jump off the wagon. But John held him back, saying, "You can wait with the rest of us and help unload."

Bo gritted his teeth and stayed put, lest he call more attention to his anxiety.

"If you're thinkin' supper, it'll be awhile," Jewell told Dru as they rolled into the yard. "Sure would be nice to see you visit and sit and not visit and run."

Dru took Junebug by the halter while they got down; he managed a halfway grin. "Well, okee-dokee, since you put it thataway. I just come over lookin' to talk at John, since it's been awhile and I get to wonderin' how ya'll are."

"We been better," Jewell responded sadly. "We had a purty nice day, tryin' to forget…"

Stepping closer to Dru, she said in a me-and-you voice, "We hain't told the boys 'bout Lonny yet. Know you won't either…"

"Uh-huh. That was terrible awful. Got me so upset, I almost… Well, Jewell, I think you know how I feel. Marybelle and Buttombottom, I reckon they must be goin' crazy."

"They are, Dru. I was over there yesterday, after they'd got themselves together and were tryin' to be brave."

Arlis had wrapped himself around one of his tall uncle's legs, and Dru was mussing his hair while talking to his sister-in-law. She watched, smiled sadly, and went into the house. Relieved to see her go, Dru continued to play with Arlis.

"Gracious, boy, you're gonna be as big as your brother if'n he don't start eatin' more."

He winked at Bo, but Bo didn't see that it was funny, no how. He was boiling-over happy to see his uncle and tried to get him to take a walk with him.

"Got something important to talk about," he said, trying to say every word just right so as not to show his anxiety.

John cut Bo short, telling him to go inside and help his momma.

"But Daddy, I gotta talk to Uncle Dru. I just gotta."

John ignored him and Bo ignored his daddy's order; instead, he went to the side yard, far enough away so he wouldn't be a bother to the grownups, but close enough should his uncle become available to him.

He also hoped he might hear some of the man talk.

"So what's bothering' you, Dru," John asked, after they'd seated themselves in the yard.

"Nothin' special," Dru said, ejecting his chaw and rolling a cigarette. Both watched two white legging' chickens fight over the tobacco quid and, after deciding it was unpalatable, mosey off in opposite directions.

John broke the silence. "C'mon now, Dru, I know you well enough to know something ain't right. You can tell your little brother."

John grinned. Referring to himself as "little brother" always annoyed Dru. This time, however, Dru pointedly ignored the teasing. He tossed a burnt-out match toward a chicken, rolled the cigarette between two fingers and tried to mask his anxiety.

"John, how well you know Del?"

"Del? Buttonbottom's oldest boy, Delphi? I reckon I know him 'bout as well as any white man hereabouts. Seems to be a nice enough fellow. Always helps when asked, and sometimes when he's not asked. Sometimes he comes 'round looking' to help when it seems like he just wants to have somebody to talk to."

Dru knew all that; he moved uneasily in the chair, knowing he was about to be asked why he was asking.

"Why you askin', Dru?"

"Oh, no reason special," Dru responded, thinking maybe he'd done so too quickly. "I see him 'round over at Sara's, ah, at Old Man Boru's ever' now and then and I was just wonderin'."

"Ah-ha," said John, staring with raised eyebrows at his brother. "You ain't..."

"I ain't nothin'," said Dru, leaning forward in the chair and picking up a stick.

John grinned wryly, but said nothing; a blind man could tell Dru was suffering about something, and suffering real bad. John waited.

Dru stirred sand with the stick and cast sideways glances at his brother a couple of times. Finally, he threw the stick out into the road, sat back and resumed talking. He did not look at John.

"I mean, would you think he might be payin' a mite too much attention to, ah, Old Man Boru's daughter? I can't think of 'nother reason he'd hang around there. Boru don't like him; I hear-tell he's even chased him off the place once or twice, maybe more…"

John's wry grin became an out-and-out smirk. Shaking his head from side to side, he said, "Dru, why don't you just come out and say it: You think Del is sparking Sara and you're jealous."

Dru bounced out of his seat. "Doggone you, John, that's hogwash! Wouldn't matter if it were Sara or 'nother white woman. Same dang thing; a colored man ain't 'lowed to go lookin' at a white woman; not like a dog in heat, anyways. Del's my friend, too, but he's a colored man! I ain't…"

Dru didn't finish; he felt a twinge in his belly, like maybe he was getting sick. He knew why; he'd never had anything but good feelings for most colored folks, since they'd always been nice to him for what he was. And here he was saying things which caused him to walk away when others said them.

With his back to John, Dru began rolling another cigarette; John reached into the top of his sock, pulled out a store-bought pack of Camels.

"Here, brother. Have a real cigarette. Calm you down some…"

Dru declined, wondering how John always seemed to have a nickel or two to buy Camels when no one else did. He also wondered where John had come by the cigarette lighter he carried. Made of brass, it had a thumb spinner that scratched a flint and sparked the flame. A retractable shield hid the flame, and John said that had been to keep the enemy for spotting the user in the dark and taking a pot-shot at him. He'd said it was a "trench lighter" used by soldiers in the Great World War. Dru figured it must have cost his brother a pretty penny, since John had been too young to be in the World War I and souvenirs such as the lighter didn't come cheaply.

Once he'd asked John how he'd gotten it, but the response had been a smile, a shrug and a mystifying question: "I've got it, don't I?"

The evening breeze stirred the pine needles above the brothers, and hundreds of bats swept back and forth above the cotton field. The chickens made their way to the coop, clucking softly and pecking at the ground as they moved along. In the pasture to the east, the two cows already were bedded down, their legs tucked against their bodies and their teeth squeezing the last of the sweetness from their cuds.

"Dru," John finally said, "I doubt if Del's being over there has anything to do with Sara. He's too smart for that, and old Buttonbottom wouldn't tolerate it, and Marybelle surely wouldn't. Seems to me it's more likely that Old Man Boru, being' the lazy SOB he is, has talked him into bending' his back over some work or something."

"Maybe so," Dru said, very quietly. "Maybe so. But why would he be over there at…"

He didn't finish; he wasn't even sure the man he'd seen leaving the Boru house was Del, and he didn't want to think that any man, colored or white, would be there at night when she was alone.

"Dru," John went on, "I don't know what you got in mind, but let me say this as a brother who cares 'bout you. If you're getting' some of Sara, and I think you are, that's fine and dandy. But don't go losing your head over a woman's ass. Sara just ain't worth it."

Dru sat upright and was glad the dimming shadows masked his face.

"Reckon as how I didn't get to askin' your 'pinion, John. Appreciate it mightily if'n you'd keep it to yourself."

Now John shrugged. "Okay, Dru. That'll be easy enough. Besides, there's something I've been wanting to ask you about, something that may be real important to all of us."

Dru leaned back. "What's that?"

"Well, I got this letter from Bantry down in Florida just yesterday, and it's about something I'd been wondering' over for quite a spell."

"Jewell's brother, Bantry, what went down there to work in them shipyards in Jacksonville?"

"That's right. He says what I always knew: there's a lot of money being made down there and jobs are goin' begging. They can't work fast enough and hard enough to build all the ships – they're calling them Liberty Ships – they need to whip the Japs and Germans.

"But he says if a man wants to get on the wagon he'd best hurry, 'cause all of south Georgia seems to be moving down. Some are even coming from over Alabama way."

"That's likely all right for you, John, you havin' been to that fancy school and in the Air Corps and all. But I'm a farmer and always will be…"

"It's me I'm talking about, Dru. Farming is just as important as building ships. The boys over there gotta eat and so do we folks back home. Trouble is, you know I ain't never really cared for farming and that's why I went off to Emory and joined the service and…"

John stopped in mid-sentence and stirred the sand with the toe of one boot. Dru knew he was thinking about the plane crash and the hurt it had brought him and the rest of the family; John was, and wished he'd taken a different tack.

With each man lost in his own thoughts, a wee voice from the darkness broke the silence.

"You done, Uncle Dru? You got time for me?"

"Not yet, Bo. Just you hang on."

Startled, John called out, "Bo! You're supposed to be helping your momma. How long have you been listening?"

"I haven't, Daddy, honest Injun I haven't. I was just watching and waiting til you looked like you was done…"

"Lordy," John muttered, "I hope not."

The silence returned, broken only by an owl's hoots down near the woodlot, by the inharmonious sounds of an inestimable number of frogs and crickets and, closer still, by the whirr of mosquito wings. The sharp-winged bats continued to sweep back and forth across the darkening sky, feeding off insects invisible from the ground; Dru sensed the memory was eating away at John's soul and probably did each time he allowed himself to watch. It looked too much like aerial combat – for which John had trained, but had never experienced.

At last, John spoke, after looking over his shoulder to make sure Bo was not close enough to hear.

"Bantry says it's so crowded down there, what with all the people coming down, that he and Agnes and the kids – they got three – have just one big room to live in. But he says there's room enough for at least me, if I want to come."

"You? What'd he say about Jewell, his own sister?"

"Oh, he mentioned her. But he knows somebody's got to watch the farm and the boys need takin' care of."

"You talk to her 'bout it? The letter? Was it just for you?"

John lied. "Yep, Dru, it was. And I hope you won't mention it to her, or no one else. I've got a lot of thinkin' to do, and I'd rather talk to her when the time's right and proper."

"Well, I'm a' hopin' you'll think real good and proper. There ain't no way I can see Jewell runnin' this farm by herself, even if it ain't got but 40 acres. The boys ain't no problem. We all watch 'em anyways."

"Well, Dru, she wouldn't have to do it for long; maybe just the winter when there ain't much to do but watch over the livestock and stay warm. I'd send money to tide them over and I'd send for them as soon as I could.

"Living out here like we are, away from everything, most of us don't even realize how important the war is, and how we all got to help win it.

"But being in the Army Air Corps like I was, I was trained to know what was coming and what we'd have to do when it did. We ain't going to beat them tree apes and cabbage eaters unless we give the boys something to do it with!"

Dru winced at John's firmness, but wondered how he'd be able to sit across the supper table from Jewell and not tell her about the conversation. There was little question in his mind that John's mere mention of leaving the farm would set her off, and he couldn't imagine how she'd react if he said he wanted to go ahead alone.

"John," Dru whispered, "you done lost your mind. And you may be 'bout to lose your whole head with it."

"Yo-ho, fellas! Supper's on…"

Dru glanced over his shoulder at Jewell, who was outlined in the doorway. There was more he wanted to say, and ask, but decided he'd best let it go – for the time being, anyway.

They stood up and John put an arm over his shoulder; he spoke softly, as if he were sharing a secret.

"Dru, if Jewell mentions Beatrice, you listen. It's very important that you listen."

Dru's shoulders tightened; John felt the change and withdrew his arm. "It's late and I'll stay 'n eat," Dru said. "But I ain't listenin' to nothin' 'bout that woman."

"Okay, Dru. But it doesn't hurt a man to listen. You try to keep an open mind and remember what I said: "If Jewell mentions..."

"Dagnabbit, John. I heard what you said!"

As they started up the steps, Bo came hustling around the corner of the house.

"Uncle Dru, you just gotta let me talk to you. Please..."

Dru turned and walked to Bo's side. "For certain," he whispered to the boy, "it's gotta be better'n what I been listenin' to."

"Whatever it was, Uncle Dru, I got somethin' really, really 'portant to talk about. There ain't nobody else in the whole world who can help me with the problem I got. I mean I..."

Bo took hold of his uncle's hand and they walked out into the road, just the other side of the light cast by the lamp in the front window.

When they returned moments later, Bo was smiling broadly and Dru was doing his best to stifle a belly laugh.

CHAPTER 7

'Giddiyap, Jenny! We're goin' to hell!'

— Dru to his mule

DRU WAS UP EARLY Saturday morning, stomping around the sandy yard like a chicken scratching for an overlooked grain of corn or a dawdling night-crawler. His mind was fighting his feelings; his anxiety had a throat-hold on the common sense he prized, and he was not the least bit interested in going into town with Jim, John, Jewell, and the boys.

He wasn't in much better fettle an hour later, when all were gathered around the Blue Goose, Jim's Dodge pickup truck. "Ain't feelin' up to it," he declared. Switching the morning chew into his right jowl, he cleared his throat and added, "Feelin' like a sore-tailed hog. Wouldn't be good company."

Disappointed, John and Jewell looked at one another; they'd sensed all the talk about Beatrice O'Connell the previous night had fallen on deaf ears. Bo was disappointed, but thoughts of the Dixie Theater drowned any sorrow he might have felt. Jim simply shrugged, and Arlis didn't appear to care one way or the other.

Watching them depart, Dru replayed his man-to-man with John and frowned; then he harked back to his talk with Bo and, despite his best efforts, he broke out laughing. Bo generally was good for a surprise; more often than not, it was the straight-faced, innocent questions he asked – and, almost as often, what happened when he went off on his own and checked out what he'd been told. Dru liked that about Bo, and figured it had been in the boy's nature to take hold of John's words, identify with them, and to have believed he might have gotten Magalene with child. Hadn't he told him that using common sense meant trying on the shoe to see if it fit?

But he had not liked much of what John had said to him, especially about Sara. Bo aside, she had been the most important person in his life for some time; he couldn't let go easily. He also was tired of doubt nibbling at his soul, forcing him to consider his age and his future. He was 36, past the time to put his house in order. He harrumphed at that thought; he didn't have a house and wasn't sure anymore whether his life was his own.

Dru recollected a mule he'd owned. It had refused to budge when more than one voice shouted a command, or a single voice changed the original command. Today, he reckoned that mule might have been kin, if nature allowed such. Knowing that it hadn't known what do to, the mule had done nothing.

But Dru now believed that he no longer had that option, and reminded himself that time was flying by with each passing minute, hour, day, month, year…

The thought irritated him. Nobody had to tell him about his shortcomings; he knew those. But he felt as physically strong as he'd ever been. To bolster that feeling, he raised his arms above his head, clenched and unclenched his fists several times, and relished the feel of his rippling muscles. Then he stood on his toes, reached for the sky and stretched his whole body until it ached.

"Lordamercy, that feels good," he said aloud. "Nothin' wrong with this old boy…"

Shaking his arms to relax them, he spat the chaw, aiming at no place in particular, and turned toward the barn where the half-dozen cows waited to be milked. If it wasn't done soon, they'd be bawling

Sullivan Road

and stirring up a fuss. Swollen milk bags and teats are painful and to ignore the cows too long was downright unmerciful.

Recalling again the cruel ways some folks teased him about the time he spent milking cows – and why, by his own admission, he felt so much love for them – Dru stopped to cut another chaw.

"That one's easy enough to answer," he mumbled. "Cows is sweet and gentle and hain't got no meanness in 'em. Folks could learn from 'em…"

Mostly, the wiseacres said his love for the bovines must have something to do with pulling their teats. They'd say "tits," and he knew they were mocking him.

Taking a small stool from a hook on the wall, Dru seated himself beside the first cow, patted her warm belly and gently washed each teat. Milking was a mindless act, something he'd done so often it had become routine. The washing done, he placed thumbs and forefingers on the sides of the two teats nearest him, pointed them at the tin pail, squeezed gently but firmly, and smiled as the white fluid shot out in two thin lines.

Pursing his lips, he tried to duplicate the sounds. "Pssssssttt, brannggg…" The sound changed as the pail filled. "Pssssssttt, broooommm…"

And then he quit, convinced one more time that no one could duplicate such an exciting, pleasing sound; and he contented himself with controlling the rhythm of what he'd come to regard as music. Instinctively he began to tap one foot, keeping pace with the "pssssssttt-broooommms" and varying the pulls to create a beat. The cow moved uneasily and shifted a foot; he smiled, whispered an apology, and moved to the other side to milk the two remaining teats.

It suddenly occurred to him that he had never listened to music with Sara, nor had he danced with her – or with anyone, as a matter of fact. Even the thought of dancing, especially of doing it in front of others, always embarrassed him. Nor did he envy those who did, those who didn't seem to mind if they stumbled occasionally and, to him, appeared foolish. Remembering how he'd justified his dislike

Pierce Lehmbeck

for dancing: "Nothin' but belly-rubbin' a go-between in gettin' a woman in bed! A real man don't need no go-between."

He also recalled "blip-blip gals," which is what he called women who passed close behind a man at a crowded party, whispering "'scuse me." What they were doing, he figured, was fishing with a double-barbed hook.

Without realizing that his face had reddened and that he was getting angry, he pulled both teats so hard that the cow bawled loudly and lifted a foot as though she were about to deliver a kick.

"Easy, easy now, Betsy," he said. "Wouldn't hurt ya' for the world. It's just old Dru thinkin' too doggone much again."

After a moment's silence, his face hardened again and he met his frustration headon: "But bigod it's Saturday and I ain't where I oughta be, and I don't give a damn what anybody thinks!"

Looking down the line of cows and seeing he still had three to milk, Dru decided to finish up quickly, load himself and his gumption in the wagon and go see Sara.

An hour later, Dru was around the corner and almost in the yard when he saw a Negro bending over the Boru pig pen, working on the wire fence while Sara stood over him. His heart jumped up and got caught in his choked-off gullet; his eyes suddenly glazed over.

But his mind was racing, racing toward the fear that was never too far beneath the surface, never too far from its partner, insecurity.

"Migod, it's Del…"

He managed to fight off total paralysis, however, and urged the mule to go on by.

But Sara spotted him, waved and called, "Yo-ho, Dru. Where you goin' on such a purty day? Get off and visit a spell."

Del straightened up, flexed his shoulders and grinned broadly. "Sho 'nuff, Mistuh Dru. And if'n you don't mind gettin' muddy, I kin use some he'p."

Dru did his best to smile, but wasn't sure he'd managed. "I'm headin' down to Tip's. I really oughten to tarry."

Sara frowned. "Aw, c'mon, Dru, when hain't you had time to stop a while and visit?"

He "whoaed" Jennie, but remained on the wagon seat.

Sara said something to Del, who tossed another wave Dru's way and resumed his work; then she stepped around the shallow tin- and glass-littered hole in which the Borus burned their trash and came alongside the wagon.

"I'm sorry Del's still here, Dru," she said softly. "He's heart-broke 'bout Lonny, but he come over anyways, like he said he would."

She looked as though she genuinely meant it, and Dru felt his heart go flip-flop, like a caught fish on a creek bank.

"Daddy said he'd stay home and help him fix that fence, but he went off somewheres. It should'a been done by now." Looking up, she added softly, "I was hopin' you'd come."

Dru didn't know what to say and the silence was deafening. Finally, he cleared his throat and responded, "Why didn't you ask me to help fix it?"

"Cause Daddy said he was goin' to help Del, and you know Daddy don't like you bein' 'round. Sometimes I think Daddy's jealous…"

More softly, she said, "Ain't you gonna say somethin' to Del 'bout his brother? He's really hurtin'…"

Dru stared straight ahead and didn't respond. After an awkward moment she added, "I'm sorry, Dru. I guess I should'a known Daddy wouldn't stay and help so they'd have it done early.

"It was him who told me to ask Del to help. He came all the way over here in that horrible storm just to…"

She paused, placed a hand over her mouth, and added, "That was the night Lonny got kilt. Maybe if Del'd stayed home…"

Dru's mind was galloping like a runaway mule. So that was it: *the visitor had been Del*, and he had been there to talk about helping Old Man Boru fix a pig sty fence.

But doubt, Dru's lifetime companion, had him by the throat again and would not let go. Why had they met at night, and alone? A white woman and a Negro man wouldn't think of doing such a thing – unless they had something to hide! Otherwise, they'd be courting trouble, real trouble, maybe a lynching for him and…

He didn't want to imagine what could happen to Sara if the word got out.

Still dazed, he managed to refocus his eyes and looked beyond Sara, at Magalene playing in the sand under her angel-dwelling chinaberry tree. Bertha was standing on the porch. Most Saturday mornings Sara would have sent them to play down by the pond, hidden in the woods over toward John's place. Even on rainy Saturdays she'd have them away from the shack, sometimes playing in the barn or in the shed where Old Man Boru kept the few tools which, he often grumbled, were more than he'd ever need.

For a moment their eyes locked and Dru felt a stiffness between his legs; gumption hadn't failed him there. Sara tugged at a leg of his overalls, and there was welcome in her eyes. Del waved, and there was welcome in his grin, though the grin was not nearly as broad as it normally was. Clearly Del was hurt, and Dru felt he ought to say something to him.

Dru's gaze switched from one to the other and back again. He glanced at Magalene and Bertha and didn't respond when Bertha waved to him.

What to do? What to say? Doubt danced around his head; fear was its partner. And finally his eyes settled on the blonde, calico-garbed blur standing where Sara had been.

And he heard himself saying, "Well, I'm sorry, too. Just seems there ain't much time for you'n me no more…"

"Why, Dru, you know that ain't so…"

"…and maybe I ought to find 'nother body that does have time."

She let go of the wagon wheel and stepped back.

"Well, now, if you're a meanin' that woman livin' over Munsterville way, you just go right ahead. But I can tell you it's a long ride for nothin'. 'Cause Bea is nothin' and maybe nothin' is what you got comin'!"

Dru felt terrible and his face showed it. If he could have eaten his words right then and there, he would have. He started to say he didn't mean it; but she was still reeling from his belligerence and,

Sullivan Road

instinctively, her own protective nature had taken control. Wielding a rapier tongue, she stabbed him right between his sagging shoulders.

"Go on, Dru. Just go on! I got things to do, and Del's here to help me do 'em. You just go on. Why, you've b'come as hard in the heart as you are in the head. You can't even tell Del you're sorry 'bout his brother…"

To make matters worse, Del heard and stopped work. He stood there, hands on hips while the sweat poured down his muscular black chest. Dru looked from one to the other again, and then suddenly snapped the reins, shouted "giddiyap!", and hoped neither Sara nor Del had seen his shaking hands.

Through blurred eyes Dru guided the mule down the dusty road and turned right, away from Tip Evers' store. He was numb all over and didn't want to be seen. He'd keep going, following the long way around to get back home.

Some fifteen minutes later, he halted the wagon by a creek branch, in a low spot where the road cut through some woods. A blacksnake, already halfway across the hot, sandy road, raised its head, looked up at Jennie, and slithered into the high grass on the far side. Dru ignored it and wouldn't have cared if the snake had been a rattler. Jennie stomped nervously.

He just sat there, felt hat pushed back on his head, not feeling the hot sun, not feeling anything. "Not lessen numbness is a feelin'," he mumbled after a long silence. "And bein' numb is like bein' dumb. Or scared or mad. A man can't think, can't move…"

And Momma Susan's voice reached down, softly and barely audible, as though she were a long way off.

"No son, numbness is not a feeling. Loving – glad or sad loving – that's a feeling. Numbness is when you feel nothing, and it's the Lord's way of letting you hold on tight until you can feel again, 'til you can plumb what you are made of and think like a good man oughta.

"You know that, dear, sweet Dru. Don't you remember when I told you that the first time, a long, long time ago…"

Dru was not startled; he'd gotten used to hearing her voice. His Adam's apple bobbed and a smile pushed his cheeks upward, nearly closing his misting eyes. Little by little, the mist cleared and he looked at the sky, knowing he wouldn't see Momma Susan, but hoping he might. He had shaken off most of the numbness; he was thinking now, and one thing he was thinking was that he really did not want to go home, where Liza would want to know why he was so broken up, and Jim would, too, when he got back from Mayo.

"Why's it have to be so hard," he heard himself asking aloud, as was his way. "If Sara hadn't come along, you'd most likely be doin' like you always done. You was bein' carried by the wind, stayin' where it put you down, sittin' there and doin' nothin' til it come blowin' up again."

He paused long enough to reach for his cigarette makings, but changed his mind. His eyes were focused straight ahead – glossed over, seeing nothing.

"But at least you warn't eatin' yourself up inside," he told himself. "At least you warn't hurtin' so much…"

And he heard himself answering himself, as was his way sometimes…

"But, Dru, somethin's dreadful wrong. You had two years with Sara, two long years, good years, and you never got things t'gether. She knows you better'n anybody livin' and she told you secrets so terrible you couldn't stand to hear 'em – secrets you swore you'd never tell nobody.

"She was your woman, Dru, but you never did nothin' to keep her your woman.

"Somethin's dreadful wrong, Dru…"

He placed his right hand on the spot just below his breastbone, feeling for God's mailbox and praying there'd be something in it. Though he moved the hand up and down and around in a small circle, he felt nothing; it was as empty.

Momma Susan had told him there was a reason God's mailbox was closer to his heart than to his head. Satan could and often did set up house in someone's head; but he couldn't get into their souls until he'd made them feel they no longer cared whether the Godspot was warm and comforting or cold, barren, and bereft of hope.

The soul's strength, Momma Susan had said, was that it could withstand pain and learn from it. The brain couldn't tolerate pain and, from within and without, called on everything it could to kill that pain.

"And dear little Dru," she had added, "Satan's got a wagon load of painkillers, though all of them will kill a man in the end…"

Dru had never doubted his mother, and he'd often rationalized that he was more fortunate than those who'd gone to school and studied hard. They relied mostly on what the head had learned; he relied on feelings, sealing in his soul those which brought him comfort and rejecting those which did not.

That is why, Momma Susan had said, the body and soul part company when a person dies; the body just crumbles up and sinks back into the earth, while the freed-up soul floats away on a happy cloud.

"How's that happen," he had asked.

"It's the way of the Lord," she'd replied. "You'll see it clear when the time comes."

But that kind of thinking had not always worked to his benefit. When he'd rationalized that way, he couldn't shake another feeling – that he was making excuses for his shortcomings.

John, an educated man perhaps rationalizing for his own benefit, had told him once that Sullivan family had come from a long line of depressed people, and that it was possible for a whole country to be depressed. Ireland was depressed, John had said, because it had lived for so long under someone else's heel. Societal mores and religious beliefs, pagan and otherwise, forced upon its people over the centuries had sapped the greatest of its strengths – spiritualism – by squashing spiritualism's greatest source of strength, freedom.

And, John had gone on to say, freedom for the Irish folk always had been rooted in the Celtic love of nature: the sky – he'd called it the firmament – and especially the earth and all that constituted its awesome richness. John had paused there, and what he said next had added to Dru's confusion.

"Well, even Mother Nature fails once in awhile. Those potato famines didn't help much; during the one in 1847 two million folks starved to death in Ireland. But you'd better believe the damned old English didn't do anything to help; they used it as a chicken-shit weapon in their war to wipe us out!"

Dru's response then had been, "Uh-huh," and an unexpressed feeling that John had had been drinking; when he got to be so talkative, it generally was after he had tied one on.

"Tied one on…" Dru knew about doing that; he also knew that, while liquor was one of one of Satan's tools, it *shut down a man's pain* – even if it demanded much greater pain later on.

Gritting his teeth and gripping the reins so hard it hurt, he squared his shoulders and shouted to the mule.

"Giddiyap, Jenny! We're goin' to hell!"

CHAPTER 8

'I'm sorry, boy. So sorry you have to see me this way...'
— Hungover Dru to his rescuer, Bo

MARVIN PATTERSON'S WHITE HOUSE, neat white picket fence and rose-covered trellis stood in vivid contrast to the red-clay road sneaking past them.

"Sneaking" was a word used by some wiseacre - a Sullivan, perhaps – who had opined that the house and its yards were so fine a common fellow might feel compelled to shake the dust from his overalls and sneak on by lest he get something dirty; or, since Patterson's business had survived Prohibition and still was doing very well, a visitor might sneak in and out lest he be seen by someone other than the man and his helpers.

Rose bushes and lilacs lined each side of the tidy driveway, right up to where it passed between a matched pair of weeping willows, narrowed and led to a whitewashed barn almost hidden in a stand of pecan trees. Dru knew just what to do and wasted no time. Telling Jenny to "gee" into the driveway, he guided the wagon to the barn. A moment later, a young Negro appeared and handed him a quart milk bottle filled with something that looked like gasoline.

"Tell 'im I'll be 'round in a day or so to pay up," said Dru, turning the wagon in a wide circle and heading back the way he'd come. The Negro watched him go and frowned. "Ain't no way you gonna be back 'n no day or so, Mis'ta Dru. Ain't no way…"

Back on the main road, Dru turned right and guided Jenny a half-mile north to Sullivan Road's western terminus, placing him a little more than half a mile from where his troubled journey had begun; he had almost completed a circle. There, he stopped and scanned the horizon to see whether anyone could see him. Bo's Arrowhead Hill was the highest spot visible; but flat fields lay around it on all sides and anyone in those fields could spot a man in a wagon from a long way off.

Today, there wasn't even any telltale dust rising from the way he'd come, nor the way he was heading.

Smiling now, he turned onto the road and guided Jenny down to a low spot where it cut through another stand of woods. Looking around one more time, he called again for a right turn and braced his feet on the wagon's shell as it bounced once, twice, righted itself, and groaned across a ditch. Jenny blew a protest but proceeded along the edge of the woods, obeying the reins and staying in the high grass paralleling the field. That grass, Dru hoped, would straighten itself in a short while and the wheel tracks would disappear.

With a final look back, he guided the mule under the forest canopy, lowering his head and holding his hat in place to keep it from being swept away by low-hanging limbs. Down the slope was a one-acre pond, a lot like the one in the woods between the Sullivan and Boru houses. And on this August afternoon it fit his mood perfectly: stagnant, bad-smelling, and slime-covered water in which cypress struggled for footholds and dying or dead pines groped with skeletal hands toward the heavens. Eye-stinging humidity and a stifling-hot haze hung over everything, and it appeared as if the living trees were gasping for breath, the dying were about to give up, and the dead were frozen in time.

Fearing a change of heart more than what he saw, Dru didn't linger long on the wagon seat. Hurriedly, he dismounted and tied Jenny to a tree, loose enough for her to graze off the knee-high grass in which she stood. Taking the jar, he walked down the bank, settled his back against a medium-sized water oak and unscrewed the cap. The first big swallow was followed quickly by a smaller one, and then in quick succession by a series of throat-burning swigs. He was in no hurry to empty the bottle and wished he'd asked for a second jar.

Minutes passed. Frogs croaked, insects buzzed, and sunlight flickered through leaves above him. Through watery, tiring eyes, he looked up, harrumphed, and remarked, "Hain't no angels up there t'day, Magalene. Not now, maybe never…"

The last thing Dru remembered as he floated up and away from the heat, humidity and soul-shaming anguish was that he was giggling uncontrollably. Hours later, the first thing he remembered as he descended back down into reality was that he'd been here before, and was about to feel unimaginable pain.

Unable to rise off his back, he blinked several times, trying to clear the thick sheet of mucous blurring his vision. Then he managed to guide an unsteady hand onto his forehead and take a deep breath before lowering the hand, balling his fist and rubbing his eyes. Little by little, the vision cleared and he could see that the dimness wasn't entirely the fault of his eyes. A pre-dawn mist was rising off the pond, and a frail pink color was beginning to appear through the trees beyond it. Here and there a bird twittered and a rabbit scurried from the pond's edge. Dru's skin burned and he sensed he had pissed on himself.

His mouth was dry, terribly dry, and he struggled to get off his back and reach the pond. He managed to roll onto his left side, but no further. Even that small effort left him gasping for breath, and when the blurred vision cleared again he was staring at an empty jar. Reaching out, he grasped it and shook it – up and down, from side to side. But it was empty, nearly as dry as his mouth, and he wasn't able to pull down a drop when he turned it upright, placed the jar's wide mouth in his mouth and sucked hard. Tossing it aside, he rolled onto his back and looked toward the heavens. He knew what was coming and he was resigned to it. It had happened before; not often, but enough so that he never forgot what was to come, minute by minute, hour by hour, even day by day...

Eyes relatively clear now, he looked around – by shifting his eyes and trying not to move his head, trying not to set off an explosive pain. He didn't expect to see anyone; he had covered his trail too well. But he remembered the devilish alter-ego that had accompanied him to this hideaway, this purgatory, and he knew for sure that the sonofabitch was gone. The SOB had coached him through his fantasy, indulged his schemes and dreams, and had watched him squeeze the last drop of 'shine from the bottle. Then he'd watched that bottle slide out of Dru's trembling hand, had laughed an evil laugh, and had gone away...

"You poor, poor fool. I've had my fun; now it's time for you to suffer. I have the fun, you do the sufferin'. Just like always, Dru. Just like always..."

Dru tried to speak, to tell the SOB to bring his ass back and share the pain. But his lips, parched and raw, wouldn't function. Like the rest of him, they were frozen in pain.

Pressing his forehead to the ground, he pleaded for relief. And what he got was another voice, this one coming from beneath his heart and just above his stomach. He had been wondering whether his Godspot, the mailbox from of personal God, his conscience, had abandoned him. It had not...

"Lordy, Dru, you know'd he'd do that. You know'd he'd give you a few hours of feelin' good, of ridin' on a soft cloud up there 'mong them cool green leaves and vines. You ain't no drinkin' man, Dru, and there warn't no way you could'a emptied that there milk bottle. Not by yourself, anyways.

"That other fella helped, that devil livin' in a deep, dark corner of your head, the one who crawls out and hurts you bad. Real bad. And he always tells you, after he's had his fun, that he's part of you and it's your fault and you'd better get on with the sufferin' you got comin'.

"You hate yourself, Dru, an he's tryin' to help you kill yourself..."

Sullivan Road

Dru interrupted. "Oh God! Why am I still livin'? Why hain't you let me go? Why, why, why?"

He got no answer, and for a long moment he lay still, smelling himself, feeling the wet between his legs, the burning all over his body, trying to forget the terrible, terrible thirst setting his foul mouth afire. Then he used his dulled senses to plumb the pain where his gullet reached toward his belly. He knew what could come next: dry heaves that could tear the gullet apart and fill his insides with blood that would slowly fill his gut and take the life from him. He dared not cough, he dared not. He dared not even think about it.

Dru knew he shouldn't move; that might set off the coughing, and coughing would set off the retching, and that surely would kill him... Right here, in the middle of nowhere. And he believed, honestly believed, that some folks would say it was a fit ending for a nobody.

"Go back to sleep," he told himself. "You gotta sleep..."

But sleep was a long time coming, pushed back time and time again by one nerve-searing intruder after another... Pushed back by a ray from the rising sun, cutting through the trees and stabbing him in the eyes; by an ant biting his face, forcing him to raise an arm and slap it away and, in doing that, discovering that his face was plumb full of insect bites; and he knew his face was red and ugly under the bristle of his two-day beard.

When sleep finally did come, he saw Sara's shuck-filled bed and she was in it, and her legs were wrapped around Delphi. And when Delphi stood, showing his white teeth in prideful satisfaction, he stood nine-feet tall, so tall his head was sticking through a hole in the roof of the Boru cabin.

And Dru saw himself running away from what he'd seen, running over Arrowhead Hill and through Bo's ghostly swamp. Something was chasing him, so close he could hear the pounding of its feet and feel its hot breath upon his back. He dared not look back for fear of losing a stride. On and on he ran, on and on, until he could run no longer and he collapsed, falling flat out on his belly.

Then he heard himself screaming. Something big and heavy and awful – it had to be Delphi – was on his back and smothering him in a small but awful-smelling pool. He gasped again and again, and finally slid his face to one side of the vomit. There was only a little bit of it, just a wee bit, because the pain and the fear of the retching wouldn't let him throw up more of the vile stuff.

With eyes burning and bulging nearly out their sockets, he spread his arms and lifted himself with such force that he threw the thing off him and rolled onto his back. Gasping for breath and sensing that the pain in his chest was beginning to ebb, he looked around, not daring to move his heavy, heavy, hurting head; only his eyes moved – wide, bloodshot, and fearful.

There was nothing there. Not Delphi, not a monster, not anything. He was alone, beneath a roof of green, an undulating green broken occasionally by the red and gold of a white birch changing colors prematurely. He knew that trees turning color in August were sick, sick as he was sick. And maybe dying, like he might be dying...

Dying, as Delphi's brother had died. Only much slower; Lonny had died of a shotgun blast. The sheriff said he had killed himself, but Dru knew better. In his heart, he knew better. Most everyone knew better. And he hadn't even been able to tell Delphi he wanted to share his grief, as a friend ought to. What kind of a friend would dream such a terrible dream – a nightmare, really – about someone he'd known and trusted for so long?

His Godspot answered...

"*A fearful man, Dru. A confused man...*"

Dru waited for more, but there was no more.

"Shame on me, Del," he finally muttered. Shame!"

The sun was right above him now; it was midday, with the hottest part still to come. And rain; it almost always rained on a late-summer afternoon. Maybe it would rain today. Oh, how he hoped it would rain! Sweet rain, cooling rain, rain that might extinguish the fire searing his skin and burning his stomach. He thought of something John had told him, once upon a long-ago time...

"Dru, the awful part is that the craving for escape, the addiction, the damnable need, it gets worse, even if you don't drink for years and years. You think you can do it again, but you find the pleasure is shorter and the hurt starts sooner and lasts longer. You want to stop, Dru; you beg the Lord to make you stop."

And John had added, "I sometimes wonder if it ain't in our blood, if it ain't something Poppa Niall Barnabas passed on. Like maybe he wanted us to suffer and understand why he was like he was.

"And maybe, Dru, sufferin' is what it takes. 'Cause from sufferin' comes perseverance and from perseverance comes understandin' and from understandin' comes courage and..."

He heard himself answering his brother, just as he had when John really had said it: "Oh, for God's sake, go away, John! Who cares? Who'n hell cares..."

And a lightning bolt of pain slammed into his head just above his eyes, barreled through his brain and straightened his spine. It knocked him out of the past and back to the here-and-now...

The pond! If only he could reach the pond; if he could just crawl to that pond! It was a good ten yards beyond his spread-out feet, down behind high grass, briars and brambles. He sensed he couldn't reach it with what strength he had left – but he had to try.

Painfully rolling onto one side, he dug his fingers into the dirt until they also hurt. After having lived through his body's vicious, explosive assault on itself, he sensed he was not going to die. He was just going to dig in his fingers, crawl an inch at a time, and suffer the horrible physical hurt and heart-strangling remorse, and that was that.

Dru finally managed to drag himself to the pond and, with one final, painful lunge, he was in it, on his belly with face and arms extending into the water. Nearby, a pair of startled frogs hopped off a rotting, partially submerged log. A turtle scrambled across the mud and disappeared under the pond's surface, and a few feet from where he was sprawled a water moccasin slid noiselessly into the water. A moccasin maddened by intense summer heat and diseased water sometimes becomes insanely aggressive; Dru hadn't seen the snake, and wouldn't have cared if he had.

Though he was aware it was going to make him even sicker, he willed a hand to stop resisting and clear the water directly beneath his face. He drank deeply, closing his eyes so he wouldn't see the putrid liquid, and let it course down his parched throat. Some was sucked through his nose, and it stung.

With eyes still closed, he splashed handful after handful across his face and pulled himself deeper into the pond. Because of its shallowness and the hot summer weather, it was warmer than most of his occasional baths. But it was cooler than the fire searing his body and soul, and his mumbled expressions of gratitude rose above the forest's natural sounds.

"Thank you, Lord. Thank you, Lord. Thank you…"

With a deep sigh and considerable fear, he forced his mind to examine his body – his legs, his burning stomach, his pounding chest, his arms, and his hands, the latter cramped and virtually paralyzed from dehydration. He concentrated on his fly- and mosquito-bitten face and wondered why the stubble of an unshaven face could hurt so much. Surmising that it hurt because his skin was drawn so tight across the facial bones, he shrugged and, very reluctantly, shifted the mental examination to his head, which felt like it was a full-grown watermelon about to be halved by a wood-yard axe.

Then he focused again on the bile in his stomach, and begged the Lord to keep it there and not send it surging up through his gullet, forcing him into the feared series of uncontrollable retches that could kill him. He made himself cough up some of the foul water he had ingested; it came in dribbles, trickling down his filthy, bearded chin and muddying the ghostly face staring at him from the water.

He did not want to see that image, that terrible, nether-world image, and he turned his head to one side, with mouth and nose just out of the water.

And he fell asleep once more…

Bo was standing in a ditch, head-high to the road and close by his house. When he saw Jenny, she was in the road, down where it cut through the woods. She was still hooked to the wagon, its frame snagged in the bushes and brambles and half-on, half-off the road. He dropped the shiny rock he'd been examining and ran the 200 yards to the mule's side.

"Where you been girl," he asked, rubbing the soft spot between her forelegs. "Where's Uncle Dru? He's been gone two whole days now."

Dru had been gone two days, and there was concern on both sides of Arrowhead Hill and up and down Sullivan Road. Dru often went off by himself, but seldom for longer than a day. He might not be home by bedtime, but always emerged from his bedroom come daybreak. A two-day, one-night absence was unusual, and the Sullivans had been driving around the county asking about him.

Bo, who'd spent a nearly sleepless night, studied the weed-entangled wagon. Carefully, he led Jenny to one side, then the other, until with a final "braaay" she pulled it free. And she protested mightily when he led her back the way she'd come.

Pushing through the brambles and bushes – some above his head – Bo began calling for his uncle; softly at first, then louder and louder as the fear welled up within him. Then he saw Dru, his head in the water and his arms and legs spread-eagled on the bank.

For an instant, panic gripped him; but he managed to shake off its paralysis and, with fear hurrying him along, scrambled to his uncle's side and dropped to his knees beside him. Seeing that Dru's mouth and nose were just above the surface, he grabbed an arm, dug in his heels and tugged as hard as he could.

"Uncle Dru, you gotta get up! You gotta get up! You'll drown if'n you don't."

Unable to arouse Dru, much less pull him from the water, Bo circled his body and stepped into the pond. The depth increased sharply just beyond where Dru lay and Bo sank to his waist; mud sucked at his feet and he fell twice, surfacing with raucous coughs and matted hair plastered over his eyes.

At long last he felt a root beneath one foot and, using it for leverage, he tried to lift Dru by a shoulder. That failing, he turned around so that his back was against his uncle; for a long, wheezing moment, he struggled for traction on the root and pushed against his uncle as hard as he could.

Still, Dru did not budge. And with tears cascading down his cheeks and prayers moving his lips, Bo pulled himself into a sitting position and managed to shove his legs beneath Dru's head. He wrapped his arms around the sides of Dru's face, arched his back and pressed his face against his uncle's face.

And he rocked back and forth, saying over and over again, "Uncle Dru, you gotta get up. You jus' gotta get up. I don't want you to die…"

An hour passed, and most of another. At last Dru felt the boy's grip and heard his now-infrequent, hoarse pleas. When he opened his eyes, all he could see was the whiteness of Bo's inner arm. All he could hear was, "You gotta get up…"

The pleas were very, very weak, and Dru sensed Bo was at the end of his strength. With one huge effort he pulled his elbows beneath him and rolled off Bo's lap, out of the water and onto the wet dirt. Looking up, he brought Bo's face into focus and tried to smile.

But he found that he was crying instead, and soon both were crying. Dru reached up, encircled Bo's shoulders and pulled him down beside him. There they lay, until the sobbing faded, their heavy breathing eased, and Dru could think of something to say.

"I'm sorry, boy. So sorry you have to see me this way. Lordamercy, I'm sorry."

Bo pulled loose and sat up. Biting his bottom lip and wiping his cheeks, he replied, "It's okay, Uncle Dru. I was…, we was scared 'bout you. "

"I know, I know, boy…"

"Nobody know'd where you'd gone. We was scared."

"I know, boy, and I'm so sorry."

"Aunt Sara, she said she'd seen you t'other day, but…"

"Sara? Sara? She know I been gone? Who told her? None'a her business…"

"Aw, Uncle Dru, she was worried, too. Ever'body's been worried."

Dru rolled over and pulled himself onto his elbows, shaking his head from side to side – vigorously, until the pain stabbed his brain and bolted down his spine. Then he shook it gently, more gently, and gentler still. Focusing his eyes, he struggled into a sitting position.

That pinched his burning belly, and he rolled back onto his stomach and buried his face in his hands.

"What'm I gonna do? What can I do? Good Lord, what?"

Bo stared at his uncle and at his dirty, mud-soaked clothes. Through Dru's hands he could see the matted beard and the festering insect bites. He smelled the whiskey smell, and it was so strong he felt he was going to be sick himself.

"What can I do to help," he asked, just loud enough for Dru to hear. "I can help, I know I can."

"I know, boy. Gimme a minute to think. I need to think."

"And pray," Bo said to himself. "You need a minute to pray, like I'm prayin'."

And Bo was. He was praying that his uncle didn't hurt the way he'd seen his daddy hurt, when he'd found him in the barn, smelling the same, looking the same. He'd rushed out to tell his momma, but she'd said worrying and crying wouldn't make any difference. His daddy just had to see it through.

Bo knew it had happened more than once, but he'd never again gone into the barn when he thought his daddy might be there, drinking and suffering. And he'd quit asking questions when his daddy wasn't seen for a day or two, and his momma was looking like her heart was broken.

Finally, Dru turned over and sat up. He looked into Bo's eyes and ran a trembling hand through the boy's wet hair.

"How'd you find me," he asked.

"Found Jenny first. She was up at the road."

"Anybody else know you're here? That I'm here?"

"No, sir. Not nobody."

Neither spoke for some time, and the silence hung heavy across and around the pond. It was hot, stinking, stifling hot, and the living things that could escape into a hole or beneath the water had done so.

Dru looked at Bo and Bo stared back, blankly; a blankness that Dru sensed was telling him, "It's okay, Uncle Dru. It's okay. Just tell me what I can do to help."

Dru knew he didn't have to explain anything right away, and maybe never. But he promised himself he would, when and if he ever got a better understanding of what had happened or why it had happened, of where he had gone wrong – gone wrong again and disappointed people. His face tightened and he choked off a sob.

"How do you tell a boy you ain't no good," he asked himself. "How do you tell him when he's your closest friend and you know you ain't a friend that is worthy of trust; that what folks say is right and you ain't nothin' and won't ever be…"

Bo broke the silence. "Uncle Dru, I got Jenny and the wagon tethered to a tree up the hill, waitin' to take you home. She's rarin' to go."

"Can a body see her from the road," Dru asked, wearily wiping his forehead.

"No sir. Don't think so, anyways."

Dru thought a moment. "You think you can get her'n the wagon down here under the trees? So we know it's outa sight? So we can go home 'bout dark?"

"I b'lieve so," Bo responded. He hurried up the slope and returned leading Jenny, with the wagon trailing along behind her. Dru struggled to his feet, stroked her shoulders and whispered apologies to her, too.

Then he and Bo lay down in the grass beneath the wagon bed, to wait out the heat and the inevitable afternoon rain storm. By then, Dru hoped, he'd know what to say to those who waited, even if no one believed him.

Bo didn't ask any more questions. He laid his head on one of his uncle's muddy, smelly shoulders and turned his face away from his smelly breath. His eyes remained wide open.

Before falling into a fitful sleep, Dru shed his filthy clothes, hoping the coming storm would clean them and himself. He hoped it would be a gully-washer, big enough to fill Jenny's water bucket, which always was attached to the wagon's side. And he hoped it would come and go before the sun took its clothes-drying rays and went off to sleep beyond the field to the west of his oasis of misery.

It was indeed a gully-washer and the sun did return, hotter than before the storm began. And with some hand-rubbing and some flapping against a tree trunk, Dru's clothing did get reasonably clean and wearably dry. The foul smell was less so, but his beard would have to wait.

Later, Bo stood to one side as Dru turned Jennie and the wagon around. He was happy that he'd found his uncle and that they were going home. But a terrible fear gripped him, rooted in the awareness that his beloved uncle shared the same terrible sickness as his daddy.

He was wondering whether it came with being a Sullivan, and that he might suffer the same way someday.

CHAPTER 9

Dru's terrible night: guilt, a disturbed Godspot, and a dream with a recurring message.

WHEN DRU DROPPED BO at his doorstoop, he was holding his back straight, his shoulders squared and his head erect. He ignored Jewell's questions and answered John's stare with, "Me'n the boy been ridin' and talkin'. Might say it was man-an'-boy talk. Gotta go now…"

Jewell stepped off the porch, intent upon asking one more time where he'd been. Bo blocked her path and the plea in his eyes stopped her halfway to the road.

"He's hurtin', Momma…"

Gently pulling his head against her side, she watched Dru and the wagon fade away in the tentative darkness of early evening. "I know, Bo-boy. I know…"

John had gone back into the house, saying nothing. He knew his brother was a mess inside; that he was embarrassed and ashamed, but indignant that anyone would presume to ask him about his private world.

"Damned hard-headed ignoramus," John mumbled. "Pride's gonna get him yet. Only it ain't pride; he's scared and he ain't sure who he is or who he ought to be. He says he has to listen to his feelings, but they scare the hell out of him most of the time."

John had tried often, before and after Momma Susan's passing, to talk to his brother about his solitary ways. Dru, he knew, was determined to go his own way, rejecting such social rituals as going to church, even refusing to listen when others wanted to talk about their own beliefs about life, death and the need to rely on one another to get through one more day. Oh, Dru might sit close by when others were talking about such things, listening and saying nothing; but he'd keep his own feelings and attitudes to himself.

"It's that danged conscience Dru insists on calling his Godspot," John muttered as, without thinking, he walked on through the small house and sat down on the backdoor stoop. "What he's doing is listening to himself and shutting the door on the rest of world."

Once and only once John had managed to draw Dru out about his so-called Godspot, when they were sitting on Jim's front porch having an after-supper smoke and enjoying an early-evening breeze. Reluctantly, as though knowing he'd be put down, Dru had told him it was a place where he got messages from the Lord telling him that what he was doing or thinking was right or wrong. He'd get a warm, comfortable feeling when he was on the right track; when he wasn't, the feeling would be terrible-awful, like the devil had lighted a fire in his belly.

John had countered that Dru was trying to be his own God and that was blasphemy. "What you're doing is relying on your own feelings and beliefs to justify what you will and won't do. Hell, man," John had insisted, "you are only what you've allowed yourself to be taught, and what you've experienced. You've closed the door on everything else!

'Where do you get off playing God!"

Dru had looked John in the eyes and had replied softly, "A wee spark of God is in all of us, John, and that goes for everything what lives and grows. I look at my peanuts and I see it, and I see it in the maypops flowerin' in the fields and woods and long side the road.

Them things live and die and go back into the ground to make it better for the next year's crop. That's 'cording to His ways, John, and no man can be so blind that he can't see it."

Rising, Dru had said, "And if he can't see it, his Godspot'll let him feel it. A Godspot is a place where God sends his messages. It's a box for His mail, and he don't need no two-penny stamp. Just someone willin' to listen…"

"But Dru, if you believe that me and you and all of us are like them plants, then you believe this is all there is; we're gonna live and die and… Damn man, you got a soul, a spirit! What's going to happen to that? Don't you believe in a hereafter?"

John had paused briefly to think about what he'd said; he wasn't sure there was a hereafter himself, but he knew a man or woman would feel better about life if they let himself believe there was.

"And, dagnabbit, what happens to that spark of God you say all of us got? That just don't die and go back into the ground when you do…"

John had heard the screen door close. It hadn't slammed; it had closed quietly, and Dru was gone.

Recalling that conversation, John asked himself whether Dru's brief disappearance and strange ways of acting lately might mean he was beginning to doubt his own beliefs. Is it possible, he wondered, that Dru is beginning to love some thing or some one – Sara, probably – so much that he no longer wanted to believe they might not be around forever? Most certainly he was of an age – 36 – when most people begin to become possessive of things they hold dear. Had Momma Susan's dying had something to do with the change in him? Did the realization that she might be out of his life forever make Dru question his personal faith, or lack of it?

Dru had told him more than once that he'd had "conversations" with Momma Susan; she'd start talking to him, he'd said, when he was troubled about something, and mostly she'd remind him of something she'd taught him when she was alive.

"Hell," John said now, "that ought to give him food for thought. What he's doing is carrying on a lifetime argument with himself and there's a lifetime of unhappiness in that kind of thinking."

Clasping his hands together and leaning elbows on knees, he added, very quietly, "And he's gonna want to hide that unhappiness in a jug – or worse, if there is such a thing. Lordy, I certainly know about that."

By the time Dru approached home, darkness had cast its shroud over everything, as it does on a moonless evening. Mist was rising above the wet fields and Jenny's "clip-clop, clip-clop" got faster as they approached the big house; she needed no encouragement and headed straight for the barn.

Biding his time to ponder answers to questions he expected to be asked, Dru removed the tack, turned Jennie in with Fran, and tossed both some hay. Then he stopped under the barn's shed and tried, without success, to roll a cigarette. Two days of rain, muck, mire, and sweat had rendered paper and matches useless.

He needed that smoke. He considered the deep, damnable frustration he felt, and it occurred to him that the simple, taken-for-granted things certainly got a man's attention when they weren't doing what they oughta do. Matches are supposed to burn, paper roll and cigarettes soothe; liquor's meant to drown heartache and a woman is supposed to be like you imagine her in your dreams…

Dru gritted his teeth and in a quiet but firm voice told his head, "That's e'nuff, Satan! There ya' go ag'in. I leave the gate open and you come gallopin' out, forked tail 'an all…"

Down deep, down there above his stomach and below his heart, his Godspot stirred.

"C'mon now, Dru. Satan wasn't doin' that talkin'. You was. Why can't you listen to your sober self, even if'n you are hurtin' bad. You was mostly right, 'cept maybe for that part 'bout women – and you ought to know you can be right once in a while.

"I know you and you know you were goin' to go on and say you have to take care of things that are 'portant to you and stay away from them that ain't. And the most 'portant thing is your own self. You gotta decide what's right for you and you gotta take care of it. That right, Dru?"

"Mebbe."

"And Dru…"

"Yep."

"Likker is not for you. 'Stead of lookin' for answers in a bottle, it'd be better if'n you let Jennie and Fran kick you in the hiney ever' time it crosses your mind – and let 'em do it at the same time."

Tired though he was, Dru smiled; at least the advice was in language he could understand.

"Well, what 'bout Sara?"

"Whoa now, Dru. If'n I told you one thing, you'd likely get mad. And if I told you another, you'd for sure get mad. And you know that we know that mad is angry and we know how being angry blinds a man.

"Love and lust, Dru. Preacher Pemberton talks 'bout 'em, but I wouldn't go the whole mile with the way he sees 'em, or how they're different. There's no arguin' with that man, anyway.

"Every man and woman's gotta decide what love means to 'em. Is it the good feeling you get when you see her comin' and you know you're going to bust open if you don't run and hug her? Is it feelin' that you want to be right there with her all the time? Can a man look a woman in the face and know that face still will be pretty when it's got wrinkles and the hair's looking like the mane on an old gray mule.

"And lust? Lust's a word with a bad name, Dru; and you know your own self that it grabs a'hold most animals at set times and they know to go out and find a mate and make babies. Animals is lucky; they're not bothered by the yen all year 'round. But you for sure know that you wouldn't be here if men and women hadn't felt some lust a long time ago and did what it took to make them babies.

"Nowadays…"

Dru's brow was furrowed and he'd begun to walk in a circle.

"Aw, c'mon, Dru. You been walking that circle so long you don't know how to come out of it and pick which way you oughta be goin'. What I was goin' to say was, nowadays folks expect a man and a woman to turn that lust into somethin' that's gentle and nice and fulfillin' for both of 'em. And it's supposed to make 'em feel safe – safe meaning they've shared the most precious thing they got and know it's done become more precious 'cause they did."

"But, that's the way…"

"...It feels with Sara? Dru, I'm not going to take sides on that. I been looking down on this old world for longer'n anybody and I seen all kinds of folks look at the same thing and not see it the same way. Nowadays – where you live, anyways – a man and a woman are 'spected to marry and marry where folks can see they done it. If'n they don't, those folks see lust instead of love..."

Dru had stopped circling, and the inner voice paused to give him time to digest what he'd been fed. Then it was talking again...

"You grow fine peanuts and you save the money; doin' that makes you feel safe, as though you don't need nothin' else. Now you're findin' that kind of safe ain't 'nuff. Lots of other things make up safe.

"You love Bo?"

"You know I do! And he loves me..."

"How do you know?"

"Aw, c'mon. I just know."

"There you go, Dru. That's safe. And I'll bet you'd share that there peanut money with Bo if he needed it."

"Doggone right! But for sure I wouldn'a share it with somebody what just wanted the money."

"You ever look back on how you come to love Bo?"

"He's John and Jewell's boy. He's family!"

"Now, now, Dru. Family ain't enough. You had to get to know him and trust him and miss him when he's not 'round and you need him. You hurt when he hurts and you'd give him the shirt off your back..."

"Wouldn't fit, but you know I would."

"That's love, Dru. It's the best thing in your life right now. But it seems to me Bo's the only one you've let get to know the honest-to-goodness you, and you haven't tried to get to know an honest-to-goodness somebody else..."

"There's Sara. I know Sara..."

"Do you?"

Dru paused and cogitated about that one before he responded. "I do more'n I don't..."

"And?"

"Heck, I dunno. I reckon she ain´t good for me. Not nowadays, anyways, if'n I'm to b'lieve you. Maybe 'nother time, 'nother place…"

"But this is now and we're right here in Shannon County, Georgia, Dru. Seems like you got a d'cision to make."

"Reckon so…"

"Bye now, Dru. I'll be 'round when you need me."

"I reckon I know that…"

Shaking his tin of Prince Albert, Dru whispered, "I reckon you wouldn't have a cigarette."

"Bye, Dru."

Doubly tired now, Dru looked across the barnyard to see which windows were lit up. Liza's room was dark, but a lamp glowed in the living room. Not caring anymore how he answered whatever questions might be asked, he crossed the yard, mounted the steps and headed for his own room, which was across the breezeway from the main part of the house.

As Dru had expected, Jim appeared in the living room doorway. The breezeway's darkness obscured his face, but Dru knew the bushy eyebrows were raised and that he was about to say something.

"Glad you're home, Dru. We missed you. Worried 'bout you, too."

Dru sighed, a heavy sigh he hoped hadn't been heard. "Thank you, Jim. Missed you, too. You can't know how much…"

His last words had trailed off and Dru wasn't certain his brother had heard them. He suspected he hadn't, but decided it didn't matter. Closing the door, he threw himself on his bed, cupped his hands beneath his head and stared at the barely visible ceiling.

His head was heavy and his eyes stung. He suspected they were blood-red, from the drinking, from sleep that really hadn't been sleep, and from the undeniable awareness that he had shamed himself again…

…That he had failed again.

Sara crept into his thinking, with her engaging eyes and disarming smile. He wondered whether it was possible for a man to hate a woman when he knew down deep he loved her? Was holding on to hope worth it when it hurts so much? Did any of it really matter when you feel you're walking downhill on life's long, long road? Wouldn't it be better to hurry along and get to the end?

Turning onto his stomach, he crushed a pillow with his brawny arm and cried aloud, "Sara, Sara, Sara! God knows, I love you so…" And a moment later he heard another voice, which he knew was his as well. "But I hate you, hate you, hate you! Hate you 'cause my life was peaceful before I met you and it's such a mess now.

"Why can't I get you outa my head?"

Sleep tugged at his eyes, and he opened them to resist the tugging; opened them wide, straining against the closing lids, forcing them to stay open. It didn't work, and he gave up the fight, let them close and drifted to a place just beneath the thin veil that separates restful sleep from restless, semi-conscious awareness.

And John's words kept coming' back:

"If Jewell ever mentions Beatrice, you listen…"

Asleep now, he saw himself in Jewell's kitchen, sitting across the supper table from her. She was talking and looking so serious and loving that he knew she had to believe what she was saying: that Beatrice O'Connell was a woman other women felt women should be like, and that men oughta want. Nice and neat and always carrying a hanky and…

Dru turned over and pulled the pillow over his head; he needed sleep desperately, and he pleaded for Jewell to go away. He couldn't stand another vision, another voice telling him what to do.

But Jewell didn't go away; she persisted, telling him she cared for him, knew the Good Lord cared for him, and that both only wanted what was best for him…

And then Dru saw and heard himself interrupting. "Yeah, and she's always squeezin' that hanky into a ball, like she's schemin', and squirmin' 'bout what she's schemin'…"

Hearing his own words, he cringed about how poorly he'd said them; even the way he talked shamed him.

"She's nervous, Dru, you silly man. For sure she's nervous. Any single woman would be 'round a man like you. Why, look at you. You're strong, you ain't bad lookin'.

"You ain't got a wife and you got a good crop of peanuts comin' in. Ever'body says so. And, being' the down-deep common-sense man you are, you likely got some money tucked away for a rainy day.

"Well, it's rainin', Dru, it's rainin'. You think you can't afford a wife? 'Course you can…"

He was thinking Jewell didn't talk all that well, either. And he didn't like what she was saying, even if she was right about some of the things she was saying.

"I don't need a wife, Jewell, and I don't want a wife. I'm too set in my ways."

She sighed deeply, rose and left the room. Before he could decide whether to sit or leave, she was back carrying a book he recognized.

"The Holy-Hard-to-Read Book," he grumbled. "You ain't gonna start at me with that, are ya'?"

"Hush, Dru. Listen to this."

Dru suspected she had marked the place before he arrived.

"It says right here in Genesis, Chapter 2, Verse 18. 'The Lord God said, It is not good for man to be alone. The Lord God caused a deep sleep to fall upon the man and he slept.'

"And right here in Verse 22, it says, 'And the Lord fashioned into a woman the rib he had taken from the man, and the man said, 'This is now bone of my bone and flesh of my flesh.'"

"And, Dru, it goes on to say, 'For this cause a man shall leave his father and his mother, and shall cleave to his wife; and they shall become one flesh.'"

In his vision, he saw and felt Jewell reach across the table and place her hand over one of his.

"You're funnin' yourself, Dru. Ever'body needs somebody. If'n you understood that, you'd not be so set in your ways – which don't seem to be makin' you none too happy anyways."

He saw himself sit upright, glare across the table at his sister-in-law – and he heard her close the vice.

"Dru, dear, dear Dru, you're too good a man to spend your time hangin' out by yourself in that peanut field, or hidin' in the barn doin' things. And, Dru, I do believe it's true that you've a feeling for them cows that maybe ain't…"

"Whoa," he said, taking back his hand. "You got no cause to say that 'bout them cows, and you leave Sara outa this. Sara's gone, dead gone! Right now I'm hatin' that woman."

And in his dream he heard his voice becoming softer, and word-by-word deliberate.

"Maybe, I'm wishin' she was dead. Just plain dead! What she did, the onliest thing she did, was show me a body ain't safe even when he's tryin' to do the things a man oughta do, and was meant to do. A man's got feelin's pullin' at him all the time, and if he tries to go 'long with the pullin' somebody's gonna say it's wrong and he's gonna burn in hell. And if'n he don't go 'long somebody else's gonna say somethin' ain't right and he ain't livin' right and he's goin' to hell."

His voice rose as he stood up. "Lordgodamighty, the only hell I know is right here on this earth! It's 'nough to confuse a man, make 'im b'lieve he's crazy. What ain't confusin', what's for sure, is that when a man takes a chance, any kind of a chance, somebody's gonna stomp on him. Like somebody stompin' on a flower or a bug when there ain't no reason but meanness. Or like when a cooter sticks his head outa his shell and somebody chops it off…"

Jewell waved a hand, closed her eyes tight and swung her head so rapidly that her honey-blonde hair audibly swished.

"Oh, Dru, that cooter'd never get 'crost the road or find his supper or 'nother cooter if he didn't stick his head out. That old cooter was lookin' for his t'morrow and we all pray we've got a t'morrow. But if you want it to be a good t'morrow, you gotta reach out and start plannin' for it."

Teeth gritted, Dru squeezed his closed eyes so hard it hurt and squashed the vision. Breathing deeply, he opened them and stared into the darkness. He was alone again and, as much as he'd hated to hear what Jewell had been saying, being alone felt terrible…

...Terrible, terrible, terrible! And terribly lonely, too.

"Get a grip on yourself," he said aloud. "You gotta calm down. You gotta sleep. You got a d'cision to make. The most 'portant d'cision you'll ever make…"

He turned onto his back, sensing that sleep wasn't going to wrap him in its arms and take him into sublime, mindless escape. He was alone. Alone, and with a frightful decision to make.

And over and over, John's words kept running through his heavy, hurting head…

"If Jewell ever mentions Beatrice, you listen…"

CHAPTER 10

'...*Dear Beatrice, have you set your mind on becoming an old maid?*'

– Her mother, Maria Charlotte O'Connell

AS DRU WIPED HIS red, sleep-deprived eyes and struggled from his lumpy bed, Beatrice Andrea O'Connell turned over in her canopied one and wrapped her arms around a soft but frayed goose-down pillow. Though time had eroded much of its opulence, the bed remained her favorite possession.

It also was her favorite retreat, a hideaway from the loneliness fate had placed upon her, as well as a demanding mother with an overriding concern: "Dear Beatrice, have you set your mind to becoming an old maid?"

The sun already was an hour removed from its cloud-cushioned resting place, and she'd heard the hired hand heading out into the pecan grove some time ago. But she seldom left hers before midmorning, unless her mother appeared and told her firmly the world was waiting for her smile.

Smarting at the thought and muttering, "Smile, indeed," Beatrice tucked a loose strand of blue-black hair under her nightcap and focused her dark eyes on the wall closest to her. She loved the wallpaper, and fantasized that it was her stairway to heaven – or, for the time being, at least – earthly bliss. The wall covering was a product of a grander age, featuring broad, circular golden stairs leading up through tall white columns entwined with climbing roses, breeze-kissed green leaves, and a variety of pink and blue flowers; closer to the high ceiling, angels beckoned from a blue sky that appeared to have no end.

The McConnells had a fine library, which included beautifully bound books that had been in the family for generations. Beatrice remembered a picture she had seen in one – Michelangelo's Sistine Chapel ceiling – and she imagined that her wallpaper stretched right on up into that painting. The power of the extended finger overwhelmed her; she breathed deeply, sighed fancifully and the green nightgown rose and fell in time with the small breasts beneath it. There was warmth in the tender spot between her legs and she fought the urge to touch it.

She lost the fight, however, as she had lost it on so many other mornings since she'd first seen Dru Sullivan sitting on that bench in Mayo. His shabby felt hat had been tipped back, revealing a mop of dark hair that looked as though it could defy the strongest of breezes and most certainly a comb. When he'd stood, she'd shivered; and she hadn't even tried to control the shivers or the needle pricks that had run up and down her spine.

He was, she felt, the manliest man she'd ever seen.

Reality replaced fantasy and she heard herself saying, "Why make it worse? Why get something started that nobody's going to finish?"

Briefly, she considered praying for forgiveness for yielding to Satan's insidious call. She'd looked up that word once, a long time ago when she'd first discovered that source of extreme pleasure between her legs. "Treacherous, deceitful," her Webster's had told her. "Beautiful but dangerous," she had read elsewhere.

But try as she had, she'd been unable to resist, and had decided that treachery and deceitfulness were sins with which would have to live. And she'd rationalized that forgiveness could wait until a priest somehow materialized, though she knew that was a remote possibility in backwoods Shannon County. Catholic priests simply were not welcome in this rather small and unique enclave of Irish-Americans, most of who had been told by parents and grandparents of priests' harsh, unforgiving methods in the Mother Country.

Turning onto her other side, Beatrice was aware that she had slept well, much better than anticipated. Sleep didn't come easily on long, lonesome nights, and sometimes it was a caustic remark by her mother, Maria Charlotte, that prompted her to seek escape in bed; that or the boredom of spending another evening with her mother, and of how the woman insisted they spend the evening. Sometimes it would be reading to one another from those old books; sometimes it was the meandering, one-way talk about things that meant little or nothing to Beatrice.

And more often than Beatrice could tolerate, Maria Charlotte tried to teach her the "old languages," Spanish and Gaelic. She had managed to learn some Spanish, the language of her mother's ancestors. But Gaelic was too difficult, and through prayer she asked her deceased father to forgive her for not having the slightest interest in it.

She had loved her father, his poetic way of expressing feelings, and even his singing. But when he had dropped back into Ireland's ancient tongue, she'd excuse herself and go to bed feeling the fireside evening had been ruined.

Beatrice was 32. Her mother was a slim, well-appointed woman of 54 whose dark hair was only now beginning to show streaks of gray. Beatrice's father, Andre Phillip O'Connell, had died eight years earlier, the victim of a hunting accident. He had tripped and fallen on his shotgun; his companions said he had died quickly.

But the pain had not diminished for widow and daughter. The future of the O'Connell name in Shannon County may have died with him, and that awareness fed the bitterness in Maria Charlotte's soul.

Beatrice had to marry and marry soon, she had said over and over again…

Four hundred years earlier, the O'Connell name had been a proud one in Ireland, where the O'Connells, like the O'Sullivans, had grown wealthy by trading with the Spanish. Their castle fortresses nestled along or near the southern coast, a few days sailing from the Iberian Peninsular, around the south of Wales and across the channel.

Those days had ended with the start of the 17th Century, when England's Lord Mountjoy and his forces routed the Irish at the town of Munster and went on to destroy the last clan strongholds to the south and west. Beatrice knew from studying the books in her mother's precious library that the O'Sullivans had been the last to yield, and she found that exciting.

In time, the descendents of both families had found their way to Spain, the Caribbean, to Cuba, and eventually to St. Augustine in northern Florida, and on up into Georgia and the Carolinas. Some came later, when the recurring potato famines sent them and thousands of others across the Atlantic, to Boston, New York and other ports in Virginia and the Carolinas.

It was possible, Beatrice knew, that Dru's branch of the O'Sullivan clans had come to Georgia in another way, perhaps in a southern migration from Boston, New York or Virginia. But she preferred to believe in the Spanish connection, which she now hoped to renew.

In the years since Andre Phillip O'Connell's death, her mother had held on to the O'Connell farm and its 250 acres with a tenacity that reflected Irish stubbornness and Spanish pride. But those years had begun to take its toll, and increasingly she had vented her frustrations on Beatrice.

"If only that foolish man hadn't killed himself," Maria Charlotte said so often that Beatrice could mouth it with her. Most of the time, she'd do it quietly so her mother wouldn't hear or see her; more recently she was saying it in a loud, mocking voice.

And hearing her, Maria Charlotte's would mutter, just loud enough for her to hear, "If only we'd had a son. If only you'd been a boy..."

A day had come when Beatrice, tired of the implied blame, had fought back.

"Well, why *didn't* you have a boy, mother? Why *didn't* you? You had such a perfect marriage, why didn't you? Did daddy's desire for you dry up?"

Maria had not responded, except to narrow her eyes and stare at her daughter for a long and painful moment. Lightning had flashed from those dark eyes, and Beatrice had retreated, fearful of what might come next.

Something did. It had begun at breakfast the following morning, and it had continued day after day after day: "Beatrice, dear Beatrice, have you set your mind to becoming an old maid? I know there's no man in these parts worthy of you, but…"

Pausing just long enough to let the sarcasm set its teeth, she'd added, "But don't you think you might give some thought about how you'll feel goin' to your grave an unfulfilled woman?" And after another pause to make sure her point found its mark, she'd completed the thrust: "And a poor, destitute one at that?"

Beatrice had stiffened. There it was, clear as a bell. They couldn't keep the estate unless they got money, and there wasn't enough money in the whole county to keep the farm going in the manner they wanted.

Troubled by the memory, Beatrice Andrea O'Connell rolled over on her stomach and refocused her thinking. She remembered another time she'd seen tall, gangly, quiet Dru; he'd been sitting alone on the bench outside the Dixie Theater in Mayo, whittling a stick and occasionally pocketing a splinter. Because of their shape, she assumed he was saving them for use as toothpicks.

She closed her eyes and replayed the scene…

"Excuse me, Miss Parmalee, but *who* is that man sitting by himself?"

"Oh, that's just Dru Sullivan. He'll sit there whittlin' like that til the motion picture show is over and the young'uns come out. Ask me, he'd rather spend time with the young'uns than with us grownups."

Mrs. Ida Jo Johnston had laughed at her friend's response. "Maybe it's 'cause they're simple folk like him. Hear tell, though, that he's got a fine peanut crop comin' in. And I never seen him spend a dime, so he must have lots of greenbacks stored away."

Beatrice had thanked both and said she needed to do some shopping. She'd walked toward the corner, wetting her fingers and pulling at the curls hanging around her ears, making them curl even more. Then she'd pinched her cheeks to give them color and strolled over and sat down on the bench next to Dru.

"Is this seat taken," she had asked.

She had smiled broadly and her next words had been honey-coated.

"I just can not imagine why it isn't, however. I just can not."

Dru had stopped whittling, bobbed his Adam's apple a couple of times and had excused himself.

"Pardon, Ma'm. I gotta go. I really do..."

And he'd hurried off to the Blue Goose, where he remained until the others had returned and Jim drove them home.

Smiling, Beatrice snuggled deeper under the worn satin covers and imagined again that Dru was with her. She felt, again, the primeval desires and chills running up and down her spine. Though she resisted the urge to touch her source of pleasure again, she smiled and said softly...

"And Momma Maria Charlotte, you'd be pleased to know he has a coffee-can treasure stashed away somewhere..."

CHAPTER 11

"A man's gotta do what a man's gotta do."

– Dru to his brother, Liam

HAD BEATRICE KNOWN OF Dru's dream about Jewell and its eroding affect on his stubbornness, she probably would have tossed off the quilts, shouted for joy and greeted the day with the broad smile her mother wanted.

Dru had made his decision: he would court Beatrice, with one eye on marriage and the other on doing the things he felt it would take to make him worthy of such a woman.

Those fear-based insecurities still gnawed at him like fleas on an old hound; what he had to do, he reckoned, was become more willing to let others help him identify and deal with them. He was determined to become a good man with a lot to offer.

He wasn't sure how it would affect the courting, but he had squashed during his fitful, vision-filled night any thoughts that marriage was holy wedlock; he'd seen marriages full of fussing and fighting, and his intense dislike for confrontation of any sort shouted that those marriages definitely were *unholy* wedlock.

And where was a man of his age going to make up for the school-based education he had missed? How could he learn to *like* going to church every Sunday, and maybe on Wednesday nights as well?

Would he be expected to *shave every day,* change out of his work clothes every evening, *take baths more often?* Get in bed with a woman and *stay there all night?* Lordamercy, what if he'd had beans for supper?

Overwhelmed, but determined to hoe the row he'd selected, he went to the kitchen and poured himself a cup of the still-warm coffee. He could see through the screen door that the Blue Goose wasn't in its usual place. Apparently Jim had gone off somewhere. And by keening his ears in the direction of the parlor, he determined that Liza was there, listening to the radio and probably knitting. He thought about the precious batteries that powered the Emerson, and of his sister's daily challenge of choosing between preserving them and saving her soul by listening to the morning prayers. The prayers almost always prevailed, and Jim managed somehow to keep a spare battery or two in a safe place only he knew.

Quietly, Dru sipped his coffee and then filled the metal cup a second time. He didn't care for metal cups; a man could burn his lips if the coffee was really hot. But Liza got downright, finger-waving mad if one of her china cups was taken outside, where they'd likely get broken or lost. Dru harrumphed at the thought; china cups were too small anyway.

When he arrived in the barn, he placed the cup on a shelf – next to two other metal cups – and roped a mule. He did it instinctively and didn't notice that he'd selected the older mule until he'd guided her onto the road and headed east.

"Been awhile, Abigail," he called to her. "You're needful of some work, I reckon."

Telling himself that wasn't a very polite thought to express to a woman, even if she was a mule, he added: "Good to see you lookin' so good, old gal. Reckon both of us got some time left. Let's go have us some fun…"

Though she was about 23 years old and you could count her ribs, Abigail didn't miss a step as she clip-clopped east down to the corner and, without coaching, turned north. The two-story house of his brother Liam's family stood off to the sunrise side of the gravel road and Liam was in his front yard.

Dru had mixed feelings; he wanted to be alone, but didn't want to hurt his brother's feelings by pretending he didn't see him. Except for John, Liam was the closest in years to Dru, being just two years older. He was the smallest brother, barely five-feet, six-inches in his boots.

He also was the slimmest – weighing maybe 120 pounds – and, like Dru, he didn't say much. Especially when it came to offering advice.

"Mornin', Dru."

Dru put on his best smile. "Mornin' there, Liam. Feel like a ride? Goin' down to look at my peanut crop."

Dru moved over and Liam climbed aboard. Neither said anything for the first quarter-mile and Dru was beginning to feel apprehensive; Liam was making it hard for him to be what he'd decided he'd be: warm, outgoing, friendly, considerate, and courteous.

Up ahead a small creek compressed itself and flowed quietly into a pipe laid beneath the road. When the water exited the other side, however, it emerged in a swirling, foam-topped cascade, which over the years had carved out a deep pool before proceeding into a larger swamp. Using soap made of ashes boiled with hog fat, the Sullivans bathed in the pool when the weather was warm, and sometimes when it wasn't.

Dru spoke up, trying to make a joke. "Mollie made you come down here lately?"

"Why you ask? Ain't no way you can smell me o'er yourself – or that."

Without breaking stride, Abigail was defecating, her tail hoisted to one side. "Phew," said Dru, trying to think of something else to say.

He couldn't, and concentrated on guiding the mule across a swale leading from the ditch into the creek. The ground was soft, but not enough to mire the wagon; and several moments later, Dru called Abigail to a halt beside his beloved crop, which stretched a quarter-mile alongside the wooded swamp and about the same distance back toward the main road to the south. With few exceptions, the deep green vista was as smooth and even as a well-swept yard.

Dru beamed proudly. Liam scanned the field and looked up at his brother. "You got reason to be proud, Dru. I watch this field from my front porch and it seems them peanuts is growin' like they oughta. See 'em up close and I know they are."

He paused and pulled a pipe and tobacco from the bib pocket of his overalls. "You must'a been workin' 'em purty good. How come I never see you?"

Dru's Adam's apple bobbed; he knew why Liam was asking the question. "I walk down through the corn to work it, Liam. No sense usin' a wagon to come round by the road. That's a lazy man's way…"

Liam lit his pipe and blew a smoke ring, which broke up quickly in the gentle morning breeze. "Way of a lonely man, too, Dru. Molly and me, we miss seein' you."

"You'll be seein' more of me, Liam. I promise."

"You done promised that afore."

"Road goes two ways, Liam."

"Yeah, it does. But ever' time I come down yours, I see you skeedaddlin' for the barn or to that outhouse, like you don't want to see nobody, not even your own kin."

Dru shrugged. He knew it was true, but had hoped Liam hadn't noticed.

"And 'sides, Molly, she says she's just gotta come 'long and she goes in to see Liza and they talks and talks and talks and I just gotta bide my time. No point in that."

Dru winced but didn't respond. Swinging a leg over the wagon's side, he dropped to the ground and walked to the edge of his crop. He pulled a clump of greenery from the soil, shook it clean and examined the pale white peanuts.

"Pretty soon," he said loud enough for Liam to hear from the wagon seat. "Won't be long now…"

"Reckon not."

Liam was standing at his elbow. Startled, Dru moved away abruptly.

Smiling, Liam said, "I ain't a gonna bite, Dru."

"Reckon not, Liam. Reckon not…"

"Sheriff Nobles come by the other day."

Liam left the statement hanging there, as though to pique Dru's curiosity. He did.

"What'd he want?"

"Says he's still trying' to figure out how to go 'bout lookin' into Lonny's gettin' killed. Says he thinks the boy might have done it himself, but Buttonbottom and Marybelle says it can't be so."

Aiming a boot toe at a dirt clod, Liam kicked it and added in a softer tone, "Says if the Higginbothams weren't such good niggers, he'd just forget it and let it die."

"Sounds like Nobles…"

"Did ask me if I had a .410. Told 'im yep, but it was so old I wasn't sure it still worked. Don't even know where it is, now that I think 'bout it."

"You got any thoughts 'bout who might have done it, Liam." Thinking of Lonny reminded Dru of Del and he wondered why he was letting this line of talk go on.

"I think 'bout it time to time. Can't help wonderin' if somebody from t'other side of the swamp didn't come over and do it."

"You mentioned that to Nobles?"

"Yep. Said he'd thought 'bout that, too. Didn't say if he was doin' anything 'bout it." After a quiet pause, Liam added, "Wanted to tell 'im maybe it could'a been someone who used to live on t'other side, but didn't."

Dru picked up on that right off. "Yeah, I can see why not. He'n Boru are thick'n fleas on an old hound."

Neither spoke for a moment, their attention diverted by a breeze stirring leaves in a solitary pecan tree that had been allowed to grow up wild in the field. Such trees were common in the Sullivan fields.

Again it was Liam who broke the silence. "Seems to me we got some personal catchin' up to do," he said.

It was more of a question than a statement.

"'Bout what? Not much happenin' in my life."

He regretted the lie, but hadn't known what else to say. The response had been instinctive, a form of self-protection; he shrugged it off, rationalizing that his former self had said it.

"C'mon now, Dru. We know better'n that. How's Sara?"

Dru straightened his back and squared his shoulders; he parted his lips to reply, angrily, but closed them again. Nudging the thrown-away lump of peanuts with a boot toe, he finally cleared his throat and tried again.

"Aw, Liam, why can't you leave it 'lone? Why can't you leave a dead dog dead? You know I ain't 'bout to talk about that woman, not now, not ever…"

"That bad, huh?"

Dru didn't respond.

"Well, okay, Dru. What 'bout that Beatrice woman? You gonna court her?"

A bolt of lightning shot up Dru's spine; he wanted in the worst way to tell Liam to find his own way back to his house. Doggonit anyway. He wondered why people wouldn't leave him alone – let him decide what he wanted to let them know.

Suppressing anger again, he turned his back to Liam. "Why you ask? It make any dif'rence what I do 'bout her?"

"You know it does. We, me'n Molly, care 'bout you…"

'If'n you did, you'd let me make up my own mind 'bout things like that."

"Lordamercy, Dru, you sound like you done decided to marry that woman! Don't do it, Dru."

"And why not? She's a good woman, needful of a good man. Womenfolk, all of 'em – them I get an earful from, anyways – they want to be like her, have what's she's got."

"What do they think she's got, Dru? Maybe you hain't heard what folks over to Munsterville got to say."

"What do they say, Liam, since you know so much? For that matter, what you got to say?"

"I say she wants that crop of your'n and whatever money you got hid away. Everybody knows you make good money ever' year, but ain't nobody seen you spendin' it?

Dru turned and faced his smaller brother. "That for certain the way you feel, Liam?"

Liam dropped his eyes and banged his pipe against the palm of his hand, shaking out ashes. "That's the way I feel, Dru. Molly, too."

"How 'bout Rufus and Glenn?"

"You know they don't pay no 'tention to nothin' but their own doings. Glenn, he ain't got the smarts to think for hisself, anyways. All he ever says is, 'A man's gotta do what a man's gotta do.' You know that."

Dru turned away and walked some distance into his peanut field, carefully stepping over each row. He felt good among his plants; they were his, he'd done right by them, and they meant freedom to him, dollar-wise and otherwise. Used to be they were his only security, except for the way he felt when he was among maypops and honeysuckle vines, or being with Bo and maybe with milk cows.

Dru stood motionless for a long time, so long that Liam finally walked back to wagon and mounted the seat. Moments later, Dru wiped a tear from his cheek, blew his nose with his red bandana, and went to join his brother. He was talking softly to himself, trying to convince himself that the decision he'd made was the right one...

"Thing is," he whispered for his own ears, "it's one thing to tell yourself you oughta do somethin' and another to get your heart in it... Specially if your heart seems to want to be doin' somethin' else."

He paused as he reached the wagon.

"You say somthin', Dru?"

"Sho did, Liam."

"Well, is it a secret?"

"Nope. I said, 'A man's gotta do what a man's gotta do.'"

Liam looked at him long and hard.

"Ohmigod," he finally said.

CHAPTER 12

'I'm goin' to learn to read, write and talk normal, Bo…'

ANOTHER WEEK PASSED AND Dru stumbled through it, going from one small chore to another and pulling the few weeds that dared show themselves among his peanuts. Like those damnable intrusive weeds, Liam's unwelcome, unsolicited advice had dampened his spirit; with each new sunrise, he found a reason to put off visiting Beatrice O'Connell.

For the better part of a week he dealt with the older brother's qualms. What if Liam was right? What if he was about to step into a honey-coated bear trap? What if his initial feelings about the woman had been on the mark? The "what-ifs" were driving him crazy and his Godspot already had told him it was sitting this one out…

But then one morning he rose from his bed, set his chin and told himself emphatically that Liam was a latecomer in a fuss already settled. He had made his decision, by jiminy; all he needed was a plan and time to round up his often-elusive gumption.

The nagging question that bothered him most was how to talk to educated women, which Beatrice O'Connell surely was. Why, he'd overheard others jesting that his English was so poor that even the mules got uppity with him. Dru knew the smart alecks were having fun at his expense; but then he'd asked himself why else would those mules snort when he was confiding his troubles to them?

"Yep," he told himself over and over again, "proper schoolin's gonna be a hard'un to handle, like tryin' to pasture a bull by hisself when it's matin' season."

Recognizing the irony of what he'd just said, Dru allowed himself a soft laugh; and since that felt good, he looked around to see whether anyone was watching, and laughed again.

It was Sunday afternoon, with dinner done and Liza and Jim napping in their rooms. He'd stepped onto the front porch and was looking down toward Banshee Swamp. Sometimes on this day of rest, Bo would escape his afternoon nap and come racing through the tunnel in that tangle of moss-covered trees, palmetto clumps, briars, and stagnant pools.

When he didn't, Dru knew Jewell had managed to head him off. Dru laughed at that thought, too, and told himself, by golly, he was feeling pretty doggone good. And maybe that was a good omen; maybe he'd find a way to…

"Lordamercy," he suddenly whispered, "where've I been? I got my answer right out there in that barn! Oh, Bo, you just gotta come t'day. You just gotta!"

Dru needed Bo. Needed him badly, and figured maybe he should go to the swamp's far side in case Bo had made it to the edge but was too scared to come on through. That still happened occasionally; sometimes a snake'd be lying in the road, or a strange new sound would be coming out of the swamp. Bo was growing quickly, but he still had some of a boy's fears.

Dru had guessed correctly. Even as he reached the place where the road tunneled through the swamp, he could see the boy standing at the other end, beyond the dangling vines, rain-filled mud holes and scoured-out roots. Bo had changed out of his Sunday best and wore bibbed overalls his momma had snipped off at the knees. Dru knew he was barefoot so he could run faster, when and if he got up the gumption to challenge the swamp one more time.

"Yooo, Bo," he shouted. "Stay there and I'll come get ya'."

Bo flinched and retreated a few feet from the swamp's southern edge. He'd heard the yell, but not the second part, the part about his uncle coming to get him. Instinctively, Dru suspected that Bo hadn't seen him and thought his yell was a banshee-scream or ghost-cry warning him to stay out of their domain. He broke into a trot and shouted again.

"Stay there, Bo. I'm comin' to get ya'."

This time Bo saw him and returned the wave.

"Figured you might be comin' over," Dru said as he arrived alongside his nephew.

Staring at him with a question spread across his face, Bo said, "That's real nice, Uncle Dru, but I warn't afraid. You know'd that, didn't you?"

Many times Bo got to talking like his uncle when they were together, and it'd take his daddy a day or two to get him talking "normal-like" again. Dru ruffled his tow-head. "I know'd, boy. But I needed the walk. The run, too. Come 'long, I got somethin' to show you."

Taking Bo by the hand, he led him back through the swamp, doing his best not to look down to see whether the boy had closed his eyes.

Bo withdrew the hand as they came out into the sunshine, and he followed his uncle to the big house. An L-shaped porch, head-high to a grownup, stretched around the front; and if you were tall enough, you could stand in the front yard, look through the breezeway and see the water well and storehouse out back, both a short walk from the kitchen.

The privies – Uncle Jim had two, both two-holers – were behind the storehouse and Liza's giant fig trees.

Dru skirted the house and led Bo straight to the barn. There, he climbed a ladder attached to a wall and sat down atop the massive pile of loose hay. It was hot, but Dru didn't seem to mind and Bo decided, that being the case, he'd also ignore the heat.

Clearly excited, Dru turned to Bo, leaned close, squinted his eyes, and looked very secretive. Though they were alone, he spoke in a whisper. "Now, Bo, I'm gonna show you somethin' I hain't show'd nobody else and don't intend to. You hafta promise you'll keep it a secret. You gotta swear on it."

Curiosity overwhelmed Bo. He raised his right hand and whispered some gibberish he felt might serve as swearing that he would keep his uncle's secret a secret: "Abba-dabba-do-wittle, the devil take me if'n I tell this secret."

"That'll do fine," Dru said. "Jus' don't forget it."

Dru reached down into the hay, so far down that his arm disappeared right up to the shoulder. Feeling around, he smiled broadly and withdrew the arm. "Look'a here," he said. "Ain't this somethin'?"

He was holding a thick book with a drawing of some strange-looking people and several big words on its front. Taking the proffered book in both hands, Bo recognized some of the words and read them aloud.

"Human ... Book One ... And ... "

For a boy about to go into the third grade, the other words were too big to say, much less decipher. Annoyed and somewhat embarrassed, Bo thumbed the pages, pronouncing words he did know and telling Dru the others were too big for him.

Dru looked disappointed, but sympathetic. "That's okay, Bo. I was a'thinkin' some of 'em might be. But ain't this the greatest find you ever saw?"

"Find? Where'd you find it, Uncle Dru?"

"Next to the railroad tracks in Mayo. I figure it fell off a train passin' through."

"Well, it sure is nice. Wish I had it."

"If I got it, you got it, Bo. I was a'hopin' we could read it t'gether."

"We can try, Uncle Dru," Bo replied enthusiastically. "We sure can try."

He leafed through more pages, and his eyes got wider and wider as he came across pictures, drawings, maps, and, best of all, words he recognized.

"Why, look'a here, Uncle Dru. This says 'peanuts.' It tells 'bout peanuts. You know 'bout peanuts. You got the best crop in Shannon County. Everybody knows that."

Dru beamed and leaned over the boy's shoulder and looked more closely. "Yeah, Bo, I know that word. Seen it on a seed bag lots'a times. What's the book say 'bout peanuts?"

Bo wrinkled his brow and became very serious. Running a finger over the words, he said, "That's 'school boy,' that's 'school girl,' there's 'new,' and that's 'grew'. It says 'peanuts' lots'a times. Here's one I just know I know. "N-e-g-r...

"Uncle Dru, it says 'Negroes'. We call 'em 'colored folk.'"

"The heck you say," Dru said, his eyes following Bo's finger to the word. "What's it say 'bout color..., uh. Ne-groes?"

"Well, I'm not sure, Uncle Dru. But I'll try..."

Placing his finger over a word, he began.

"Lessee, that's 'the' and that's 'Negroes' again. That word's too big for me. That one is 'peanuts,' and there's 'with them from...'"

Frowning, he stared hard at the next word.

"I don't know that one, Uncle Dru. But it looks like the name of some place, like maybe where they came from. That big word right there – 'b-r-o-u-g-h-t' – could help us, if I knew how to say it and what it means."

"Well, Bo, can't you try to say it? Maybe it looks like 'nother word, but means somethin' differ..., uh, but ain't got the same meanin'?

Dru was so excited that he nudged Bo very hard, knocking the book from his hands. Recovering it and rubbing his shoulder, Bo said, "I reckon so, but you gotta help me."

Finding the word again and placing his finger on it, he began very carefully. "Bro... brou..., broug... I dunno, Uncle Dru."

"Couldn't it be 'brought,' Bo? Like I brung this here book home. Your daddy tol' me onct it warn't 'brung.' It was 'brought!'"

"You're right, Uncle Dru! It's gotta be 'brought'."

Bo ran his finger along the familiar words once more, saying them out loud. "The Negroes brought peanuts with them from.... There's that word again, and I don't know how we're gonna figure it out without some help."

Dru was now sitting very erect and he'd pushed his felt hat to the back of his head.

"That's okay, Bo. We knows it says them Negroes brought them peanuts from someplace, but I ain't a'gonna b'lieve that for one tick of a clock. Not for one minute, I ain't!"

"But it's in the book, Uncle Dru, and you gotta believe it's so if it's in the book."

Dru arched his back, reached into his hip pocket and pulled out his red bandana, which he sometimes wrapped around his neck when he was sweating real bad. He wiped the sweat from his brow and his eyes, pulled at his nose with the bandana, and switched his stare from Bo to the book and back again.

"I reckon you got it right, boy. I ain't a'goin' to argue with no book, 'especially a big 'un like that." Squeezing the perspiration out of the bandana, he replaced it in the pocket and looked across the barn's breezeway at an identical hay mow on the other side. Bo knew his uncle always stared 'way off when he was thinking deep thoughts.

Finally, Dru shifted his eyes back to Bo. "You said awhile ago we needed some help, boy. Who'd you think we could trust with this here book?"

Now it was Bo's time to think, and it didn't take long.

"Why, Missus McGraw, Uncle Dru. My schoolmarm."

Nellie McGraw was a woman of Scots-Irish descent married to a man of Scots-Irish descent. Her maiden name had been McIntosh and she had inherited the finest characteristics of her ancestors: a pretty face and inviting green eyes above a freckled nose. She also had the countenance of a 24-year-old, happily married woman very satisfied with her chosen field. Though she had no children of her own as yet, she loved them and was a natural-born teacher.

Nellie and her husband, James, had come down from North Carolina's western mountains in 1934, looking for a place he could practice his trade – blacksmith, or smithy – and she could practice hers. There had been a teacher in the McIntosh family for generations: in North Carolina, in the family's 110 years in Northern Ireland, and in the lowlands of Scotland, where it had originated. She was proud of her heritage and used it as a tool in teaching geography to the oldest of her six grade-levels of pupils.

She was genuinely fond of Bo and had been able to deal positively with his mother's firm demands that he be given every opportunity to build on what she'd already taught him.

"I only went to the sixth grade, but I've learned a lot more since I had to leave school," Jewell Sullivan had told her when she'd brought 4-year-old Bo to the school on Sept. 3, 1940, three months before his fifth birthday.

"His daddy went to college and he's helped teach him, too. He knows his alphabet, can read the days of the week and all the months. He can count to 50 and he can read in that primer over there."

Turning to Bo with a "you-better-do-it" smile and a firm blue-eyed stare, she'd said, "Say the days of the week and spell them." He had, and she'd turned back to Mrs. McGraw and smiled even more proudly.

"Well, that's wonderful, Beaujames," the teacher had responded, matching Jewell's smile. "I'll bet you'll be moving out of that back row quicker'n a kitty can blink its eyes."

The schoolhouse, built by the Sullivans and other families living in their part of Shannon County, was equipped with homemade desks arranged in six rows, each with three or four desks across. The back row was for young'uns just beginning their formal schooling, and they were moved forward each year until they reached front row. Most left school after the sixth year, a practice Mrs. McGraw had vowed to eliminate.

The school schedule was arranged around known needs – planting, harvesting, and general crop-care requirements such as hoeing and weeding – and unscheduled natural occurrences, mostly storms, unusually heavy rains, heavy insect infestations, and deaths. The school year ran from the middle of September through late April or early May, though there would be extended periods of absences throughout the school year, especially among older pupils. Increased farm chores required their time at home.

Nellie McGraw, however, had been quite willing to take advantage of rainy days or downtimes on the farms, when she might lure pupils to the schoolhouse or her home.

She quickly agreed to Bo's plea, delivered on shaky legs and with some stuttering, to help them read Dru's treasure. Surprised but with renewed confidence, Bo went on to explain that his uncle had sworn him to secrecy and that he'd probably want her to take an oath as well.

"Why, Beaujames, that'll be just fine. I'm just as excited as you must be. I love secrets."

Bo thanked her profusely and started toward the door. There he hesitated, turned back, and made a request that he'd wanted to make since first day he had walked into the school.

"Missus McGraw," he asked timidly. "Do you think maybe you could call me Bo? I get an awful lot of teasin'…"

She smiled and wrinkled her nose, like he'd seen rabbits do. "Why, of course, Bo. I've been meaning to ask you about that anyway."

They met the following Sunday afternoon in Nellie McGraw's home, a small, whitewashed house within sight of the schoolhouse. Bo knocked on the door and Dru stood several paces behind him. Seeing his anxiety, the teacher smiled, extended a hand to Bo and stepped out to greet Dru.

"I am so glad to meet you, Mister Dru Sullivan," she said. "Don't you worry one bit. Our secret is safe. Mister McGraw is out back doing some work in his shop. I told him he absolutely could not come back until I told him he could."

Dru had noticed that she had put special emphasis on *"our secret."* He decided that making her swear to an oath wasn't necessary; nor, he was thinking, could he have gotten up the gumption to ask her.

"Lordy, what a pretty woman," he whispered to Bo as she led them through a parlor and into the kitchen. There, on the eating table's blue-checkered oilcloth, sat three glasses of tea, a loaf of home-baked bread and a plate of sugar cookies.

Once they were seated, she went to an oaken icebox sitting near the hand pump which brought water into the house, both quite rare in Shannon County. She lifted the icebox door, chipped some shards into a bowl and returned with it to the table.

"Help yourself," she said.

Dru had brought his precious book wrapped in a newspaper and carefully placed it on the table in front of the teacher. "There you are, Ma'am." He was going to make every effort to talk more like the schoolmarm and less like his normal self.

She smiled and carefully removed the paper. "Well, I do declare, Mister Sullivan. This is indeed a fine book."

More enthusiastically than he'd intended, Bo leaned forward and said, "Please, Ma'am, could you tell us what it says on the front. I could read some of the words, but..."

"Surely I will, Bo." Pointing to each word as she reached it, she began in a soft but audible voice. "It says 'Human Geography, by J. Russell Smith, Book One, Peoples and Countries, State of Kansas."

"Wow," Bo exclaimed.

"I've heard 'bout that there Kansas, but don't know where 'tis, er, it is," Dru said, his facial expression split between awe and pleasure.

"Oh, I believe it's 'way out west somewhere," Mrs. McGraw replied. "I am sure we can find a map in this book that will show us where it is. It's a state, like Georgia, but I really don't know much about the place. I guess this book was used in Kansas schools."

Opening the book to what she said was its "frontispiece," she added, "It was published by the State of Kansas in 1927. And look right here, where somebody's written some names in it: William Lehmbeck, Goldie Lehmbeck, Norman Lehmbeck, and Byron Lehmbeck."

"It must have belonged to them," Bo said, looking at his uncle.

Dru frowned. "Well, I told you I found it next to the railroad tracks and figured it must'a fallen off'n a train. I don't see how I could get it back to them folks, seeing as how we don't even know where this Kan… that place is."

"Kansas, Mister Sullivan. And I wouldn't worry about returning it. I'm sure they got another one."

Dru relaxed his shoulders and breathed a sigh of relief. Bo grinned. Turning the pages, Mrs. McGraw said, "Gracious, this book was meant for pupils much older than you, Bo. Maybe even high school pupils."

"But it's got some words about peanuts in there and Uncle Dru's growin' the best crop in the county. You can ask anybody and they'll tell you it's so."

"Well, Bo, I don't doubt that one bit. I surely don't." She smiled at Dru.

Being extra polite, Bo asked her to turn to a page marked with a piece of newspaper. "Please read this part right here. See, that word right there is peanuts."

"I ciphered that word, too," Dru chimed in. Immediately he blushed, thinking maybe he'd said more than he should.

Mrs. McGraw, who'd known Dru couldn't read, smiled knowingly despite her best efforts not to do so. Clearing her throat, she told them to stand behind her and follow her moving finger. She promised to read slowly.

"Peanuts. Every school boy and every school girl has surely seen something that came from North Carolina, for everybody has eaten peanuts…"

Though he tried not to, Dru interrupted. "North Care'lina? Why'nt it say Jaw-ga, uh, Georgee?"

"Well, I suppose it's because the book was written 'way out there in Kansas and they didn't know about Georgia," Mrs. McGraw said. She looked over her shoulder and smiled at Dru. He blushed and looked away.

"The Negroes brought peanuts with them from Africa, many years ago, and grew them around their cabins on the plantations. White people soon learned how good they were. One of the reasons we all like them so well is because they have almost as much oil in them as there is in butter. In fact, one of the leading uses of this nut is to make peanut butter."

Now Bo interrupted. "Momma makes it some time and stores it away," he said. "Once I had a store-bought jar…"

The teacher smiled and returned to her reading. "The nuts grow under the ground…"

"Uh-huh," said Dru. "If'n it don't rain too hard and wash 'em out or cause 'em to rot…"

"…When they are ripe, the whole plants are plowed up and stacked to dry. Then a threshing machine knocks the pods loose from the plants, just as wheat grains are loosened from the straw. There are…"

"'Scuse me, Missus, but I saw one of them thrashers onct over in Owen County and sure wished I had one," Dru interjected. "Cost a man a lot of money, more'n anybody I know has got."

Looking disconcerted, Bo said, "Well, I hain't seen any wheat 'round these parts."

"It's for making bread, Bo," the teacher said.

"We use corn," Bo went on. "For cornpone, hoecakes, and if there's fish, Momma sometimes makes hushpuppies. Hushpuppies is better'n all the rest."

Mrs. McGraw paused, smiled gently, and turned to look at Bo. "Bo, we are going to have to work some more on 'are' and 'is'…"

Embarrassed, Bo wished he'd never opened his mouth. She changed the subject. "Isn't it nice, though, that we can learn from books like this about what other people have and do?"

Dru's excitement was showing. "Is that why all them folks on the front of the book look so diff'runt?"

"Probably so," she replied, preparing to resume her reading. "Follow my finger, now… There are several counties southwest of Norfolk where…"

She placed the book on the table. "I guess there's a Norfolk in Kansas. I know there's one in Virginia. It's got a large harbor that's always full of ships that travel the world over."

"The one in Kansas, Ma'm," Bo asked.

"No, Bo. The one in Virginia."

"Shhh now, Bo. Let her read…"

"There are several counties southwest of the Norfolk in Kansas where nearly every farmer grows peanuts. In the city of Norfolk there are great warehouses full of peanuts waiting to be sent all over the country."

"Don't send 'em here. We got plenty…" Dru blushed and added, "Sorry, Ma'm."

She laughed. "I can understand your feeling…

"After the farmer has secured all the peanuts he can from the field, the pigs are turned in to eat those that remain in the ground. The pig's nose tells him where the nuts are, and then roots them out for him. In many parts of the South fields of peanuts are grown especially for pigs to harvest, peanuts being very good indeed to make pigs grow."

Looking up, she said, "That's the end of that page. Perhaps we…"

"That's all it says," Dru asked, with some anxiety. "It's all good to hear, but why don't that there book mention our state? I figured we must be 'bout the biggest grower of them things. Leastwise, the folks over to Mayo say so."

"I'm sure that's true, Mr. Sullivan," she responded while turning the page. "But look here. Here's a picture of Georgia peanuts."

The picture was of pigs nosing through a peanut field; she read the caption aloud: "Georgia pigs harvesting a crop of peanuts without cost to the owner and with pleasure to themselves."

"Ain't that picture 'bout Georgia," Bo asked, pointing to the lower half of the page. "It's got 'Georgia' in the words under it." Pointing to the caption, he added, "I see it right there. Can you read that one?"

"Well, we can, but I think that's enough for today. There's so much to read about in this fine book and we are very lucky you found it."

She looked up at Dru and smiled her prettiest smile. Then she put a hand on Bo's shoulder.

"Bo-boy, would you mind taking that glass of tea and a cookie or two out front? I would like to talk to your uncle, if you don't mind."

Bo grinned and left; when Dru emerged with Mrs. McGraw several minutes later he had a sack of cookies in one hand, the book in the other, and a proud but anxious look on his face.

Nellie McGraw waved from the porch. "I'll see you and your uncle next Sunday at the same time, Bo. Bye, now, Mister Sullivan."

When they had reached the road, Bo asked, "What'd she say, Uncle Dru? Is it 'nother secret?"

"For sure it is," Dru responded. "But not from you."

He turned away, ran a hand across his face and seemed to have difficulty putting his words together. Finally, he spoke.

"I'm goin' to learn to read, write and talk normal, Bo. She's gonna teach me."

CHAPTER 13

'I'm lookin' for my t'morrow.'

–Dru to passersby

Pumped up by his Sunday experience and smiling like a Cheshire cat, Dru headed out the following morning to call on Beatrice O'Connell. He hummed with the humming of the Blue Goose's engine and waved at those he passed. Slowing when he saw a familiar face, he leaned out the window and called out, "Good to see ya. I'm lookin' for my t'morrow."

Most grinned and returned the wave; some looked puzzled, as though wondering if Dru had been hitting the 'shine again.

Though he'd been sure he'd find Beatrice O'Connell's big old Victorian house without difficulty, he passed through Munsterville on a road that dead-ended at a cypress-dotted marsh. Missing a second time, he asked directions from a Negro fishing the Tallapaloosa River from a bridge.

"Go back through town 'n take the fust road on yo' right. No 'way you gwine a'miss it. Biggest house in dese parts, right dere in the middle of a big old pecan grove."

Grinning, the man added, "Reckon you ain't from 'round dese parts. Else you'd a sho' 'nuff known..."

Dru frowned and drove off, with wheels spinning and gravel flying; the man quit grinning and went back to his fishing.

Immediately, Dru regretted what he'd done; perhaps the Negro hadn't recognized him, but that wouldn't have made any difference. He felt ashamed, knowing that, among themselves, some colored folks still called the town "Monsterville," a descriptive that time had not erased. A scattered few were old enough to remember when the plantations surrounding the town had been worked by their parents; to Negroes, the word slave was as abhorrent as nigger."

"Monsterville..."

Dru said the word aloud, so he could feel it, while sensing that he'd never be able to feel it like the Negroes he knew: Buttonbottom, Marybelle, Del, gone-to-Heaven Lonny...

Half an hour later, he saw the O'Connell place, right where the old man had said it would be: in the middle of a pecan grove that stretched away from either side of an imposing two-story white house. Looking south, Dru barely could see where the grove ended.

The sight left him with mixed feelings. On the one hand, it increased his anxiety; on the other, it set him to thinking that maybe courting the woman might be worth all the changes he'd begun and was determined to complete. A middle-aged man doesn't go back to school and church and become well-mannered and pleasant unless there's a reward, and a pretty substantial one at that, he reasoned.

Ooops. For the briefest of seconds, he'd felt an uneasiness in his midsection; had his Godspot been about to raise an objection to that kind of thinking? He hesitated, felt nothing more, and decided maybe it'd only been a warning.

"Dagnabbit," he mumbled. "That's twice in one morning. Bad thinkin', thinkin' that ain't like me... Gotta watch it."

Halting the truck in the circular driveway, he left it several feet short of where the circle topped out at the doorsteps. He didn't want to appear too bold – which he truly did not feel.

The porch extended the width of the house. Geranium-filled pots sat on either side of the green-painted steps, and lush green ferns hung from one end of the porch to the other. Rocking chairs were scattered about, and a swing hung motionless at the porch's northern end. Impressed with what he saw, he took a deep breath, nervously removed his new felt hat, checked the soles of his shoes and brushed the seat of his pants.

Then he gathered his gumption, climbed the four steps and knocked on the door, having overlooked the tarnished brass bell and the brass, chain-attached ball used to ring it. The wait seemed interminable, and he was about to reach for the bell's chain when the door was opened partway.

A woman stared at Dru and he stared at her. He figured it was Beatrice's mother, though he never had seen her, and to his knowledge she'd never seen him. Pulling up his gumption once more, he said, "Ma'm, I'm hopin' Miss Beatrice is home. I'd like to visit awhile. My name is Dru. Dru Sullivan, from over Mayo way."

"Why, Mr. Sullivan, I've heard about you. Some real nice things, too. My daughter's in, of course, but she may need some time to prepare herself for a visitor. I know you'll understand..."

She stepped back and, with a gracious sweep of an arm, invited him to enter the foyer. "Why don't you just wait there in the parlor? I'll go tell her you're here and get you some tea while you are waiting."

"Lordamercy," Dru thought as he followed the tall, erect woman through a wider, draped doorway and sat down in the seat she indicated. "Lordamercy, I'm really here. I'm doing it..."

Staring at another draped doorway through which Beatrice's mother disappeared, he rechecked his shoes, then told himself it was too late anyway. He looked back at the path he'd followed across the floor, but the light was too dim to see whether he'd left a trail and soiled it. Dim and cool, it was, just as he had imagined a parlor in such a large house would be; smelled nice, too, as he had imagined a lady's perfume would smell.

Sara's smell was different. Sometimes it was like homemade soap; sometimes it was like a man's smell, but that was when she was all excited and making love.

Dru gritted his teeth, shook his head, and vowed again to forget her.

Mrs. O'Connell reentered the room, walking so softly that she startled Dru. "Beatrice will be down soon and she is pleased you are here." Smiling secretively, she added, "Don't you let on I told you, but she is very, very pleased."

Dru told himself he oughta be pleased at what the older woman had confided. He tried to be, but truth be known he was trying to visualize the woman he was about to meet. Though he'd seen her several times, he'd never really given her a close look; he'd always been too busy looking for a way to get away from her.

Was she really as pretty as other women, and some men, said she was? Could she arouse a man she once had terrified, and likely still did? Or was she going to be one of those dainty little hankie-clutching women who looked up at a man with a superior-but-tolerant gaze? Lordy, how he disliked women of that sort...

Beatrice arrived several moments later, smiling, curtsying, and extending a hand. Dru wasn't sure what to do, so he extended one of his own and touched hers lightly, as he'd seen gentlemen do in picture shows. Though she'd taken his hand and held it for a long moment, as though she was expecting more, he did not kiss it. He had seen men do that in the shows, too, but he never had been able to figure out why; seemed like it might be unclean, specially if a farmer like him did it.

When she finally released Dru's hand, her smile broadened, her eyelashes fluttered, and she took a seat on the sofa where he had been sitting.

"Sit yourself down, Mister Dru Sullivan. Right here next to me." She swirled her floor-length blue dress and gently sat down, leaving, he felt, little room for his wide shoulders and long legs.

Seeing his unease, she grasped the folds of the dress and tucked it up close to her body. He sat down, hoping his anxiety wasn't showing; he still had trouble knowing what to do with his long arms and size-11 feet.

"I am so surprised I hardly know what to say," she continued. "I just never expected you'd ever come visitin'. I am so pleased, really I am."

He'd heard women talk like that before, but the talk always had been directed at somebody else. He blushed, grateful for the room's dimness.

"Well, Ma'm," he said, better than he'd thought possible, "I've been meanin' to call on you for some time. And it'd please me a lot if'n you'd call me Dru."

He was pleased at the way he'd pronounced his words, except for "if'n." He'd have to work on that one, and a whole lot more. He also was pleased when she smiled broadly and patted her hands together. One held a hankie; he tried to ignore it.

"You have? Oh, Mister Sullivan – I mean Dru – that just makes me feel so good down deep inside. I swan, it gets so lonely in this big old house and nobody ever seems to come callin', even on mother. And daddy's been gone so long…"

Her words trailed off, hanging there like a cork bobbing on a fishing pond. Why, he asked himself, was he suddenly feeling as though he wanted to run while there still was time… Had he been fooling himself; could be go through with this?

After an awkward silence, he managed to refocus his thoughts and said, as softly and with as much compassion as he could muster, "I know how you must feel, Ma'm. Our daddy, who was Niall Barnabas Sullivan, he's been gone a long time, too. We've tried to make up for him, us bein' five brothers and a sister, who is Liza. She don't go nowhere much."

He knew he had mispronounced some words again and hoped they'd somehow gone unnoticed.

"Five brothers and a sister. My goodness, that is one large family. You are so fortunate to have such a family."

"I reckon so. An' 'nother brother got killed by a train. We miss him, as you might 'magine. Him an' his wife an' little boy, they was killed, too."

Though the light was dim, he saw the compassion in her eyes and found himself wondering what color they were. He also felt her hand, as she placed it on his.

"Oh, Dru, that must have been terrible. I swan, is there any family that trouble don't visit?"

Despite himself, Dru gulped audibly; he found himself wondering he might be visiting trouble. For the briefest of moments Sara's face sat atop Beatrice's shoulders, a pained, woeful expression in her eyes. Liam's warnings echoed in his ears. He decided to ignore them, and apologized for gulping. She withdrew her hand. "Oh, gracious, Dru, no need for that. Are all of your brothers married? I mean, I've met Mister Jim and Mister John an' I think I've seen Mister Liam, but I've never asked about…

"My goodness, forgive me for askin' such a personal question. I…"

"Nothin' to 'pologize for. Yes, Ma'm, all my brothers took a wife, though Jim lost his awhile ago. Liza married, but she lost her man to the cholera. Me, I hain't, er, have not had the chance, what with all the chores an'…"

He didn't finish and neither spoke for a long moment, during which the parlor clock chimed 11. She smiled, a kind of a half smile, while he prayed she wouldn't ask more questions.

She did, but he was relieved to hear this one, which indicated she'd sensed his discomfort and his need to move.

"Would you like to see the grounds? There are some nice horses out back, though they've been getting old and cranky since daddy passed on. And I just love to walk in the pecan grove, but it's no fun doing it alone and mother isn't up to walking most of the time."

Pausing to look him straight in the eyes, she added sorrowfully, "I'm so alone most of the time I'm afraid to go out there. Specially summertime. I worry so much about snakes, even green snakes. I saw a coach-whip snake out there one time and it was longer'n your arm…"

"I know what you mean, Ma'm. Far as I'm concerned, the only good snake is a black snake. He kills rats and other pesky varmints. I tease them when I can. They get so long that when they crawl into the bushes they'll sometimes leave their tail sticking out. I like to grab it and pull on it..."

"Well," she said, placing a hand at her neck and looking nonplussed, "I reckon that could be fun – for a man, anyway. Uggh. I'd just as soon not see them at all. Gracious me..."

Dru frowned and his Adams apple bobbed again; he sensed such talk wasn't meant for a real lady's ears.

But Beatrice wasn't about to be sidetracked by such, and she quickly regained her composure. Taking his left arm, she squeezed the muscle; Dru avoided her eyes, sensing he'd see in them an invite he wasn't ready to accept. Not yet, anyway.

"I know how you feel, Ma'm... er, Beatrice. Truth be told, I don't like snakes either. Any of 'em..."

"Oh," she exclaimed. "That's one more li'l ole thing we have in common."

Dru wondered about the others, but didn't ask. He was glad to be able to stand up and move somewhere else. Sitting so close he'd been overwhelmed by the sweet smell of her and he wondered where a woman in these parts could find such perfume, if that was what it was.

He also was glad her mother had not shown up with any tea. Iced tea would have been all right, but he suspected it would have been the hot kind that came in a cup too small for a big hand. He'd seen such on the screen at the Dixie.

"I'd like to see the horses an' walk under them, er, those pecan trees, Ma'm. I surely would."

She led him through the dining room and onto the back porch, which she called a veranda. It was quite large, and the well-used cushions on the several chairs indicated Beatrice and her mother spent considerable time on it.

Beatrice was feeling apprehensive herself, and at one point she knew she was blushing. She also knew why: Everything was going so much better than she could have anticipated and she sensed Dru was ready for picking; already she was thinking of ways to get him into her bedroom, which was just above where they were standing.

As they left the porch and strolled into the yard, Dru managed to extricate his arm and get a step or two ahead of her. He felt somewhat better, though some anxiety remained. Looking for things to say, he pointed to the barn and remarked, "Looks like you could use a shingle or two to fix that roof."

"Oh, we simply have not been able to keep up with things since Daddy died. There's an old tractor inside an' it needs fixing, too. I'll wager you're good at such things."

Blushing, he said, "Yes, Ma'm, we still use mules to do our plowin', but I've been 'round tractors enough to know how to work on 'em. Jim, he says we could 'ford one, but he ain't much for change."

"Well, now, you get that one to runnin' and maybe he will change his mind. You most certainly can use it, whenever and wherever you want to."

She had caught up and taken hold of his arm again.

Jim was sitting in his rocker on the front porch when Dru drove into the yard. He looked up from the newspaper and waited for his brother to park the Blue Goose beside the house and come up the front steps and report on his visit.

Dru didn't. He simply waved, called out, "Afternoon, Jim," and disappeared around the side of the house.

Jim heard the backdoor slam, heard the kitchen cabinet being opened, and heard the clink of the soup kettle lid being laid on the iron stove. A moment later, he got up and went to the kitchen, trying his best not to look too curious.

"Saturd'y," Dru said without looking up from his soup. "Saturd'y's gonna be a long day. She'd like to go to Mayo with us and maybe see a picture show. An' she'd like to listen to the radio, to the Grand Ole Opry, with us Saturd'y night. Says she really likes Roy Acuff..."

Dru took a deep breath and looked at his oldest brother. "That is, if I can borrow the truck again. I'd need to pick her up real early an' come back here for ya'll – you, of course, an' John, Jewell, an' the boys, if'n they're goin'."

Dru switched positions and looked through the screen door toward the barn. "An' I'd have to take her back home later…"

Jim's heart was swelling and his eyes showed it. Both men looked straight at one another til it got to be uncomfortable. For the first time in a long time, Jim wanted to hug his brother.

Dru sensed it and went to his room. There, he hugged his pillow; hugged it as hard as he could, and sent up a prayer…

"Dear Lord, if you're listenin', please give me the gumption to hoe the row I've done started."

CHAPTER 14

'I just hope she'll understand...'

— John, as he buys a single bus ticket to Florida

COME TUESDAY DRU AND the setting sun had crossed Arrowhead Hill and told John and Jewell of his visit with Beatrice. "Maybe not my dream woman," he said, "but I reckon sleepin' in her bed might change things..."

He winked; Jewell blushed and hid her excitement by looking away. John seemed seriously preoccupied, however; he nodded, half-heartedly returned Dru's wink, and said, "Uh-huh."

Dru was disappointed, but reasoned that John had been hitting the bottle, was feeling under the weather, or both.

The truth was that John was dealing with his own problem: did he truly believe that the one-way ticket to Florida, which he'd just hidden in the barn, was going to lead to a better life for his family; or was it simply a way of escaping what he felt was a confining, unfulfilling life? Hadn't he prepared himself for something better than a backwoods dirt farm, as a non-participant in the great world conflict for which he had prepared himself?

After a night of tossing and turning, he'd risen before the sun and sauntered to the top of Arrowhead Hill, leaving a meandering path of dark footprints across the dew's silver blanket and the moist sand of a late-night shower. With a 360-degree view of the surrounding landscape, he pondered the pros and cons of the decision he'd already made…

Overall, life was good among Shannon County's hills, forests, swamps, and fields; September had graced Sullivan Road with blue skies, warm days, cool, starlit nights, and the promise of bountiful harvests. Pink, lavender and white boles decorated healthy green cotton stalks and weevils were few. Golden tassels waved from atop head-high corn, and thousands of golden ears already were stored in bins that would be overflowing before cold weather settled in; then livestock would be turned loose in the fields, to consume missed ears and stalks and replenish the earth with trampled refuse and their own excrement.

Green acorns wearing wee brown caps peeked from among oak-tree leaves, and squirrels sat upon the limbs, exclaiming their impatience with switching tails and rasping squawks. Green pecans the size of man's thumb had begun the metamorphous that would turn them dark brown and ready to fall within eight to ten weeks.

Rainfall had been plentiful and August's Dog Days generally had been pleasant for man and beast. The thick, slimy, disease-producing algae that normally covered the ponds in late summer wasn't nearly so widespread. Mosquitoes still whined and bit as the sun prepared for sleep each evening, but insect-eating bats were plentiful and had reduced their number.

Sadly, the Higginbotham family appeared fated to lose another child to a wheezing, feverish illness that Satan apparently had created for the newborn of colored folks. Lonny's murder still tortured their daily lives, though they pretended it did not.

Jewell's mother, the boys' Grandma Dunaway, remained quietly comfortable, and that demeanor appeared to have graced her with good health; she was going on 74 and was seldom sick. No one questioned Grandpa Jack's health; he seemed as an oak tree, tall, serene and ageless.

The older Sullivan brothers, Jim and Glenn in particular, were slowing down, in physical stamina and mental sharpness. Liam and Rufus simply walked through each day as it came and seemed to emerge unchanged.

Increasingly, the Boru family had distanced itself from the community. Old Man Boru was meaner; Sara was a sad, sickly woman, and Magalene appeared lost in an imagined world of angels sustained by the God they served and requiring no food. In the child's mind, neither did she.

Sweet, sensitive Jewell was visibly concerned about all of them: her kin, the Higginbothams, Sara, Bertha and especially Magalene. She tried not to think about Old Man Boru. Her smiles remained warm and deeply engaging, clearly coming from her soul. However, she had become subject to occasional periods of depression, which took her down into a gray world of quiet detachment.

John had noticed without comment; when she learned of his intentions, he reasoned, the depression either would become deeper, or it would disappear altogether when the shock reawakened the innate fight in her character.

Pulling Tom's soiled, wrinkled letter from a shirt pocket, he read it one more time…

"Money to be made… Plenty of jobs for everyone, but you've got to hurry…"

Dropping the letter-holding hand to his side, he looked out across the land: most of it Sullivan land, tied together by narrow, clay-red and sand-yellow Sullivan Road. Liam's two-story farmhouse could be seen two miles to the northeast; Jim's was a half-mile to the north, beyond Bo's Banshee Swamp. On the south the woodlot separated his house from the Boru shack. Half a mile to the west a stand of pines stretched north and south, broken intermittently by the rounded green tops of water oaks and cypress. Beyond them loomed the tops of the Patterson and Johnston houses.

All around him green, bountiful fields stretched away, some reflecting the awakening sun and others emerging from beneath morning mists rising from swamp waters, farm ponds and that treasured fishing stream, Redbreast Creek, a half-mile back of Jim's house.

Sighing deeply, he looked to the south again, at the little tin-roofed house he and his brothers had built a scant 10 years earlier. Cedars and those infernal, too-prolific chinaberry trees – "sex-mad monsters," he called them – sheltered the western edge of the clapboard structure; four pecan trees flourished on its sunrise side. Two of those valuable trees stood in the small pasture that backed up to the woods and wrapped around the south side of the house, separated from it by a small, sloping backyard.

After the pecans ripened in late October and November, pigs would be turned loose to root out those that had fallen and escaped discovery and bagging. The high-protein nuts added to their weight; some were being fattened for slaughter during the winter, when temperatures often sank to freezing or below and there was less chance of contamination or spoilage of the meat.

Despite the physical and mental pain that seldom gave him respite, John was not and never had been a hard man. Not when sober, anyway, and he had not had a drink since Grandma Susan's funeral four months earlier.

Mentally, his stare penetrated the walls of his house and took him back inside. Jewell had, of course, ignored his suggestion that she sleep late and let the boys do the same. For sure, Bo and Arlis were on their pallets; but he sensed she was fully dressed and, basket in hand, was about to go out the back door toward the garden. When she appeared in the yard, he grinned, felt a tug at his heart, and blew her a kiss.

Such a wonderful woman, he thought; such a hard-working, wonderful, loving woman…

Then he took another sheet of paper from the shirt pocket, this one a single, soft-green sheet of folded paper. It was a few months older than the house.

MEMORIES
A poem written Tues. night, March 15th, 1932, by Jewell

I

The words I use to tell him that I love him
They have all been true, I know them to well.
The kisses that I keep for him are the same kisses.
I've got the onlyest heart for him, because I can tell.
John W. Sullivan, a boy good and kind, he's always the same.
I have choosed for my lover, out of a long list of names.

II

But I care for his heart only, and for no other one.
He has kept his love as fair as mine.
I'll be true and wait for him, until his work is done.
For God is the onlyest one that knows our hearts, and He'll send him back to me some time.

III

No thoughts are as faithful as my thoughts of him
That travels from my heart to meet his own.
Each night I say my little prayer alone.
God hears and answers, for He always guides His children safely home.

IV

Now as I sit here and look out my window,
I see lots of little stars.
And all of prayers that I ask are—
Lord, take care of John W.,
Because he is away so far.

V

There is a dear old gray headed mother
Waiting with her heart filled with pain.
She and his Lover,
Trusting that soon the one they love
Will return in health again.

VI

Thus I write on and know
That when he sees this,
Something will tell him
Why I write and how
Between the lines I'm saying that I love him
Just as I always did – as how I do now.

Turning away, John took a corner of the blue bandana wrapped around his neck and wiped his eyes. "Yep," he said aloud, "you're crying some. But it's okay, it's okay. They're gonna be okay. I swear to God they'll be okay. And they're going to have a better life than they've got here…"

He looked down toward Banshee Swamp and beyond it to Jim's house. And without looking back, he headed that way off Arrowhead Hill.

Some 10 minutes later John climbed the back-porch steps, opened the screen door and went into the kitchen, where he found Jim staring at a nearly empty coffee cup. He wasted no time.

"Need to borrow the Blue Goose. Have it back by noon. We need some things that can't wait til Saturday."

"Okay," said the older man, after a brief pause to consider the request and John's abruptness. "But maybe me or Dru oughta go in with you. There's some things we could use."

"Make a list and I'll just charge 'em for you. You and Dru need a day off, and it's gonna rain most all day, I'd say."

Jim frowned. "Well then, we need some two-penny nails and a gallon of whitewash. I could use some Feen-a-Mint. Maybe some Cal-o-Side for my corns. But we can get 'em next…"

"I can remember those things," John said abruptly. He took the keys off a hook, waved a salute and was out the door.

Jim pushed his coffee cup aside and started to get up, but decided against it. "Whatever you're up to, I guess it's important," he mumbled.

Jim always gave his brothers the benefit of the doubt; this time, however, the doubt troubled him.

The rain began even as John turned onto the Mayo road. It was the soft, misting kind, the kind that could indeed last all day and perhaps into the night. Unusual in late summer, such a rain was welcome in farm country; it soaked into the ground and didn't run off like those afternoon cloudbursts, which sent water rushing to the low spots and taking precious topsoil with it.

It was his kind of day. Cool, dark, and maybe a little tearful, when a man could relax and be alone inside himself; when he could stick an arm out the window and feel the cool raindrops sting his skin and know he was alive.

Sometimes, at home, he'd lean his head out of a window and turn his face into the rain; sometimes, when there was no rain, he'd do it to feel the strong, gusty winds that occasionally swept in from the open fields.

He thought again of the lines Jewell had written and patted the shirt pocket to which he had returned them. She had been 15 or 16 when she'd written them, a year or two after quitting school following the sixth grade to help at home. He had ignored the words she'd misspelled, and had been proud about those she had written correctly. And most of all, he had grabbed hold of the sentiment and held tight, even as he had held onto and squeezed his pillow each night up there in that Army hospital.

He tried not to think about the plane crash, but today he couldn't block it out. From the blurred road ahead, a vision emerged of a squeaky clean, sandy haired youth fresh out of Emory Academy in Oxford, Georgia; he saw the boy welcomed by Army Air Corps officer who, despite his military bearing, was unable to disguise his pleasure about John's letters of support from Shannon County officials and some of its prominent residents.

Pretty little Jewell was waiting back home, responding to his love letters with the same fervor he put into his. She'd been very good at drawing cute little hearts and flowers in the margins, and he'd never asked where she got the different colored inks; especially, he'd loved the green ink, which reminded him of the fields and woods and of home.

John's thoughts switched to the reading he had done in the hospital. He'd borrowed books about famous aviators of the Great War from a Captain Ribault, a flight-school instructor. He'd read about Albert Ball, the Briton who'd shot down 44 better-made German aircraft before disappearing into a cloud during one dogfight, never to be seen again. The Germans claimed he'd been shot down by Manfred von Richtofen, the infamous Red Baron. Later, they claimed he'd been brought down by Manfred's younger brother, Lothar von Richtofen.

The British hadn't believed either claim. Nobody, they said, could have shot down Ball. He'd simply disappeared into that cloud and gone on to the Valhalla reserved for brave men who'd already earned their wings down here on earth. He felt somewhat better when he remembered that Lothar's brother, that damned "Red Baron," had been shot down and killed by Canadian flier Arthur Brown. The Baron had crashed amidst a battalion of Australian soldiers, who claimed he'd fallen to their anti-aircraft guns. An Australian Flying Corps battalion had buried him with full military honors.

"Whoever runs Valhalla doesn't take sides," John whispered. "And it's not for me to question that."

The book said allied officials had given the credit for the Baron's death to Captain Brown, the Canadian. "That Brown must have been one helluva man, or just damn lucky," John mumbled. "Too bad he didn't get to him before the bastard shot down all those 80 planes the Germans said he did."

As John drove on, a crossroad appeared through the mist and he let the truck roll to a halt. Then he swung it into the wider dirt road, pushed down hard on the accelerator and slammed the gear into first. The truck roared, the wheels spun, and John shouted through gritted teeth: "Go, you goddamn bird! Go like the wind, down and down and down and scare the hell outa those damned Krauts! Go, go, go…"

The truck careened from side to side, and the realization that he was about to lose control brought John out of his spell. He turned the steering wheel in the direction the truck was sliding, and it came to a halt less than a foot from a ditch. He gripped the wheel so hard the broad backside of his hands were white while his knuckles were a fiery red.

"Yeah, it was like that," he mumbled, after a long moment during which the only sounds were the "swish, swish" of the windshield wipers and the rumble-rumble of the idling Dodge engine.

"Damned plane wouldn't pull up like I asked it to. Told 'em we'd have to build better ones before we could even think about fighting another war. Nobody with half a mind really believed the 'war to end all wars' had ended anything. They *knew* we'd have to build better planes. Damn President Hoover! Damn Congress! Damn the blasted economy!"

John had been pulled out of the wreckage and had spent a year in a military hospital in New York, where doctors repaired his body and counselors, chaplains and friendly nurses tried to repair his soul.

Remembering, he smirked at the irony; not a sneer, though he felt angry enough to sneer, but a halfway grin, a helpless sort of grin, as though he had come to realize, and accept, that he had had no real control over what had happened in that terrible, painful year.

Going into the hospital, he had been a young lay preacher and a tee-totaler, and one of his letters of recommendation had come from a sheriff he'd helped find some unusually elusive 'shiners. Coming out, he'd craved the good liquor he'd been given, mostly by an adoring nurse, and in time he knew he had become addicted to alcohol. He smiled at the memory; though he'd asked often, the nurse never had told him where she got such good whiskey during Prohibition, which had not ended until 1933.

He had been sent home during the summer of 1932, with a medical discharge and reports which said – to him, anyway – that he was no longer of any use to his country. Something in his spine kicked out often when he forgot he wasn't supposed to be lifting things, such as a bale of hay; his knees seized up in cold weather, and when the pain got too much he drank and his soul suffered most of all…

…As it was doing now, even though he was telling himself that he finally had a chance to do something about it.

With chin set, he backed the truck away from the edge of the ditch, shifted into first gear and resumed his journey at a much slower speed, one that covered the miles as if it were in step with the somber day and John's introspection.

"Maybe down there, in Jacksonville, I can straighten out," he told himself. "Maybe I can find what I'm really meant to do and I'll feel like I'm worth something again.

"I just hope she'll understand…"

CHAPTER 15

John fesses up, Jewell is furious, and Bo recalls a terrible secret

JEWELL DIDN'T understand. John told her of his plans shortly after Dru left, and now she was stomping around the front porch telling him he'd lost his mind.

He retreated to the front yard, hoping he was out of range of anything else she might throw. She'd missed with a book; but then she'd headed toward the kitchen, where firewood was stacked against one wall and iron skillets and pots hung on another.

"Jewell, for the sake of God and the boys, calm down. You haven't heard my thinking…"

Reappearing on the porch empty-handed, she put her hands on her hips and shouted, "Thinkin'? Thinkin'? What kind of thinkin' could come outa your head that would have you going' off and leavin' me and Bo and Arlis alone? You been drinkin', John? I might understand that!"

"No, no, I haven't been drinking. I've been thinking a long time and now I'm doing what I believe is best for all of us. I'm just asking you to hear me out…"

She didn't respond right away; with undisguised anger, she stood in place, hands on hips and staring daggers. Then she reached down and picked up the thrown book, prolonging the silence while inspecting it for damage.

"John, I really could understand if'n you'd been drinkin'. I hope you hain't, but I'd understand if'n you had. That'd be better'n havin' to think you've gone plain loco."

Jewell turned away and reentered the house; John walked out onto Sullivan Road, pulled a Lucky Strike from the package in his socks, lit it, and walked off into the gathering darkness. He figured it'd be best to wait til she'd gone to bed; missing supper was a far greater option than facing up to more of her wrath.

With a final glance over his shoulder, he mumbled, "She really oughta do something about that temper." He walked deeper into the darkness, down past the mailbox and up Arrowhead Hill, where he sat down on a rock and lit another cigarette.

"Hell," he said, "I'm getting it from both ends." The rock was wet, and the sky promised more rain.

Jewell, meanwhile, was preparing supper for the boys by rote, paying little attention to what she was putting on the table. Bo had overheard the argument and, based on prior experience, didn't ask questions. He also acted as he generally did in such circumstances: he tried to be a peacemaker.

"The eggs is good, Momma. Thank you."

Arlis frowned. "Din't we have 'em for breakfast?"

"Shhh, Arlis. Can't you see Momma's busy..."

"Shhh both of you," Jewell said. I'm thinkin'..."

John had waited til after Dru had left before dropping his bomb. Jewell had mixed feelings about that; Dru might have tried to talk some sense into him as well. Now, at least, she understood why John had been so quiet of late, and suspected that his plans likely had something to do with his leaving the house so early.

So much she didn't understand... Maybe he was right and she oughta calm down; maybe she oughta hear him out...

John, meanwhile, had his own concerns. Quarrels, or conflicts of any kind, were the worse kind of threats to his sobriety. For four months now, he'd managed stay clear of the half-filled jug in the barn. Sitting in the dark on a rock on Arrowhead Hill, he noticed that the red glow of his cigarette was dancing in agitation; his hand was shaking, he knew, and he flipped the butt into the darkness.

When John did venture in, the only lamp burning was the one in the small front room. He left it alone, peeked into the bedroom to see if she was asleep; then he retraced the few feet, blew out the lamp and dropped his overalls, shirt, boots, and socks where they fell. He found a resting place – on the make-do settee – and was still tossing and turning when Jewell spoke to him, very calmly.

"You really goin' to Florida?"

"I am, Jewell. It's for the best…"

"Just you? Without me'n the boys?"

"For a little while, anyway. Til I get a better picture of the possibilities down there."

"You'd go without me'n the boys?"

"Julie, honey, be reasonable. We can't all go at once. You know that."

He usually called her Julie at such times, or when they were sharing a moment of intimacy. She knew it was one of his ways of trying to bring her to his point of view.

"You're askin' me to be reasonable? After you promised that when you got back from that Air Corps and that New York hospital we'd never be apart again. I got it in writin', John."

She was crying now. Bo stirred and sat up on his pallet, but said nothing.

"What are you tryin' to do, John? You want to run off to that…, that place 'way down there and leave us here alone, to bring in the crops and kill the hogs an…"

"Oh, I didn't say I was going right away. You're just imaginin' things. I'll stay til winter and then go. That's still more'n three months away…"

"And how did you get to this way of thinkin'? Who put you up to it?"

"Your brother. Bantry. He wrote and said folks like him are makin' $10, maybe $15 a day working in those yards. They need welders and carpenters and sheet-metal men, and they're working shifts around the clock."

"I didn't hear no mention they need farmers."

"Aw, Julie, they train a man. If Bantry can do it, you know I can."

"Don't you go talkin' down on my brother, John. And how come my brother wrote you? He never cared much for you. How 'bout me? What'd he say 'bout me?"

"Well, he really didn't…"

"Where's the letter, John? I hain't seen no letter?"

"I haven't got it right now."

"You hain't? And you expect me to b'lieve you? Lordamercy, John. Don't play me for a fool."

"Honey, I'll get the letter in the morning. I put it away for safe keeping."

He paused and let out a resigned sigh. "Come to think of it, it was addressed to both of us. I'm real sorry; didn't want to bother you til I'd thought it through."

John tried to remember the precise wording of Bantry's letter. It was hidden in the barn, next to the jug, his coffee-can bank and the newly deposited one-way ticket.

"I get so sick of the way you do things, John. I truly do. You say you gotta think things out first. How 'bout us? How 'bout me'n you? Don't you think I oughta be part of the thinkin'? Where's all the sharin' you promised?"

Neither said anything for a while; then Jewell began again, so quietly he had to lift his head to hear her.

"And you won't be leaving til winter, til after the crops are in and the hog-killin's done. Well, that's all well and good. But you'll be gone Christmas, leavin' me and these boys alone at that holy time. How do you think the Good Lord's gonna see that? You know He's already down on you, the way you sneak around drinkin' when you think nobody knows, and the way you beat on me when…"

Thinking of the boys, she stopped abruptly. Arlis might be sleeping, but she knew Bo was not.

Sullivan Road

The rain had started up again the next morning, but the dismalness was nothing like the mood in the house. After breakfast, Bo took Arlis to the barn and they sat down in the rear of the wagon. From there, they could look across Sullivan Road and see the white cotton bolls grinning from the greenery; it wouldn't be long before there'd be bent-over backs moving down the rows, straining backs hauling big bags made of sewn-together croaker sacks.

Moments later, the field disappeared beneath the gloom of a creeping fog bank. Arlis began to sniffle and soon was crying outright. Though he was about to break down himself, Bo tried to calm his brother. Neither feared anything so much as a confrontation between their momma and daddy.

"It's gonna be okay," he said, putting his arm around Arlis' shoulders. "You know how they are, fussin' and then kissin' to make up." Trying to smile and make Arlis smile, he added, "Sometimes fussin' is better, ain't it? I mean, you'n me, we don't need the kissin'…"

Despite himself, Bo thought about the terrible secret he shared with his daddy. He'd had not known it was so terrible until he had reached an age where he could begin to understand that there were many kinds of hurts, and that when the outside and inside hurt at the same time it was terrible awful. And a boy, even a brave boy, wanted to cry and pray and do both at the same time…

…Jewell had been on the bed in the front room, the one right off the entry porch and closest to the road. Though he was still a month shy of being three years old, Bo had known something was very wrong. His momma was moaning and occasionally she'd scream and arch her back; her face was wet and between screams she held her teeth tightly together.

Crying, Bo ran outside, where a colored man passing in a wagon found him standing in the middle of the road. Hearing Jewell's cries, the Negro removed his hat, limped to the door, knocked, and then stepped inside. A moment later, he stumbled back out, placed

Bo in the wagon and whipped the mule two miles to Doctor Arlis' house.

When the doctor reached the house in his automobile, Bo's brother had been close to being born on his own. And once he had been born, Doctor Arlis had come back outside, stomping around and cursing while he waited until the Negro and Bo returned in the wagon.

"Where's John," he demanded. "There's welts all over that woman's body and she didn't put 'em there herself!"

The Negro – Bo'd been too young to remember his name – shook his balding head from side to side and, clearly terrified, responded, "I doan know. Truly, I doan. It's de way I said: I wuz jus' passing by and…"

"Oh, the hell with it! Goddammit, she says she knows where John's at, and if she ain't gonna say, the hell with it!"

The anger also scared Bo, who resumed his crying and threw a screaming tantrum when the doctor restrained him from going to his mother's side. He was a long time calming down; and though Doctor Arlis remained until long after the Negro fetched Liza to help with Jewell, Bo remained too scared to tell what he knew…

…John had gone into the barn's hayloft that morning and had not come down, as he had done lots of times, mostly when Jewell was visiting kin or off helping somebody who was sick in bed.

Bo had tried to suppress the awful memory of that terrible day, and with the passing of more time it might have faded altogether. But John, in a fit of guilt during another drinking episode, had called him aside.

"Bo, boy," he'd said, "you remember the day Arlis was born and I was out there in the barn and ol' Doc Arlis was looking for me?"

Embarrassed and anxious to get away from his daddy's foul-smelling breath, Bo had responded quietly: "Yes sir. I do."

"Well, you hain't never mentioned it to no one, have you?"

"No sir."

"Well, since you're my good buddy-ro as well as my big boy, you won't ever mention it, will you? It'll be our own little secret?"

"Yes sir. It'll be that. For sure…"

Sometime later, during one of their visits under the live oak tree in Jim's yard, Bo had told his Uncle Dru about John's request, and of what he remembered about the day his brother was born.

Dru had let the story sink in, and then pulled Bo onto his lap and hugged him. "Son," he'd said, "there's all kind of ways to put a load on someone, 'specially a lovin' and carin' boy like you. They say the Good Lord don't give a body more'n he can carry, but sometimes it's a head-scratchin' wonder…"

Bo never knew whether Dru had ever talked to his daddy about it, and it never occurred to him to find out why Liza had apparently had not told anyone. He had prayed often that the Good Lord would take the memory from his own mind and bury it somewhere he'd never find it.

It had not happened, and never would…

Jewell had named Arlis for the doctor, a common practice among the poor. Some said it was partial payment for the doctor's services; others joked that it was a way of letting others know they'd been able to afford a doctor.

CHAPTER 16

*'The Good Lord's ... opened the door, Jewell
We gotta walk through it...'*

IN THE DAYS FOLLOWING John's declaration, the little house on Sullivan Road was as somber as a sunless midwinter day. Jewell alternated between shallow anger and deep depression; John sulked and stayed out of her way, and Bo and Arlis retreated into themselves.

Bo had a double-dose of upset – at the way his momma and daddy were acting and at word that his beloved Uncle Dru was going to marry that Munsterville woman, Miss Beatrice What'shername.

Neither Jewell nor John ventured off the property; they simply weren't up to dealing with others. Jewell was determined to wait until John had changed his mind or, at the very least, agreed to take his family with him; John didn't feel up to facing the objections and ridicule he suspected he'd face, especially from his brothers and sister.

Jewell prayed a lot. Though she knew she wasn't acting as the Good Book said a good wife should, she did something she'd seldom done: she tried to justify her vindictiveness and anger. What else could a wife and mother do, she asked; how could You, Dear Lord, allow this to happen; what have I done to deserve to be left behind like an unwanted cat?

She read the Bible on the porch by lamplight, after John had gone to bed on the make-do settee; he wasn't welcome in her bed any more. She searched the pages for justification, thinking it might be hidden among those big words she'd never quite managed to comprehend, much less pronounce.

And then one day she stumbled across some well-worn pages John must have torn from a book during his academy days. On one page, someone had underlined the words: *"Women sometimes forgive a man who forces the opportunity, but never a man who misses one."* Below was a man's name the likes of which she'd never seen: Charles Maurice de Talleyrand-Perigord, 1754-1838.

Quickly, Jewell put the tattered pages back where she'd found them. Though the message was not one she'd sought, it grabbed hold and wouldn't let go. Didn't John say he was looking for opportunity for the whole family? Could he possibly be right? Would he be missing a great opportunity because of her stubbornness? Was this why God was not telling her that she had a right to be resentful?

She also had begun to wonder whether God purposefully had led her to the tattered page containing the message; maybe it was another of his miracles… She wasn't sure, but she knew she was not happy and could not go on this way much longer.

Finally, she relented. Weary from arguing, tired of crying, and uncertain of her position, she pulled him off the make-do settee on a frosty mid-November night and told him to come to bed. There, she placed her gown-covered body against his and melted the frost between them.

"John?"

"Uh-huh?"

"You know I love you, don't you?"

He didn't respond right away. "Well, I don't know, but… Lordamercy, you'd have to if you felt about me half as strong as I feel about you."

"I do, John, I do. An' I know you're doin' what you feel is best for all of us. 'Specially for me'n the boys."

"I am darlin', I am…"

"And if I hadn't fussed so much 'bout you wantin' to go without us, you'd have felt I didn't care one way or t'other. John, darlin', I fuss because we love you so much and 'cause the world's gonna be a harder, lonelier place with you gone."

Rolling over, he kissed her long and hard. "Julie, honey, I know you've been hurting bad that I'm goin'. But you're right about why I'm going, and that is the only reason I'm going."

Running her fingers over the bristles on his cheek and feeling the dimple in his chin, she didn't respond right away. He sensed what was coming.

"John, I know it's been awhile since you drank, but are you sure you'll be able to stay off'n that likker down there. I mean, bein' alone and all…"

"Jewell, I won't be alone and you know how Bantry feels about my 'likkerin''. That was the first thing he asked about in his letter."

"Which I hain't seen yet."

"I know, I know. I'll try again to find it. Maybe tomorrow… But Julie, honey, there's one thing I want you to know and believe. I've tried to do better and I'll keep on trying no matter where I am. But being here, feeling I've failed everyone, I just feel that I, that we… I feel we have to try somewhere else.

"Even if I could stay sober here, it wouldn't change the way we live, doing back-breaking work from sunup to sundown and sometimes after. We'd still be poor, sitting out here in the middle of the woods and fields, knowing full well that the best we could expect was that the next year and the year after that the crops might – and I say might, Jewell – carry us through another year.

"I've been out there and I've seen the way others live, and while it hasn't been so good anywhere lately, it's still been better'n what we got or can expect to get here. I've ridden in motorcars that would make the Blue Goose seem like a rickety old wagon. Even with the rationing and them damned coupons, I've been in A&P stores that have things Tip Evers' store will never have. I want my own radio and I want my family to have one.

"I want…"

He paused, and his hands tensed upon her back. And in a whisper, he added, "I want things we haven't got. Things we'll never have here; things we might have down there, away from this infernal red-clay, sand-filled Sullivan Road and swamps and gnats and snakes…

"And I want our boys to get good educations and to be able to hold their heads high, not having to feel they're not as good as others. I want them to have the chance to make something of themselves, like the chance I had and, and…"

John paused, and Jewell could sense he was trying not to cry. Getting hold of his emotions, be added firmly, "And I don't want them to fail and have to apologize to anybody or anything. Like I failed…"

"But, John, you hain't failed. You still got us." She'd said it softly, almost prayerfully. He squeezed her, squeezed her hard.

"I know, honey. And I want you, us, to have all that I think the Good Lord wants us to have. He's opened the door, Jewell. We gotta walk through it and see what's on the other side."

Come morning, Jewell rose with a smile; but it was a sad smile, rooted in resignation, and she knew she'd have to try hard to be happy if she was going to look happy.

Dru had set her to thinking that way, an unexpected result of another of their debates about why he didn't go to church.

"Jewell," he'd said, "if you pray the same thing night after night, it's bound to come 'bout; you're jus' gonna walk in that there d'rection. I can do that in the fields or woods and don't have to wear no fancy clothes or lissen to that Pemberton rattlin' on 'bout things…"

She'd understood his thinking about prayer; but the bickering had continued til Dru had gone off by himself to repeat, several times, his prayer that Jewell quit trying to save his soul. Lordamercy, he was about to give it away anyway, to Beatrice O'Connell.

Through the front window, Jewell saw that John was on the front porch, looking out across the fields with a determination she had not seen in a long time. She decided she oughta get busy helping him prepare for the fall harvest and to fatting the five hogs for killing when cold weather set in for the long haul.

She also figured this might be a good time to suggest, for the umpteenth time, that maybe he could build a privy...

Moving to another window, she looked down at the woods to the southwest and decided they needed moving back some so there'd be more room for crops. She'd made up her mind that she and the boys would be following John to Florida come spring and there was nothing he'd be able to do about it. She'd need to find a tenant to farm the 40 acres, and reasoned that it would be easier to find one if there were more tillable land.

And she was of a mind to pick and sell most of the velvet beans growing among the corn stalks. Normally they were left for the livestock to eat when they were turned loose in the field after the corn had been harvested. Picking the beans could be a horrendous task; when freezing weather sets in, the soft velvet on the pods freeze into thousands of short, blood-letting needles, and even a pair of good gloves don't last long.

With John gone, there'd be more eggs to sell in Mayo. Arlis didn't like them anyway. And maybe this year she'd try real hard to get the boys to pick up as many overlooked pecans and walnuts as they could, before the hogs were turned loose on them. Mister Jamison, who'd opened Mayo's first drugstore during the spring just past, had told her he could use them at the soda fountain for banana splits and such. She'd never had a banana split, but Mister Jamison said the nuts would "enhance" them, whatever that meant.

When she told John about adding more planting space in the southwest field, his open mouth showed his surprise and he asked, "Well, now, who's gonna do the cuttin' and the digging-out and burnin' of all those stumps."

"I will, of course," she declared. And she promptly picked up an axe and headed out across the field between the house and the woods, a distance of some 500 yards.

"Migod," he said aloud as he watched her go, "she'll do it, too."

John got a warm feeling inside and his Adam's apple bobbed a couple of times. Jewell was special, he knew, and always had known. What he was feeling now was that he'd better find a way to let her know it.

Maybe come Saturday in Mayo…

CHAPTER 17

Mayo, tall stories, and Julie's revenge

TWO SATURDAYS back, Dru and Beatrice O'Connell had gone along on the ritual jaunt into Mayo, with Jewell and John sitting in the truck bed with the boys. Jewell hadn't minded; neither had John, though he wasn't about to pass up an opportunity to rattle Beatrice's straight-laced bearing.

For much of that five-mile trip, he had good-naturedly kept up a running harangue: "Doggone, we're smotherin' in the dust back here!" followed by such shouts as, "Hey, Dru, Julie's dryin' up in this wind! She's 'bout to blow away…"

Knowing John, Dru had turned a deaf ear; Beatrice, however, hadn't known what to think, and on this Saturday the couple rode to town in a one-horse surrey borrowed from Liam. Knowing Liam's feelings about Beatrice, Dru hadn't said why he needed it; not wanting to talk to Dru more than necessary, Liam hadn't asked.

Upon arrival in Mayo, the grownups browsed the stores along the town's only shopping street, meeting friends and trading information. Depending upon the sharer, the tittle-tattle could be gospel or it could be gossip; most knew the difference, but enjoyed it anyway. Simply smelling the new overalls in the dry goods store was worth the trip into town.

Almost everybody looked in on Sid Jamison's shiny new drugstore. Built atop the remains of a burned-down barber shop, the drugstore had a long, marble-topped counter, stools, glass-topped tables, iron-framed chairs, tiled floors, ceiling fans, and so many unfamiliar "cures" and new drugs that it was awe-inspiring for all and confusing to many, especially those who had difficulty reading the labels.

Then there was Missus Kimball's Dixie Theater. The small red-brick building was several hops, a score of skips and an impatient run across railroad tracks cutting north and south through the broad town square. Mayo's shopping block was on the sunset side; the theater and the Southern Rail Road's (SRR) huge warehouse on the opposite. Missus Kimball showed westerns, cartoons, and serials every Saturday. Bo liked Gene Autry movies best, in part because he liked to sing Gene's songs when no one was around to hear.

Mexicali Rose was his favorite. He also cottoned to Lash LaRue, Tom Mix and Monte Hale, and he didn't mind Roy Rogers and Dale Evans, mostly because of Gabby Hayes, a funny, tobacco-chewing old man whose beard was always dirty.

Grownups loved Missus Kimball, too. For a nickel, they could deposit a child in the Dixie about 11 o'clock and she would watch over them the whole day through, if need be. She didn't tolerate orneriness; misbehavers often listened to the picture show from a mock jail in the lobby. Only for a time, however; she ran the shows three or four times a day, making sure the "outlaw" and latecomers saw the complete program.

"You know, old Mayo is gettin' to look so much like a carnival that I wouldn't be surprised to find somebody sellin' tickets one of these Saturdays," John remarked as Jim guided the Blue Goose onto the open field next to the Dixie.

"You reckon?," the normally taciturn older brother remarked. "Betcha it'd be that Halbertson fella. Never saw a man lookin' for so many ways to earn a nickel."

"A nickel is fertilizer for growin' a dollar," Jewell chimed in. She helped Arlis to the ground and told him to stay close to Bo, who had vaulted from the truck bed and was racing toward the theater. One of his Buster Brown's came off, however, and toddling Arlis caught up. Both hated store-bought shoes, preferring the croaker-sack lace-ups Jewell made for them. Those they wore on cold days and for school; the store-boughts were for Sundays and trips to town. Despite the expense, Jewell had pinched pennies to insure that Bo have one good pair of shoes – "shoes that'll last and be Arlis' when he gets big enough."

Jim took his time getting down, waved to Dru and Beatrice and wondered about John's unusually good humor. Stepping to Jewell's side, he spoke just loud enough for her to hear.

"What's goin' on with John? Seems too happy."

Jewell didn't have time to respond. John already was leading her across the railroad tracks; with his free hand buried in a pocket, he was fondling the two dollars and change he'd taken from his secret cache in the barn.

"Julie," he said, "I know you're gonna go down to the dime store and visit with Mauve Shaughnessy and that Helen woman, but I hope you'll find some time for me to take you into the mercantile later on."

With an Irish twinkle in his blue-grey eyes, he added, "I got something in mind."

Warily she looked at him. "You? Askin' me to go the mercantile? What's goin' on, John?"

"Oh, I was just thinking you might need a new dress for Sunday. Or maybe a pair of them new shoes, maybe ones with high heels. You'll need them once you come down to Florida…"

"John, you know we can't afford anything like you're talking about," she said, halfway hoping he was serious. "You hain't been holdin' back, have you?"

"Smart folks always save for a rainy day, and there's been a lot of rain lately," he said, smiling secretively.

She returned the smile. But she was thinking, "Smart folks? Lordy, what do you take me for, John? You want to go to Florida and you think it'll ease your mind if'n you buy me a purty or two?"

Still, she couldn't wait to tell Mauve, Helen Riley and the other ladies. She wasn't sure, however, that she'd be telling them about John's coming trip to Jacksonville. By asking around, she'd found that it was more than 200 miles away.

John was at his best in Mayo. Maybe not always on his best behavior, but he had a way of charming folks, and he did it so well that it sometimes made them forget his shortcomings. With a dry tongue, his wit was sharp; sometimes it could be downright biting.

John headed straight for the hardware store owned by Harry Hilldebrand, a well-educated man who had attended the University of Georgia in Athens. If a fellow could get by some of the big words, he'd say Harry's wit was even sharper than John's.

As he entered, the usual four or five men were standing around Harry's rolltop desk. Of average height and slim, Harry was leaning back in his chair, with one foot propped on the desk and the other on the floor. His fingers were tucked under his suspenders, and he was listening with a straight face to James Walker tell of how he'd just moved a house to a new site three miles distant. John stopped behind Walker, unnoticed by him.

"Why, I tell ya', Harry," Walker was saying, "we got that old house up on four sleds, all tied to Jason's pickup, and we moved that whole thing without losing so much as a plank..."

Instinctively, John cleared his voice. "I know that for sure, Harry," he said. "I was right behind him pulling the water well and didn't spill a drop."

Big, burley and still on the shy side of 30, Walker turned abruptly, even as John continued.

"And when James asked a man of color where to find the place he was goin' to set that house down, that Negro told him he reckoned it was about a mile and a half before you got to the bridge and..."

Sullivan Road

"Why, John Sullivan, you bastard! Are you mockin' me? I oughta…"

"…And he asked that fella, 'How'd I know when I was there,' and the Negro says, 'Well, I reckon you gotta get to the bridge and come back a mile and a half. Elsewise, you likely gonna miss it.'"

Walker raised a clinched fist and waved it menacingly.

John backed away, raised an arm and put on his most engaging smile. "Why, no, James, I'm not mocking you? Nary a bit. You're in the company of the town's biggest liars and I just naturally figured…"

While the others protested, Walker's glare melted and he lowered the fist. "Well, now, my story's true and if'n you don't believe it…"

Harry dropped his foot to the floor and stood up. "Aw now, James, we believe you. Sure we do. I've seen the house sittin' this side of Hicks Road and I ain't one to believe it just grew legs and walked over there."

Pausing, he winked and added, "Specially since it's a mile and a half from that bridge…"

When the laughter subsided, Harry added, "John's John and he takes some gettin' used to…"

"I'm used to him all right," responded James, a proper, church-going man who preferred to be called James rather than the more informal Jimmy. "I understand he's a drinkin' man with a smart-ass mouth."

John's face turned a deep red and for a moment he considered raising his own fist.

But Harry spoke up again. "Now, James, that ain't no way to talk about no one. John didn't mean no harm to you. He didn't. And if you want to know about a real drinkin' man, let me tell you about old Mr. Sampson and about…"

He stopped momentarily, to allow the nervous laughs to have their affect. Walker's composure returned; John saw the change, grinned, and said, "Yeah, Harry, go ahead. And don't leave none out."

"Well," said Harry, sitting down again, "it was back before John there went off and tried to kill himself by becoming a one-man

Army Air Corps. Yessiree. This old organ grinder name of Sanchez'd come through town ever' now and then and he had a monkey that he prized like you'd prize your only milk cow, or even your wife. Old Sampson, he was part Cherokee and he'd get hell-raisin' drunk and when he couldn't stand it no more he'd take himself home to bed where he'd spend four, maybe five days sleepin' it off. Lived right over there behind the Dixie.

"Well, me'n John and one or two others – Sean Cleary and Ronnie Houser, if I rightly recall – got on the same hellish bent and borrowed that organ grinder's monkey one day and we took it in and tied it to the foot of Sampson's bed. With us standin' just outside his bedroom watchin' and listenin', old Sampson opened one eye and saw that monkey. Then he opened the other eye and he said right out loud, `Fella, if you're not a monkey I'm in gosh-awful trouble. And if'n you are a monkey, you're in trouble!'

"And he pulled a pistol from under his pillow and he shot that poor monkey dead! Dead as a polecat that had the effrontery to turn its stink-shootin' hindside to a shotgun-totin' coon hunter!"

Harry paused to let the laughing subside. "Cost us $20 to pay for that monkey and Sanchez didn't think it was funny at all. Not at all. He never did come back to this town, and word got back that he was goin' 'round tellin' folks Mayo was a hellhole full'a drunks and folks who were goddamn crazy."

"Well, hell," said Harry Blivens. "That's a good story, and true, too. But lemme remind you of the time you'n John and that Stuart boy and half a dozen other fools went and put old John Hartley's mule up in his hay loft. Ho, boy…"

"Yeahwellhell, I reckon he must'a been 'bout as mad as that Carter fella who was so young he was just learnin' how to plant beans o'er t'ward Munsterville," chipped in Harvey Dreyfuss. "'Member when we tied his wagon to the back of his barn wall, down low so the rope was outa sight?"

Dreyfuss waited for the new round of laughter to subside. "He like'ta wore out that mule tryin' to pull that wagon outa that barn. And what's worse, his new wife got tired o' waitin', walked straight in there and cut that doggone rope!"

Sullivan Road

The men were beginning to repeat themselves when Jewell stuck her head through Hilldebrand's door, way up at the front of the long, narrow store. Knowing that ladies didn't get within earshot of such gatherings, she leaned in just far enough to make herself heard.

"Yoo-hoo, John, you 'bout ready for me? I hain't forgot what you promised."

Harry feigned horror. "You promised somethin', John? You lost your cerebral matter?"

John ignored the guffaws and winked secretively. "Sure did, Harry. Tell you about it another time."

Jewell had indeed told Mauve, Helen and others about John's generosity, as well as the probable reason. They had urged her to go ahead and squeeze him like a pinched penny and deal with the reason later on.

When Jim drove them home that night, Julie sat in the middle beaming with pride; John sat next to the window, holding paper bags containing a $1.39 Kitty Fisher cotton print dress; a 99-cent blue skirt and a 49-cent white blouse; a 47-cent black ladies' bag; a 93-cent pair of high-heel shoes, and a 5-ounce bottle of Buddha Oriental Toilet Water costing one dollar. Ralph Farmington, owner of the mercantile, had accepted John's $2 and change, plus an IOU for $2.23. Sid Jamison at the drugstore had an IOU for a dollar.

Altogether, Julie Sullivan had spent $5.23 on herself – an amount that caused Jewell Sullivan, God-fearing country wife with a sixth-grade education, to drop to her knees at bedtime and pray for forgiveness.

John had another concern. Before he had left Harry Hildebrand's store, Harry had called him aside and asked, "Did you know that Sheriff Nobles has been around asking about Dru. Wants to know if he owns or ever has owned a .410. Also wants to know how he's been spending his time these days. Says he don't for a minute believe he's gonna marry that O'Connell woman."

"Damn," John muttered as he'd left Hildebrand's and walked to the Blue Goose. "Nobles ain't the smartest of men, but he thinks he is...."

"Wonder what he's thinking?"

CHAPTER 18

A cold winter, ill omens and far-reaching changes

NOVEMBER RACED AWAY AND winter followed with changes that were to alter, drastically alter, the lives of several Shannon County families forever, as well as the lives of those not yet touched by events in this wee, obscure part of backwoods Georgia.

John Sullivan waited until after Thanksgiving, and Bo's seventh birthday, then went to Jacksonville alone. His present to Bo was a Gene Autry belt, the finest gift Bo said he or anybody else could ever get.

Shortly before Christmas, Dru Sullivan married Beatrice O'Connell and went to live with her and her mother in the big house on the far side of Munsterville. Family and friends wondered why they hadn't waited until Christmas and celebrated with a really splendid affair. Dru told Jim they hadn't because the O'Connell women hadn't wanted to spend money on a big wedding – not even his money which, he said, they already were spending as their own.

The Deep Springs Methodist Church was nice, Beatrice allowed, but Judge Homer Winslow in Munsterville could marry them just as well at the O'Connell plantation. Knowing her love of fancy things and of putting on a show, Dru was hard put to understand her decision. But since he didn't care for fancy things and shindigs, he accepted her decision and felt good about it.

He also tried to learn about Catholicism, with which Beatrice said he would have to be familiar before they could marry. After a while, however, she stopped teaching and the wedding went on. Reluctantly, her mother agreed; she had participated in the aborted instruction, appreciated the reasons, and was a genuinely happy woman at the wedding.

If Sadie Boru had been a stay-at-home before, she became a virtual shut-in after the Sullivan/O'Connell nuptials. Word spread that she'd taken to drinking heavily, and folks tied into Shannon County's gossip line simply shrugged and said, "Well, what would you have expected?"

Sadie's older daughter, Bertha, made it to school every now and then, but Magalene was seldom seen, even in her own yard. Those who did see her said she seemed to be living in a fanciful world of her own making and might be losing her mind.

Old Man Boru got meaner and meaner, and wasn't even welcome any more at the weekly card game at Tip Evers' store. Passersby said they'd seen him in the yard at night, waving a jug and howling at the moon, even when there wasn't a moon. He'd disappear for days; apparently he had taken to going to the other side of Big Springs Swamp, from whence he'd come and old cronies remained. Men and women from the other side of the swamp were seen at the Boru house, an altogether new development. It was something proper folks openly worried about, and which sometimes got mentioned from Preacher Pemberton's pulpit.

The Higginbothams weren't seen much. Mostly, folks figured they didn't come around because of the cold weather and there weren't many odd jobs after hog-killing time. They still mourned Lonny's death; most still believed he had been murdered, despite the Sheriff Nobles insistence that he had killed himself.

Perhaps to ease his own conscience, the sheriff had visited the Higginbothams occasionally as the weeks had rolled into months.

Always he reported that his "'vestigatin'" just supported his belief: that the death had indeed been a suicide.

"Hain't even been able to find anyone, white nor colored, who can 'magine anyone wantin' to kill that boy," he said, so often, the Higginbothams believed, that it sounded rehearsed. "Why, I didn't know so many folks 'mired Lonny much as they did. You had a lotta reason to've been proud…"

One man who definitely didn't believe Lonny had taken his own life was Jacob Faulkner, the insurance man. He showed up one day with a $25 check, saying it was the payoff on the policy on Lonny. Buttonbottom and Marybelle said they didn't recall having a policy on Lonny, and couldn't have afforded one anyway.

"Our company doesn't make mistakes," Faulkner had insisted. "This check's made out to you and I ain't 'bout to send it back."

The weather had turned very cold in mid-November, a downturn John had jumped on quickly to hasten his departure. Cornering his brothers on a Saturday in Mayo, he had convinced them to move up the hog-killing tour and start at his farm so he could get on down to Jacksonville and help out with the war effort. Wisely he had added that it also would relieve Jewell and the boys of the responsibility. None of the Sullivan brothers felt he should be going to Florida alone…

When the clan gathered on November 20, 1942, the Higginbothams also answered the summons. With Lonny's pet pig gone, they had a single hog of their own and relied on what they'd get for helping others to get them through the winter.

Marybelle was especially popular when the fattest of the Sullivan hogs were rounded up and slaughtered. She didn't mind stripping out and cleaning hog guts; then she'd stuff the long, translucent entrails with ground-up hog meat, herbs, and other seasonings she'd gathered in the woods and swamps. And at day's end she'd stand beaming over a tubful of choice pork sausage, weary but unable to mask her pride.

Liza Sullivan told her the same thing year after year: "I just never got the hang of that. I can't for the life of me 'magine how you do it!"

Marybelle accepted the flattery, but knew the last place Liza and the other white women wanted to stick a hand was in a dead hog's steaming belly.

During that quiet off-season, Del did get into Tip Evers' every now and then, and one time he asked whether everybody enjoyed seeing the stars through the ceiling as much as he did, or sleeping with one finger stuck in a hole in the wall to cut down on the draft. Because it was Del and he was grinning, the half a dozen in the store laughed with him.

John, Jim and Liam laughed as well; but then they looked at one another, followed Del down Tip's hand-hewn log steps and caught up with him as he headed out the yard, on foot.

"Get in the back of the truck, Del," Jim said. "That fallin'-down shed over at Glenn's has got some nice wood on it. And he's been meanin' to chop up them trees that August storm took down…"

Del grinned, nodded and told himself, "A colored man's gotta ask fur whut he needs in dis world. Whut he needs, not wants." He completed the thought as he stared at the three Sullivans, already sliding into the truck's cab.

"Mebbe someday a colored man'll get a li'l of whut he wants, too. 'Jus' as long as there's good white folk."

Del remembered something Marybelle had told him, when he was a small boy learning his first prayers: "Allus be askin' the Lord to take good care o' the good white folk, Delphi. And always ask Him to make more of the good uns."

Del tried not to forget, but sometimes he felt uncomfortable praying in such a way. He wondered whether white folks ever prayed for more good colored folk, and whether they prayed to the same God.

He had asked Marybelle about that one night, when he was ten. "Shore dey do," she'd responded, after an uncomfortably long wait. "Dey just doan know it."

Being a married man, Dru didn't visit Bo like he used to, nor was he able to meet as often with his nephew and Mrs. McGraw. Bo missed him terribly.

On those days when he did top out on Arrowhead Hill and come strolling on down, he'd sit and talk for a few minutes and Bo would get to feeling sad about how sad he looked. Bo tried asking him about it, and even tried to find out just how far he could go in asking. One day, he slapped him on the backside and asked, "Uncle Dru, why's yore face nigh on to as long as a mule's…"

Dru didn't say anything, but his sideways glance froze Bo right down to his toes. And it hurt deeply.

Come early January the Christmas-New Year's recess ended and Bo was relieved when school started up again. His mind was kept busy with studying, and his hands were kept busy with helping his momma during the short January afternoons. His heart never seemed to rest, however, and it worked hardest during the cold winter nights.

With their daddy gone, he and Arlis were put to bed shortly after supper, before the fire died down and the cold took an even harsher grip on the wee clapboard house. Bo felt he shouldn't be treated the same as Arlis, since he was now the man of the house. Jewell kept telling him that's what he was, and she always was praising him for doing a man's work. But she also said he needed his proper rest to do a man's work.

After a while, Bo figured she needed those early nighttime hours to be alone and read the Good Book, which she was doing every night, and to say her prayers. He suggested a couple of times that she let him read and pray with her. But he stopped asking when she told him one very cold night, "Bo, you sweet young man, your momma really does need some time to herself these nights. You'll understand one day."

He'd gotten a mite indignant. "Momma, you know I understand. Ain't that part of bein' grown up? Ain't I gettin' ahead of all the rest in school?" Then it came to him: She was missing his daddy very, very much. And, he reasoned, a man oughta know that a woman like his momma wouldn't want to be seen crying.

Still, he watched her from the bed when she'd be sitting on the floor using the fire for a reading light. One night, he watched as she took two letters from inside the Bible. The thinner one she read quickly, paying special attention to one part of it:

"There is no telling when he will be released, and he remains in great pain after all these months. He says he wants to stay with you until he is well when they do release him. If he has to come back up here (to this New York hospital) it will kill me. For I have seen how it is now. They just brought in another boy and he was dead. His plane fell and burned up with him in it...."

It was dated March 31, 1931, and signed (Mrs.) N. B. Sullivan, John's Mother. In time she had become Jewell's beloved Grandma Susan. Everyone's beloved Grandma Susan.

The second saved letter, dated nearly six months later, was from John and much longer. Jewell read it for some time, laid it aside, cried audibly, and began reading again.

U.S. Army Hospital,
Langley Field, N.Y.
Monday p.m., Sept. 11, 1931

My dear darling Jewell,
After a long time I am once again able to write you, the dearest one in all the world.

Dear, you will never know how I have suffered. It has been awful, and I still suffer greatly but not quite so much. Dear, you sure like to have lost John that time. I guess mother has told you all about it, as she has been here ever since Friday a.m. At least she was here when I woke up.

I was unconscious from Thursday til Saturday. I think, dear, that it was my love for you, and your prayers, that kept me alive. It was so terrible for me to breathe, and it hurt me so and does yet. My side and my back hurt me so bad and every breath is like a knife is in my side, but they say I can get up by the last of the week. That is, if my knees don't give out on me. They still hurt real bad.

But dear your two sweet letters came this a.m. and oh how proud I was. They did me more good than all the doctors in New York could ever do.

Jewell, darling, you are the sweetest thing in the world. One of your letters was the dearest, sweetest letters in the world. Understand, dear, they were both sweet, but the last one was the sweetest.

You said, dear, that one of my letters made you feel bad. I'm sorry, s.h., I did not intend for it to do so. I must have been worried about something else. My little girl has (meaning Jewell} been sick and I hope you won't be any more.

I won't ever fall in love with any of the girls up here, and or anywhere else.

It was here that Jewell broke into tears. She had read the letter scores of times and always cried when she reached this part. Not because of the sentiment expressed; that genuinely was welcome, and it was beautiful. But why, she wondered, had John even mentioned other girls? He'd done that in the past, before he'd gone off to what she thought of as that "awful old Army." She had wondered then whether he was hiding something, or just trying to make her jealous.

Jewell, dear, please believe me when I tell you that there is no other girl for me but you. Won't you do that? I could not love anyone else, dear, you were made for me. I believe God sent me down there to you. And oh how I wish I was there today, to lay my aching head in your lap and you could brush my hair back. I think that I could go to sleep, for I haven't slept any since about 3:30 Sunday morning and then for just a few moments.

And so I lay here hour after hour, thinking of my dear blue-eyed girl waiting for me, and looking at your little picture.

Dear, you don't know how much I love you. You don't realize the torture that I go through here, away from you...

The fire did as it usually did so late at night: the wee, blue and gold flames struggled as though gasping for breath and became too dim for Jewell to see John's penciled words. She tucked the letter back inside the Bible, got to her feet, stoked the dying embers, and added another log. She knew John's 12-page letter almost by heart, and never failed to be proud of him for telling her in an earlier one not to take a job in the shoe factory in Sligo until he had come home and discussed it with her.

But her sister, Annie Mae, lived in Sligo and had a spare bedroom. Jewell had taken the job. "Never told you that, and reckon I never will," she said as she went to bed.

As she lay beside Bo and Arlis, Jewell told herself for the umpteenth time that everything was going to be all right – or hunky-dory, as she often said. The crops had been good, bringing in almost $450 for the cotton, peanuts, corn, and some dried vegetables from her garden. Most of it already was owed, for seeds, flour, cornmeal, salt, pepper, sugar, and other staples, as well as repairs and essentials needed to keep a small farm going.

She'd heard once on Jim's radio that truck drivers in New York sometimes earned $9 a day, or $54 for working every day but the Sabbath. Even with her poor education, she had been able to figure the driver could earn as much in two months as the farm brought in for a whole year. That had rankled her – but it also had rekindled the feeling that John may have been right about going to Jacksonville.

Turning over and pulling the quilt under her chin, she mumbled, "Way past time to bury that fuss, anyways..." And her last thoughts as she drifted toward sleep were of the day when Jim drove John to Pine Shadows to catch the Greyhound to Jacksonville...

Jewell had sat in the front seat between them. Though a cold and unrelenting wind was blowing, Bo and Arlis threw such a fuss that they were allowed to go along, with Bo hunkered down in the open back of the truck and Arlis squeezed into a ball on his mother's lap.

Despite his best efforts, Bo had cried like Arlis when the bus had departed, with John waving from a window seat. Jewell didn't and Jim hadn't. But she had cried going home, and Jim almost had while trying to comfort her. She'd also cried herself to sleep for several nights thereafter. Bo and Arlis had heard her and in time even Arlis understood that she needed to cry and he could help her best by holding back his own tears.

And Bo, being the man of the house, continued to get up first and rekindle the smoldering ashes. The sun slept later now; he envied it and sometimes told it so. And he performed his last nighttime chore with special care, heating the bricks for tucking under the covers just before going to bed with Arlis.

He'd tried once or twice to get up and re-heat them when he heard Jewell coming to bed. But she'd put a stop to that, saying he should have been asleep a long time ago. For some time afterward, he'd feign sleep until she came to bed, so he'd be available if she changed her mind.

They still didn't have a privy, and they still had to use the bucket under the bed to relieve themselves at night; and if the weather was too cold or too wet to go into the woods or fields, they used it daytime as well.

John had said he'd be making good money and would send some to hire Del or somebody else to make them a privy. The money hadn't come and Jewell rationalized that he hadn't been gone long enough to get settled and get a job.

Bo figured that even if his daddy had sent any money she'd probably hidden it to buy their tickets come spring. And, spring, he now knew, was going to be a long time coming.

CHAPTER 19

'Lord, why's it gotta be so?'

– Jewell, after Little May's death and
witnessing Magalene's pathos

JEWELL DREAMED OF THE Higginbothams one January night, and the dream began with a vision of Marybelle's small black fingers struggling to insert the wavering end of a length of thread through the eye of a needle. It reminded her of a biblical allegory – that it would be easier for a camel to crawl through the eye of a needle than for a rich man to enter the Kingdom of Heaven.

Compared to the Higginbothams, her family was rich – at least in having enough food, warm clothing, more land to cultivate, good health… And then she remembered May, now two years old, as she had looked on that cold, hog-killing day back in November; she'd been a fragile, coughing child with a runny nose and eyes glossed over with mucous.

Was the dream an omen? Was it a reminder that she hadn't visited the Higginbothams in some time? Were they in need of vegetables? Did little May need medicine? Were Marybelle´s home remedies sufficient to keep the child alive through the winter? John had said some came from her African heritage; most, however, had been passed to her by a Choctaw squaw who knew the benefits of herbs created from yellow daisies, wild turnips, comfrey roots, and dandelion roots.

Rolling back the covers, she shushed her startled older son and stepped into the freezing January morning. "Go back to sleep, Bo, an´ let me get the fire goin'," she whispered. "We oughta be switchin' off chores ever' now and then, anyways."

Rubbing his eyes, Bo reluctantly agreed – and Jewell was alone to talk to her heart. She carried with her the dream and its visions, but left on her pillow the increasingly worrisome concern that John wasn't keeping his end of the bargain; he still hadn't sent any money.

"I want to walk with the Lord today," she whispered in the pre-dawn darkness. "I've got good deeds to return, good deeds that are lovin', and I don't want to hear no mean thoughts."

Touching a match to a stick of fat lighter'd, she shoved the resinous pine chip beneath the triangular end of a cleaved chunk of wood and willed that it accept the hissing blue flame. It did, and quickly: a yellow finger stood up, danced around in the cold air, and then stood tall.

Jewell walked to Bo's favorite morning window and stared across the dark woods at the soft blue and yellow light pushing up behind them. She smiled tenderly, and with cold fingers closed the nightgown at her neck. She had not yet worn her new chenille robe, a Christmas gift left by John. It was too nice to muss up, she felt, and it could wait until they were together again.

Reminded of John, she whispered, "Some of the favors I've got to give back are for you, John. Those Higginbothams, they love you, too. And it seemed they loved you best when you was drinkin', like they could see the sufferin' an´ it was somethin' they knew about."

Plumbing the deepest recesses of her feeling self, she added, "Like maybe they knew you in a way I never could. Like maybe they knew a man don't bring sufferin' on himself 'less'n there's a worse sufferin' he needs to hold down…"

She crept back into the bedroom, donned her old flannel robe and shook it into place. Then she went to the kitchen, struck a match and lit the fire; the kerosene-doused woodchips and corncobs ignited quickly. Smiling, she said aloud, "Well, now, it looks like we got a good day comin'."

Taking a slab of bacon from a ceiling hook, she turned back to the stove and, very gingerly, felt to see whether it was sufficiently hot. She sliced the bacon and laid the slabs side by side in an iron skillet, wondering as the meat sizzled whether the slab and sausages given Marybelle for her work during hog-killing had lasted this long.

She hoped they had. But she knew she was slicing bacon from a slab hung in the smokehouse the previous winter; it had had time to cure properly and was safe to eat. Bacon not cured for at least seven or eight weeks was not safe to eat.

Had the Higginbothams been able to wait that long? Had they been eating uncured meat, meat that wasn't safe to eat? Pausing, she remembered that the two Higginbotham children who'd already gone to their Maker had been ill of some kind of stomach trouble, the same kind of an illness that now threatened May's life. Was there a connection?

"Lordy, you'd have to think so," she whispered. "Trouble is, they ain't gonna tell what they been eatin'… or not eatin'. And they ain't gonna beg for what they hain't got. They're too proud to do that, ever…"

An hour later, with the sun up and melting the frost. Jewell climbed onto the seat of the wagon Junebug had brought to the front door. Bo had hooked her up, but Junebug had learned what was expected of her and generally cooperated. Bo begged to go, but was told he had to stay home, watch over Arlis and await the mail man.

"Maybe there'll be somethin' from your daddy," she said.

"If so, can I open it? You know I can read…"

She pondered the question and looked down into Bo's pleading face. "For certain, Bo. You can do that."

Jewell patted the burlap sack on the wagon seat, and prayed there was something in it to help the sick child. Among its contents were eight eggs and half of the bacon slab, from which she had prepared their own breakfast.

To Jewell's knowledge, none of the Higginbotham young'uns ever had been seen by a doctor, and Marybelle had brushed aside suggestions that she call one for May, even when the child was retching and throwing up blood. "Mebbe later," she'd said. "God's gotta have his chance to do wif her as He will…"

Though she had no doubt about Marybelle's faith in God, she knew the real reasons: There was little money in the Higginbotham household and Negroes just did not go to a white doctor in a white man's world. There were no Negro doctors in Shannon County.

Jewell patted the sack of medicines she also had packed. It contained a half-empty bottle of Creomulsion – good for coughs and colds, she knew, but probably not the right thing for a two-year-old. It could tear up the stomach of a man or woman and make them crazy in the head, if the dosage was too great.

The bag also had a container of Requa's charcoal tablets, for indigestion and sour stomachs, as well as a nearly empty bottle of Roche's Embrocation, for croup and whooping cough. Both Bo and Arlis had gotten some help from that medicine, but Jewell worried whether it was too old to be good any more.

Then there was the bottle of castor oil, which always seemed to work for the boys, John and sometimes for her, when nothing else would. It was Kellogg's, which Mister Sampson, the druggist, had sworn was nearly tasteless and the best available. The bag also contained some of the garden harvest Jewell had canned last fall.

Marybelle met her at the cabin door, accepted the bag and, clearly embarrassed, thanked her. But she did not invite Jewell inside; "Doan want the sickness spreadin'," she said.

Over and over Jewell said, "I understand, Marybelle. But you know I'm willin' to chance it…" Over and over Marybelle apologized.

And Jewell finally left, telling Marybelle, "I understand," and telling herself she did, but did not want to.

May passed on a few days later, and nobody outside the Higginbotham home knew about it. Not until several days later, when Marybelle went into Tip Evers' store looking to trade homemade soap for hominy grits. Asked about the child, she responded, "May? Oh, she's gone back to her Maker. We done took her to dat Holy place in de woods and put her next to her sisters, Susie an' Belle."

Jewell cried when she got the news, during one of her visits to the store. And she was still wiping her eyes on the return trip, as she approached the Boru shack and saw Magalene standing in the yard, barefoot and wearing a thin, sleeveless cotton dress. She called Junebug to a halt, and then had the mule pull the wagon beneath the chinaberry tree under which the child stood, looking up.

"Your mama know you're out here without a coat 'an bonnet," Jewell asked softly. "You'll catch your death of the wintertime sickness."

Magalene didn't respond. She ignored the fine sleet bouncing off her upturned face and continued to stare at the tree's bare limbs, starkly grey and naked, and whispered a question just loud enough for Jewell to hear: "Where's all the angels? Did they die like the leaves?"

With arms wrapped loosely around the trunk as far she could reach, Magalene circled the base, looking up and saying, over and over, "Where's all the angels? Did they fly away 'cause they're scared? Did they die? Angels can't die…"

Jewell shook her head, sadly, and bit down gently on her trembling bottom lip. Dropping down from the wagon, she took Magalene by the hand, stroked her long, matted hair, and led her to the front porch.

"You go on inside, now," she said. "If you need anything, or you just get to feelin' lonesome or hungry, you come through them woods and visit me. It's wintertime and there ain't no snakes to bother you."

Magalene still didn't look at her. But she smiled at something only she could see and went into the house. Jewell watched her go, and returned to the wagon. Snapping the reins, she set her chin and gnashed her teeth; gnashed them so hard that it hurt, and she forced herself to relax and let Junebug pick her own pace.

"Such an awful old world," she told herself as her own home became visible through the falling sleet. "May, who probably didn't have to die – and Magalene, who probably will die if somebody don't look out for her. And John gone off and me and the boys pining away.

"Lord, why's it gotta be so? It just ain't possible this is the way you want it to be…"

CHAPTER 20

Jewell's divine reassurance, Bo's satanic confrontation

JEWELL SLEPT LITTLE THAT night. A firm but loving voice kept telling her to be kind to herself; she wasn't responsible for tragedies only an all-seeing, all-knowing God could understand and permit.

She hadn't lived long enough, the voice said, to realize that faith flourishes in a middle ground shared by pain and the need to survive; and that if faith does not grow, the pain kills it.

She rolled about the bed, bouncing off Bo on one side and squashing Arlis on the other. She spoke aloud, saying, "Is that you, Momma Susan? If it is, what you're saying is beyond me; I'm findin' it hard to understand…"

"Oh but you do, sweet Jewell. You must. You've got to have the faith to believe that God has a reason for everything, the good and the painful. When you truly believe that, your faith will grow, the pain will dry up, and you will live."

"Is that what Marybelle is doin'? Buttonbottom? Is that why they can just take a child out an' put it in a cold hole and go on livin' and pretending' everything's fine? Is that what they do?"

Though Bo was shaking her and begging her to stop talking and crying, she struggled to hold on and get a response. "Don't go 'way… Please don't…"

From faraway, the voice answered…

"Just keep on loving and caring, dear Jewell." And from further away, it concluded. "But remember you can't do it all; leave the Lord some room. You can help, but let Him tell you how…"

Jewell sat up, reached into the darkness for Bo, and pulled him to her breast. Whatever she said was muffled by the embrace. He remained still for a long moment, then asked to be let go.

"You okay, Momma? You was ravin' somethin' awful…"

"I'm okay, Bo. Let's try to go back to sleep. Looks like it's the middle of the night…"

"It is, Momma. But let me put on 'nother log and I'll come right back."

The sun was up and peeking through the frosty window panes when Jewell heard the boys coming into the kitchen; without looking up from the frying bacon, she said, "Bo-boy, I'd like you to go 'an see Magalene."

Though he was still wiping the sleep from his eyes, Bo suddenly became very alert. "Aw, Momma, why'd I want to do that?"

"Cause she's been a good friend to you and she's needful, that's why."

He screwed his mouth around, like he'd just tasted something sour, closed one eye and shook his head from side to side. Sensing what he was doing, she turned away from the stove, put one hand on a hip and wagged the spatula at him with the other.

"Don't go play-actin' with me, boy," she said. "A boy your age oughta have friends and, bein' older, she done you a big favor when she took the time to play with you. Now she's actin' strange-like and you oughta try to help her feel better…

"If that Sara ain't still mad about Dru and will let you come 'round, and if her crazy old daddy ain't there…"

The last part Jewell said mostly to herself; Bo was on the verge of having a fit, but not so his mother could see or hear. To himself he mumbled, "Done me a big favor? Done me a big favor! If you only know'd what she was doin', and who was makin' who feel good…"

Aware that he was mumbling and not caring what he was mumbling about, Jewell turned back to her cooking. "You do it, boy! Right after breakfast."

Bo didn't hang around for breakfast. Saying "Aw, Momma," again, he slipped out of the house and, by habit, headed for the chinaberry tree. But realizing that was the last place he wanted to be, he turned about and wound up standing by the road.

Picking up a rock, he chunked it across the far-side ditch and groaned when it clipped off a boll of cotton the pickers had missed. Remembering the trouble he'd caused, and the pain he'd felt, when he'd killed the mother bird with a similar throw, he suddenly felt sad. A quick look around assured him no one had seen his proficiency this time. Not that it made him feel any better; he still had today's problem and it wouldn't let go…

Magalene. A girl, just a girl and a bothersome one at that. But, he recollected, before she'd started that Doctor Pete stuff it'd been more fun to be with her than waste his time trying to teach Arlis how to do things. She was a good tree climber and she liked to look for shiny rocks and arrowheads almost as much as he did. She wasn't always asking silly questions like Arlis and, being older, she'd actually been helpful in some ways; like showing him that the Boru pig purred like a hoarse kitten when scratched between the ears, and how he'd learned to roll over when she offered a carrot or potato.

"Momma, she says pigs are smarter'n most folks," Magalene had told him. "Specially if you're nice to 'em. Nothin', even a pig, likes to be poked at and kicked 'round. Bein' nice is so 'portant, don't you think so, Bo?"

Yep, she said it just like that; he hadn't answered her question, figuring it was mostly girl talk and he didn't know quite how to reply, being a boy.

Bo had another rock in his right hand, and he tossed it up and down and jiggled it around, looking for a place to throw it that wouldn't get him in trouble. He walked up the road a bit, and looked toward the Boru's house beyond the woods. Feeling a twitch in his stomach – likely from being hungry – he remembered his Godspot and asked it what he oughta do. It didn't answer; he'd always taken that to mean it didn't agree with him, so he decided to forget he'd asked.

His Uncle Dru popped into his mind, though, and reminded him of something he'd once said: "If what you're thinkin' don't feel right, think 'nother way. Maybe that'll get that Godspot up and goin', and if your new thinkin' has you goin' the right way you'll feel all warm inside."

Resigned, Bo tossed the rock into the weeds, hoping there wouldn't be anything in there that might get hit and killed. Except snakes. They didn't matter. Then he spotted a shiny stone, sticking out of the red clay over by the ditch, and he went over and picked it up.

"Magalene, she'd like this one." He felt good and warm saying it, right down there above the tummy. And smiling about how nice the stone felt when he rolled it around between his fingers, he decided to take it through those woods and show it to Magalene.

Several yards and a lot of bushes, brambles and fallen trees later, he was halfway through the woods, where he paused and pondered the warm feeling. Part of it still was up there around his Godspot, but another part had slipped down into his groin. His peter was swelling and he found himself remembering that Magalene's Doctor Pete game really had not been that unpleasant...

The path came out just behind the pig pen, and Bo stopped long enough to shush the occupant and make another decision. To the right was the shed where Magalene took him to play her game; to the left the path skirted the pen and led straight out into the yard, in clear view of the house.

Bo went left – and wished he hadn't. Old Man Boru was standing at the woodpile, scratching his behind and leaning on an axe. That was scary and, though it was clear the man had been splitting firewood and hadn't seen him, Bo began backing off.

He did it quietly, but not quietly enough. Reaching back with one foot, he stepped smack-dab on a pile of cans in the burned-over trash pile. The cans rattled, and Bo thought he was going to die.

Old Man Boru, a big man with a huge belly and wide, sloping shoulders, looked over one of those shoulders and spotted him. The only part of Boru's face visible to Bo was his brow, his steel-gray eyes and his big red, round nose. The rest was covered with a matted black beard that sagged onto his chest.

Slowly, the man revealed another of his features – his great teeth, one of which was gold and all the more visible because the teeth on both sides of it were missing.

Lifting the axe and wrapping the other hand around its handle, Boru turned to face Bo.

"You," he said, "whut'er you doin' over here? There ain't nothin' over here for you!"

Bo gulped but couldn't respond. He wondered why the old man – he must have been 50 – acted nice when he was with his momma and daddy; he'd smile without showing his teeth and take off his hat and reveal the bald corridor stretching from the front to the rear of his head. It was all the more pronounced because of the long hair bushing out on either side.

"Asked you a question, boy. You gonna answer ta'day?"

Bo tried to open his mouth, but it wouldn't budge. With great effort, he did manage to remove the foot from the pile of cans and began to feel with the other for open ground behind him.

"Now I reckon you got it in mind to run, boy. Well, you just do that. Old as I am, I'll betcha your ass I kin catch you afore you hit that there tree line."

He raised the axe and took a menacing step; then he took two more, patting the handle over and over against the palm of his other hand.

Bo stopped feeling for running room. "If I'm gonna die," he told himself, "there's some things I wanna say first."

Then he put his hands on his hips, frowned and shouted, "You're a mean old man, Mister Boru, and I don't care what you do to me. You'd have to answer to lots of folks, me bein' just a boy…"

Boru stopped, and his furrowed brow relaxed. He halfway grinned.

"Whut's that you say? I'm a mean old man? Boy, you don't know the half of it…"

"I know you treat Aunt Sara bad, and you won't let the girls come out to play like they used to."

"I treats Sara bad? Boy, you don't know whut you're talkin' 'bout an' it hain't none of your goddamn bizness, anyways. They're mine, an' I do with 'em as I wants to do with 'em, you hear! You goddamn Sullivans, whut the hell do you know? Goddamn tater-eatin' Irish!"

"If my Uncle Dru was…"

"If your Uncle Dru wuz here, boy, we wouldn't be talkin'. You'n your Uncle Dru would be high-tailin' it back through them woods, an' I'd be a whalin' the air an inch behind his butt. Both your butts!"

"No sir, you wouldn't."

"Y'as boy, I would. Bigod, I would!"

Bo stood his ground, and Boru appeared to have decided to stand his. Neither moved, but Bo sensed that his gumption had about run out.

Boru surprised him. He stuck the axe handle into the ground and leaned on its cutting end. For what Bo felt was an eternity the man stared at him, with one eye closed and other squinting.

"Boy," he finally said, "you got some gumption an' I likes that."

Bo tried to hide his trembling and believed he succeeded. "Thank you, sir. My Uncle Dru's got gumption…"

"Fergit your Uncle Dru, lessen you want to tell me why he don't come 'round here no more. Couldn't be 'cause he married up wit' that there hag o'er Munsterville way?"

Bo felt the hackles rising on his neck and back, but he sensed this wasn't the time to pay attention to them.

"He does too come 'round. To visit us. He don't say nothin' 'bout Aunt Sara."

Bo knew he was lying, and figured the old man also did. "'Ceptin' he does ask about her, ever' now'n then. Wants to know if we've seen her and things like that."

"Don't he ever ask how she's doin'? Hell, ever'body knows he's had a hankerin' for my gal."

"Yes sir, he asks that. But I never know'd he had a hankerin' for her."

Now, Bo *knew for sure* he was lying and figured his bobbing Adam's apple was betraying him.

Boru grinned again. "Hell's faire boy, I reckon you wouldn't know a hankerin' man if you saw one…"

He paused and the grin went flat. Then he threw back his shaggy head and laughed aloud.

"'Ceptin' Sara, she did say…" He paused long enough to close off another loud laugh and catch his breath. "…She did say she caught you'n Magalene in the shed over there doin' what you ought not a'been doin'."

"She didn't see us doin' nothin'. She didn't!"

Boru stopped laughing and stared hard at Bo, who took a step backward, expecting the worse. But the old man shook his head from side to side, closed one eye and squinted through the other.

"I already said you got a man's balls, but don't go pushin' it by callin' me a liar. As you grow bigger 'uns, you'll larn to git it wherever an' whenever you kin, an' if you ever git to be a real man you'll be danged proud to let on you did git it. But as fer your Uncle Dru, if he ever comes round here ag'in, I'll kill his sonofabitchin' ass."

He took two steps toward Bo and slapped his left palm with the axe handle, very hard. To Bo, the first slap sounded like a shotgun blast, and the rest were almost as loud. The old man kept talking, but Bo didn't hear him. He had skirted the pig pen and was too far into the woods to hear anything but his own thrashing feet and heavy breathing.

Frowning, Boru watched him go. Then he walked around to the other side of the pigsty and, using the axe handle, spread the limbs of a young water oak. The grass beneath was flattened to the ground, like somebody had been sitting or kneeling there. He reached through the lower limbs and picked up one of several cigarette butts scattered about. Some were brown with age.

Boru noted that all were handmade. Frowning, he said aloud, "You got balls, boy, an' you may be old 'nuff to smoke 'em. But you for sure ain't old e'nuff to be rollin' 'em like that…"

CHAPTER 21

'I'm a'scared of that man, Bo.'

– Dru, after hearing of Boru's threats

WHEN BO STUMBLED INTO the house and told Jewell about his confrontation with Old Man Boru, he was red-faced, breathing hard and talking so fast that she had to restart him several times.

After he got most of it out – all but the part about him and Magalene – she went to the back steps and looked toward the Boru house which, John had said, peeked through the leaves-shorn wintertime woods like a bad dream. She stood stone-still and straight, hands on hips; Bo thought she looked as rigid as a dead pine that didn't have any needles and couldn't bend in the wind.

"Or won't," he muttered. Likely, he reasoned, she was thinking about walking right through those woods and giving Old Man Boru the what-fors; and if she'd wasn't going to do that, she might go get his Uncle Dru and maybe Uncle Glenn and turn them loose on the monster, Dru being the strongest Sullivan and Glenn the biggest. Dru was back home at Uncle Jim's now; he said he couldn't stand dealing with those O'Connell women day after infernal day.

"What you gonna do," Bo asked again. He was about to ask a third time when she closed the door, leaned down and looked him in the eyes.

"I'm gonna pray some more. Seems sometimes that's all a body can do."

She rumpled his hair, the way his daddy did, and smiled sadly. To Bo, it looked as though she hadn't heard a word of what he'd said about his head almost being chopped up by a madman with an axe. He was about to say as much when she spoke up.

"I know what you're thinkin', Bo-boy, but the best thing we can do is pretend your fuss with the old man never happened and stay away from him. We can't be lettin' his mean old ways turnin' ours away from the ways of the Lord.

"Nothin' wrong with turnin' the other cheek, like the Bible says. But you can do it without bein' close enough for him to slap you…"

Bo was flabbergasted. Turn the other cheek? Let him be? Let that old bear of a man get away with scaring a boy out of a year's growth? Ain't no way!

Bo didn't say those things, but he sure was thinking them. He also was thinking it was time to gather up his gumption and brave that infernal Banshee Swamp one more time.

There was no sign of Dru when Bo loped into the yard, gasping for breath after his race through the swamp and the deep sand of the rut road leading out of it. Halfway through another fearsome thought had put more "git" in his get-up-and-go: Was it possible that Old Man Boru had been born in the swamp? Was that where he went when he'd disappear for days on end?

He'd ask Uncle Dru about that, too…

Bo found him in the barn, currying the mules, and he didn't waste any time getting to the point.

"Uncle Dru, Old Man Boru just about killed me with an axe and if you're my best buddy-ro like you say, you'll go take one to him. I was…"

"Whoa, boy. What's this you say? Old Man Boru 'bout to kill you with an axe?"

"Yes sir, he was chasin' me with it and sayin' all kind of mean things. Said 'em 'bout you, too. That man don't like you none at all, Uncle Dru!"

"Don't care none what he thinks of me, Bo-boy, but I don't want him messin' with you. Slow down now and tell me what you're talkin' about."

The man and boy sat down on a bale of hay and Bo repeated the story he'd told his momma. When he'd finished, he looked up to see Dru staring at the straw-strewn floor, holding his fingers against one another; the man was silent and Bo figured that whatever he was looking at was in his mind and not on the floor.

"You gonna do somethin', Uncle Dru? You ain't gonna let him…"

Dru draped an arm around Bo's shoulders. "Bo, Bo, let's just calm down a mite and think this thing out. Got some questions of my own, like what he said when you was standin' nose-to-nose with him."

"Uh-huh."

"When he mentioned me, what was it he said, and how did he say it?"

"He said if you came 'round he'd chase your, er, your hiney all the way back to where you come from. And he was shakin' that axe and shoutin' when he said it."

Neither spoke right away. Then Dru cleared his throat, removed his arm from Bo's shoulders and spoke so quietly that Bo had difficulty hearing him.

"I'm a'scared of that man, Bo."

"But Uncle Dru, he's a big old fat man and you're a big strong man. You ought'na be afraid of him. Why, you could…"

"Not that kinda scared, Bo. I mean I'm scared of what he might do, of what he might have done already."

"Well, I don't know 'bout that, 'ceptin' I ain't as big as he is and I am scared of him right down to the bottom of my feet."

"It's good to be scared at the right times, Bo, and it's good you're scared of him. No tellin' what he might do if he got on a likker tear. But I'm thinkin' 'bout Sara and them girls. Magalene hain't gone crazy by herself, and I for sure don't know how Bertha 'pears to be walkin' a straight row…"

Dru paused, marked the ground with a toe of his boot, and added, "And Sara. Poor, poor Sara…"

"I know, Uncle Dru. Maybe it's because you went and got yourself hitched to that, er, you married Aunt Bea."

Without looking up, Bo tried to hide a face full of disgust; Dru sensed it anyway.

"Now, now, boy, it's okay that you don't like Bea. Not many folks know what's hidin' behind them brown eyes, swishy skirt and that doggone smile. I do, Bo, and maybe I'll tell you one of these days."

"You ain't happy with her, are you Uncle Dru. Ma says so. Uncle Jim, he don't mention her no more."

"'Nuff 'bout her, Boy. I just wanted you to know… Well, let me put it thisaway, inasmuch as it'll help me say better what I'm tryin' to say."

"That's a mighty big word, Uncle Dru, that inaswhatever…"

"One'a her mother's words, Bo. I just picked it up – not meanin' to, a'course."

He paused to scratch his head.

"What I mean to say, and I'm talkin' 'bout Sara, now, is sometimes when a fella hears a woman say somethin' and not finish sayin' it, he'll try to make her go on and finish. There was lots'a times Sara wouldn't finish somethin' she was tryin' to tell me, but there warn't no way I could make her go on. That got to botherin' me real bad once and I put my foot down real hard and made her tell me…"

"Tell you what, Uncle Dru?"

Dru was a long time answering. How much could you tell a boy? When did a boy become a man?

Finally, he said, "Bo, I just can't tell you. I wished I'd never asked her myself…" After another long pause, he added, "And I wish she'd never told me."

"But, Uncle Dru, you can tell me. I keep secrets. You know that."

"I know, Bo, I know. Why don't we just leave it alone; why don't you just believe I'm a'scared of that man and it'd best if both of us just kept outa his way."

Though he wanted in the worst way to know his uncle's secret, Bo figured it would be best to drop the question – for the time being, anyway. So he asked his old standby.

"What you gonna do?"

"Dunno, Bo, I really don't know. I'm afraid to talk to anybody but you 'bout the feelin' I got, and that sure makes it hard. Your daddy, he might have helped, but then he didn't care for Sara no ways and he'd likely put the wool on it anyway."

Bo was looking at the ground again.

"Well, Uncle Dru, you said you could tell me when you couldn't tell no one else. If that's so, why can't you tell me what you're thinkin' and ask me what you oughta do?"

Dru smiled and, with a gentle hand, lifted Bo's face so he could see the boy's eyes again. "I know I told you that, son, and..."

Looking away, Dru dropped to one knee and picked up the stone that a few minutes earlier had held Bo's attention.

"What would you think if I went to see Sara one more time, to ask her 'bout how she's feelin' and maybe tell her 'bout my scared feelin? I hain't got no idea how I'd do it, and I for sure dunno how she'd she'd act when she saw me."

He paused, as though waiting for Bo to say something. He didn't, though he remained focused on his uncle's down-turned head.

After a moment, Dru went on. "Maybe I could sit in the bushes out behind the pig pen and wait 'til I was sure her daddy'd gone off somewheres. Or maybe I could just bide my time in them bushes 'til she comes out and 'pssst' her over. Maybe if one of the girls came out..."

Pausing again, Dru looked up at his nephew. "You think it'd be a wrong thing to do, me goin' o'er there and tryin' to see Sara? Last time I saw her, she didn't look like she could'a spoke up anyways."

Bo could see what was going on and wasn't sure he liked it; his Uncle Dru was talking his way around going to beat up on Old Man Boru by saying he really needed to go see Aunt Sara. But, loving his uncle the way he did, he closed his half-opened mouth, thought a moment, and timidly responded.

"Well, Uncle Dru, if you think that's what you oughta do, I reckon you oughta do it."

Dropping to one knee himself, as though he were a grown man sharing his thoughts with another, Bo went on.

"But what would Aunt Bea, er, that Bea woman think, Uncle Dru? Wouldn't she raise a ruckus? And if she did, Sara's mean old daddy for sure would find out and…"

Dru interrupted so suddenly that Bo was surprised, by the interruption and the firmness with which his uncle spoke.

"I don't give a tinker's damn what Bea thinks, boy. She's always talkin' at me, tryin' to find out why I thought Sara was worth messin' with. Oh, she's a smart 'un, she is. Ever' time she's 'bout to make me good'n mad, she backs off and turns on the sweetness and light. Makes me so sick to the belly that I wanna… Well, you oughta know what I mean."

"Reckon I do, Uncle Dru. Truly I do."

Calmer now, Dru chuckled and addressed Bo straightaway. "Well now, Bo, since you agree that that maybe it would be a good thing for to me try'n and see Sara, I reckon I will. And I for sure will let you know what I find out.

Bo was struggling for words; he sensed their man-to-man was about to end, and he wanted desperately to prolong it.

"Do you think Aunt Sara's daddy – Old Man Boru, I mean – might'a been born in Banshee Swamp?"

Surprised, Dru stood up, looked down at Bo with mouth wide open and said, "What's that, Bo? Born in Banshee Swamp? Well, I never give it…"

"Seems like he belongs there. Lordy, I'm as scared of him as I am of that doggone swamp…"

"I reckon as how none of us will ever forget that swamp, Bo-boy. Thinkin' 'bout it'll always remind me of you; ain't no two ways 'bout that."

The grin dissolved and, and Dru's eyes glazed over, as though he'd had a vision, a spiritual awakening of some sort.

"But you know what else? Maybe we need a place like that there swamp; maybe we need it to blame for everything bad that happens 'round here.

"I mean, we got Godspots, which we know are good. Why shouldn't we have somethin' else as bad as Godspots is good; somethin' we can look to for explainin' why somethin' bad happens and it don't make no sense that it happened..."

Bo interrupted. "Like Lonny gettin' murdered, and May dyin', and Sara and Magalene bein' so sick and sad, while a mean old man like Boru keeps on livin'?"

Dru didn't respond right away. And when he did, he was moving the straw around with the toe of his boot, like his mind was a thousand miles away.

"Yep, Bo, I reckon that's one way of lookin' at it."

"So, do you think Old Man Boru was born in there?"

Again Dru was pensively quiet. Then he smiled weakly and said, "Not really, Bo. I think it's likely he come rarin' up out of Big Springs Swamp. Banshee Swamp is ours, it's special, and he ain't earned his way in."

"But how'd be earn that?"

Dru looked beyond Bo with unseeing eyes, as though he was picturing rather than seeing.

"Only one way I know," he said, quietly.

"But Uncle Dru, ain't you gonna tell me?"

"Oh, Bo, I'm just mumblin' to myself. Let's call it a day. I still got some chores to do."

Bo returned home, disappointed that he hadn't stirred his uncle into action against Old Man Boru but determined to follow his thinking; after all, that's what best buddies did.

Jewell was waiting on the porch for him. "Hey, young man," she said, "it looks like a good day for burnin' some of that brush you piled up down there where we're widenin' the west field. I'll fix us some lunch and we'll make a party out of it."

She was talking to herself as she turned away, but Bo heard her anyway. "And maybe," she said, "it's best we hurry up and get ready to go join your daddy…"

Bo beamed, clapped his hands and went looking for Arlis. He found his brother curled up on the bed, knees tucked under his chin – a position that suddenly sent shivers up Bo's spine. It reminded him of the time two years earlier when they'd nearly lost Arlis, in such a terrible-awful way that they would never forget or quit blaming themselves.

John had carried a fruit crate holding one-year-old Arlis to a field that needed plowing and placed it on the ground; Bo was to stay beside Arlis while John joined Jewell in trying to run down Junebug, who was kicking up her heels and dragging the overturned plow across the field. A harsh winter's cold winds were gone, the air was brisk and clean, the sun bright and warm, and the delighted grownups purposely prolonged the chase, laughing, falling down frequently, and finally letting the mule stop when she had run out of her own playful energy.

In his excitement, Bo had followed them, leaving Arlis and the box where John had left it – smack dab on a bed of fire ants. Arlis' screams had gone unheard for some time, and the horribly bitten child had barely survived the long drive to the Sligo hospital and a week of treatment by an appalled doctor and compassionate nurses.

Time had eliminated Arlis' scars, but he never would overcome his fear of crawlers, or anything resembling them. John, Jewell and Bo still carried the scars of shame-based guilt, and vowed they would watch over and be grateful for one another so long as they lived.

John had phrased the vow, as they sat in the hospital's waiting room.

"And in the hereafter," Jewell had added. "Don't ever forget 'bout Heaven."

January crawled into February and day after cold day Jewell put on two pair of overalls and went to the woods bordering the now-bare fields to the west. There she blistered her hands, chopping down pines and shrub oak, stacking brush, and burning the stumps and undergrowth. Bo helped when he got home from school, and on the warmer days Arlis tagged along to help stack the brush.

Since his terrifying meeting with Old Man Boru, the school bus driver, Elsa Peters, made her pickups and dropoffs of Bo a quarter-mile up the road from the Boru house. Bo had told her about the standoff, and she didn't like the old man, either. Every school-day morning, Mrs. Peters still halted the bus outside the Boru house on the chance Magalene, Bertha or both would be there. Once in a while Bertha would be waiting; Magalene never was.

Bo always hunkered down in his seat until the house was out of sight.

Sometimes Jim intercepted the bus on his side of Banshee Swamp and Arrowhead Hill and brought Bo home in the Blue Goose. Jewell figured he had ulterior motives, and he did. Not usually a grumbling man, he set to grumbling one day about the work she was doing, work he said even a man wouldn't undertake.

"Why you want a bigger field, anyway? You ain't gonna be here to work it, and..."

She stopped chopping and looked him straight in his concerned, empathetic eyes.

"Jim, if you're gonna help, then help. But don't go tellin' me this is too much work for a woman. I ain't just any woman, and I got my reasons and you know what they are."

Sometimes Del came to help, bundled in an old knee-length coat with his long arms and gloveless hands swinging at his side. Generally, he'd call out while some distance away and Jewell liked that; it gave her the opportunity to see the flash of his snow-white teeth, which got larger as he trotted toward her.

The visitors also gave her a chance to catch her breath and massage her aching, sometimes blood-spotted hands. She carried a packet of salt in her overalls pocket for when the bleeding got especially bad, a habit she'd picked up from her Negro friends during cotton-picking time. The salt stung, but it worked...

Marybelle sometimes came with Del, bringing a pail of biscuits and fussing when anyone tried to help her down from the wagon. Jewell had learned not to do that.

Jewell's velvet beans were ready for picking right on schedule, when February's nights coated everything with frost so thick it took the rising sun half the morning to melt it away. When three successive days brought a slate-grey sky and sleet, however, the "velvet" on the beans froze into needles that shredded her cotton gloves and bloodied her fingers. Despite the pain, she cleaned the three acres of vines in less than a week, and set the remaining two hogs and the cow to foraging among the corn stalks and vine for what was left.

Jonathan Ramsey, owner of the Mayo feed store, bought all of her beans. Ramsey hadn't needed them and she knew he hadn't; but her pleading blue eyes and torn fingers closed the sale and both felt good about it.

Pushed by reminders that they were paying their way to Florida, Bo and Arlis filled one burlap bag with what pecans they still could find and a good part of another with walnuts. Sid Jamison at the drugstore said he was glad to get such fine nuts, and he paid a good price.

The druggist appeared genuinely pleased; Jewell felt good about the sale and rewarded her sons with an ice cream cone each. She also thanked them profusely, telling each separately that they were well on their way to becoming young men. Secretly, she regretted that they had little choice; and her prayer that night was that, at some point in their lives, they would be able to retrieve the childhood they were sacrificing to family need.

Every weekday Jewell went to the mailbox, looking for letters that seldom were there. When they were, she'd read and re-read them to Bo and Arlis. More often a postcard arrived; when she read those to the boys, she'd do so very slowly and try to make them appear longer. Sometimes she'd add phrases that weren't in them; when she did this, she'd hide the card so Bo wouldn't find it.

When Bo was able to get his hands on one, the first thing he looked for was the "Love, John," at the bottom, and it always was there. That made him feel very good, and gave him added incentive for being his daddy's stand-in.

Then one day Bo overheard his momma talking to Jim…

"But he ain't sendin' no money, Jim. Not much anyways…"

"Didn't you save some from the crops and the extra stuff? After you'd paid up your accounts in Mayo and Sligo? I hear Buttonbottom and his family'd like to sharecrop the place when you're ready to go. Del says he'd even live over here, if you'd agree to that. Said he know how to keep a place clean."

"I did, Jim, I did. And I've already talked to Del 'bout living here for a little of what he can squeeze outa the place. But it'd mean so much if John would send money for the tickets. We're havin' to live with the little he does send. Sendin' more would show us he really wants us with him."

"Likely he's savin' up to send you ticket money all at one time. Likely he's doin' that, Jewell."

Though he tried to make her believe it, Jim wasn't sure he succeeded. He was thinking, as he knew she was, that money in the hands of a drinking-prone man is a dangerous thing.

And as March came on, Dru started coming by and lending a hand. That pleased Bo greatly, though he wasn't at all happy that his uncle didn't smile much any more. Dru's sadness made Bo sad, though it did not sadden him so much that he forgot to tell his uncle, again, about the run-in with Old Man Boru.

When Bo did, Dru looked east toward the Boru house, and looked sadder still. Watching him, Bo eased up close and said quietly, as from one man to another…

"How come that old man is so mean? How come he don't like you? How come he says you still got a hankering' for his gal? How come he says you'd best stay 'way from her?"

Remembering that his uncle was now a married man, Bo paused to catch his breath and think some.

"Maybe," he finally added, "he wouldn't feel so if you wasn't married."

Dru squatted and juggled a couple of stones. Without looking up, he said, "That's a wagonload of how-comes, Bo, and I ain't sure I kin answer any of 'em."

He tossed away the stones, one by one, and talked some more, very quietly. "Some I reckon maybe I could answer. But the time ain't right. May never be…"

Another pause, and Dru looked directly at his nephew. "You know, Bo, I sometimes forget you're still just a boy…"

Seeing Bo start to object, he raised a shushing hand. "Whooa now, don't take it thataway. It's a nice thing I'm sayin' and you'll know why one day."

He paused a third time, picking up more stones and considering Bo's questions. Finally, he tossed the stones away and stood.

"So I don't want to answer them questions today, Bo-boy. I'm just gonna have to think on 'em some more. And I promise this: Before you go we'll have us a good, long talk.

"Man-to-man or boy-to-boy, Uncle Dru?"

"Had my druthers it'd be boy-to-boy. What's the good of bein' a man anyways?"

Dru turned on his heels, mounted the wagon and headed back toward Jim's, over Bo's Arrowhead Hill and through Bo's Banshee Swamp, that narrow strip of woods Dru had made so fearsome with his stories about banshees, ghosts, ghouls, and intruders who went in but never came out.

And he was thinking that the few special things in his life were special because Bo had made them so.

"Lordamercy, I'm gonna miss you, boy. God knows I will."

CHAPTER 22

Another pigsty murder; Dru disappears

TWO WEEKS LATER JEWELL and the boys were returning from burning brush in the west field and saw a green Chevy sedan parked in front of the house. She knew at once it belonged to Sheriff Nobles.

Though she tried to restrain them, Bo and Arlis ran ahead and were standing with the sheriff and Jim just off the front porch when she arrived. Despite the cold wind, stony-faced Nobles had removed his hat; her brother-in-law stood a few feet behind him, hat in hand and looking bewildered.

Beatrice Sullivan, nee O'Connell, sat in the car.

"Something wrong," Jewell said, her curiosity aroused even more by the concern she saw in all three faces.

"Sorry to bother you like this, Jewell," Nobles said. "We're lookin' for Dru. He warn't at home in Munsterville and Jim says he ain't seen him in day or two."

"Well, now, I haven't either. He don't come around like he used to."

Gesturing toward the car, she asked, "Why's Beatrice here? She never comes here."

"Well, Ma'm, she's here because she hain't seen Dru in some time, she says, and she's got plenty of reason to be worried."

"Worried? Why? What's this all about?"

Clearly anxious, Jim reached out and started to step forward; but Nobles extended an arm and held him back.

"Jewell," Jim said, "this whole thing is crazy and don't you believe one word of it. I know for sure Dru wouldn't…"

"Wouldn't what?"

Nobles interrupted. "Jewell, Sara Boru's been murdered an' somebody's done stole her body. We got reason to believe…"

Stunned, Jewell struggled to the front steps and sat down. Jim pushed by Nobles and hurried to her side.

"Jewell, he ought not be tellin' it to you like this. He's talkin' like he's lost his mind…"

Still dazed, Jewell took Jim's hand and managed to say, "Hush, Jim. What are you sayin', Sheriff? When'd this happen? What's Dru got to do with it?"

"Happened last night, best we know. Mister Boru, he found her in his pigsty, like the Higginbothams found Lonny. Said she'd been beaten up terrible and her body was shoved down in the muck and mire. Face down, too. After he come and got me, we went back out there and her body was gone…"

Crumpling his hat with both hands, he added, "But there was blood all over and it didn't look like no hog's blood. The hog was in the woods. Somebody had let him out, or maybe the killer left the gate open."

Jewell found herself thinking of Magalene.

"Oh, dear Lord," she whispered, suddenly remembering a passage from the Bible she'd read after May's death.

'She's weary – Go down, Death, and bring her to me…'

"Is that why Magalene's angels were gone? Did they take her with them?"

Jewell shook off the trance and looked at Jim. "This can't be happening, Jim. Sara can't be dead! What're the girls gonna do? What're we gonna do?"

Exasperated, Jim squeezed Jewell's hand harder than he'd intended, and apologized. Looking at Nobles, he said, "If Sara was dead ain't it likely some animal come and drug her off while Boru was gone? Nobody'd steal a dead body, specially not Dru. He got sick just lookin' at somethin' dead…

"Lordy, everybody knows you don't like Dru and never have. He wasn't the kind to bow to you…"

Ignoring the second part of what Jim said, the sheriff responded, "Don't you think we thought 'bout that? Only a bear would do something like that and there hain't been no bear seen outside Deep Springs Swamp in years. An' I never seen a bobcat or a panther big enough to do it.

"They might hang 'round an' gnaw on somethin' dead, but they couldn't just haul off a body. There'd be something left…"

Jewell put both hands over her mouth as if to keep from throwing up. Her eyes were glazed and she said nothing. Jim stepped toward Nobles as far as holding her hand allowed.

"Why have you got to talk like that? That ain't nothin' a civilized woman can stand to hear. And who is *we*? I hain't ever heard of you takin' anybody's word for anything…"

Showing no emotion and still holding his hat, Nobles took a deep breath.

"Mister Boru, he said he's got plenty of reason to b'lieve Dru beat the life outa her, and maybe came back and took her remains. He showed me some cigarette butts in the bushes back of the sty and figures Dru'd been sittin' out there watchin' the house. Some of 'em were so old they'd turned yeller."

"Dru ain't the only one 'round here who smokes," Jim said. "Anybody could'a left them butts. Why'd it have to be Dru?"

"Well, that's true, Jim. But Boru, he says he's seen Dru hangin' 'round like a dog in heat an' duckin' outa sight when someone come out in the yard."

Pausing momentarily and acting as though he was embarrassed by what he was about to say, he added, "We all know'd that Dru still had the hots for Sara, even after he got hisself married."

After another pause, he went on. "An' Boru says it got so Sara was 'fraid of goin' outside for fear he'd be there..."

"Dear God," Jim said, "that just ain't so. If Dru was there, Sara'd be glad to see him. It stands to reason that..."

He quit in mid-sentence and looked beyond Nobles; Beatrice had gotten out of the car and stood a few feet away.

"Beatrice," Jim said, "you don't believe..."

"I don't know what to believe, dear brother-in-law." She hunched down in the fur-collared coat, and added, "He's been actin' so strange-like for some time, goin' off for days at a time and not sayin' where or why."

Looking at Nobles, she added, "If it hadn't been for Jim tellin' us at church, Mother and I likely never would have known he'd been stayin' at his house. And us treatin' him with the kindness we did..."

Bo, meanwhile, was fit to be tied. Standing to one side, he'd heard it all and couldn't believe any of it. Suddenly he moaned loudly, burst into tears, vaulted onto the porch and disappeared into the house.

Jewell got up to follow, but Jim intervened. "Let him go, Jewell. You know how he feels 'bout Dru."

Staring hard at Nobles, he said angrily, "Lordamercy, man, haven't you got any feelin's at all? Nobody ought to have to hear about such a thing this way, let alone a church-goin' woman and her young'uns..."

Pale and staggering somewhat, Jewell got off the steps, called Arlis to follow and entered the house. She ignored Nobles' pleas to be allowed inside; Jim told him he'd better leave and take Beatrice with him.

"All right," the sheriff responded. As the door slammed behind Jim, he shouted, "But I'm gonna find Dru an' he's gonna be charged with Sara's murder. An' maybe with Lonny's, too, since he seems to have this thing 'bout pigsties."

Jim stopped at the door. "Thought you said Lonny killed himself, Sheriff. You changin' your mind, now that you got somebody you think you can lay it on?"

With hardened eyes and a rock-hard face, Nobles returned Jim's stare. "Maybe," he said quietly, "I suspected him all 'long…"

Throwing up his hands, Jim responded, "Oh, for heaven's sake, you know as well as I do that ain't possible."

Bo had thrown himself onto the make-do settee and was crying uncontrollably. When Jewell tried to sit down beside him, he pushed her away and ran into the kitchen, where he crawled under the table. Arlis stood to one side, trembling, confused, and looking as though he were about to cry as well.

Jim watched from the doorway separating the kitchen and the bedroom. And as he had learned to do since Abigail's passing, he tried to ignore his own emotions. It didn't work; his hands trembled, his stomach knotted and, try as he did, he was unable to staunch his own tears.

With a final glance at Bo under the table, he went to join Jewell, and he cried with her.

"Oh, Jim, dear Jim, what are we gonna do? Prayin' don't seem to do no good, the Good Lord forgive me. First Lonny, then May, and now Sara. Magalene's gone crazy, wonderin' where her angels has gone. What's gonna happen to her and Bertha without a momma?"

Placing her face against his chest, she went on. "John's gone off and we haven't got the money to go to him. Now they're sayin' Dru killed the woman we all knew he loved – a woman deservin' better'n she got…"

Despondently, she turned to her brother-in-law; and as if asking for forgiveness, she said, "Maybe we was to blame, Jim. Maybe we ought'na messed where we had no business to mess. Maybe we oughta left Dru and Sara and Beatrice to do for their own selves…"

"Aw, Jewell, we did it thinkin' it was best for Dru; we did it 'cause we loved him."

Jewell shook her head from side to side. "I had a dream the other night," she said softly, "and Momma Susan was sayin' we can't do it all; we gotta leave to the Lord what is the Lord's to do."

Neither spoke for long moment, while Jim thought of what Jewell had said and she tried to recount the dream. She began to tremble again. "What're we gonna do, Jim? Are we livin' in purgatory? Is it right here, on Sullivan Road?"

Clearing his throat, Jim responded, "We're gonna pray some more, I reckon, Jewell. Prayin's all we got left."

When Bo finally emerged from beneath the table, the sun and Arlis had gone to sleep and his momma and Uncle Jim were sitting together before the fire. Silently he crept out the back door, into a cold and moonless night. He still wore his coat; that and numbness kept him from feeling the cutting cold of an unusual nighttime breeze, and the not-unusual cold pushing up out of the yard's bare ground.

With little awareness that he was doing it, he made his way to the barn loft and burrowed down into the hay. There, he managed to clear his head enough to realize that he was angry and oughta be. Uncle Dru wouldn't just run off without coming to him first; he couldn't have done what the sheriff said, and of that he had no doubt.

He tried to talk to his Godspot, but it didn't respond. He figured it was angry as well and didn't know what to say.

Momma Susan's passing, Lonny's murder, May's dying, Sara's killing… All had occurred within the last ten months; except for Spot's passing two years ago, his only exposure to death and its impact on the living had been at hog-killing time – and that had been a time for celebration. He'd seen death in movies and read about it in books, but that was death of a different kind; sometimes it was sad, but mostly the dead were bad guys and had it coming.

But Aunt Sara, Magalene's momma? That was too close to home, and it hurt bad, real bad. And the sheriff saying his Uncle

Dru killed her, and in such an awful way... That was too much to take, way too much.

For the first time in a long time, he wished he could talk to Magalene. She'd likely know who killed her momma, and what really was going on at her house. Nowadays he couldn't even ask Bertha. Like Magalene, she'd quit coming to school; and, like Magalene, she had begun to act crazy-like.

Then he remembered what he'd overheard his own momma say to herself one recent night: that Magalene's angels may have run off because they knew somebody else was going to get killed.

Did Momma believe in Magalene's angels? Gracious, he reflected, this is getting as scary as Banshee Swamp...

Suddenly aware that he was sitting in the darkness, in the barn loft and alone, Bo began to fidget; after all, wasn't this where the snakes wintered? The cogitating had cleared his head and helped ease the paralyzing shock of what he'd seen and heard; but now a new awareness gripped him, and it was a fearsome one.

Though he was still a boy – and hated to admit it, even to himself – he had not been one to sit by and not take action. Uncle Dru, his momma and his daddy, they'd taught him to think things through and do what had to be done; idle hands were no good to anyone.

But what? What could *he* do? None of what was happening made any sense; all of it was stupefying and, when things got that way, his momma said, it'd be best to back off and add some praying to the thinking.

He'd wait. He'd do as his Uncle Dru had said; he'd keep the faith, and he'd believe, really believe, that Dru hadn't run off and left him alone. He knew, without question, that his Uncle Dru had not killed Sara.

He was around somewhere, and probably close by...

CHAPTER 23

'A man's gotta do what a man's gotta do...'
—Resigned Dru to heartbroken Bo

BO PRAYED TO HIS Godspot that night, and when he awakened with the sun it contained a message telling him to go to the pond where he had found his uncle, drunk and helpless, on that steamy day last summer.

Dru stood as he approached and cast aside the blanket in which he'd wrapped himself. They embraced, then Bo stepped back and asked, "Where you been, Uncle Dru? They're sayin' you killed Aunt Sara. Tell me that ain't so."

Exasperated, Dru responded, "Bo, you know that ain't so. I went over there like I said I would and found her in that pig pen. She'd been beaten terrible awful. I been cryin' most all the time ever since."

"But where's she at, Uncle Dru? Old Nobles, he said she'd been drug off and nobody knows where to."

Dru turned away. "I don't know what to tell you, Bo, and if I did I likely wouldn't – or couldn't. I just couldn't..."

"But you said you trusted me when you couldn't trust nobody else. Why can't...?"

"I can't, Bo, and there ain't no two ways about it."

"But..."

"That's enough, Bo," he said firmly. "You gotta know I didn't kill her – Lordy, you *know* I didn't – and you gotta leave it alone. For my sake and for yours..."

"But Uncle Dru?"

"Hush, now, I got things to tell you and I ain't got a lot of time."

"Like what?"

"Like I've got to go away, go somewheres else where nobody can find me, where nobody knows me."

"But runnin' away ain't gonna..."

"Lookee, Bo-boy, I was standin' right there in your front room when Nobles drove up with Jim and Bea. I heard everything he said and, up til then, I didn't know he was lookin' for me."

"Well, where you been? Why didn't you come right out and tell him he was crazy as a loon?"

"I've been off hurtin' and cryin' a lot, if you must know. After what Nobles said, and when you was about to come in the house, I snuck out the back way and come down here. It's as good a place as any for a man to hide and think. Figured you'd be comin' sooner or later..."

"But you just can't up and run away..."

"Please, Bo, you just gotta hush, now. Nobles is scared to death of Old Man Boru, and he's got a right to be. They used to be good buddies, got drunk t'gether and all that. He's gonna stand by that old man, no matter what.

"Maybe," he added, "he's afraid Boru'll be the next to wind up dead in a pigsty..."

Seeing the hatred in his uncle's eyes and doing the best he could to understand, Bo screwed his face into one big question mark. "What are you talkin' about, Uncle Dru? You ain't gonna...?"

Bo paused right there, wiped a horrifying thought from his mind and heard himself ask, "Who did kill Aunt Sara? You got any ideas?"

Dru's response shocked him. "I think Old Man Boru killed her, Bo. And I think he killed Lonny when that boy caught him stealin' his pig."

"But if that's so, why have you got to run away? Why can't you stay and show that Old Man Boru did kill them both?"

Dru knelt and placed a hand on his nephew's shoulder. "Bo, there's so much you don't know, so much I can't tell nobody. I was told some terrible-awful things, things I swore I'd never tell nobody, and I gotta keep that promise."

Desperate now, Bo pushed the hand away. "You said you'd never keep no secret from me. You did, Uncle Dru, so why've you changed your mind?"

Dru dropped down from the kneeling position and sat on the grass; he felt and looked helpless, like a beaten man. He heard the desperation in Bo's voice and saw it in his eyes. Though his lips were trembling with indecision, his inner voice was shouting at him…

"With the Good Lord's help, you and this man-boy has come so far together, been through so much together. You just can't shut him out now. It'd pain you the rest of your days, and you know he'd never forgive nor forget…"

Finally, Dru looked up at his nephew and said, "Bo-boy, I reckon as how all of us has got a Banshee Swamp in our lives. You got yours, and I reckon your daddy and I put it there for you with stories about ghosts and such."

He thought about what he'd said, and shook his head as though he might have done a bad thing.

"For my part, I did it 'cause I thought it'd help you growin' up, let you see that things ain't always as bad as they 'pear to be, and that you can whip 'em if you've a mind to.

"Womenfolk say that ain't the right way to teach a boy, scarin' 'im like that. I reckon it ain't, but I never know'd no other way. My pa did it. His pa did it."

Responding softly, so softly Dru barely heard, Bo said, "To teach a boy, Missus McGraw says you gotta catch his attention. Was that what you was doin', Uncle Dru?"

"Yup, I reckon that says it."

Clearing his throat, Bo said in a firm voice, "But you gotta tell me what…"

"Thing is," Dru went on as if he hadn't heard, "it does seem to me that all of us got some swamps. And, truth be known, most of us didn't put them there. Somebody else did, some of 'em well-meaning, like me and your daddy, and some just not knowin' what they was about."

"Who's got their own swamps, Uncle Dru? Are they like mine?"

"Well, your daddy's got one, a real big one. I recollect a time when he'd be the first to stand up and preach about buryin' the jug. That's his swamp, and the mud that's miring him down – the jug.

"Somebody, somewheres, put one in front of him thinkin' he was needful of it; like maybe he was hurtin' awful bad and somebody gave him somethin' to make him forget the hurtin'.

"Maybe," he added after a brief, thoughtful pause, "maybe they just wanted to help, too. Trouble was, they didn't know they was settin' out to make him sick, real sick, inside and outside."

To Bo, it sounded as though his uncle was trying to avoid his question; but he also had strong feelings about what he was hearing now and blurted, "But Uncle Dru, he beat up on Momma somethin' awful. He liked to have killed her one time…"

"I know, son, I know. That's the worst part of it, and it's the part we can see. What he's doin' to his own self, that's the part we can't see, and it's doggone awful, too.

"Nobody, most of all me, wants him to beat up on your ma and make you and Arlis feel bad. Not to mention your ma. But nobody seems to care that he's beatin' his own self nigh on to death."

"It's Momma, Uncle Dru. She don't like to be called ma."

Bo had whispered that.

Dru lifted a hand, ruffled Bo's hair and went on without looking up. "And them that don't know what to look for can hardly see what it's done to you and Arlis and the rest of us what love him. Easy to see how it hurts your ma; ain't so easy to see what it's done to the rest of us – specially you, who holds back the hurt more'n you oughta."

"Please don't call her ma," Bo said, aloud this time. "Please don't. She's too purty and smart to be called plain ole ma. And what's it done to the rest of us, specially me'n Arlis? You said we were gonna grow up and be men before our time. What's wrong with that?"

Dru shook his head again and frowned; he rubbed a weary eye and tugged at the bristles on his chin. "Oh Bo-boy, I also told you that bein' a young-un – before someone's done messed up the way you think and feel – is the best it'll ever be.

"Don't you remember your maypop, the one I said was like you and was gonna grow up and sprout a lavender flower and everyone would be pleased to see it? You ever think of that maypop?"

"I do, but it's dead by now. Winter kills maypops."

"Reckon so, Bo, reckon so. But it ain't ever gonna die if you can see it the way it was. It was purty and growin' when you saw it last; that's the way you'll always see it.

"One thing I know for sure: Your ma, er, your momma, she's a fighter and you're a fighter. The more your daddy hurts her, the more he keeps from you and Arlis, that makes her more set on makin' the way better for you boys."

Dru extended a calloused hand and ran it over Bo's hair. Some of the boy's apprehension slipped away, and he moved closer to his uncle; gently, as if asking permission, he placed a hand on the man's extended knee.

"And then there was Sara," Dru finally said, softly and with head down. "She had so many swamps you couldn't count 'em. Nobody know'd about the biggest one, and it was just as well."

"Lord knows nobody should ever know..."

"What was it?"

Dru raised his head and stared at Bo. Bo stared back.

"Some things," Dru said, "are meant for God and them that's hurtin' – and sometimes for them that's hurtin' with 'em. This is one of them things, Bo. I'm dreadful sorry I made mention of it."

"But Uncle Dru, I'm hurtin'. Hurtin' bad, and you know I am – hurtin' for you and for Aunt Sara. And for Lonny and his ma and pa and Delphi and the rest. You gotta tell me what you're hidin'. You just got to."

Dru dropped his head again. He knew Bo was about to start crying. He didn't want to see that, and he knew Bo did not want to be seen if he did break down.

"Bo, I just don't know. I just don't know that you'd know what to make of it."

"But Uncle Dru!" Bo fairly shouted the words, then shushed himself and looked around uneasily, as though somebody might have heard. The pond was still and there wasn't even a breeze to stir the dead broom grass.

Taking a deep breath, Dru felt he had no choice; the time had come. Whispering, he said, "Bo-boy, Sara's pa is Magalene's daddy."

Bo jerked his hand off his uncle's knee, bewilderment contorted his face. "You mean Old Man Boru? But he's Magalene's grandpa. That can't be! That's wrong! That's terrible-awful..."

"I know that, boy!"

Dru had spoken more harshly than he'd meant to; lowering his voice, he repeated himself. "I know that. But nobody else knows the truth about it. Now it's me, it's you, and it's God. And I just know she's with Him now, if He really is what everybody thinks and is some place she can be.

"It'd be a dreadful thing if He ain't and she ain't. She didn't get no love down here..."

"But you loved her, Uncle Dru..."

"I know I did. I just didn't know how to let her know; not really, anyways. I don't know what keeps me from tellin' someone how I really feel; it's something inside me, maybe. Like maybe I'm afraid they'll go 'way if I did. Or maybe they'd laugh.

Bo's face asked a silent question; Dru saw it and responded. "Oh, Bo, I ain't talkin' 'bout you. You know how I feel 'bout you, just like I know how you feel 'bout me.

"But I shore couldn't tell nobody else about my deep-down feelin's..." "They'd a' laughed for certain. Your daddy, he once said she wasn't worth a..."

"Wasn't worth a what? What'd my daddy say?"

"Aw, forget it, Bo-boy. I'm just ramblin'."

Both were silent for a long, long moment. Bo removed his hand from Dru's knee and wrapped both arms around his own knees. With his chin resting on them, he tried to imagine Sara being with her own daddy, like he'd been with Magalene, who was Old Man Boru's..."

Bo shuddered and Dru sensed what he was thinking.

"It wasn't her fault," he said, quietly. "He made her do it. After she'd had Bertha, with somebody else bein' the pa, he made her bed down with him over and over again. All that time, for a whole two years after Bertha came. Said if she was goin' to be a harlot she might as well be one at home."

Dru slammed a fist against the ground. "Bo, there was one time when I saw her come right outa that house and go to that chinaberry tree and fall down on her knees and start prayin'; with her arms wrapped 'round it, she cried and she prayed."

"At the tree where Magalene's angels live?"

"Yes, Bo, that one. And there was one time I could hear what she was prayin' about, and that's when I did go to her, and that's when she told me, just blubbered it out, what was happenin' and what had been happenin'.

"I tell you, Bo, it scared the voice right outa me and I couldn't say nothin; didn't know what to say, truth bein' what it was."

Dru shifted his knees again. "Then her daddy, he come on the porch lookin' for her and I skittered 'round behind the tree. When he did see her, he laughed, laughed right out loud, and shouted she'd best be gettin' her ass back inside if she know'd what was good for her."

Apologizing for the off-color word, he added: "Bo, I swear I almost went up there and whaled the tar outa that man. Ceptin' I was afraid I would kill him, kill him with my bare hands!"

Pausing to get control of himself, Dru added quietly, "I would have too if it hadn't been for her. She saw my face and waved me off, movin' her lips like she was sayin' I oughta stay put and it wasn't worth it; that I oughta wait, then go 'way and come back when he wasn't home."

"What'd you do?"

"I did go 'way and I did go back, the very next day when he likely was sleepin' off a drunk. She came into them bushes and she told me everything. That's when we know'd we were two peas in a pod when it came to wantin' people to leave us alone and let us live with our own feelin's – the way we wanted to, with nobody judgin' and playing' the Lord when they hain't got no right to."

"She told you Old Man Boru was Magalene's daddy? She really said that?"

"Yes she did, Bo. She said she know'd I'd never understand, and that I'd never want to so much as touch her again. But she asked me to forgive her, and maybe in time I could forgive her daddy.

"Forgive her daddy! God forgive me if ever I did, or even thought about it!

"But I did try to forgive her, and finally I did. Told her and the Lord I did. But even if it means I'm goin' to swim in the devil's burnin' river forever, I'll never forgive that goddamn old man!"

"You ain't goin' to the devil, Uncle Dru. The Lord's gotta understand."

"I know, boy. I know. What the Good Lord did do was let me'n Sara get real close and love one another and hope to marry some day. Maybe it can still happen…

"You gotta believe that, Bo," he added that after a thoughtful, soul-searching pause. His brow was furrowed and he wiped both eyes – too hard, Bo felt, for it not to have hurt.

Bo didn't respond right away, and when he did he spoke softly, with his own brow furrowed. "I reckon I do, Uncle Dru."

But a trace of doubt had snuck onto Bo's face; it was hard to imagine someone marrying a dead person, even if his uncle said he would. Then he remembered his talks with Grandma Susan, after she had died and gone to Heaven….

"Grandma Susan, she says most anything's possible, if you believe it is."

"Bo, it's easier for womenfolk to believe there's a forgivin' God in Heaven, and do like He does and forgive bad things, too. For men, it's harder, specially for men like me.

"What makes it so hard, and so confusin', is some men, and I'm one of 'em, gotta think 'bout it over and over again; and after a while a man knows part of lovin' is listenin' without letting on how much it hurts to hear what he's hearin'."

Dru paused, and Bo waited. "Anyways, Sara told me she finally got up the gumption to tell that old man that there was someone who knew what he'd been doin' and if he didn't stop that someone'd tell Sheriff Nobles and anyone else who'd listen.

"She said he laughed and told her he didn't worry about that; him and Nobles was buddies, and he didn't give a damn about what others thought. Why, he told her, Nobles sometimes went with him when he went back to T'other Side for a night of drinkin' and such."

Dru paused to wipe his brow, though the morning was cold and he wasn't sweating. "He beat her bad, real bad, when she said it, Bo-boy, but not any more after that. She scared him real good."

"Didn't he try to find out who know'd?"

"He did try, Bo, he did. But Sara, she didn't tell, no matter how much she feared he'd whomp her."

Bo didn't say anything right away. Then he shook his head to deal with lingering bewilderment and asked what he'd already asked: "Was it you that was gonna tell on him, Uncle Dru?"

"No, Bo. It wasn't nobody. Not then, anyways. She just told him, hopin' he'd stop. And he did. He stopped... For a while, anyways."

"Didn't he ask her some names? Like your name, Uncle Dru?"

"She said he did. Asked about me. Asked about Delphi and even your daddy – even Lonny, if you can believe that..."

He reached out and slapped Bo's shoulder, harder than he'd meant to. "It was her mention of Lonny that made me see that it likely was Old Man Boru who killed Lonny. And Lordamercy, that he must have killed Sara, too! Maybe he was beatin' on her ag'in and just couldn't stop!"

Then, suddenly, there was fire in Dru's eyes, the flames fed by a deep, dark realization. Bo started to say something, but Dru squeezed his hand and the squeeze told him to wait.

"Strange, wasn't it, that I was so blind, that everybody was so blind. They was both left in a pigsty. And I heard Boru tellin' Tip Evers that a boy like Lonny didn't deserve such a fine pig. As for Sara, he'd nigh on to beat the life outa her lotsa times."

Letting go of Bo's hand, he cupped his face in his own hands. "Lordy, lordy, lordy!"

Realizing Bo was full of more questions, Dru reached out and squeezed one of the boy's arms. Bo accepted the message, and both were quiet for awhile; the cold crept back into their awareness.

"Didn't you think about tellin' Sheriff Nobles about Old Man Boru bein' Magalene's daddy, Uncle Dru? about all the beatin' on Aunt Sara he done? Maybe about wavin' that shotgun at you?

"Maybe about him wavin' that axe at me?"

"No, boy, I'd never do that, not about that old man and Sara; never in this world would I do that. Sara's gone, and folks got a mem'ry of her that ain't good.

"But it ain't as bad as it'd be if they heard what really was goin' on; most likely, they'd say it was all her fault anyways.

"And Magalene and Bertha. They got their lives to live and they don't need more trouble than they already got. Specially Magalene. No, Bo, I'd die before I'd tell that; I promised Sara, and I promised the Good Lord."

To Bo, it seemed like his uncle was talking more about the Lord than he was used to hearing him do. Pushing the thought aside, he said, louder than he had intended: "But everybody'll think you killed her if you run away..."

"That's enough, Bo!" And he said it a second time, very gently. "That's enough."

Though gentle, the rebuke slammed Bo's heart; he realized that his beloved uncle really was going away, out of his life, and maybe forever.

"What're you goin' to do? Where're you goin'?"

In an emotion-choked voice, Dru responded: "I got my own swamp, Bo, and it's showed me that I'm what counts when all's said and done; what I think of myself, anyways, and what those who love me think. A man gets judged – and judges himself – by how he faces up to what he has to do; he gets a bad mark when he runs away from it."

"What're you talking about, Uncle Dru? You're about to run away and I don't understand what you're talkin' about...."

Waving a hand, Dru said, "No matter, Bo, no matter. Like I told Liam, 'A man's gotta do what a man's gotta do.' After I do what I gotta do, maybe you'll understand and maybe I will have a better handle on things. There're other places I can go and maybe start a whole new life.

"I ain't that old for an old dog, and I can read and write some now. Thanks to you'n Missus McGraw."

He reached for Bo and pulled him against his chest. Nestled there, Bo could smell the man-smell, like he hoped he smelled.

"Don't you worry none," Dru said. "I'll write you from wherever I am, and I'm gonna come see you, too. You keep listenin' for that knock on your door, and you keep on listenin' to your Godspot; remember that maypop that's yours and yours alone, and you care for your ma and Arlis."

Bo had been trying to hold back the tears, and what Dru had just said caused him to straighten his shoulders and hold them taut. Clear-eyed, he squeezed his uncle's neck and shoulders and repeated himself:

"It's Momma, Uncle Dru. It's Momma, and she's such a purty and smart woman. She went through the sixth grade."

Smiling and misty-eyed, Dru ran a hand through Bo's hair, real hard and rough, like he was giving him an Injun haircut.

"I'm sorry, Bo, and I will remember that."

Grinning, he added, "And Bo, I won't ever forget that we was boys together. I thank you for that."

Releasing Bo and getting up off his knees, he handed him the blanket and said, "Give this back to your momma. I took it last night. Reckon there'll be some where I'm goin'."

He walked off through the underbrush and broke into a trot. He didn't look back, he couldn't bear to look back; Bo was still there, and he couldn't bear to see him standing there alone.

"Not to worry, Bo-boy," Dru whispered. "I'm always gonna be close by, and one day I won't have to hide."

He had one more place to go before he left Shannon County, a sacred place that would give him all the incentive he would need to do what he felt he had to do.

He would visit a grave, hidden beneath a canopy of green overlooking the Big Springs ford, the revered swimming hole. The grave lay at the foot of a magnolia tree, among ancient cedars and spreading, moss-covered oaks. Only he knew it was there, and he felt in his heart that Sara's soul was watching from somewhere and would welcome him whenever he appeared to reaffirm his love.

He wanted to believe that they would be together some day … but he was not sure that would be possible if what he'd always believed about life and death was true.

BOOK II
FOLLOWING THE FRIGHTENED ANGELS

Magalene remained in her faraway world, staring, seeing what only she could see, her eyes alternately reflecting disappointment and elation; occasionally she whispered to herself: "Angels. Where have the angels gone? There's gotta be...""

"Scared," Dru interjected, very softly. "They been scared away..."

"Frightened's a better word," Gladys said, also whispering. "I reckon we're gonna be following the frightened angels..."

CHAPTER 24

Celestial indecision, earthly expectations

DRU DIDN'T LEAVE SHANNON County right away. For the first week he watched the Boru place from a storm-cut gully in an overgrown field across the road. He was afraid he would be discovered if he hid out in the undergrowth at the edge of the woods separating the shack from the John Sullivan household. He had done that in the past, but he didn't want to press his luck.

The old man, Bertha or Magalene rarely appeared outside, and Boru never came out of the shack without looking in all directions before he stepped through the front door. When he did, it generally was to go to the woodpile, the outhouse or the smokehouse. Sometimes he'd step to the side of the porch and urinate. So much for having an outhouse, Dru thought, dryly...

Once, Boru returned from the smokehouse – a log structure built low to the ground, with dirt piled high along its sides – carrying a sizeable haunch of beef; Dru couldn't imagine where he'd gotten it, but he was glad the girls were not going hungry.

To feed himself, Dru occasionally slipped out of the gully and dug up peanuts that had escaped the harvest the previous fall. Pecans were plentiful; most had survived the wintertime freezes and were scattered under trees growing wild back in the woods and in the yards of an abandoned house some distance off Sullivan Road. He also chopped out the hearts of palmetto palms. Called "swamp cabbage," the firm white heart resembled the flesh of a turnip; it could be sliced like a hunk of cheese and eaten raw. Water was no problem; a quarter-mile away, the gully reached a creek feeding into the Big Springs ford.

After a few days, Dru's spying on the old man drifted from active interest to boredom to gut-wrenching self-examination. Why, he asked himself, was he doing it? His heart remained heavy and his eyes occasionally got teary. The nights still were cold, and he wished he'd kept the blanket he'd told Bo to take back to Jewell. The mind-numbing hatred of the man, and the gritted teeth expressing that hatred, caused excruciating headaches.

One reason, he knew, was that he still had not decided what action to take. One moment he was thinking of choking the life out of Boru, or axing him to death. Or perhaps he'd simply take a piece of firewood and beat him to death and dump him into the pigsty, which seemed an appropriate – and rightful way – to do away with him.

But then he'd remember that killing anything wasn't in his makeup; he had always managed to be absent at hog-killing time, and he had come to ignore those who joked about it.

Still, he had sworn on Sara's grave that he would revenge her brutal murder. And Lonny's too. How could he back out on that? How could he leave Shannon County unless he'd kept his promise and was able to walk out with his head held high?

So he kept to the gully, watching as the days and nights drifted away with painful slowness. Eldest brother Jim passed in the Blue Goose a couple of times, and Dru had to force himself to resist the temptation to flag him down. There were things he needed, which Jim could provide. But he was determined not to involve anyone else in his plan, even if he had not decided the specifics.

Jewell passed by in the wagon three times, posing the same dilemma. But he managed to remain hidden, even when she stopped in the Boru yard one morning; after looking at the silent house for several minutes, she snapped the reins on Junebug's haunches and went on her way.

Then one morning, when Dru was about to give up, Boru appeared in the door, looked around as he usually did, and started walking across the field less than 50 yards from where Dru was hunched down in the gully. For a brief moment, Dru considered rising and confronting him, with the outcome to be determined by how he felt when they were face to face.

"Think it through, think it through," he told himself through pursed lips and with clenched fists. Instinctively he knew this was neither the time nor the place for the kind of revenge he envisioned, the kind he hoped he'd have the gumption to carry out. They were too close to the road, the girls were alone in the house, and Grandma Dunaway's house was in full view, only a few hundred yards to the south. He didn't want to be seen by anyone, family or friend, and certainly not those he knew were searching for him.

He wondered why Sheriff Nobles had visited Boru only once during the week, and why their discussion had been confined to the front porch. That meeting had taken place the previous afternoon; it had been an active one, with the men alternately waving their arms and walking in circles, until Nobles had driven away in apparent anger. Perhaps, Dru surmised, Old Man Boru's action today had something to do with the Nobles' visit.

Some three hours after Boru disappeared into the woods behind the field in which Dru was hiding, he reappeared sitting next to another man on a mule-pulled wagon. Together they loaded Boru's belongings into the wagon, and with dusk falling they headed back the way they'd come. Bertha and Magalene sat atop the pile in the wagon bed, huddled under blankets with their backs to the men.

Obviously, Dru reasoned, they were heading toward the other side of Big Springs Swamp, from whence they'd come some four years earlier.

Sara had been with them then…

Dru knew he would be going across the swamp himself soon; he had made a vow he now hoped he would be able to keep. But, again, he remained haunted by the feeling – indeed, the knowledge – that there were too many unresolved considerations, too many hidden obstacles...

If Boru were alone, that would be one thing; but the girls were with him and that was a major complication. Dru found it hard to believe that some other family hadn't offered to take the girls, after they had been left without a mother when Sara was murdered and her battered body left in the pigsty. Perhaps someone had and Boru had refused.

Then, too, it had been years since Dru, or any other Sullivan, had gone to the swamp's other side, and he did not know what to expect. The best approach, he figured, would be to do as he had done for the past week: find a hideout close enough to spy on the settlement and plan accordingly.

As Dru watched the wagon carrying the Borus pass Grandma Dunaway's house and turn left toward the fording place, he thought again of Sara. They would be passing within 50 yards of her grave, hidden above Big Springs Ford among thick green cedars, scattered pines, and mossy, vine-covered oaks, their leafs shorn by winter's freezes but numerous enough to help hide and protect the site. Dru hadn't visited her since he'd begun his vigil in the field. He'd had a lot time to think, about so many things, and he was hurting, inside and out...

Dru wanted with all that was within him to believe that Sara's soul was watching from somewhere, and would welcome him whenever he appeared at the grave to reaffirm his love and to assure her that, if there really was a heaven and he might somehow be accepted, they would be together some day, and for all eternity.

But still he was wracked by doubt, a doubt rooted in a lifelong belief that all living things shared the same fate: they were born, lived out of their lives as best they could, died, and returned to the earth to replenish the soil and feed the crops and flowers and trees and the humans and animals and other forest creatures and all the living things that would come to take up where they left off. He had spent much of his life alone, walking fields and woods, watching birds and other creatures, examining their nests and dens, observing their habits. His beliefs were based on what he *saw*, and what he *felt* down there in his Godspot, which he regarded as a mailbox for messages from his personal God.

Often he had wondered about the irony of that belief; it did indeed seem odd that he would ask, in prayers directed to God, to be with Sara in a hereafter in which he had never been able to believe. Others, Momma Susan among them, had assured him that God would grant him eternal life if he would go to church and believe, really believe, that there was a paradise waiting at the end of the earthly journey.

That, they had said, was all you had to do be happy down here and, if you pleased God as you did it, you were headed for heaven, reunions with loved ones, and immortality.

Immortality? The way Dru saw things, it meant that a person or a beloved pet or cow or mule or even a flower would be immortal so long as someone still living loved and remembered them. Some American presidents – George Washington and Abe Lincoln being the best examples – were immortal because no one would ever forget them, though he'd run into some who weren't sure they loved Old Abe. Mostly they were ones who didn't have much truck with colored folk.

As he walked into the woods above the ford and ruminated about his beliefs, Dru soon found himself standing over his beloved's grave, which he'd dug with his own hands, and the full impact of his lifelong beliefs hit him hard; he suddenly felt very cold, very forlorn, and very helpless.

Sara was dead. Would he ever see her again?

And for a long, silent moment he stood motionless, one hand clutching his battered felt hat and the other alternately wiping a moistened cheek. Little by little, a quivering that began in his chest passed into his stomach and reached his knees; weak and rubbery they became, and, as pent-up emotion finally broke loose in a torrent of body-wracking sobs, his legs gave way and dropped him to the ground.

"God, dear God," he wailed, "how's it come to this? Why, why, why ain't it me down there, 'stead of her? Damn it all anyway! What's the use of livin' if'n it's gonna wind up like this anyhow? What's the reason, the damnable, mind-defyin' reason for it all?"

Dru crawled around the grave and pulled himself beneath the brambles on the other side; using his hands as rakes, he made himself a bed of dry grass and leaves and lay down upon it. He dried his tired, tear-saturated eyes on his sleeves and, as the sun headed for its own bed and twilight drifted into darkness, he slept.

CHAPTER 25

Fevered sleep, gentle awakening...

DESPITE THE COLD AND hard ground, Dru slept. But it was a fitful sleep, as nightmares intermittently assaulted his increasingly fevered mind. He moaned often and struck out at imagined assailants; at some point, he curled into a fetal position and wrapped his arms protectively around his head.

Then birdsong awakened him, that and the first rays of the rising sun piercing his bramble shelter. His first thought was that he had never heard so many birds singing at one time; they seemed to be everywhere, and he was only mildly surprised when a blue jay appeared in the greenery above him and abruptly switched from singing to scolding.

He remembered where he was, and why, and he focused on the chattering bird. Smiling weakly, he whispered, "It's okay, little fella. I'll be gone in a bit. I got me some things to do."

His gentle self... Somehow, it was still there, and he imagined that the little bundle of fluffy blue and grey feathers was urging him to get off his duff and join the world of the living.

Dru smiled and crawled from beneath the shelter, carefully pushing aside thorn-barbed briars, and stood up. Brushing leaves and dirt from clothing he had worn for more than a week, he sniffed his armpits, ran a hand over the insect bites on his face, and listened for the sound of water rushing through the ford below the hill. He needed a bath, his clothes needed washing, and he was hungry.

For a long, meditative moment, he knelt at Sara's grave, the pain expressed in his eyes sharing space with a determination that had not been there the night before. He was tired of being mired in uncertainty, and of the paralysis by which it held a man. Though he couldn't remember specifics of his nightmares, he sensed they had been telling him to get on with his life, and be careful of the dangers to come.

Some two hours later, with body washed and clothes laundered but still wet, Dru left the ford and its icy-cold water. Shivering, he hastened into the sun's warmth, running in place until he had scanned an open field and determined that no one was about. The hunger remained, but he was certain he'd find swamp cabbage when he traversed Big Springs Swamp. He thought about snaring a rabbit, but rejected the idea; he wasn't the killing kind.

That thought still troubled him; but he set his chin, said "Not yet, anyways," and headed up the hill away from the ford and Sara's grave. He could have gone by the road traversing the ford; though it ran a good four miles around the swamp, the road would have saved time and, as he was about to find out, a lot of misery. But what he had in mind would require secrecy, time to observe the backwoods community of purposeful exiles, and surprise. It had been years since he had been over here, and then he had passed through on a wagon.

His chosen track took him through a well-kept but ancient cemetery a few hundred yards off the main road, and on down through a heavily wooded area of oaks and assorted other hardwood trees, cedars, shrubs, and jack pines. Half an hour later, the first cypress appeared, and soon he was wading knee-deep in water so black he couldn't see the bottom. His progress slowed as the water got deeper; he had to feel with his feet for roots that would keep him from sinking to his waist or disappearing altogether in unseen mud pits scattered beneath the water throughout the swamp.

He knew about those. A few years earlier, he'd gone into a swamp to rescue a mired calf and found himself being sucked down in a hole that had no bottom. A solitary root, the remnant of a long-dead cypress or water oak, had saved him, after he'd sunk to his armpits and had exhausted himself by using his arms to remain erect while probing with his feet and calling for help. Jim had heard his calls and pulled him out with a thrown rope.

The less-weighty calf finally had wallowed onto solid ground and trotted off to find its mother.

The sun was hovering at about 3 o'clock when Dru struggled onto the south side of the swamp, to the sucking sounds of heavy, water- and mud-soaked boots being pulled from the muck and mire. He stomped both on the solid ground, then sat down and used the stub of a broken tree limb to remove what he could of the adhering dregs. He smelled smoke, wood smoke, and knew he was getting close. Pausing, he thought of the name of the alien community he sought; to those on the side from which he'd come it was known simply as T'other Side. He reckoned he'd keep on thinking of it that way.

After resting briefly, he crept upward through the tangled undergrowth growing beneath oaks, magnolias and cedars, which in time were joined by such upland vegetation as pines, chinaberry trees, live oaks, wild plums, and acres of palmetto clumps. Winter was only now beginning to release its hold on the forest, and the signs of its invasion were everywhere; the dominant color was the brown of freeze-burned wild grass and weeds, and the stems of dead broomgrass snapped loudly when he forgot to go around it. He knew he'd have to be more careful, if he were to succeed.

Succeed? He wasn't sure what that meant. Finding Old Man Boru was his goal, but what would he do when he found him? Deep down he wanted to kill the man, but deeper down he wanted to see justice done in the appropriate way and the girls in a safe place.

Time and circumstance, he finally decided, would determine his actions...

As he inched further up the slow incline, he could see the smoke hanging above chimney pipes of various sizes and shapes; then he could see rust-marred tin roofs and, finally, the grey, weathered siding of shacks lining a sandy road, gouged out by dry mud holes and liberally sprinkled with protruding tree roots. Pulling aside a palmetto frond to get a better view, he counted more than a dozen domiciles, strung out in disarray and clearly thrown together with no thought of anything but functionality. Some leaned against tall trees for support; only a few had front porches or door stoops. All appeared to have been there a long time.

Except for the chimney smoke, there was no immediate sign of human habitation. Briefly, he pondered that, then decided those existing here likely were abed, sleeping off hangovers or, with nothing else to do, simply having no cause to be out and about. Then he heard a boisterous laugh, one so loud that he ducked deeper into his hiding place. That was followed by other laughs, accompanied by voices saying things he couldn't make out. Little by little, the voices became more subdued, until he couldn't hear them anyone.

Maybe the breeze carrying them had turned; maybe he'd better remember that any sound he made would be carried as well...

Looking from his hideaway again, he saw two men exit a large, barnlike structure at the other end of the cluster of shacks; he figured it was about a hundred yards from where he sat and, from the way the men were staggering, it likely was the local watering hole.

Animals. He'd forgotten to look for animals, which could detect his presence much more quickly than a man, woman or child. Cautiously, he pulled aside the frond again and looked back out. What he saw alarmed him, especially since he realized they'd been there all along. Two dogs were dozing in spare sunlight penetrating the tall oaks, magnolias, and leaf-stripped sycamores. A cat emerged from beneath one shack, stretched itself and lay down in the sand. Warily, be backed off and crept further back into the undergrowth.

Wouldn't it awful, he thought, to have come this far and be discovered by a dog... Patient. He needed to be patient, and think things through. The sun's position told him nightfall was still about two hours away. Time to think, time to doze… He burrowed more deeply beneath the palmetto branches.

"Why, Dru Sullivan, what in tarnation are you doin' over here? You lost your way, or somethin'. Or maybe it's your head you lost?"

The voice seemed to be coming from a long way off, and Dru was slow to react. Blinking his eyes, he looked up into eyes that were looking into his, from beyond a held-back palm frond and vaguely outlined against the paleness of descending darkness.

"C'mon, now, Dru, c'mon on outa there. If you was a'hidin' you been found… I ain't gonna bite."

Dru rose to one elbow, shook his head to clear the cobwebs, and rubbed his eyes with the free hand. He had dozed off, and the voice, while tremulous and sometimes wracked by a cough, clearly was that of a woman.

CHAPTER 26

'Should auld acquaintance be forgot…'

HER FACE WAS LINED and her eyes were tired. Her matted, gray-streaked hair hung below her shoulders, and she wore an ankle-length flowered dress which, like her, was of an uncertain age. A gold tooth, barely visible in the twilight, sat between a pair of yellowed incisors.

But she was smiling, and Dru managed to return the smile.

"Evenin', Ma'm," he mumbled, embarrassed and a little fearful. He had been found, which was exactly what he had been trying to avoid.

"Well, just don't sit there, Dru Sullivan. Come out'a them bushes and explain yourself. You happen to be sleepin' on ground some folks use for the outhouses they hain't got. Hope you were careful where you walked…"

Extending a hand, she looked at him more closely, and said, "You are Dru Sullivan, ain't you? I'd never forget the Dru Sullivan I knew, but that there beard's hiding your face…"

Dru accepted her hand and got to his feet, brushing off the dead grass, brambles and dust. He was tempted to sniff himself, but decided it wouldn't be polite.

"No problem, Ma'm, far as I can tell. Er, do I know you?"

"Lordamercy, I hope so. We grew up together." Pausing and looking him up and down, she added, "It's been a long time, though. Sure has..."

Unable to see clearly in the descending darkness, and hoping not to startle the woman, Dru stepped closer and stared hard into her face. There definitely was something familiar about her; she stood pat, grinned, and even pushed her face closer so he could see it better.

"Well, I swan," he finally said. "Gladys Thompson. You're Gladys Thompson, who moved with her folks to Tifton... Gracious, how long ago? Twenty years, maybe?"

"That sounds 'bout right. And you'd better not be forgettin', what with the good times we had skippin' school and all.

She laughed. "'Course, it was the 'and all' I like to remember. Lordy, Dru Sullivan, we learned what *it* was like and I just never could get over it. Or quit doin' it, either..."

Now Dru was embarrassed, red-faced embarrassed. Gladys had been a pretty girl, too pretty for her own good, folks said; she'd been older them him – his Magalene, sort of – and one of his secret excuses for avoiding school, which in time had become habit. Her pa and older brothers had been poor farmers, inclined toward laziness; the men drank excessively, their own liquor when they could afford it and stealing it when they couldn't. Her worn-out ma had given up caring. Eventually they had up and moved 70 miles south to Tifton. Other than Dru, few had sorrowed over their departure.

Though he had always remembered Gladys Thompson fondly, he had forced himself to put her on the back shelf of his mind as the years had passed. The word coming back to Shannon County was that she had become a whore, and a notorious and unashamed one to boot. He didn't like to think of the role he had played in her life, that maybe she had helped set the course for his own life...

Sullivan Road

Refocusing on the present, Dru realized Gladys was still staring at him, but that her grin had faded during his long, contemplative silence. Her disappointment was evident.

"Why, Dru, hain't you got nothin' to say? You just gonna stand there like a lightnin'-struck tree? Say somethin'!"

Reacting quickly, Dru responded, "Aw my goodness, Gladys, I was just remembering our times together and how I missed you all them years. You wouldn't begrudge that, would you?"

Her face brightened. "Well, now, that's more like it. Why don't you come up to my place and we can catch up on things, like what you are doin' here. Lordamercy, I can't imagine you comin' to this place…"

An hour later, after he had explained himself and after a moonless night had settled on the cluster of shacks, Dru sat on a rickety, cane-backed chair at Gladys' grease-rubbed pine table; she said it was her most prized possession, and one of the few things she had managed to haul up from Tifton after failing health had forced her out of her chosen profession.

"Men don't like to do it with a coughin', hackin', mewlin' woman," she said, without further explanation. He didn't ask, and assumed from her rasping voice and too-frequent coughs that she might have a lung sickness. He felt he should respond, but couldn't. What, he wondered, could a man say to a woman who openly acknowledged being a fallen woman, but whose face revealed the furtiveness of someone who had suffered greatly and was ashamed.

She was feeding Dru from a huge pot of stew cooked up on a blackened wood-burning stove, which took up about one-fifth of her small shack. The table, three chairs, a bed and a 'shifferroll" of drawers – her description – filled the remainder. The dwelling sat a few yards back of the others on the north side of the road, a location which pleased Dru. It had been empty for almost a year, she said, until she had arrived several months earlier and had been told it was hers for the taking.

"Mostly men said that," she'd mumbled to herself. He had heard, however, and had grimaced when she'd added, "That was before they got me in that bed over there and decided I was damaged goods…"

"Hain't got no coffee," she said, after contemplating the story he'd told her and watching him woof down the stew and a hardened chunk of bread she'd come up with from somewhere.

"Water's fine," he responded. "Maybe I'll be able to find some coffee while I'm here." He felt he should say more, but didn't know what; both were thinking personal thoughts and biding their time.

Pulling up a chair and sitting down opposite him, she asked, "You wouldn't have the makin's, would you? I run out a long time ago."

Feeling in the bib pocket of his overalls, he pulled out a bent tin of Prince Albert, shook it, and said, "Might be some left in this. The papers are long gone…"

"Don't matter," she said, taking the tobacco. "Newspaper will do."

Moments later, she blew smoke from her raised nostrils and leaned back. "What you gonna do, Dru? Boru is one mean SOB and even this place has gone downhill in the few days since he come back."

Dru raised a questioning eyebrow.

"He never really left, you know. Now that he's back fulltime he stays drunk most of the time, and when he's so drunk nobody'll have any truck with him, he goes looking for a fight. Found 'em for a while, but he don't fight fair and folks just walk away when he starts up.

"If there's a chunk of firewood or a rock he can reach, he'll lay a'hold of it and lay somebody out…"

She paused, blew a smoke ring, and stared directly at him, as though she was asking a question. "There ain't much food in this place, but us that's got some been sharin' it with them girls he brought over here. Bertha and Magalene, he calls 'em"

He still did not respond, nor did he show any reaction. He just sat there, examining his hands.

Finally, she stood up and circled the table. "Goddamit all, I know it's true 'cause you said so. But it's beyond me to think that that old man was daddy to his own grandchild! And that he killed his own daughter!

"Good God almighty, the devil's gotta have a special treat for that man…"

"And I reckon I'm the man who'll have to take it to him," Dru said softly. Lifting his voice some, he asked, "Where's he hang out most of the time…"

"Down there with the rest of 'em, at Satan's Hideaway. Ol' Jack Barker may have thought he was funnin' when he made up that name for his drinkin' place, but he was calling it right…

"Most of the women stayin' here don't go down there much. Their men won't let 'em, for one thing. I went in for a while, til they figured out I wasn't much good no more…

"I still get in there once in a while. The likker ain't the best, and sometimes some new fella who don't know me will buy me a drink."

Her voice had trailed off, and Dru didn't say anything for several moments. Then he looked up at the still-walking Gladys, and said, "I think I know what I'm gonna do. I sure will need your help, though…"

With a toss of the hand, she indicated that was a given.

"You any good at play-actin'," he asked.

"Been doin' that all my life. Leastwise, ever since them good times when we was young."

CHAPTER 27

'This here's hell, Boru, and I'm the devil...'
–Dru to Old Man Boru

MUCH LATER, WHEN THE raucous noises coming over from Satan's Hideaway had reached a crescendo, Dru and a scantily dressed Gladys snuck along through the woods until they were directly behind the place. After a whispered exchange, she strolled jauntily to the open door, looked in, and flashed him a high sign.

Dru signaled back, and then headed to the shack Gladys had said the Borus occupied. Peeking inside, he saw Bertha sitting on a stool and reading by the light of a coal-oil lamp; Magalene sat on the floor nearby, with arms wrapped around her knees and her eyes staring blankly into a darkened fireplace.

Quietly, Dru entered. Bertha looked up and immediately jumped to her feet. Magalene looked his way, but did not move.

"Shhh," he said. "It's only me, your Uncle Dru. I'm here to help you."

"Why'd we need help," Bertha asked, frowning and stepping back against a wall. "You killed Momma. We don't need no help from no one, specially not you."

She bolted for the door, but Dru intercepted her. Holding her by the shoulders, he looked directly into her eyes and said, "Whoa, now. I didn't kill your momma, and you know I didn't. That's a lie your grandpa's been tellin' you…"

"Ain't so! Your killed her! Grandpa says so; the sheriff says so!"

Dru opened his mouth, but didn't know what to say. He noticed that Magalene had risen and was creeping up behind her older sister. He hadn't counted on this kind resistance; he knew he should have, but he had not.

Bertha struggled to break his grasp and reach the door. He shushed her again, saying, "Please now. Bertha, hear me out. I didn't kill your momma. I loved her and she loved me. She did. God knows she did, and He knows I wouldn't hurt a hair on her head."

Bertha quit struggling, but her body remained rigid and she began to cry. Her face was dirty, her hair matted and she smelled of not bathing. Her dress was filthy and torn on one shoulder. Magalene looked much the same…

"Bertha, Bertha, listen to me, now! You know you don't belong over in this here place and you're smart enough to wonder why you was brought over here. I come to get you, and with the help of somebody who loves you I'm gonna get you out of here and back where you can get proper care…"

Bertha sagged and, feeling dead weight, Dru feared she was going to faint away. Poor child, he thought; she's got to be starving and perhaps ill. Magalene, too.

He shook her again. "You listenin' to me, gal? We're gonna get you outa here, but you got to help…"

"You, you killed Momma," Bertha said again, so softly he could barely make out her words. "Grandpa said so…"

"I didn't kill Sara," he said through gritted teeth. "You gotta believe me. You just gotta!"

From behind him came a voice, saying, "He didn't, Bertha. Honest he didn't. Come here to me and I'll explain why Dru's here. I brought you somethin' to eat…"

As he turned and released the girl, Gladys told him, "Old man's ready for the takin', Dru. Probably best you wait til he's left that place and comes home. Ain't nobody gonna be wantin' to come with him. He's stinko…"

"Okay, Gladys. You take them out the back way and to your place. I'll wait her."

"What you gonna do after that?"

"Depends. You said you had a mule and wagon…" It was more of a question than a statement.

"I do. Keep 'em both over at the corral we all use. Sometimes someone else will use 'em, but they was there day or so ago."

"Help muchly if we know for sure they're there."

"I'll look when I take the girls home. We go right by the corral."

Bertha resisted when Gladys approached her, shrinking back against the cold stove and mumbling, "Why you with him? I ain't goin'…"

Magalene, however, looked from one to the other, and finally said, "But Bertha, she says she's gonna feed us. Why would she say that if she didn't mean it."

Bertha's eyes, rebellious and uncertain, swung back and forth between Dru and Gladys; even when she moved, she stepped around them as far as the small room would allow. Reaching Magalene, she took her by the hand and, edging past Gladys, she led her out the door and into the dark night.

Alone in the Boru cabin, Dru searched beneath the mattress and other likely spots for a hidden weapon. Finding none, he checked the unwashed eating utensils and assorted dishes sitting on one end of the stove. Strange place for those to be, he thought; but, looking around, he noticed again that the only table in the room was a small one, holding a water pail and a wash basin. Turning back to the dinnerware, he removed a butcher knife and placed it out of sight, on a cross-beam separating two poles helping support the ceiling.

Suddenly, his attention was diverted by someone coming up the road and singing loudly.

And he couldn't help but grin as the noise got louder...

"Oh my darlin', oh my darlin', oh my darlin' Clementine, you are lost and gone forever, dreadful sorry, Clementine.

"Ruby lips above the water, blowin' bubbles soft'n fine..."

Dru heard a loud thump, the cabin shook slightly, and the singing stopped abruptly. Boru had stumbled and fallen against the outside wall near the door; Dru visualized the man, smiled and almost laughed. Catching himself, he stopped and mumbled, "T'ain't funny. Nothin's funny about this. Let's get on with it."

Striding to the door, he reached out and grabbed the surprised Boru by the arm and hauled him in. The man almost fell, but Dru took him by the shoulders, shook him, and looked straight into his blurred, dazed eyes.

'This here's hell, Boru, and I'm the devil," he said, with teeth bared and grinding on one another. Deep furrows cut across his brow, and he shook Boru – forward, backward, sideways...

The huge man, as tall as Dru and much heavier, simply sagged toward the floor, his eyes unseeing, his mind shut down in an alcoholic blackout.

"Damn," muttered Dru. "Damn, damn, damn!"

He drug Boru across the floor and threw him on the bed. Then he sat down to wait...

CHAPTER 28

Old Man Boru's Banshee Swamp...

BORU WAS DEAD TO the world, his mouth opening and closing and spouting loud snores, assorted gibberish, and the foul odor of beer and hard liquor. Time passed, and Dru sat and remembered Sara and Lonny, visualizing them in the best and worst of circumstances: Sara smiling and running ahead of him up a cedar-lined road and down through the ravine leading to the fording place, their Eden, a place where they could be alone and feel complete; Lonny grinning broadly when John told him he'd been cleared to enter his prize pig in the previously all-white 4-H exposition.

Then he cringed, as he saw again Sara's battered body lying in a pigsty, the only movement a breeze playing with her filthy, torn dress; and Lonny, blood oozing from a jagged hole in his head and mixing with the muck of a rain-sodden pigsty.

Grimacing, Dru arose, picked up the butcher knife he'd placed on the cross-beam, and walked to the side of the bed on which Boru sprawled. The minutes clicked away, in time with the changing expressions on Dru's face, expressions which alternated between a hate-fed, soul-searing desire for revenge and a Godspot-fed awareness that he could not, would not, be judge, jury, and executioner.

He could not assume the role of the God he was finally beginning to sense, indeed to believe, was an all-seeing, all-powerful deity whose grand design a mortal could neither understand nor question. Backing away from the bed, he sat down again; and he remained there quietly, slapping the knife with one hand against the open, trembling palm of the other.

He sat and he dozed and he arose and walked around the room; he repeated the process several times, waiting for the monster on the bed to awaken. A pre-dawn sprinkle settled the dust in the road beyond the front door; Gladys reappeared, curious and anxious, and returned to her shack and the girls after Dru assured her nothing had happened, that he was waiting for the man to awaken from his drunken stupor before confronting him.

Boru finally did, when the sun had risen to a midmorning level and Dru was anxiously watching through a grimy window, hoping, praying, that no one would show up in the yard. Hearing Boru's snores give way to pained utterances, Dru turned and their eyes met.

"You," the prone man said sharply. "Where'd you come from? Got no business here. Man needs his sleep…"

Dru stared back for a long moment, and then spoke softly.

"You gonna get more sleep than you ever dreamed of."

"Whut? What's that? Who the hell are you?"

Raising himself to on elbow, Boru rubbed his bleary eyes and stared hard at the figure outlined against the window; seeing the knife clutched in the figure's hand, he threw both feet to the floor and sat up.

"Move to where I can see you," he demanded. "Don't hide in that damned light…"

Dru took two steps, one forward and one to the side. He said nothing.

Suddenly, Boru recognized him. "Dru Sullivan! What the hell are you doin' in my house?" Looking around the room, he shouted, "And where're my gals? Where they gone?"

"Gone is right," Dru said in a barely audible voice. "Gone where they're safe from the likes of you; gone and you'll never see 'em ag'in."

Boru gripped the side of the bed, as if about to spring from it. He looked again at the knife and changed his mind.

"What you want?" Moving one hand to the back of his neck, he rubbed it and shrugged his shoulders. "I'm thirsty," he said, after Dru didn't answer. "Mind if I get some water?"

"Hell yes, I mind," Dru said firmly. "You can suffer, you bastard, suffer like you made Sara suffer all them years! You move and I swear I'll kill you, right now, right here, the way you killed Sara… And Lonny, too.

"Only you didn't give 'em the chance I'm giving you. You took no mercy on them! You just killed 'em and left' 'em in them turd-filled, filthy pigsties. You…"

"That ain't so," Boru interrupted. Shifting his eyes from right to left and clearly looking for a way out, he added, "It ain't so and you can't prove it if'n I did kill 'em…"

"Oh, I'm gonna prove it alright and you're gonna help me, you goddamn slobberin' old SOB. You're gonna admit you done it or I'm gonna beat you to death. Maybe do some cuttin' on you while I'm about it…"

Boru was holding the side of the bed again, harder and with fingers gripping, letting go, gripping again, squeezing harder each time; hatred-fed flames danced in his dark eyes; they danced from side to side, reflecting the fear that was in him as well.

"I'm gonna give you a choice, old man," Dru continued. "You can fess up and come with me to the judge over in Carey County and take your chances in court…"

"You're crazy, that's whut you are! Goddamn shanty Irish Sullivan…"

"…Or you can get up off'n that bed and I'll cut your gullet out and let you bleed to death. You d'cide what you wanna do! Truth be known, I don't give a tinker's damn no more…"

Suddenly Boru bolted for the box behind the stove, grabbed a chunk of oak wood, turned to face Dru and began pounding it in a beefy hand.

"I made my d'cision," he sneered, "and it's to splatter your fool brains all over this place. That knife ain't gonna do you a bit of good."

He lunged, swinging the split log in a roundhouse motion aimed at Dru's left shoulder. At the same time, he picked up the stool and held it between him and Dru's knife-holding right hand. Dru threw the knife aside, took the blow on the shoulder, and tackled Boru at the knees.

Boru dropped the firewood, and the pair rolled over and over one another, swinging punches when they could and scratching and gouging when they couldn't. Dru was amazed at the older man's quickness; he knew Boru was a strong man, but he hadn't counted on his speed – and certainly not after seeing him so hung over from a night of drinking.

Dru was the first to regain his feet, and he caught the rising Boru with a balled-up fist smack on the tip of his chin. Dazed, the older man dropped to one knee and raised his arms too late to avoid an arching left-hand punch Dru aimed from the ceiling. Desperate, Boru grabbed one of Dru's legs, pulled him to the floor and, despite the punches raining down on the back of his head and neck, he crawled atop Dru's legs and sank his teeth into a thigh.

Dru growled in pain and began pounding Boru on both sides of his face, trying to disengage his teeth from the fabric and the flesh welling up beneath it. He succeeded, but Boru, with face held down, managed to deliver an overhead blow on Dru's crotch. Stunned and paralyzed with pain, Dru lay helpless for several seconds, while Boru lashed out at him with lefts and rights that turned his head from side to side.

Then, spotting the knife on the floor a few feet away, Boru scrambled off Dru and grabbed it. Turning, he rose to one knee, and sneered savagely. "The tables is turned," he said through bloody lips. "Now I'm gonna cut your balls off..."

Launching himself with the knife extended, Boru was on top of Dru before he could roll out of the way. But he'd managed to get a clutch-hold on the wrist of the hand holding the knife and turned it away from his body. With the free hand, Dru pounded at Boru's face; but the much-heavier man absorbed the blows and, gritting his teeth, forced the knife closer and closer to Dru's face.

Just as it appeared Dru was about to collapse under the pressure and take the knife in an eye, he slammed a knee upward into Boru's crotch and rolled from under him. Boru still held the knife, but he also was holding his crotch and screaming in pain. Dru had run out of mercy; he picked up the chunk of wood Boru had dropped and, rolling from side to the other, he used the momentum to smash the wood down on Boru's forehead. He couldn't have scored better if he'd had time to aim the blow. Boru was out cold, with blood spurting from a gaping wound above his eyes.

For some time, Dru lay on his back, breathing hard blinking his eyes. Had he killed the man? He prayed that he had not; he wanted Boru to live long enough to admit his crimes and suffer the legal consequences for them.

Rising finally to his hands and knees, Dru crawled over to Boru's sprawled-out body. The man was breathing heavily and a quick examination of the gash on his head indicated that it probably was not fatal.

"You bleed like the hog you are," Dru mumbled, "but I reckon you ain't gutted yet…"

Bone-weary, Dru remained sitting while he took stock of his own wounds. Aside from skinned knuckles and a cut on the right side of his face, he did not appear to have suffered severely. His left thigh, where Boru had sunk his teeth, ached terribly, but no blood oozed from the fabric. Though his crotch still throbbed, the pain was easing by the moment.

His eyes hurt badly, however, and he rubbed them as hard as he dared. Then he scanned the room, until his eyes finally focused on the pail of water and tin basin sitting on the small table near the door. Struggling to his feet, he took a ragged towel hanging from a nail in a stud, soaked it and scoured his face and the wounds on his hands. Then he sat down next to Boru and began cleaning the old man's face and head wound.

Knowing he would be unable to lift Boru onto the bed, he left him where he was. Then he returned to the basin, picked up the knife and sat down in the chair.

"That's round one," he muttered.

Boru was out for about three hours, during which Gladys came by again, this time with a bowl of stew. Seeing Boru stretched out on the floor, she grimaced and said, "Ouch. This goin' to be over soon? I had to head off a couple of his drinkin' buddies who'd heard the noise and was headed this way…"

"Hope so. He's a tough old turkey."

"Sure is a big fella. If he didn't look so mean, I'd say he looks like that there Burl Ives I heard sing over to Albany few years back. Sang a song about lavenders bein' blue."

"I thought they was purple."

"You'd a'said they was blue if you'd a'heard him…"

She stood by his side long enough to touch a welt on his cheek, smiled sadly, and left.

"The girls is fine," she said.

An hour later, with thunder building up in the southwest and the skies becoming darker, Boru moaned. Touching the gash on his forehead, he moaned louder and tried to sit up.

Then he noticed Dru, sitting on the stool casually tapping the knife in an open hand. Dru was frowning.

"Welcome back, old man. I reckon you know you been at death's door, and it leads straight down to hell."

He wanted to frighten Boru, to bring an end to the bloody standoff.

Feeling his crotch, the older man licked a swollen bottom lip and mumbled, "You don't fight fair…"

Their eyes locked and neither said anything for a strung-out minute. Then Boru's eyes focused on the knife.

"You ain't the kind to use that," he said.

"Try me," said Dru.

More silence. Then Boru got to one elbow and pushed himself into a sitting position.

"So you want me to 'mit I killed Sara and that lousy nigger kid," he said. "I'll die first."

Dru got off the stool and took stepped toward the man.

"You made the choice. It's likely you're a'gonna."

Boru looked to his right, left and then behind him. He mumbled something, but a thunder roll and the splatter of rain on the tin roof drowned him out. Dru was now standing over him; Boru looked up, then crab-walked backward until he pushed up against the bed.

Dru let him go, and went to the window. It was raining hard, pounding the tin above their heads and making further talk almost impossible. Finally, Boru spoke above the din.

"I smell food. You been eatin'?"

"Stew. Had some stew. Plenty left for you, if you want to git straight with me ... and yourself."

Turning, he added, "Give you some water, too. You must be really needful of that by now."

Boru didn't respond.

"You got any family, Boru?"

The old man cocked his head. "Why you want to know?"

"Thinking of the girls."

"My girls? Where they at? You got no right..."

"They're fine, Boru. You got more things to worry 'bout than Magalene and Bertha. I'll ask ag'in: You got any family?"

Boru rubbed his bashed forehead, thinking. "Got a sister down in Blackshear..."

"She anything like you?"

Looking up and wondering where Dru was going with this line of questioning, he mumbled, "Nope. She's a good God-fearin' widow woman. Hain't seen her in some time. Younger'n me by a few years."

"Blackshear's down there close to Floridy, ain't it?"

"Yep. Closest big town is Waycross. Railroad town."

"Blackshear?"

"Some. Waycross is the big 'un. Railroads cross there. Mostly farmers and niggers in Blackshear."

"Black folks don't farm?"

"Hah! Not so you'd notice. But a white man can't farm without 'em."

Dru sauntered back to the stool and sat down and stared at his captive; Boru stared back, then asked, "Why you wanna take me to Carey County? The judge there, he hain't got no juris... ah, he got nothin' to do with Shannon County."

"Judge Crawford's said to be an honest man and he's the circuit judge. Folks say he knows about your pal Nobles and don't care for him. He'd likely make sure everybody gets a fair shake.

"This keeps up and you sure as hell ain't gonna get one from me," Dru said, rising from the stool and moving toward Boru, knife in hand. "...and I'm runnin' out of patience."

Boru moved as if to take a seat on the bed, then stopped and raised an arm.

"Alright, alright! So I killed 'em. One was a no-good nigger and Sara... Well, I was crazy outa my mind. Drunk. Don't hardly 'member doin' it.

"She had it comin' anyways... Worthless harlot..."

He paused, looked up at Dru and said, "But you know'd that better'n anyone..."

Dru lashed out with a fist, striking the cringing Boru on the jaw. The man tumbled onto one side and Dru kicked him in the ribs. He raised the knife above his head, poised to plunge it in Boru's unprotected belly.

Then he stopped, stepped back, breathing hard and struggling to regain control of himself. "You ain't worth it," he whispered bitterly, his teeth gnashing. "You just ain't worth it..."

Turning away and walking to the window again, he said, "Git yourself some water. We'll go when it quits rainin..."

Dru opened the door, wondering how he was going to alert Gladys. The girls? They'd have to stay with her while he took Boru into Sligo, the Carey County seat, about 16 miles to the southwest. Somehow he'd have to get Gladys' mule harnessed, hooked up to the wagon, and get out of T'other Side without being seen.

He'd need to tie up Boru, but realized he hadn't any rope in the shack. Would bedsheets do? Damn it all, anyway. So many things he hadn't thought of...

Dru heard the sudden movement behind him, but he was unable to react quickly enough. He managed to turn and instinctively raise one arm, a movement which likely saved his life. Boru was charging him, swinging the hunk of wood with both hands and screaming his anger.

Once more Dru's shoulder took the brunt of the blow, though part of it caught one side of his head. He fell, dazed and unable to move. The chunk of wood glanced away and rolled against one wall. For a crazed moment, Boru looked around, cursing but unable to find it. Then, seeing the open door, he kicked Dru in the ribs and raced out through it.

Dru hurt, hurt really bad. His right shoulder and arm were so numb he had to feel to make sure they were still attached. He was bleeding from a cut on his head, just above an ear covered by the thick mat of his black hair. Recovering quickly, however, he struggled out to his feet and, using the door jam for leverage, he pushed himself out into the downpour. The deluge blurred his eyes, but he wiped it away and looked up and down the darkening road. Seeing nothing, he stepped to one side of an oak tree, using it to partially shield him from the blowing wind and rain.

From behind the shack Boru suddenly emerged, jumped on his back and began pounding Dru's head with his free hand. Dropping to one knee, Dru reached deep down inside himself for what strength he had left, and, with a loud, angry shout, slung Boru over his shoulder, leaving him sprawled on his back in the mud. But Boru, again with remarkable agility, was on his feet, cursing and stumbling away, across the road and headed into the palmetto clumps, brambles and other undergrowth leading to the dark swamp.

Catching his breath, Dru followed. "You don't wanna go down there!" he shouted. "You damn fool! Come back here..."

Boru, weakened by exertion and the beating he'd taken and also winded, struggled on, with Dru close behind and closing the distance. Down they went, down through the pines and oaks and magnolias. Dru finally was able to make a grab for Boru, but fell short. Rising to one knee, he saw the old man crash through a looming wall of foliage. Weeping willows, Dru knew, with the cypress-dotted swamp on the other side.

Pushing through their supple, pliant hanging branches, Dru halted at the swamp's side. In the dark, he couldn't see the morass he knew began at his feet and stretched for nearly a mile across. It was the way he'd come just the day before; there was no way he was going to follow Boru into the muck and mire on such a dark, rainy night. He stood there, feeling helpless and listening hard but knowing the rain would make it virtually impossible to hear any sound at all...

But then he heard it, a screaming, plaintive voice begging for help. Modulated by wind and rain, the screams rose and fell; it was difficult to determine the distance to the source or from which direction the cries came.

Dru stood in place, listening...

"Help! Help me ... drowning... Dru, Dru ... For pity's sake ... goddamn shanty..."

The calls, increasingly mournful and fading away, finally died. The wind raged on, as did the desperation wracking Dru. Twice he stepped into the swamp water and pushed ahead until it was up to his waist; each time he retreated.

"Mud hole without a bottom," he whispered. "Just like the quicksand in them Tarzan picture shows..."

He started to add, "Nobody oughta die like that..." But he changed his mind and, after a several more minutes during which he heard nothing but wind, rain and his own heavy breathing, he turned and began picking his way back up the hill.

"Reckon," he mumbled, "you found your Banshee Swamp, old man."

CHAPTER 29

'A man's always got a choice, Dru..."
— Gladys, as they set out for Blackshear

DRU AND GLADYS WAITED til after midnight to leave T'other Side and head southeast, the direction in which the now-departed Sylvester Boru had said they'd find Blackshear and the only surviving relative he had known: a younger sister named Imogene Rafferty. Obtaining the information about the sister had been difficult, but getting Boru's given name had been much more so.

Mercifully, the rain had stopped; but the rut roads were full of water-filled mud holes and the wooden wagon seats were soaked through. So was the wagon's body, where Bertha and Magalene slept fitfully atop worn blankets which did little to smother the dampness.

Even Satan's Hideaway was muted, as though the likker lappers – Gladys' description – had decided collectively that the inclement weather provided an opportunity to sleep off accumulated hangovers and related ills; perhaps the consensus, she joked, was that a rainy "dry" spell had its advantages.

Dru guffawed at her attempts at humor, but remained stone-faced and mute for the most part. He knew she was trying to get her mind, their minds, off what had transpired and onto what might be down the road.

Gladys' mule, named Hiram, was a pleasant-enough fellow, despite being rousted from his stall at such an unusual hour and in such inhospitable weather. Without complaint he plodded along in the darkness, picking his way with some sort of sixth sense with which animals apparently are gifted.

They had not told the girls what had happened to their grandpa. Bertha didn't ask; and in one emotional moment, she told Dru that, yes, Grandpa Boru was a bad man, that he had beaten them often and their mother most of all. "Hated him," she'd said, avoiding Dru's eyes. "Scared of him…"

Dru had wanted to ask her whether she'd witnessed the fatal beating of Sara; but that would have been too painful, for Bertha and for him. Instead, he'd pulled her head to his midsection, hugged her and stroked her hair. She had cried, and she had returned the hug.

Magalene remained in her faraway world, staring, seeing what only she could see, her eyes alternately reflecting disappointment and elation; occasionally she whispered to herself: "Angels. Where have the angels gone? There's gotta be…"

"Scared," Dru interjected, very softly. "They been scared away…"

"Frightened's a better word," Gladys said, also whispering. "I reckon we're following the frightened angels…"

Dru pondered that for a silent moment. "Where'd you get to be so 'phisticated? That's a word with lots of feelin'…"

"Dunno, Dru. I read a lot, when I can find somethin' to read. Wasn't much in T'other Side, as you call it…"

Looking at him in the dark, she whispered, "And where'd you get to know feelin's?"

He shrugged; she added, "Maybe we both growed some…"

Hiram plodded on, instinctively turning when the black passage ahead turned; he seemed tireless.

But Gladys and Dru were very tired; with a blanket wrapped around her shoulders for warmth, she leaned against him and dosed occasionally, awakening when the wagon hit a rut or bounced over a root. The heaviness in her chest remained, and she coughed frequently – deep, retching coughs that caused Dru's brow to furrow and his lips to twitch nervously.

"I can always tell when there's rain comin'," she remarked once the attack had subsided. "My chest feels like I swallowed a great big rock and can't spit it up."

Compassionately, Dru placed a hand on her knee and squeezed softly. "It'll get better," he said. "It's got to…"

Once, when Gladys yawned and stretched her arms above her head, he said, "You oughta quit dozing so much and do some driving. He's your mule."

"How can you talk like that when you're so worried 'bout my health?"

He guffawed and said, "You recollect the date?"

"Date? Not sure, but I think it's comin' on to April. Maybe it's already April…"

"'Bout time Jewell and them boys oughta be leaving for Floridy," he said. "Lordy, I'm gonna miss 'em…"

Softly, he added, "Specially Bo. I'm sure gonna miss that boy."

He remembered the times, when spying on the Boru shack, he'd seen Jim drive slowly and he had resisted the temptation – extreme at times – to hail him down. He remembered seeing Jewell pass in her wagon, too. Bo and Arlis had been with her, and the temptation to call out had been strongest when he saw the boys…

He wondered now whether he had been right to avoid his family. But he had not wanted to involve any of them for fear of what might happen to them.

Nobles, like Boru, was a crazy man.

And so was Beatrice O'Connell Sulli… But he had closed off any thoughts of her almost as quickly as it had popped up. He wondered whether he was still married to her. Perhaps she had done as she had said she would and divorced him.

He hoped so. He prayed so.

Gladys was yawning and pressing herself against his arm again. "What we gonna do, Dru? Where we goin'?"

"To Blackshear. To give these girls to their aunt…"

"That really what you wanna do, Dru?"

"What else can I do? Seems to me I got no choice…"

"Man's always got a choice," she said, softly. "He just has to decide what it is…"

Dawn found them coming into a crossroads hamlet, which a crude sign told them was Pineview. A woman emerged from a frame house, the water-soaked, unpainted siding black from the overnight soaking. She dumped a pail of water, watched them approach, and then came to the side of the road.

"There's young'uns sittin' up in the back of that wagon," she said, "and they gotta be cold and hungry. You want to stop and come in a while?"

It went that way for the next six days, as they meandered south and east over unpaved country roads, avoiding the occasional paved ones when they could. The intermittent cars and trucks and prying eyes made them nervous, and they were uncomfortable even when they came upon a wagon or somebody on foot. The anxiety lessened, however, as time passed; it became evident that those traveling the back roads in the old ways shared camaraderie that did not require explanation.

Exeter, Haverford, Fitzgerald, Smytheville, and even smaller towns and crossroads communities whose names – if they had names – they could not remember slid by to the clop-clop of Hiram's hooves. But they were met in almost all with kindness, and twice spent the night as guests of farm families. The wagon's empty bed filled each day with old clothing, housewares and other items, prompting Gladys to remark, "If this keeps up, we'll have enough to set up our own house when we get there…"

Dru just looked at her, and returned to his own thoughts.

Finally, after almost a week on the road, they rounded a bend and began descending a hill. The wagon rocked in the ruts and their bodies ached. Off to the left, a stream appeared and in time it broadened into a river. Railroad tracks extended across the road and, stopping on it and looking along the rails, they saw a depot in the distance. A large, aging sign painted near the top of the two-story structure told them they had reached their destination.

"Blackshear," Dru and Gladys said in unison. She squeezed his arm, and turned to the girls.

"We're here," she said. "This is gonna be your new home."

Without being specific about Sylvester Boru's fate, they had told the girls of the journey's purpose. Bertha, aged 14 now, may have understood more than she'd been told, but had not let on.

Magalene had simply wanted to know whether there were angels in Blackshear.

"There's angels everywhere," Gladys told her. "We'll find some in Blackshear for sure…"

"Have to find the right trees," Magalene responded. "They live in special trees."

CHAPTER 30

"Oh, that's gotta be where angels live..."
             —Magalene, upon arrival in Blackshear

DRU WAS ANXIOUS TO head for the railroad depot, thinking it looked large enough to be a town center in which they might find out how to locate Imogene Rafferty, and perhaps learn something about the woman. But he yielded to Gladys, who wanted to look around some before doing that.

"Looks like a nice little place," she ventured. Seeing his inquiring stare, she added, "You're not in all that much a hurry, are you? After a week on the road, seems like we don't have to rush into things..."

"Lessen it's a bathtub," he mumbled.

The railroad tracks and a bridge crossing the river – the Altahaba, a sign told them – were on the left of the partially paved main thoroughfare they traveled. Beyond the bridge was a clump of oaks, sycamores and some pines, and beyond that were fields recently plowed for spring planting. He "geed" Hiram to the right, onto a sandy side street leading past clap-board houses and small bungalows, which soon gave way to several two- and three-story Victorians which bespoke of wealth.

Pierce Lehmbeck

"Oooo," Gladys remarked, "wouldn't it be somethin' if…"

"Yep," said Dru, "but don't go countin' on it. "

With a gift blanket draped around her shoulders, Bertha sat in the back, on a rocker they'd also been given during the journey. She was silent, but her eyes brightened as Hiram clip-clopped past one of the larger houses; it was three stories tall, had steeply a pitched roof, pointed-arch windows, elaborately carved trim along roof edges, high dormers, and lancet windows.

Pointing to a tiny porch extending from a narrow door near the top of the structure, Bertha said, "Lookit that. What is it, Uncle Dru? I never saw such…"

Gladys responded. "It's a widow's walk, honey. I read somewheres it's for wives whose menfolk have gone off and they're watchin' for them to come back. Read it in a sea-farin' book, but I reckon they'd have a reason for bein' here, too."

"Can't see far with all them trees," Bertha said, turning her head and continuing to watch as the wagon passed on by.

"Decoration," mumbled Dru. "Probably put up there for looks rather'n anything else. Darn if I can figure why they'd need all them curvy things on a house anyways…"

"It's filigree," said Gladys. "Or somethin' like that. And it is for decoration. Like twirly lace on a fine curtain or tablecloth. Why, I read once where they even put heads of monsters and ghouls and things like that on some houses, in overseas places we hain't been…"

Attracted by the talking, Magalene looked up from a picture book and saw the house. "Oh, that's gotta be where angels live," she said excitedly. "It's purty…"

"Well, honey, I don't know 'bout that," Dru said softly, "but if that's what rich folks spend their money on, I reckon there's just as many crazy rich folks as there are crazy poor folks…"

"Awww," said Gladys, giving his shoulder a shove. "You're just bein' jealous."

"Hain't never been jealous of a crazy man," he mumbled. "Ain't gonna start now."

Besides, he was thinking, the houses along this street reminded him somewhat of the O'Connell place…

"…Without the fili… or whatever that was."

Suddenly, Gladys placed a hand on her breast and began coughing uncontrollably. Dru halted the wagon, took the reins in one hand and soundly slapped her on the back, watching with concern as her face turned crimson. For the better part of a minute she leaned over the edge of the wagon, wheezing and occasionally bringing up blood-stained phlegm.

"Lordamercy, I got to get over this some ways," she muttered when the retching subsided. "What'd you say, Dru?"

"Said reckon it's time we find 'nother street, one leadin' back into town. And we gotta find you a doctor. One of these times you ain't gonna make it through one of them fits."

Bertha had moved up to place both hands on Gladys' shoulders. "I'll take care of her," she said. "You shouldn't be hittin' her so hard…"

Magalene had moved to the back of the wagon. There, she sat on her knees and watched as the big house began to disappear behind trees along the road; it disappeared altogether when Dru turned onto another side street.

Several minutes later, Dru "hawed" Hiram into the yard of the depot. It was more than that; the huge building had a cotton gin built into one end, and most of the rest was given over to warehouse space. A small stack of cotton bales, left over from last fall's picking, occupied one corner. Most of the space was taken up by stacks of sweet-smelling, freshly cut lumber, and Dru surmised there was a sizeable sawmill operation somewhere around Blackshear.

A few workers moved about, mostly Negroes; a few whites were among them, but they were mostly older folks you'd expect to see sitting on a front porch and avoiding work if they could survive without it. He flagged down one of them and asked, "Ain't there no young folks 'round here to handle this kinda work?"

"Nope. Them that can and wants to work have gone off to the shipyards down in Jacksonville. Just picked up and left, taken' their families and all. Can't hardly blame 'em. Pays awful good down there…"

Looking Dru up and down, he said, "Talkin' 'bout wars, you look like you've done been in one. You need to see a doc? Old Doc Hardy's right good, when you can find him…"

Looking at Dru again, he added, "You new 'round here? Don't recall seeing you before…"

Dru, recalling John's reasons for going to the shipyard city, didn't respond right off; he was thinking John apparently had known what he was talking about.

"Answered your question," the man was saying to Dru. "Gonna answer mine?"

"Huh? Oh, yessir, didn't mean to be unsocial-like. Just got in town and I'm a mite weary. Lookin' to find a woman named Imogene Rafferty."

"Miss Rafferty, who lives down the tracks there a'ways? Yep, I know her. Sure do. You kin?"

"Ahh, no, I'm not kin. I know some of her kin, though, and I need to talk to her. You say she lives down the track a'ways?" Dru pointed looked in the direction the man was pointing. "Thataway?"

"Yep. Thataways. Third house once you go round that bend in the road. Right on the tracks. Used to be white. You ought'na have trouble findin' it."

Dru turned away, intending to return to the wagon, which he'd tied up outside and in which he had left Gladys, Bertha and Magalene. He paused, looked again at the man and said, "I'm a farmer and a good one, and don't reckon I'd care to build ships, even if it was to help win the war." Motioning to the stacked lumber, he added, "I got a strong back, though, and I could handle that. You reckon they need an extra hand?"

"Haaah. For certain, *we* do. I'm the foreman and my name's James. James Pulaski. It's gonna get real busy 'round here come growin' time, and we got lumber still sittin' here and back at the sawmill 'cause there ain't enough men like you to move it out. This here warehouse has gotta be cleaned out by the time the summer crops come in. Cotton bales and tobacco's gonna take up all the space you see here."

James Pulaski smiled broadly, showing one tooth missing and a couple more that looked as though they were hanging by a thread.

"When can you start?" he said.

"Oh, I'm just asking right now. Don't even know if we'll be staying. But it's nice to know there's work to be had here..."

He doffed his felt hat, shook the man's hand and headed back to the wagon.

"What'd you find out," Gladys asked.

"Lots. But most important thing is Imogene lives down the road apiece.

'Anybody say what she's like?"

"Nope. And I didn't ask."

When James Pulaski had said the Rafferty house sat on the railroad tracks, he wasn't far off. The house's rear looked as though it had been sheared off by a passing train.

"Migod," Gladys remarked, "that house had to be there before them tracks. You think maybe the owners was stubborn and didn't wanna move?"

From his perch on the wagon seat, Dru pushed his felt back on his head and, despite himself, grinned at the thought. "Hard to imagine they'd lay them tracks so close," he said, "but it's harder to imagine what it's like to be in there when a train takes off your tail."

"Dru! For shame. Think of the girls. You'd sure have to paste down any good dishes, though. And you'd need cotton for stuffin' in your ears..."

Momentarily silent, Dru sighed deeply, dropped down off the wagon and reached back to help Gladys down. "Well, let's go do it," he said. "We come a long way for this."

Bertha was about to vault to the ground, but stopped when Dru held up a hand; she already had one foot atop a rear wheel.

"Nope, not yet," he told her. "You'n Magalene wait here til we see what's what. Might not be anyone home…"

He had parked the wagon on the shady side of a tall magnolia, where it was almost out of sight from the house. Looking skyward, he added, "You'll be out of the sun and we won't leave you too long."

Gently touching one of Bertha's cheeks, he said, "I promise."

CHAPTER 31

Visiting Mrs. Rafferty

NO ONE WOULD HAVE picked her out as Sylvester Boru's sister. She was a short woman, grey of hair and demeanor; her eyes also were grey, and they were deep. Deep, in that you'd have to look deep into them if you hoped to find out what she was thinking, or was trying to think.

They stared and she stared back, through a door she held partially open.

"Ya'll lookin' for someone," she finally asked.

"Imo...," Gladys began.

Dru spoke over her. "Missus Rafferty? We're lookin' for Missus Rafferty."

She looked them over again, focused on the felt hat Dru was squashing between both hands, and said, "Even old hats needn't be treated thataway."

Stepping to one side, she added, "I'm Imogene Rafferty. Ya'll come on in."

Once inside, she closed the screen door but left the wooden one ajar. "Gettin' on into springtime," she mumbled to no one in particular. "Time for some fresh air in here."

Looking at them again, she said, "Who'd you say you was? I fergit."

"I'm Norm Foley," Dru said quickly, squeezing Gladys' arm. "We come from up, er, Tifton way and was asked to look you up, if we passed through Blackshear."

"Well, likely you just did." She pointed back the way they'd come, and added, "More'n I done in awhile. Don't git outa the house much no more. Don't care to."

Motioning them to a frayed settee that, like her, was of uncertain age, she sat down in a well-used, well-cushioned rocker; then, abruptly, she rose again.

"'Scuse me and my manners. Would ya'll like some sweet tea? Young Bob, who lives up the road apiece – I believe that's his name – sometimes I fergit things – he goes to the store once in a while – I just can't no more – and he brought me back some sugar. So it's real sweet, my tea…

"No ice, though. Can't 'ford no ice. Weather's been cold anyways. Comes right through them walls, like they wasn't there…"

The interior was bare of sheetrock or paneling of any sort, and a quick glance showed light coming through half a dozen knotholes.

Dru started to decline her offer, but stopped when Gladys waved him off.

"Why, Mrs. Rafferty," she said, "we'd love some tea. It's so kind of you to think of it…"

"Reckon I could heat it up, but I like mine cold."

"No, no, cold will be just fine."

While she prepared the tea, Dru and Gladys looked around the small living room. The door to a bedroom stood open, revealing a sagging, unmade bed. The two other doors leading from the room were closed, and Dru had to stifle his surprise when he saw that one obviously opened onto the railroad tracks. Gladys was unable to stifle hers – "Oh, dear," she muttered – but Mrs. Rafferty apparently did not hear her.

A moment later, she returned with two pint-sized canning jars containing the tea. She sat down, and abruptly moved to get up again.

"Lordy, I forgot mine…"

Dru was on his feet immediately, retrieving the third tea and handing it to her.

Looking them over once more, she leaned back and said, "Now what was it you said you wanted? I swan but I done fergit…"

"Oh, we didn't say," Dru responded. "But we…"

"We didn't say…" Gladys had spoken at almost the same time, but yielded to Dru.

"…we was wonderin' if you was, or are, related to a fella named Sylvester Boru?"

"Sylvester? Sylvester Amos Boru? Why, yes, I had a brother by that name. Hain't seen hide nor hair of him in a long time…"

Focusing her grey eyes on Dru, then on Gladys, she asked, "He ain't in trouble is he? He always found ways to git inta trouble…"

"Er, no Ma'm, not that we know about," Dru lied.

"Well, how come you know him," she asked. "The Lord knows he's been gone outa my life for a long, long time, even ere Alvin died."

With considerable difficulty, she had risen from the rocker as she spoke and was walking toward a table against one wall.

"Alvin, Ma'm?"

After picking up a black-covered book and heading slowly back toward her seat, she stopped next to Dru.

"Alvin. My husband. He's been gone more'n 10 years now. Sawmill mishap, they said. I never was sure. Alvin, he was a lot like Sylvester. He'd go off for days and then some one would bring him home drunk. Most times it was Sylvester."

After staring down at Dru for a long, silent moment, she sighed, and moved on back to the rocker.

"Now, what was I sayin'?"

"You were telling us about your late husband, Alvin."

"Ohh. Yes, seems he was always late. Specially when he and Sylvester went off t'gether somewheres…"

Pausing again, undoubtedly to collect her thoughts, she went on.

"Waycross. That's where they'd go. Only nine miles down the road, down there close by that old Okey-fe-noke Swamp. Place had more gin mills than this little biddy town…

"And I didn't want to know what else it might'a had. Still don't."

More quietly, as an aside to herself, she added, "Likely warn't even white…"

She sipped her tea, and asked, "You folks like somethin' stronger. Young Bob, he brings me back some blackberry wine once in a while…."

"No Ma'm, tea's just fine," said Dru.

Looking a mite disappointed, she grinned naughtily and said, "Well, now, if'n it's somethin' real strong you want, I think I got some of that, too. Most days I wait til evenin' to get inta that, but…"

Dru glanced from Mrs. Rafferty to Gladys and back again. Ignoring the question and clearing his throat, he said, "Ma'm, do you know if your brother ever had a family of his own? A wife, maybe?"

Lifting her head, she looked straight at him. "Sylvester? A wife? Not that I know'd of. Can't imagine a woman wantin' him."

Gladys was leaning forward. "Then he wouldn't have had any children, would he?"

"Not that he'd admit to… Why you askin' these things? I, I, er, I get mixed up real easy. You ain't funnin' me, are you?"

"No, Ma'm," said Dru, standing up and taking his empty glass to the counter. "No way we'd do that. We must be the ones confused, and for certain we ain't funnin'."

"He's right, Missus Rafferty. He surely is. The Sylvester we knew never mentioned no place called Waycross and, lessen I'm wrong, his middle name was Andrew. Ain't that right, er, Norman?"

"It is. Most folks called him Andy, for short. And I reckon we done took up enough of your time, Missus Rafferty. We really should be goin' now."

"Well," the woman said, lifting the book and trying to get out of her rocker at the same time, "I went and got the family Bible, thinkin' it might help you…"

Looking at them, she smiled weakly and added, "Reckon it won't though…"

Mrs. Rafferty took a couple of steps, the Bible clutched to her breast. "I do wish ya'll would stay and visit awhile. I get so few visitors an…"

Her words were drowned out as a steam-driven locomotive approached from the south. A moment later, the train rumbled by the back door, bell clanging and tracks rattling. Suddenly there was the high-pitched screech of a whistle. The clamor forced them to cover their ears. The whole house shook.

Mrs. Rafferty stood mute and smiled apologetically, until the train passed.

"Old Sam Carlson was drivin' that one," she said. "He's the only one who blows that whistle. He knows how much it pesters me, and that's why he does it. Thinks he's somethin' special, I reckon."

She sighed and walked to the front door. "Never did get used to this house," she said. "Never have, never will. But it was the best Alvin could do. No one else wanted it…"

Dru and Gladys stood by the wagon, gesturing for the girls to stay out of sight until Mrs. Rafferty waved a final time, closed the door and disappeared behind it.

They stared at one another for some time, then Dru helped Gladys and the girls mount the wagon.

"What you thinkin', Dru? We can't give them girls to that crazy old woman, no matter how sweet she is."

"Shhh," he whispered. "I know that. Reckon we gotta talk some…"

CHAPTER 32

Time's miracle and spirituality's decision...

"WHAT WE GONNA DO, Dru?"

"We're going' to find someplace to feed these girls and ourselves and we're gonna think it through."

Clicking Hiram's reins, he turned the wagon back toward town. With shoulders sagging and brow furrowed, he was the picture of dejection.

"Kinda expected it'd turn out thisaway," he said, mostly to himself.

"Truthfully," Gladys replied, softly, "so'd I." Her disappointment showed.

"Clip-clop, clip-clop," Hiram's hooves beat out a cadence as they moved from sand to red dirt and sand again. He snorted, tried up look back over a shoulder, then snorted again.

"Believe he's likely hungry, too," Gladys said. "Maybe you oughta find a livery first. Maybe we can find out there where there's a good place to eat."

As an afterthought, she added, "And a cheap place, of course…"

"Ain't necessary," Dru mumbled.

"What? Ain't necessary to eat? Why, Dru…"

"Ain't necessary to find a cheap place. I got some money."

Looking crosswise at Dru, Gladys opened her mouth to speak, closed it, then spoke. "You got money? Where'd you get any money?"

"Don't you worry 'bout it. I got money…"

Dru set his chin and clicked the reins again, as if to say he had no more to say. Gladys decided to leave him to his thoughts … while she weighed her own.

Adam's Stable was a block off the main drag and three blocks north of the depot. Owner Adam Sadansky, who also was the town blacksmith and veterinarian, welcomed Hiram and told them Maggie's Inn served good country cooking.

Looking them over, he chortled and added, "Also got some nice rooms, by day, week or however long you need. Don't mind my saying so, Ma'm," he said, looking at Gladys and casting a sideways glance at the girls, "ya'll look like ya'll need a rest, and a good long one.

"You," he said to Dru, "you look like a man who knows what he needs…"

"Yep, but you're right," Dru cut him off. "We'll eat and come back and get our stuff if it looks like somethin' we oughta do."

"Nice fella," Dru said, as they headed off.…

Maggie's Inn was a neat, two-story white clapboard house with a white picket fence and a trellis at the gate. They paused at the gate, Dru and Gladys looking at one another and communicating an unspoken question: "Do we dare go in, looking as we do…"

Maggie Fitzpatrick answered for them; opening a screen door and waving them on, she said, "C'mon in. You look like you need a place to sit a spell."

"We're hungry," Bertha called from behind Dru and Gladys. Surprised, they looked back at her and frowned.

"Well, we are. You said we was gonna eat…"

Miss Maggie laughed. "That's the way, young lady. I got some chicken n' dumplin's waiting inside."

All were hungry, ravenously hungry. In their haste to cover the remaining miles to Blackshear, they had pressed on without pausing to eat; the girls had finished off any leftovers during the night.

Though the dining room table and its place settings were the nicest they had ever seen, they were not so awesome as to intimidate the travelers. When the food arrived, brought in by Miss Maggie herself, they attacked it vociferously. Magalene ignored the fork and dug in with her spoon; Gladys tried to correct her, but the girl cried out and shoved her away.

"Forks is new to us, Miss Gladys," Bertha said, quietly. "She don't know no better. I ate at Aunt Jewell's once. She showed me."

Dru said little during the meal. When he had finished and was wiping his plate with a biscuit, he ignored Gladys' condemning glare and turned to the younger sister.

"Magalene, honey, you miss your momma?"

"Momma?" She looked at Bertha, as though looking for her to respond for her. "My momma?"

"Uh-huh. Your momma. Sara."

Again she looked at Bertha, who returned her stare, looked at Dru and said, "Sometimes she's like that. She forgets things…"

Arching an eyebrow and switching his eyes from Bertha to Gladys and back again, Dru said, "Forget things? How can she forget her own ma?"

"She forgets and I try not to remember," Bertha added, sorrowfully. "Not Momma, though. I'll never forget Momma…"

Bertha remained silent for the better part of a minute, looking at her hands, then rubbing them together. When she finally looked up at Dru, she spoke softly.

"Sometimes I wish I could forget. Not Momma specially, but most everything else." Reaching over and touching her sister's shoulder, she added, "It ain't hard to figure why she's always lookin' for them angels…"

Gladys reached across the table and touched Bertha's stringy, uncombed dark hair. "Oh, honey, I don't know what to say…"

"Don't need to say nothin'," Bertha responded. "It's been good, our bein' with you and all. You hain't asked questions, til now, and you hain't shouted at us or called us bad names; you hain't hit us, not once."

Smiling softly and clearly trying to hold back tears, Bertha halfway laughed in embarrassment. "It's taken me a while to see that I don't have to worry 'bout duckin' every time one of you comes near me, or her … that we don't have to worry 'bout bein' hit, or worse…"

"Oh, honey, we never would…"

"Magalene, she ain't as tough as me; and Grandpa, he hated the way she'd call for angels and such, and he'd whomp her bad some times…"

Dropping her eyes, she added, "Momma, she'd try to get him to stop and he'd just beat her, too, only worse."

The four remained silent for some time, each plumbing inner thoughts. If was midafternoon, and they were the only diners in the small room. Miss Maggie had gone off to handle other chores.

Dru finally broke the silence. "You 'member Bo, Magalene?"

"Bo? Bo-boy?"

"Bo-boy…"

"Uh-huh, he's gonna marry me when we're all grow'd."

"He tell you that? How you know he will?"

"I just do."

"Why?"

"Can't tell. It's a secret."

"A secret?"

"Uh-huh."

Dru glanced at Gladys, who returned his stare with a knowing half-grin. She didn't know about Magalene's special relationship with Bo, though she knew that young girls often talked that way.

Magalene's secretive smile became a sad frown. "But Bo stopped comin' to play with me, longer ago than I can remember." Looking at her sister, she said, "Bertha, she said it was likely he was scared of… er, of Grandpa."

She paused, then looked from Dru to Gladys, stuck out her chin and said firmly, "He was a bad, bad man! I don't want to talk 'bout him, ever!"

Her hands were balled into small fists, and she squeezed them so tightly turned red.

"Easy, now, honey," said Gladys, reaching across the table and covering both hands with one of hers. "It's okay. He won't bother you no more."

Bertha looked at her quizzically, her lips drawn thin across her mouth and one eyebrow arched. She started to say something, but didn't.

"Somethin' wrong, Bertha?" Dru had been afraid she was about to ask the obvious question.

"No, no," she finally said. "It don't matter."

Dru met the girl's stare and, after a considered delay, he said, "Bertha, honey, I want to you know I gotta lot of good feelin's 'bout you. I think you're a lot smarter than you let on…"

He paused. "How old are you now?"

"Goin' on 14. Birthday's in August. I think…"

Silence returned, a pervasive silence, broken only by Dru's fidgeting and his tapping of a spoon on the table. Finally, Gladys spoke up. "Dru, why are you so quiet? Seems to me…"

"Norm. Name's Norman Foley, if that's what I told that Rafferty woman."

Looking askance, Gladys leaned toward him, but didn't have a chance to say anything.

"Ain't Dru no more, not 'round Blackshear, anyways. Time for a new name and a new life."

"Here?" Gladys looked confused, but hopeful.

Dru raised his elbows off the table. "Yup," he said. "Here's good as any place." Talking mostly to himself now, he went on: "There's work here, nice folks, and we passed a nice looking church back up the road. We got some money…"

Making direct eye contact with Gladys, he asked, "You still with us?"

She opened her mouth to respond, but closed it and placed a hand on her breast; she made no attempt to hide her surprise. "Why, Dru, uh, Norm Foley, you know I am. What else would I do? But…"

"Then you sit right here while I talk to Miss Maggie." Abruptly, he got up and headed for the foyer, into which the portly, white-haired woman had disappeared.

Bertha, who had been listening the whole time with hands clamped on the sides of her seat, watched him go. Then she turned to Gladys and said, "This mean we gonna be a family?"

"Lordy," said Gladys, prayerfully, "I hope so. I gotta believe so."

"Good," said Bertha. "He's a nice man."

Both looked toward Magalene, who was idly playing with her fork and humming to herself.

Dru had been deep into himself ever since they had crawled on the wagon and left T'other Side a week earlier. And he had had much to think about: Home, or what had been home; his brother Jim and sister Liza, his other brothers; Bo, Jewell and Arlis, with John off in Florida and them about ready to go; the Higginbothams, silently bearing up under the loss of Lonny to a sociopathic murderer and too many children to diseases they couldn't understand; and there was his beloved Sara, lying in her secret grave back up there close by the Big Springs Ford.

Time had performed its miracle, and spirituality – that enigmatic wisp you can feel but not physically touch – had taken over his soul; he now believed there was more to life than a simple, sometimes joyous, sometimes painful journey which, in God's grand design, was but a wee crawl.

His body, soul and life's rhythm finally were one. He would be with Sara again. And in the time he had left on earth, he would take care of her daughters. He now saw that opportunity as a gift he could not, and would not, decline.

Then there was Old Man Boru, gone now but leaving behind two troubled children: one about to become a young woman whose only tools for dealing with life were those of survival learned in an unbelievably monstrous existence; the other a beautiful but severely wounded child of 11 whose survival had been in the creation of a make-believe world in which even the angels came and went with the sunshine.

There was no question in his mind – and apparently in Gladys' mind – that the home of lonely, absent-minded and embittered Mrs. Imogene Rafferty would be no place for the girls to be shown a new and better life. In a very real sense, he had known that even before they'd visited the woman in her humble, trackside home.

He would have to write Jim and tell him what had happened. He hoped the elder brother and family patriarch would be able to convince someone, if not Sheriff Nobles, that Boru was dead and gone and that he had admitted the murders. In his heart, though, he sensed that was not going to happen, and that he – Dru Sullivan – would remain a wanted man. The passage of time would be his only hope for closure on that question.

Though he'd thought about it along with everything else, he did not know what to do about Beatrice O'Connell Sullivan – if that's who she still called herself. He didn't have to worry about her getting his "coffee-can treasure" peanuts money any more; he'd dug that out of ground before leaving and had it strapped to his waist in a money belt. There was a lot of it, and he'd added to it by taking a stash of about $50 he'd found hidden in Boru's mattress.

It hadn't bothered him one whit to take it; it was, he thought, small payment for getting the girls safely away.

A major factor in Dru's decision to settle in Blackshear and create a home for the girls and Gladys had a great deal to do with his beloved nephew, Beaujames (Bo) Sullivan. He had figured Blackshear would be close to Jacksonville, Florida, where he hoped Bo, Jewell and Arlis would soon be reunited with John.

But he had not expected it to be only about 80 miles away, nor had he known that the Atlantic Coast Line railroad passed through Blackshear and that it hooked up with several other railroad lines in nearby Waycross. Jim, he knew, would write him back and give him their address in Jacksonville. He already knew they were to stay with Jewell's brother Bantry and his family, and figured he'd be able to find them regardless.

He had promised seven year-old Bo – with whom, in a very real sense, he had experienced a second childhood – that he would see him again, and he intended to keep that promise.

"Yep, thank you for lettin' me be a boy with you, Bo," he whispered to himself as he approached Miss Maggie. He'd told Bo that the last time he'd seen him, and it had felt good. He also remembered the sad feelings he'd had, about his role in Bo's having had to grow up faster than a boy should. He stopped a few feet short of the woman, shook his head, sighed and whispered to himself, "But he'll always have his maypop, and both of us will have memories and feeling's nobody else might understand."

Miss Maggie smiled as he looked up again and closed the distance between them.

Yes, she had a room available for as long as they'd need it; yes, she knew of a small farm that was up for sale, and yes, "James Pulaski down at the depot is a good man to work for…"

After proudly signing the register – as Norman Foley – Dru hurried back to the dining room, with chin set, eyes shining and a firmly held room key in one hand.

CHAPTER 33

A heavenly sendoff...

AS THOUGH BY HOLY manipulation, four figures stood a day later in a morning mist alongside a highway and watched in awe as a heavenly spectacle unfolded before them. The woman clasped the hands of her two children, and a tall man reverently reached down and took the hand of the smaller boy.

For the rest of their lives, Jim, Jewell, Bo and even four-year-old Arlis would remember and talk of how God was there with them on that balmy predawn April morning in 1943. With the sun still sleeping, a full moon's glow and the cumulative brilliance of countless stars bathed woods and fields stretching away from the bus stop a mile south of Mayo. Across the two-lane highway, the radiance danced along the spine of an iridescent fog, tip-toed across the concrete, and wrapped the four of them in a heavenly embrace.

Then a great circle of light began to form around the moon. Little by little, the circle changed shape, in a gleaming, flickering metamorphosis from which it emerged as a great towering cross, with a central beam anchored in the fog and two others extending

Pierce Lehmbeck

as shimmering arms on either side; the fourth emerged from atop the moon and inched toward heaven, climbing straight and true and clearly knowing the way.

"I've heard of such things," Jim managed to whisper, after clearing his throat and reverently doffing his straw hat. Jewell was praying, her lips moving but emitting no sound; her misting eyes were needful of the store-bought handkerchief buried in the bottom of her borrowed cardboard suitcase; she had placed it there the night before, feeling it was too nice to soil.

Cautiously, awkwardly, Jim struggled for words that might explain the phenomenon, but the swelling in his chest had blocked his breathing. What he saw and felt were so overwhelming that his tongue and mind could not immediately communicate; both had been rerouted through his heart and conditioned by his deep religious convictions. It was some time before he was able to speak.

"And, er, I've read 'bout 'em, too..." Even those few words had been hard to say and hard to hear. He spoke no more until he could breathe normally, then added: "But I never seen such. If John was here, he'd likely say the moon's light is playin' off the fog and them dew drops that hain't took to earth as yet is reflectin' the light..."

"Maybe so," Jewell whispered. "But I have to believe it's the Good Lord sayin' He's goin' with me and the boys, and we're gonna be alright. He meant for us to see it."

"And you may not ever see it again, Jewell. I like your reasonin' better'n what John'd say. The Good Lord's got to be tellin' us somethin' good. There can't be no bad in what we're seein'."

"Shhhh, Jim. It's a miracle, for certain. Let's just enjoy it while it lasts."

Arlis squeezed her hand and said he was scared. Bo shushed him. Now seven, he was telling his knees to stop shaking and telling himself a man wouldn't let on he was scared, even if he were.

Then they heard the growl of the Greyhound bus, and turned as one to watch its headlights emerge from around the corner a quarter-mile to the north. Jewell, Bo and Arlis were about to begin their journey to Florida, to a reunion with husband and father and, perhaps, to experience a new life much more wondrous, Jewell prayed, than anything they had dared imagine.

She thought of John, wondering how he really was doing, and especially whether he was staying away from the bottle. As of his last letter, he was still living with Bantry and his family, and that was the best indicator that he was remaining sober. When Bantry laid down the law, he stuck by it. And he had no truck with a drinking man, even if he was his brother-in-law.

She thought of Dru, wondering where he was and whether he was safe. Though he was in her nightly and morning prayers, she often felt it strange that she wasn't as worried about him as perhaps she ought to have been. Maybe, she reasoned, Dru was a wiser, smarter and more complete man than anyone had ever given him credit for being.

As she hugged Jim and prepared to board the bus, Jewell Ellen Sullivan paused one more time to look back at heavenly, celestial spectacular. It was beginning to fade now, but it still was awesomely beautiful and heart-stopping mesmerizing.

Though she had to overcome her paralysis to do it, she smiled prayerfully, and said, "Did you cause that, Momma Susan? Was that you?"

THE END

CPSIA information can be obtained at www.ICGtesting.com
Printed in the USA
LVOW091411010612

284278LV00001B/84/P